ANY OTHER WORLD WILL DO

ANY OTHER WORLD WILL DO

A NOVEL

ALEX LUBERTOZZI

TOP FIVE BOOKS
OAK PARK, ILLINOIS

A TOP FIVE BOOK

Published by Top Five Books
521 Home Avenue
Oak Park, Illinois 60304

Library of Congress Cataloging-in-Publication Data

Names: Lubertozzi, Alex, author.
Title: Any other world will do : a novel / Alex Lubertozzi.
Description: Oak Park, Illinois : Top Five Books, [2021]
Identifiers: LCCN 2021005720 (print) | LCCN 2021005721 (ebook) |
    ISBN 9781938938580 (paperback) | ISBN 9781938938597 (ebook)
Subjects: GSAFD: Science fiction.
Classification: LCC PS3612.U233 A85 2021 (print) | LCC PS3612.
    U233 (ebook) | DDC 813/.6—dc23
LC record available at https://lccn.loc.gov/2021005720
LC ebook record available at https://lccn.loc.gov/2021005721

ISBN: 978-1-938938-58-0

Cover & book design by Top Five Books

Printed and bound in the United States of America

For my Dad,
who taught me sarcasm.
Thanks.

ANY OTHER WORLD WILL DO

Barcelona

The untented Kosmos my abode,
I will pass, a willful stranger;
My mistress still the open road
And the bright eyes of danger.

— *Robert Louis Stevenson*

1.

October 1986

VIKRAM BHAT weaved his way down the corridor, the train's swaying motion making him appear drunk, and stopped at a half-full compartment. He looked inside and found what he'd been looking for—a potential recruit. The young man, shabbily dressed and a bit pale with a tangle of dark brown hair, was not much more than a kid. Vikram had been casting around for fellow travelers for years with little success, but, he figured, what the hell. He slid open the door with a *kershhlunk* and stepped inside.

The train had pulled out of Gare Saint Lazare just before dusk, and Vikram now noticed the elderly couple sitting across from the kid in the dim compartment. He greeted them all with an *"Hola!"* and fell into the seat beside the kid, Spain in front of them, the setting sun on their right. The young man glanced away from the book he was reading to appraise him. Vikram, a leather satchel slung across his shoulder, wore a linen sportcoat and pants that looked slept in, blue sneakers, and no socks. He had an open, friendly face, and appeared to be Indian and fortyish, despite being neither.

"Are we all heading to Barcelona?" he asked them, repeating it in French for the benefit of the old couple, who nodded tersely, the stern look on the old man's face inviting no further small-talk.

"Madrid actually," said the kid.

"Oh."

Vikram was inured to his presence being politely ignored, so it didn't bother him. He possessed the detachment of a perpetual observer, a tourist light-years from home. He raised an eye at the pulpy cover of the paperback the kid was trying to read. Though he didn't recognize the cover, with its half-naked blue alien staring back at him, he knew the title.

"Is that *Skygarden?*" he asked.

As it was printed in large block letters across the cover, the kid could hardly say no. "Yeah," he said. "You've read it?"

"Years ago," said Vikram. "The author—Tor Bass—he was rather an odd goose, as I recall. Ever read any of his other books?"

The kid shrugged. "Just *Blue Moon,*" he said. "It was good."

Vikram smiled a crooked, approving smile. "I'm Vikram, by the way," he said.

"Miles."

"I'm surprised you can still find his books," said Vikram.

"I inherited some of my dad's old paperbacks," said Miles, closing the dog-eared book and resting it in his lap.

"I think his best was *The Harpies of Ganymede,*" said Vikram. "Do you know it?"

Miles shook his head.

"It was never one of his more popular books," Vikram admitted. "It was sort of an homage to Dante's *Divine Comedy,* set on the moons of Jupiter."

"I never took Bass for being very religious," said Miles.

"Well, no, unlike Dante, Bass took a fairly dim view of heaven."

Miles nodded. "That would make sense," he said. "Skygarden is kind of like a version of heaven to the colonists...at first."

"Right," said Vikram. "The idea of paradise is a fairly universal religious delusion."

"Well, what about, uh..." Miles began. "I mean, don't Hindus believe in reincarnation?"

"I guess," said Vikram. "That is, I assume so, but I'm no expert. I don't go to temple, or wherever it is Hindus go."

"Oh." Miles smiled, disarmed. "I never really went to church regularly, either," he admitted. "When I was little, though, my parents did make me go to Sunday school. One time, I remember my teacher was going on about what heaven would be like, and I started crying. When she asked me what was wrong, I said, 'I don't wanna go to heaven!' She said, 'Why on earth not?' And I said, 'Because it sounds so *boring.*'"

Vikram blinked in surprise. "I bet the other kids loved you," he said.

"I remember my teacher said, 'Well, you probably won't have to go there for a long time, anyway.'"

"Hah—*probably*," said Vikram. He liked this kid. He was thinking Miles showed real promise as he drew a pack of smokes from his breast pocket and shook one up to his mouth. He started patting down his coat and pants looking for a light when the old man cleared his throat and gestured at the sign just above the ashtray that read NE FUMEZ PAS. "*Ah, oui. Merci*," he said. Stowing the cigarette back into its pack, he said to Miles, "Say, I take it from your clothes and backpack up there that you're poor. Buy you a drink?"

"I mean—" Miles's eyes darted unconsciously up at his second-hand backpack and back at Vikram, seeming momentarily lost for words. "Okay," he said.

In the bar car, Vikram smoked freely while they talked well into the night over several drinks. Because he never bothered to modulate the way he presented himself to different people, Vikram came across as guileless, and so near strangers would open up to him as if he were their therapist. Miles told Vikram about the death of his father a year earlier, the story of the last time he saw him, and how he spent his last year of high school and the summer after back in Chicago working odd jobs, saving up money so that he could fly to Europe once he turned eighteen.

"So you ran away from home," said Vikram. *Like me*, he thought.

"I guess so," said Miles.

Aimless, young, and untethered, Miles seemed ideal. Vikram already felt a strong attachment. Of course, he wasn't immune to flattery, and resurrecting the name Tor Bass, someone he hadn't thought of in years, might have colored his judgment. If Miles worked out, though, Vikram could have a matched set to bring home. But he was getting ahead of himself now.

"You should come to Barcelona," he said.

"Yeah?"

Vikram told him about where he was living, a shared apartment above the Hotel Kashmir, a lively and cheap establishment with a bar and a revolving group of young backpackers. Miles looked interested and seemed agreeable.

The next morning, however, a rail strike detained them just over the Spanish border in the town of Portbou. Vikram, accustomed to this sort of thing, assured Miles that it would last no more than twenty-four hours. But when Miles learned that Portbou had a beach, he decided to leave the station and explore the town, try to see if he could camp out by the sea.

"Oh," said Vikram. "See you in Barcelona?"

"Maybe," said Miles, sounding more noncommittal in the light of day.

So the two went their separate ways—Miles to camp on the beach, and Vikram, not wanting to force things, to stay in the station awaiting the next train, wondering if he'd ever see the kid again.

2.

BY THE NEXT DAY, Miles Townsend had tired of salt air and of sand working its way into the crack in his ass, and itched instead for city lights and people. The trains had started running again the night before, as Vikram said they would, and Miles thought about Barcelona. He didn't know anyone in Madrid—he'd only chosen it in the first place because it was the first city in Spain he could think of. But maybe not knowing anyone there was a good thing. He'd spent six weeks traveling around Ireland and France without getting too close to anyone, and part of him clung to the freedom of it.

Yet something drew Miles to Vikram. Despite the crush he suspected Vikram had on him, he was easy to confide in. Maybe it was simply the fact he'd shown an interest in Miles, or that he managed to listen without judgment. Whatever the case, he had a way of making Miles feel like less of an idiot.

So that evening, after a short train ride down the coast and a long walk soaking up the charms of the Ramblas—which included dead-eyed, middle-aged prostitutes loitering down by the harbor and the legion of drug dealers who brushed past him every few seconds with offers of *hash-coke-speed*—Miles found himself in the bar of the Hotel Kashmir made idiotic by love.

He had fallen in love with the bartender. She was an older woman— at least twenty-two or twenty-three—tall but not too tall (that is, not taller than him), lithe and graceful, with dreadlocks that just brushed her eyelids. It wasn't merely that she was pretty—Miles preferred to think he wasn't that superficial—but she was quick to smile, had an easy laugh and a kind way of regarding people she talked to. He decided he had better calm down, find out her name, perhaps speak to her. She might turn out to be a moron.

Miles made his way across the small, crowded bar—a narrow galley off of the common room—and overheard her conversing in English, Spanish, and German with various patrons. The thought that she was probably out of his league now occurred to Miles. But he managed to squeeze in at the bar and catch her eye. She leaned across the bar to hear him over the din.

"Hi," he said, "I'm looking for a man named Vikram. He said I might find him here. Do you know him?"

"Oh, I know him," she said, her smile revealing faint dimples on her cheeks. "He's my flatmate."

"Oh."

"I haven't seen him since this morning, but he's probably not far." She spoke with a slight, hard-to-place accent. "How do you know Vikram?" she asked.

"I met him on the train coming down from Paris," he said, and she nodded, picking up empties as he went on. "We ended up talking over a few drinks in the bar car. I told him I was going to go to Madrid, but he said I should come to Barcelona. So...I did."

"Let me guess," she said, leaning a hand on the bar, "you poured out your life story while he just sat there, chain-smoking and nodding his head."

"Uh...yeah, pretty much," he said, laughing. "How'd you know that?"

"It's his M.O.," she said. "I'm Anna, by the way."

"Miles," he said and shook her hand across the bar, the touch of her hand sending a tingle up his arm. "His M.O.?"

"*Modus operandi.*"

"Ah," he said, pretending that helped.

"Vikram doesn't always tell me where he's going," she said. "But he tends to stay in town for at least a few days after returning from one of his excursions—also part of his M.O."

Miles nodded. "Isn't an M.O. something a criminal has?"

"It is," she said. "But Vikram's crimes are, well...showing up late for drinks, making inappropriate small-talk with strangers, a tragic lack of awareness...that sort of thing."

The man on the stool next to Miles, hearing their conversation, turned and squinted at Miles, unsure if they'd already met. With a shaggy mustache and goatee and prominent canines that flashed whenever he smiled, he had a slightly wolfish appearance.

"He just got in," Anna explained. "He's looking for Vikram, have you seen him?"

"I saw him down in the plaça a couple hours ago," the man said. "I didn't ask where he was headed, though." Then, extending a hand to Miles, "I'm Tom."

Miles introduced himself, and they shook hands as Tom downed the remains of his wine. "You staying here?" he asked.

Miles nodded.

Tom asked the two young women sitting on the other side of him if they'd seen Vikram, but they both shook their heads.

"Pour you a beer?" asked Anna.

"Yes, please."

Anna drew Miles a pint of beer from the tap and refilled Tom's glass from the giant box of red wine behind her. It was a no-frills bar—no rows of liquor bottles lining the wall, no array of tap handles emblazoned with colorful logos, no bowls filled with nuts or wedges of lime—just one generic beer on draft, and your choice of red or white wine. Still, it was a popular spot and was soon standing-room only, so Tom suggested they take their drinks and head into the common room to find a table. Miles would have liked to talk to Anna more, but she was now swamped by customers anyway, so he followed Tom and the two young women out.

The Hotel Kashmir's common room looked down onto Plaça Reial through large half-moon windows that echoed the arcades ringing the square. Cracked open, they let in snatches of conversation from the people gathered around the fountain below, as well as the odors of roasting meat and smoldering hashish.

The hotel was in fact just a rather grungy hostel, without any of the customary youth hostel rules intended to maintain an aura of wholesomeness. It attracted a certain kind of young backpacker, as well as quite a few older travelers and transients in need of a bed and hot shower for three hundred pesetas, or about two bucks, a night. Its three-word description in Miles's guidebook had read simply: "Watch your things."

The Kashmir's guests, along with a few stray cats, were gathered around the long wooden tables and benches of the common area, talking and drinking, or cleaning themselves, according to their wont.

Tom, Miles learned, was a New Zealander teaching English at the Escuela de Lengua, and had been in Barcelona for nearly a month. He seemed to know most everyone in the Kashmir and introduced Miles to more of the "regulars," as he called them, despite the fact they were all just passing through. Krissy and Tawny, the two who'd been sitting with Tom, were on holiday from university in Brisbane and had arrived in Barcelona a few days earlier. Tawny, the taller and thinner of the two, was very blonde, tan, and pretty. Krissy, shorter, sturdier, sun-freckled, and sandy-haired, was not unattractive, just similar enough to her friend, it seemed to Miles, that she didn't benefit from the comparison. Tawny was quieter, more aloof, whereas Krissy was more forward—quicker to laugh, quicker to take the piss out of someone.

"Tom, what the hell does *that* mean?" she asked him, pointing at the red circle-A symbol sewn onto the sleeve of his army-surplus jacket.

"It means I'm an anarchist," he said.

"You're an Antichrist?" she said. "Crikey, I thought there was only the one."

"An *anarchist*, not the Antichrist," he said, smiling. "I mean, I'd hardly advertise it if I were."

"I would," said Tawny, as if this were obvious, which made Krissy laugh.

Miles met a few other regulars. They all knew Vikram and seemed to regard him with a mixture of affection and curiosity. He was a figure of some mystery, it turned out, as nobody really knew what he did. Someone said he had been in academia once, but he seemed to be on permanent sabbatical. He'd just shown up one day at the Kashmir with his leather satchel and was now a fixture. A real regular.

Then a large blond head appeared, supported by a six-foot-four frame, broad shoulders, and the noble, neatly chiseled features of an Aryan Übermensch. The large head and body, Miles learned, belonged to a Dane named Anders.

Tawny perceptibly straightened when Anders sat down, unconsciously thrusting her chest out and blinking at him. He didn't seem to notice, but his ears pricked up at the mention of Miles's connection to Vikram. Miles told him about parting company after the short-lived rail strike.

"Ah, labor strikes," said Anders, "the bane of these Mediterranean countries. There's a definite disdain for authority here. I suppose it's part of what attracts people like us."

As Anders was dry and the glasses around the table nearing empty, he offered to buy a round, and Miles offered to help carry. Standing up next to Anders, he felt the contrast. Despite being just over six feet tall, Miles had yet to fill out his frame and compared to Anders looked like a sapling whose limbs might snap in a strong wind. Miles also had that distinctly adolescent combination of not enough meat on his bones and baby fat. Anders rubbed a hand over his square jaw, thick with manly stubble, and looked Miles over as they fell in step and walked toward the bar.

"Have you met Vikram's roommate, Anna?" said Miles.

"I think so," said Anders.

"She seems nice," said Miles. "Pretty too."

"I hadn't noticed."

When they got to the bar, Anders continued around and behind it, ducking in beside Anna and greeting her with a prolonged open-mouth kiss, pulling her body against his. Anna leaned her head back and laughed, her hands pushing gently on his broad chest. "*Hola*," she said, as Miles looked for a trapdoor he could jump into.

As Anna filled two pitchers with beer, Anders asked her, "So you don't know where Vikram is, either? He's not in the apartment?"

Anna shook her head no. "You know Vikram. He comes and goes like a stray cat."

"Well, if you'd stop feeding him," he said.

The sweaty metal pitchers filled, Miles reached for one, but Anders simply wrapped his meathooks around their middles and hoisted them both. He gave Anna a peck on the cheek and proceeded toward the common room. With a backward glance and a wistful *bye*, Miles followed him out.

After another round of drinks—and still no sign of Vikram—Krissy, Tom, and the others adopted Miles's mission of finding Vikram as their own and determined that they should head out to search for him.

Miles, recalling the reason he'd come to Barcelona in the first place, said, "Where should we go?"

"Wherever the four winds take us, Miles," said Krissy. "Probably a bar."

*

THEY HEADED OUT, losing Anders in the process, who said he'd meet them later on, and made their way down to the plaça. From the square they moved into one of the narrow alleys of Barcelona's Gothic Quarter—the Barri Gòtic—which had sprung up around the fourteenth-century Cathedral, the basilica before it, and the Roman forum before that.

They wound their way through the crooked lanes of the medieval labyrinth, ending up at a bar Vikram haunted, though not this night. It was quiet as a church in there, and they lasted no longer than it took to down one drink before they found themselves dancing in a subterranean discotheque back near the Plaça Reial. Tom managed to wrangle a bottle of absinthe at the bar and proceeded to drink most of it, which would turn out to be the second worst idea he had that night.

In a couple of hours, they were back on the street looking for a place to eat, having failed so far in their quest to find Vikram. They did find Anders, lurking alone down a side alley when they ran into him, and dragged him along to a late supper. At the restaurant, Miles ate and drank and chatted with Tom and Marie, a college student from North Carolina. Across the table Anders sat next to Tawny while Krissy was deep in conversation with a couple of girls from Yugoslavia both named Katya. They were all at least a few years older than Miles, and at one point Anders narrowed his eyes at Miles and asked him, "So, did you get separated from your school field trip or something?"

"Um...," said Miles, slow to take Anders's meaning, "I'm between schools at the moment, actually."

"How old *are* you?"

"Eighteen," he said.

"That's young," said Marie, who was in her early twenties.

"You don't look nearly that old," said Anders.

In spite of Anders, Miles felt strangely at home among Vikram's friends. The feeling extended to the others in the room, including a group of college students at the next table who were seeing off a friend that night and trying, with Tom's help, to remember the words to a familiar Irish blessing.

"May the road rise up to greet you…" said one, raising his glass.

"*Meet* ya, not *greet* ya," said Tom.

"Ah, right. And may the sun always be—be always—at your back."

"Sun's on my face," said the man whose last night it was. "*Wind's* at my back."

"Wind blows out yer arse," said another.

"Close enough!" And they drank to his health.

One of the group told Tom about an after-hours get-together at some students' apartment near the Plaça del Tripi, and that was all the persuasion it took to move them in that direction and prolong the festivities after the check arrived. Maybe they'd run into Vikram there.

The apartment was only a few minutes' walk away, down a side street that looked narrow enough for you to reach out and touch the buildings on both sides. The flat was on the second floor, and people had spilled out the door onto the landing and down the stairs. Some unholy fusion of jazz and world music wafted around the room, receding into the background and filling the gaps in conversation. The apartment itself was small—a narrow main room with whitewashed walls and a high, wood-beamed ceiling, a kitchen at one end and open french doors leading to a wrought-iron balcony at the other. Guests crowded onto and around the large L-shaped sofa that dominated the living area, and open bottles of wine covered the small kitchen table. Tom grabbed one of the fuller bottles of red by the neck and, not finding any glasses handy, took a swig and offered it to Miles with an apologetic shrug.

"So how d'ya like Barcelona, yer first night heah?" asked Tom, his accent thickening as his blood-alcohol level rose.

"I like it," said Miles. "Is it always like this?"

"Weell…it is the weekend."

"Actually, it's Thursday," Miles pointed out.

Tom flashed his lupine grin. "Close enough," he said with a shrug, adding with a nod to the balcony, "I think I'm genna grab some fresh air."

Krissy and Marie wandered over, and Miles offered them the bottle. Marie took a short swig, then wiped a dribble of red wine off her chin with the back of her hand. She handed the bottle to Krissy, who eyed it suspiciously. "Ah, well, when in Rome," she said with a chuckle and finished it off. Anders was leaning against the kitchen counter, talking to the two Katyas, while Tawny sat on the arm of the sofa, listening to a good-looking, dark-haired young man make his case.

"Looks like Tawny's made a new friend," said Miles.

"Yeah, she has to practically beat them off," said Krissy, who blushed when Miles laughed at the unintentional innuendo. "You know what I mean."

When Miles looked up again, Tawny had ditched the guy who'd been chatting her up and was now in the kitchen talking to Anders. Tawny seemed a more obvious match for that overgrown Viking than someone as interesting as Anna. Anders was the only guy in the place taller than she was, for one thing, and her face lit up whenever he looked at her. From time to time, Tawny would wet her lips or tilt her head in rapt fascination while Anders spoke. It was like watching a baboon display its ass. He wondered how immune to temptation Anders really could be.

"I'm gonna see if there's anything else to drink," Miles said to Krissy, as he headed over to the collection of bottles on the kitchen counter. He smiled at Katya and Katya and pretended to test bottles for fullness as he tried to listen to Anders's and Tawny's conversation. Somehow, they'd found glasses and were drinking some kind of booze. Tawny laughed at something Anders said, and he finished his drink and excused himself to use the facilities.

Miles casually sidled over, a mostly empty bottle of white wine in his hand. "Where'd you find that?" he said, motioning toward her glass.

"Dunno. Anders found it," she said. "Scotch, he said. Quite nasty, but it does the trick."

"Anders seems nice," he said, hoping he sounded like he meant it.

"Quite nice," she said, "but spoken for." Miles knitted his brow as if he didn't know that. "With Anna, the barmaid."

"Oh," said Miles, "I thought they were broken up."

"Who told you that?"

"I'm pretty sure Vikram had said that," he lied.

"How does he know?" she asked, skeptically.

"Well, he's her roommate, isn't he," he said.

Tawny turned her head in the direction Anders had gone. She turned back to Miles and raised her eyebrows. "Hmm…food for thought, that."

"Mmm…" Miles said and nonchalantly swallowed the remains of the bottle, which included a cigarette butt, causing him to double over in an unproductive hacking fit, his eyes watering as Tawny looked on in bored distaste. "Well…" he managed finally to gasp, "nature calls."

With that, he headed out of the kitchen, passing Anders on the way with a queasy smirk, and found the bathroom, a small closet under some stairs where a commode and sink were crammed. In the mirror above the sink, his reflection caught him in its glassy stare. If someone had asked him why he'd told that pathetic lie, he couldn't have told them. So he wondered why he did it. And he wondered why it was that drunken encounters with bathroom mirrors always forced him to question his life choices.

When Miles emerged from the loo, there was an excited commotion coming from the other end of the flat. Tom had climbed atop the balcony's iron railing, one hand holding onto the ledge of the balcony above, the other pointing across the street. *I know 'at balkenny*, Miles heard Tom say, *I was in 'at flat lest week*. Miles could hear other voices alternately pleading with him not to or egging him on to go ahead and do it. *Iss only sex feet away*, Tom was reasoning as only a drunk can, *Iss lower down, see…theeah's plenty of room to land…I'm not genna break the gless*.

Miles struggled his way through the crowd now gathered around the open french doors to the balcony. He called out, "Tom! What the hell are you doing?"

"Whozat?" Tom called back, scanning the expectant faces below.

"Me. Miles." He raised a hand and caught Tom's eye.

"Ahh, cheers, Miles."

"I really don't think this is a good idea," said Miles.

"You don't think I ken jump *that*?"

A few people parted to let Miles through. He looked across the street to the other balcony. It really wasn't that far—about seven or eight feet away straight across and a couple feet down. "You could probably make it three out of four times," said Miles.

"Right on, mate!" said Tom.

"It's that fourth time that worries me."

"I'm only genna do it the once."

Miles wasn't doing a very good job of discouraging him, he realized. He could hear Krissy from back in the apartment call, "Oy, is that you, Tom? Get down off theah, ya Kiwi bastard."

Miles tried a different tack. "How will you get back? You gonna break into their apartment after you make it over?"

Tom scoffed, then hesitated, considered. "Ehh…I ken see yer point."

While it was certainly doable in theory, whether it would have been after the amount of beer, wine, and absinthe Tom had consumed that night—not factoring in the force of his weight landing on the other balcony, nor the question of whether he'd go crashing through the french doors or bounce off them, or what he would do once he got there—would forever remain moot because, as Tom was weighing his options, one of the students who lived in the flat came out of the stairwell through the front door, saw where he was, and screamed, causing Tom to jerk his head around, lose his grip on the upper ledge, and fall over the railing straight down to the pavement below.

Miles rushed toward Tom and the iron railing too late. He looked over the side. Sure enough, gravity worked the same here as it did everywhere else. Tom's form was inelegantly sprawled on the stones below, where the road had risen up to meet him.

3.

VIKRAM LIKED HIS cigarettes unfiltered, allowing all of the smoke's spicy notes to warm his mouth and lungs while the nicotine entered his bloodstream to do its thing. He was alone in flavor country, enjoying this intoxicating mix of poisons, when he saw Tom drop over the railing of the balcony and onto the paving stones in front of him. He'd been hoping to run into Tom and the others here but hadn't expected to be met so dramatically.

Vikram rushed over to find Tom flat on his back, his eyes closed, his body slack. He knelt down next to him and glanced up to see the people on the balcony starting to scatter. Vikram didn't have much time, and it didn't appear Tom did either. With a quick check in either direction, Vikram tapped the thumb and middle finger of his right hand above his left, and the palm of his left hand suddenly glowed with a cold artificial light. He proceeded to scan Tom's supine form, his hand inches from his face. A clean fracture of the spinal cord was all it found. Child's play—fixed in a few moments by Vikram as he waved his hand over Tom's neck, illuminating his features with the bluish light.

Tom opened his eyes, shook his head, and Vikram helped him to his feet. He stood next to Tom, a hand under his elbow in case he needed it, and looked up again to see Miles alone on the balcony staring down at him as though he'd just caught him *in flagrante delicto*.

The sight of Tom lying broken on the ground had left Miles light-headed and a little nauseous. He licked his lips, his mouth dry, feeling the gooseflesh on his arms despite the sultry temperature. The sight of Tom now standing and apparently unhurt would have been a relief if it weren't for the spooky way it seemed to have been accomplished.

Vikram, momentarily frozen in Miles's bewildered stare, the cigarette still dangling from his lower lip, smiled uncertainly and waved hello. "You made it," he called up.

ALEX LUBERTOZZI

"Uh-huh," said Miles.

Krissy and Marie burst out of the building and ran over to Tom, stopping short of him, more than a bit surprised to see him standing. They started looking him over, reaching out to touch him as if he were Lazarus risen. More people emerged, relieved to discover their night hadn't taken a tragic turn. A few of them laughed and started slapping a disoriented Tom on the back.

Miles made his way down in a haze, wondering what could explain the black magic he'd seen Vikram perform. Was it merely a trick of the light—a reflection from a streetlamp or a scooter's headlight? He'd drunk a lot of beer that night, but beer had never made him hallucinate before. Maybe it was the wine-soaked cigarette butt he'd ingested? By the time he found the others in the street, he concluded that there had to be a rational explanation for whatever he thought he saw.

"*Hola*, Miles," said Vikram, "I was looking for you."

"We...we were looking for you," said Miles.

"Well, Tom found me."

Miles turned to Tom and asked, "How are you feeling?"

Tom shook his head and smiled. "Like I coulda made it," he said.

That snapped Miles out of his daze, and he laughed. "You wanna head back up, try again?" he said.

"No!" said Krissy.

Tom and Vikram laughed, as they all started slowly heading in what Miles assumed was the direction of Plaça Reial. The only evidence of Tom's fall were his clothes, the back of which were scuffed and dirty—or at least moreso than they had been when they left the hotel. Vikram walked behind the others, and Miles fell in step beside him.

"I saw him fall," he said, hoping to prompt a response. Getting none, he continued. "Looking at him lying there, I thought he might be dead. Or have a broken neck."

"Well, he wouldn't be walking around now if he had," said Vikram.

"Did you...do anything to him?"

"Just, uh, checked his pulse."

"Were you shining a flashlight or something on him?" asked Miles. Vikram shook his head. "I coulda sworn I saw this strange light when he was on the ground and you were next to him."

Vikram shrugged. "I didn't see anything," he lied.

"I can't believe he's not hurt." Miles shook his head. "I mean, he's lucky to be alive, but he doesn't look like he even has any broken bones or anything."

"It is remarkable," Vikram said, as though it were in fact hardly worth remarking on. "But it was only the second floor, about a five-meter fall."

"Yeah, but onto a stone street," Miles countered.

"Well, I have an inkling he'll feel it more tomorrow," said Vikram. "The alcohol probably helped."

"Yeah, I'd say it was partly responsible," said Miles.

"No, I mean…the alcohol tends to relax your muscles, makes your body better able to absorb a fall."

"Well, his muscles must've been very relaxed."

"I had a friend once back in Madras," Vikram began. "He was passed out drunk in the passenger seat of a car. The driver, also drunk, drove off the road and hit a stone barrier, and my friend was thrown clear through the front windshield and landed in the weeds off the shoulder. He walked away with a few cuts and bruises, that was all."

"Wow, that's…incredible," said Miles, who wasn't inclined to challenge Vikram's rather unbelievable story, much to Vikram's relief, as it wasn't strictly true.

"What happened to the driver?" he asked.

"Um…he died." (That part was true.)

"Huh."

*

ANNA STABBED AT a puddle of beer between the cat's legs with her washcloth. The ginger tabby was a scrawny thing and had a bite-size chunk of its right ear missing, but managed to carry itself with an air of dignity. One of the hotel's regulars, the cat was named Esteban by the Kashmir's manager and subsequently called Steve by most of the guests, despite its being female. She was on all fours atop the bar, tail swishing back and forth, staring intently at the activity in the common area, and hissed when Anna's wet rag bumped her, shooting a warning swipe at Anna's hand.

"Bad Steve," she said. Steve glared at her a moment and then went back to ignoring Anna, keeping her vigil over the common room, now shifted into a more casual position with her hind quarters down and tail wrapped around her front paws.

Anna snuck a peak at her watch: a quarter till two in the morning—only a little over an hour left before quitting time. A platoon of drunken Brits had descended on the Kashmir, and now only the most inebriated remained. They were singing, badly, along with an American playing an almost unrecognizable version of "Peace Train" on a beat-up acoustic guitar. The tunes of early seventies-era singer-songwriters were the only ones these guitar-toting backpackers ever seemed to know.

The early morning crowd at the Kashmir was usually a lively one, but that was not always a good thing. The more Anna worked behind the bar, the more time spent as the only sober one in a roomful of drunks, the less endearing it all became. Anna grew up around enough alcoholics and addicts to know the difference between a good drunk and a bad drunk. A lot of people thought they were good drunks—those were the drunks you had to watch out for.

Anna de Wit had been born in the capital of the Dutch colony of Suriname, a backwater called Paramaribo—referred to as "Parbo" by the locals—on the Caribbean coast of South America. Raised by her mother in a neighborhood of ethnic East Indians and Creoles, Anna never knew her father. She also never knew she was poor until she emigrated with her mother to Amsterdam in 1975, an immigrant quarter of the city known as Southeast (Zuidoost), which on a map of Amsterdam hung off the city proper like a ripe dingleberry. Not for Southeast the quaint canals, gabled brick façades, stone bridges, and tree-lined streets of central Amsterdam. The austere, brutalist high-rises of Southeast remained half-empty after being completed shortly before Anna and her mother arrived, attracting mainly residents who could afford nothing better, and crime. They were two among hundreds of thousands who left their home for the Netherlands when Suriname was granted its independence.

Holding Dutch citizenship and speaking the language helped Anna and her mother to assimilate, but the color of their skin marked them as strangers in a strange land, even a land as progressive and free-thinking as the Netherlands.

The most valuable thing Anna possessed was her mind. As a young girl in Paramaribo, she had displayed an uncanny knack for languages. It was the perfect place for a polyglot, in some ways, as most people spoke both Dutch and English, and there were a dozen other languages spoken regularly on the streets of the capital, including Sranang Tongo, a local mélange of Dutch, English, Spanish, Portuguese, French, and an African creole dialect known as Saramaccan. At the age of four, Anna came home one day and tried out a few snatches of the Hindi she had picked up from a neighbor on her mother. Anna's mother, Eveline, just shook her head and worried that the poor girl would grow up speaking a mixture of all languages and hence none.

"Don't you know what it means?" Anna asked.

"No, sugar, I don't. Why don't you tell me?"

"I think it has something to do with food," she said.

"Good to know."

Anna soon absorbed the meaning behind the new words and phrases she learned, then sorted and categorized them into their proper languages, mentally flagging the words many of them shared in common, which tongues derived from the same root language, which ones were older, which used different alphabets, and so forth.

When twelve-year-old Anna arrived with her mother in Amsterdam, she adapted to the colder climate and the alien surroundings. She found things to love about her new home, though the impersonal, monolithic apartment complex was not one of them. Living in Amsterdam allowed Eveline to take Anna on short weekend trips to the cultural centers of Europe—Paris, Cologne, Bruges, London—whenever she could afford tickets on the train or ferry. Anna loved being a tourist, soaking up the unique atmosphere of each city or town and practicing her French, English, or German on the locals.

Anna never truly considered Amsterdam her home—not in the way she had once thought of Parbo. But she understood the move as her mother's attempt to provide her with the life choices she never had, and she did appreciate it. They lived on little, but they didn't need much. Or, at least, they appreciated what they had more than they missed what they didn't.

Anna's mother was educated enough (high school) and sharp enough to get and keep a string of low-paying office jobs. But, without a university education, white skin, or a penis, her opportunities for advancement were limited. Of the two of those three things Anna *could* acquire (a penis or a college degree), she opted for the degree. She passed her exams and entered the University of Groningen, a couple hours from home, with a double concentration in linguistics and Spanish, a language she did not yet speak or read fluently.

After earning her degree, she came to Barcelona to enter the university's doctoral program in anthropology. It was warm and sunny, which suited her, but after a year of bartending and studying primitive cultures, she was thinking of switching back to her first concentration, linguistics, or to something between the two.

And that's where she was, cleaning up spilt booze around a stray cat in a bar at two in the morning, when her flatmate Vikram and a few other regulars popped in.

"*Hola!*" they all yelled.

The young guy who'd been looking for Vikram earlier was with them. *What is his name?* He looked a little tipsy and a bit rattled. Some of the others were buzzing about something. Steve jumped down off the bar and darted into the common room past Vikram, causing him to flinch in barely concealed terror. He hated cats.

"You found him," she said, to which both Miles and Vikram nodded.

"Did Anders come back with you?" she asked.

"Hm? Oh, I think he stayed behind at the flat we just came from," said Vikram. "I imagine he'll be back soon. The party was starting to break up."

"Anything interesting happen?" she asked.

"I'd say so," said Miles. "Tom nearly killed himself falling off a balcony." Anna raised an eyebrow and emitted a *hmph* while drying a beer mug, as though she heard this type of thing a lot.

"Tom's a bit shaken up," said Vikram. "Fortunately, it was only a second-floor balcony. I wouldn't let him drink anymore, though."

"What happened?"

As Miles and Vikram were explaining what they each saw at the apartment, Tom and Krissy floated in, making straight for the bar.

"Anna, medear," Tom said, "Ah've cheated death. How 'bout a drink to c'memorate the miracle?"

"Thanks, I'm good," she said, looking him over curiously.

"...Ah mint...for meself."

"How about water? You can turn it into wine."

"Ah...at'll do."

Tom raised his glass of tap water in toast and wandered off into the common room with Krissy in tow.

"Well, I wouldn't mind a beer," Miles said.

"Not for me," said Vikram. "I'm off to bed." Anna slid a foamy mug of beer over to Miles and exchanged a quick cheek-to-cheek embrace with Vikram—*'Night, Rumbi*—as he said his good-nights all around.

Miles was too wired to go to sleep. Besides, he was alone with Anna now with Anders off somewhere. She was trapped.

Remembering what he'd wanted to say, he asked Anna, "Say, is Vikram a doctor or something?"

"Just a doctorate in anthropology, I believe."

"So not a medical doctor."

"Not that I know of. Why?"

Miles tried to explain what he saw Vikram do when he ran over to help Tom in the street, his fuzzy memory already fudging the more bizarre aspects of what he'd actually seen.

Anna agreed it sounded strange, though she was practiced at humoring drunks.

Miles shrugged. Maybe it wasn't so remarkable. "So Vikram's a professor, then?"

"Yes...well, he was. He says he's on sabbatical now, though he's no longer at his university. He was on the faculty at Manchester. And in India before that...I think..." Anna dropped a cluster of beer mugs into a sink filled with soapy water. "He's actually the one responsible for my being in Barcelona."

"How's that?"

"When I was an undergrad in the Netherlands, I was doing research for my thesis in linguistics. I came across a journal article Vikram had authored about a group of hunter-gatherers in East Africa, the Ndzada. Their language is an isolate—not related to any other language. He'd spent a month living with them."

"That sounds interesting." It didn't especially, but she could have read the phone book to him, and Miles would have found it interesting.

"It was," she said. "They've lived the same way for thousands of years. Their way of life—they live almost entirely in the present. They don't dwell on the past or worry about tomorrow."

It sounded familiar to Miles.

"They have no possessions, no laws. He made it sound rather idyllic, I must say," she said and smiled. "Though he did tell me later that the flies drove him crazy. Anyway, his paper was a big part of the reason I decided to pursue anthropology in grad school and come here."

"So you knew him before he was your roommate," Miles said.

"No, actually, I only knew of him," she said. "Our meeting was complete kismet. It's a small world, I guess."

"I guess so."

"I forget," she said, "did you say where you're from?"

"No—Chicago, one of the suburbs."

"You like it there?"

"Not really."

Steve jumped up on the bar just then, startling them both. The skinny, lop-eared cat stared at Miles, as if she were sizing him up. "Hello," he said. "What's your name?" The cat climbed down into his lap.

"That's Steve," said Anna.

"He's a friendly kitty," he said, scritching her behind the ears.

"He's a *she*, actually," she said.

"Oh."

Miles nodded, not bothering to ask why she had a boy's name, and rubbed his knuckles under Steve's chin. She slowly closed and opened her eyes, then snapped her head around, distracted by a noise, bounded down off his lap, and bolted back into the common room.

"So," said Anna, "are you on a break from university?"

"Sort of," he said. "I haven't actually started yet. I got accepted one place, then decided not to go there. My plan is to go, but I'm not sure where."

"Hm."

"My father passed away last year, and I guess I just needed...to get away."

"Oh, I'm sorry," she said. "I never knew my father," she added matter-of-factly, then, regretting it, laughed, something she did when she was nervous.

Miles laughed, a little relieved. They shared a brief comfortable silence.

"Anders—"

"Hm?" Miles said, turning around to see the giant slab of Danish beef parked in the doorway.

"—there you are."

Anders looked surprised to see Miles there. "Miles," he said.

A brief *aha* expression flashed across Anna's face.

"You ready?" Anders asked her.

Anna checked her watch. "It's three already? *Miles* and I were just having a nice talk." He smiled his humblest smile at Anders. "I should close up. You staying at the Kashmir for a few days, Miles?" she asked, tossing his glass into the sudsy water.

"Uh, yeah, at least," he said and got up.

Anna had been clearing things away while they talked, so there wasn't much to do but lock up. Miles walked with Anna and Anders through the common area, where a small group remained playing cards, past the empty reception desk, and up the stairs. They said their good-nights as he turned and entered the third-floor dormitory, while Anna and Anders continued up to her fifth-floor flat.

*

IT TOOK NO TIME for Miles to fall asleep, nestled in his sleeping bag on one of the bottom bunks and dreaming. He was having the same dream he'd been having for the past year. In the first part of the dream, he relived the memory of the last time he saw his father alive, three days before he was run over by a delivery truck.

It was just the two of them in his father Nate's North Side apartment for one of his dad's two weekends a month, his younger sister Sara away at band camp. It was after dinner and Miles was asking him again why he wouldn't let him borrow the car.

I told you already, his father said. *Look, we could go see a movie. Why don't we see what's playing?*

I don't wanna go to a movie with you, Dad.

Fine, he said. *How about a video?*

I don't wanna watch TV either, said Miles. *This isn't fair. Mom lets me use the car on weekends when I'm home.*

It's an hour's drive from here.

Forty-five minutes. Besides, whose fault is that?

You're not driving my car to some party with your friends where there's gonna be drinking—

I don't drink, said Miles, though he could hardly say it with a straight face.

—where the best-case scenario is I only have puke to clean off the upholstery.

Miles frowned.

The answer's no, said Nate. *Don't ask me again.*

This is bullshit, said Miles. *I don't even know why I still have to stay with you every other weekend. What's the point? Nobody wants to. The only reason Sara stays in band is because it allows her to go to camp twice a year instead of coming here.*

That was a low blow. Miles could see his father's fists clench and unclench.

Why don't you just…go to your room. It had been a few years since Nate had sent Miles to his room, but he was clearly out of ideas.

Why don't you make me? Miles made his way toward the front door.

Whoa—where the hell do you think you're going? said Nate, watching his son defy him, an expression of anger mixed with defeat etched on his face.

Out, he said. *And you know what? Fuck this. And fuck you, Nate.*

After that, the dream always segued into the hazy time period just after his father died and then into one of a number of surreal scenarios, usually involving Miles being questioned by the police without any pants on.

He was woken up this time before the pantsless part by the couple in the bunk above him, humping with loud determination. They were making the rickety bed frame creak and sending puffs of plaster dust and crumbly, unidentifiable bits of mattress innards into Miles's face.

Miles had always had a phobia about being on the bottom bunk, afraid that the person above would fall through and squish him. Now there were two people on the bunk above him, doing everything in their power to test the integrity of the already flimsy-looking structure. After an eternity of this, finally a drawn-out crescendo of moaning and groaning. Then blessed silence. Miles began to drift back into the beginnings of unconsciousness. Then—

"Again?"

"Mm-hmm."

4.

VIKRAM AND ANNA'S apartment had only two doors—one for the main entry off the hall and the other for the bathroom. So Vikram was accustomed to waking in the middle of the night to the sounds of passionate lovemaking coming from Anna's sleeping area, separated from his only by a low wall in the kitchen and a red Japanese screen. But last night was curiously silent.

That or Vikram had learned to sleep through it.

When he woke she was already gone, downstairs to open the bar, where they served coffee and hard rolls at the start of every day. Vikram lazed on his futon, gazing out the window across the plaça, the sun creeping above the buildings and throwing its angry morning light against the beige walls of their flat. He pulled a pack of unfiltered Chinese cigarettes from his brown leather satchel and lit one, blowing out the match with a stream of smoke and dropping it into the overflowing ashtray on his bedside table.

Dragging himself from bed, Vikram let the sun warm his bare flesh as he stretched into a parenthesis and dropped his blanket in a pile on the floor. He looked down into the square, then caught his reflection in the glass. He had a thick, luxurious head of wavy jet-black hair, large brown eyes, and full lips on a perpetually crooked mouth. The caramel brown complexion of his face still retained the smoothness of youth, but lines were working their way deeper into the skin around his eyes and mouth. Still, he was happy with the body he'd been given, though he sometimes missed his old self.

He didn't miss home, despite not having been back for some time. He would be happy to never live through another tsunami or dust storm, or endure the intense heat and drought followed by the neverending rains and occasional cyclones. Yet home was frequently on his mind even as he had made Madras, Manchester, and now Barcelona his residence.

Throwing on a faded pink cotton bathrobe, he headed for the shower, where he spent an eternity basking in the hot spray, enjoying the warm prickly sensation before washing up and rinsing off. He toweled himself dry, burned some toast, smeared it with apricot jam, quickly downed it, and finally got dressed. Quickly pocketing a cellophane-wrapped hard candy and a piece of fruit from the bowl on the counter, he headed out the door. Downstairs, he waved *hola* to Paco, the Kashmir's Andalusian front desk clerk, and slipped into the common area to find Anna angrily scrubbing one of the tables, head down, arm working a filthy rag hard enough to remove the finish.

"*Hola*," he said, plopping onto the bench beside her.

Anna threw down the rag and turned to look at Vikram, the rims of her eyes red from crying.

"Oh," he said, "what's wrong?"

"Anders," she said. "That's what's wrong."

"I see," he said, though he didn't.

She exhaled audibly and sat down across from Vikram. "He fucked that blonde Australian girl last night," she said.

"Krissy?"

"No, Tawny!" It was clear Vikram didn't understand why the distinction mattered. "So that's over," she said.

"When?"

"Early this morning, just after he told me."

"No, I mean, when did he have time to fuck somebody other than you last night?" he asked.

"Back at your party, I assume," she answered, a look of irritation on her face plain but not plain enough for Vikram to pick up on. "Shortly *before* he told me about it."

"Oohh...that was quick."

"Well, he wouldn't need long."

"Ah...sorry."

"It's all right. Nobody's died...yet. I just wish it didn't bother me so much. It isn't as if I wanted to settle down with him." She sighed. "He could've handled it better, though. Now I feel foolish."

"Why?" said Vikram, "he's the fool."

Anna smiled weakly and squeezed Vikram's arm. Out of the corner of her eye she could see Miles stagger in and groggily pick up a piece of bread from the bar, looking round about him in a haze, and laughed despite herself. "If you're looking for the coffee," she said, "it's on your right."

Miles hadn't slept well. Between the alcohol, his unsettling dreams, and the orgy in the bunk above his, he was still half-asleep. He swiveled his head around like a bobblehead doll bobbling in slow motion. Spotting Anna, he nodded weakly and turned deliberately to face them, feeling the pain he wasn't feeling last night. "Hi. I'm a little dehydrated. Is there any orange juice?"

"Sorry, no," she said.

"Here," said Vikram, pulling a small orange from his coat pocket and tossing it to Miles, who watched it sail past his head, hit the wall behind him with a splat, and land with a thud on the floor.

"Now we have orange juice," said Anna.

*

ANNA HAD A SEMINAR later that morning but agreed to meet up with the two of them in the afternoon. Vikram offered to show Miles some of the more interesting parts of the city.

"What would you like to see first?" he asked Miles.

"I'm not really sure," he said.

"Do you know anything about Barcelona?"

"I know it's where the waiter on *Fawlty Towers* was from."

"Anything else?"

"I think his name was Manuel?"

Vikram looked at Miles with a crooked smile.

"Nothing else," Miles said.

"This should be fun then."

For the next few hours, they wandered around the old city and into the Eixample. Vikram would stop intermittently, seeming to be caught off guard whenever his meandering led them to someplace noteworthy. A market. A park. A church. A museum. A block of flats. A hospital. Another church, more impressive but still unfinished after a hundred years.

"Gaudí's modernista masterpiece," said Vikram. "Or kitschy Euro trash, depending on your point of view."

La Sagrada Familia's massive towers and façade sprang from the more finished side of the sprawling construction site, concrete molded in organic shapes, dripping down like melted wax from giant candles. For a fee, they climbed one of the towers' spiral staircases, the inside decorated with decades-old graffiti. Near the top, an opening with a small stone balcony offered views north and east. They were all alone, and Vikram stuck a foot in one of the holes of the parapet and hoisted himself up higher, his feet balanced now on the edge of the balcony, a hand on the tower the only thing to steady him hundreds of feet above the ground.

"Um," said Miles, fairly certain this wasn't safe.

A spark lit in Vikram's eye as the sun beat down on his face and a breeze ruffled his hair. He stared out at the city and the ground below, a bead of sweat forming on his brow. It seemed to require all his self-control to resist the urge to launch himself off the tower. Unsure what was going on, Miles didn't know if he should reach a hand out or say something. But the sensation passed, and Vikram stepped down from the parapet, Miles grabbing his elbow to help him down.

Back on the street, Miles wondered if there was something about him that inspired people to want to jump off of buildings. As they walked back in the direction they'd come, he saw that it was ten past four already.

"What time were we supposed to meet Anna?" said Miles.

"Four."

They ducked down the nearest Metro stop and quickly caught a train to the Universitat station, Miles distressed at being late and possibly missing Anna altogether, Vikram pleased that they wouldn't be nearly as late as he usually was.

It was past four-thirty when they came upon the café where Anna was sitting reading and having a drink. Anna smiled as Vikram leaned in for a peck on the cheek. Miles waved hello as they both pulled chairs up to her table.

She brushed a few locks of hair out of her eyes, which promptly fell back, and asked about what they'd seen. Miles told her, and they compared their impressions of La Sagrada Familia and some of the other places Vikram had dragged them both to. They went back and forth comfortably, picking up their conversation from the night before as if no time had passed.

"You two sure seem to like each other," said Vikram.

Miles gave Vikram a look like he'd just flicked him in the nuts, while Anna just laughed.

Anna turned the conversation to the buzz on campus. A hundred or so students had gathered in the courtyard of the administration building and were now on their way to Plaça de Catalunya to join a protest of U.S. involvement in Nicaragua and El Salvador.

This was a good illustration of why Miles had more than once considered sewing a Canadian flag onto his backpack.

"Should we go have a look?" asked Vikram, who seemed keen on the idea of being in the thick of it.

"Um..." hemmed Miles, "I don't like the Contras, either, but being an American, I'm not sure..."

"Oh, don't worry," said Anna, "you don't look like you're from the U.S."

Miles wasn't sure if she meant that as a compliment or just thought he was too scruffy-looking to be mistaken for an American tourist, with his olive green, army-surplus cargo pants and raggedy-ass gray cotton T-shirt. Either way, they were headed to Plaça de Catalunya.

The square was mostly in shadow now, and at least five hundred protestors had congregated beside the fountains, many with signs, and a small group at the front with red bandanas covering their faces, carrying a large Ronald Reagan head on a stick, wrapped in an American flag. Miles recognized many of the words on the signs—SANDINISTAS, REVO-LUCION, GUERRA, MUERTOS, YANQUIS, CIA, and so on—and a man standing on a milk crate next to the masked protestors was leading the crowd's chants with a bullhorn. Anna, Miles, and Vikram were off to the side of the demonstration, and Vikram started talking to one of the students at the back of the crowd in Spanish.

The student, a stocky young man in a hand-painted T-shirt and spiky, bleach-blond hair, was speaking animatedly to Vikram, who was nodding vigorously. Vikram turned to Anna and Miles at one point and said, "Apparently, Reagan signed a law today to start funding the Contras again." Miles had spent the last six weeks more or less blissfully unaware of what was going on in the world, so any news was news to him.

The student continued talking with Vikram, and as Miles looked around, he could see that the crowd had grown by at least half, plus many more like the three of them scattered on the periphery, looking on. The chanting grew louder as more activists joined in, including the young man and Vikram, who had joined in at the top of his lungs. After a few minutes of this, the guy who'd been leading the chants helped the ones holding the Reagan-head effigy to mount it on the milk crate and light it on fire from its stars-and-stripes drapery.

That's when the police descended on the demonstration. The crowd reacted angrily to the cops, which impressed Miles because, in their black riot gear, toting tear-gas launchers and automatic weapons, they looked pretty scary. They went immediately for the flaming Reagan head but were impeded by masked protestors who soon had reason to regret it, getting smashed in the face with plexiglass shields or beaten with billy clubs. Now the crowd divided into camps—one loose affiliation of quickly dispersing students trying to get away from the police, and other small groups intent on causing mischief and/or aggravating the police without directly confronting them. Vikram seemed to be in one of the latter mobs, while Anna and Miles, in the former, tried to clear off as casually as possible.

Small stones and a few sticks flew in the direction of the police, and a few masked activists decided to take their frustration out on the large plate-glass windows of the Burger King at one corner of the plaça. At the sound of smashing glass, Miles turned to Anna and said, "Um...should we—?"

"Yes."

They both ran down a side street away from the square and back toward the university, while others variously followed, stood watching, or ran the other way. They passed in front of an old cinema. "In here!" she yelled to Miles. He had to double back, and they went inside.

Miles looked around, saw the popcorn machine. "What's playing?" he asked. Anna gave him a sardonic look.

Fantasia, the old standard from Disney's golden age, was playing when Anna and Miles entered the darkened theater, the sorcerer's apprentice madly chopping animated brooms to death over Dukas's symphonic poem. They found a place to sit toward the back, a sparse group spread out among the hundreds of seats. Mickey Mouse tugged on the tail of Leopold Stokowski's tuxedo jacket, the two outlined in silhouette, and said something to the conductor in Spanish. Miles and Anna smiled at each other and slouched down into the mangy upholstery of their backrests.

"I hope Vikram didn't get arrested," Anna whispered to Miles.

"I know," he said.

"At least the country's not run by fascists anymore," she offered, referring to the regime of Generalissimo Francisco Franco, who by 1986 was still dead. *Of course, if there are any fascists left,* she thought, *they'd be in the police.* In her experience, the police attracted fascists the way priesthood drew pederasts.

*

STROLLING THROUGH the alleys of the Raval at dusk after the movie let out, Anna and Miles wound their way back to the Hotel Kashmir.

"Well, this has been an interesting day," Anna said, meaning losing her boyfriend and possibly her roommate in the space of a few hours.

Miles thought of Vikram, and of Tom falling from the balcony. "Mm-hmm," he mused. "You worried about Vikram?"

"A little," she admitted. "Although, actually...not terribly much. He's like a cat."

Miles nodded, then knit his brow. "As in, he always lands on his feet," he asked, "or he has nine lives?"

"One of those."

They continued on in silence for a while, skirting round the back of the Boqueria Market and turning on Carrer de l'Hospital, where they saw a teeming Ramblas lit up in its nighttime incarnation. When they emerged from the side street, Miles looked down the mile-long boulevard from the reverse perspective of his arrival twenty-four hours earlier.

To their left, the protest in Plaça de Catalunya had ended, and the Ramblas showed no sign that it had ever happened. Miles and Anna weaved their way under the plane trees lining the boulevard, being offered *hash-coke-speed* every few minutes as if it were a kind of benediction and this was the most devout place on earth.

When they arrived at the Kashmir, there was no Vikram, but most of the regulars were hanging out in the common area. Anna was late for her shift behind the bar. She gave Miles a quick one-armed squeeze, leaving him pleasantly flushed, and headed off to relieve the other bartender, Ahmed. Paco, the desk clerk, was sitting and talking with Tom and Krissy by an open window when Miles wandered over.

"...that I from Andalusia," Paco was saying, "and Catalans think we are, ah, how you say..."

"Yobbos?" suggested Krissy.

"I no know this word," he said.

"Hayseeds?" offered Tom, but Paco shook his head. "Rubes?"

"Rednecks?" Miles put in helpfully.

"Yes, rednecks, I think," said Paco, chuckling. "Is American expression, no? But it means?"

"I think it just means someone who works out in a field every day," said Miles, pantomiming to help explain, "and he gets a sunburned neck—a *red neck*."

"*Sí*," Paco said. "Catalans think we are all rednecks."

"Westies!" said Krissy. "That's another one we say."

"Yeah, well, you're *all* westies to us," said Tom, and Krissy gave a laugh while backhanding him on the shoulder—"Ow."

"Sorry...forgot."

Paco looked a little like an extra from a Sergio Leone western—olive skin with curly dark brown hair and sleepy, half-lidded chestnut eyes. His thick eyebrows were perpetually tented in an expression of inquiry, which gave his face a meek, simple appearance. He'd been working at the Kashmir since before Vikram had moved in upstairs. People tended to like Paco because he smiled a lot, was slow to take offense at even the worst behavior, and went out of his way to help guests who had paid almost nothing to stay there.

Miles looked around and saw Marie talking with some of the Brits from last night, Katya and Katya at a table with a guy he hadn't seen before. No Anders or Tawny, though. "Where's Tawny?" he asked Krissy.

Krissy, having just taken a sip of beer, managed to swallow instead of doing an unladylike spit-take and gave Miles a look of annoyed surprise. "She didn't tell ya?"

"Tell me what?" he said. Then, "She *who?*"

"You came in with Anna, so I thought she'd've told you." Krissy took another sip to prepare for her third or fourth retelling of the story. "Tawny took off with Anders this morning. Just flippin' left me here on my own."

"What?"

"Right? We're supposed to be mates. I've known her for three years, and we've been traveling companions for two months, ever since we landed at Athens. One night with Anders, and it's hooroo to you, mate. Bitch."

Miles felt a slight pang in the pit of his stomach.

"Poor Anna," said Tom, who'd already heard this.

Paco shook his head with a sardonic smile and got up. "Back to work," he said with a wave.

"I saw you talking with Tawny last night," Krissy said to Miles, under her breath.

"Hm?" said Miles.

"I just wondered if maybe she'd said anything to you?"

"No. Not really," he said. "I mean, she said things, and I said things, you know...we were talking. But not about much of anything, as far as that goes."

Krissy gave him a dubious glance but left it at that.

Miles didn't know if he should be horrified or proud. He didn't think his feeble attempt to sabotage Anders's and Anna's relationship would actually work. It was a little like snapping your fingers on a mountaintop on a lark and watching in horror as an avalanche followed. And then benefitting from the destruction it caused. Then again, it's possible it had nothing to do with him.

Just then they heard Paco greet Vikram at the front desk with a low gasp. "*Lo que le pasó a tu cabeza?*"

"*No es nada, Paco,*" said Vikram. "*Sólo un bache.*"

Vikram walked in, all smiles, with a tattered rag wrapped around his forehead and dried blood staining the left shoulder of his wrinkled linen sportcoat. "It's not as bad as it looks," he prefaced his greeting to Miles and the others.

Anna walked in, having heard his voice, and gave Vikram a relieved hug as he winced from her squeeze. "Did the police do this, Rumbi?" she asked, lightly touching his bandage.

"This? No," he said. "I tied it myself. The shirt was ruined, so I just tore a strip off."

Anna gave him a look. "We lost you in the crowd once the police came in," she said. "We didn't know what happened to you."

"What happened to you two?" he asked.

Anna shrugged and let out an embarrassed laugh. "We went to the movies," she said.

"Anything good?"

"Yes. Were you arrested?"

"A new film? An oldie?"

Anna sighed audibly. "*Fantasia.*"

"Oh." Vikram smiled. "Yes, while you were watching your cartoon, I was detained briefly by the police. Fortunately, they weren't in a mood to be vindictive about it. They released me after an hour or so, and here I am."

"You are like a cat," she said.

Vikram scowled. "You know I hate cats."

Anna returned to the bar, and Vikram joined Miles and the others at the table, where a card game soon broke out. Miles and Tom nursed their beers, while Krissy got good and drunk, and Vikram just sat back and smoked—*best thing for a headache*, he said. Tom shook his head. *You look like I ought to*, he said. Soon Marie joined them, and later Vikram's bleach-blond friend from the demonstration, who had managed to elude the police, stopped by with his multiply-pierced, dyed, and tattooed girlfriend for a drink. Tom and the couple—Ramón and Laia—got talking anarchist politics, and it wasn't long before people started departing for anywhere but there. Miles joined a small group for an early supper, and Vikram, looking ragged, begged off to retire for the evening.

"*Vaya con dios*," he said with a smile and headed up the stairs. From behind the front desk, Paco watched Vikram disappear, his eyes betraying his curiosity about this enigmatic Indian anthropologist who'd been living upstairs for so long and who seemed to have so many secrets.

*

VIKRAM REMOVED the bloody strip of cloth from his head and dropped it in the bathroom trash. The scalp was split, bruised, and still wet from freshly oozing blood. He washed the wound in the sink, gently ministering to it with his now glowing left hand, and then dried it off with a washcloth. Already it looked better as he examined it in the mirror, the cut mostly closed, the ugly purple bump fading away. He found a medium-sized gauze bandage in the medicine chest and adhered it to his forehead.

Returning to the kitchen, he grabbed his satchel and a bar of chocolate from the table and continued on his way out of the apartment. Once in the hallway, he made a right turn and walked over to an unmarked door. Unlocking it and then closing it behind him, he climbed the stairs to the top of the building and opened the door onto the roof. He wedged a rock under it to keep it from closing and picked his way across the gravel and brick tiles to the tile he was looking for. Opening his pocket knife, he bent down and slid the blade under the tile and pulled the large ceramic square back, revealing more gravel. Digging his hands into the rough stones, he extracted something wrapped in a black plastic bag and sealed with duct tape. He blew the dust off the package and cut the tape with his knife. Carefully, he withdrew a slim black metal case from the bag, paused to admire it, and then fumbled it onto the gravel below while trying to transfer it to his right hand, kicking it for good measure as he leaned over to grab it.

Vikram straightened and sighed. His precautions were probably unnecessary, he realized, but he had never trusted any of Anna's lovers—especially Anders, even though he couldn't pinpoint why. He calmly bent down and picked the case up, brushed off the fresh dust, and examined it with his eyes and hands with a mixture of reverence and sentimentality. He slid it into his satchel, looking around him as he did. It was a clear night with a half moon, and the lights of the Ramblas glowed like a spiral arm of the Milky Way.

He made his way back down to his flat and sat down at the kitchen table. He extracted the case from his satchel and set it down gingerly in front of him. He entered a combination and opened the case. Inside was an array of recessed compartments, some filled with vials, some not; some containing rather ordinary natural artifacts, such as acorns, hazelnuts, walnuts, chestnuts, or more exotic, like the seed of a baobab fruit; some vials filled with small seedlings floating in liquid; one section cold, with dry-ice mist rising off the frozen vials containing god knows what. The case's interior actually appeared deeper than its exterior would allow, there was so much crammed in there. Vikram removed a vial from the pocket of his sportcoat draped on the chair opposite him. He found the available spot in the case and inserted the tube gently. Each vial or object wore a handmade label written in a script that vaguely resembled Sanskrit but flowed vertically like Japanese kanji—elegantly angular characters with swooping arcs, punctuated by squiggles and dots, and connected by bold lines. Vikram finished filling in the label and stuck it on the vial. He turned to look behind him out of habit before reclosing the case, locking it, and stuffing it back inside his satchel.

Once again, he made the palm of his left hand glow, the brown skin now a blue backlit screen. There was a message this time, as expected, a reminder he'd written to himself a long time ago.

5.

ANNA WOKE BATHED in the red glow of sunlight seeping through her folding Japanese screen. Imprinted on the other side of the screen was, aptly, a giant red rising sun. A rare day off from both work and school, she was luxuriating in having the whole bed to herself for once and in no hurry to get up.

She was allowing herself to think about Anders, picturing him throwing off the covers and sitting up, the muscles of his back and shoulders rippling under pale rough skin as he stretched his arms to the ceiling. She decided she'd gotten everything she wanted out of the affair. Well, all but one thing. She would have liked to have been the one who did the dumping. She was good at it, anyway, and would have done a better job than that oaf. A handsome oaf, certainly, but an oaf in the end.

More than one male guest of the Kashmir had made it up to her apartment, and she always knew how to let the fellow down gently before sending him on his way. In most cases, the feelings were mutual—he was passing through, and their romance came with a predetermined expiration date. In other cases, Anna could tell the guy thought they would continue the affair long distance, while he bounced around Europe or returned home, absence making the heart grow fonder and all that crap. In either case, she usually managed to leave it on friendly terms, without hurt feelings. She even maintained a platonic correspondence with a few of them.

Being jilted by Anders only reminded Anna of the transient nature of her existence here. She loved the city, the hotel, and the people. But few stayed longer than a couple of weeks. Then there was school. Though she'd made some friends there, she sometimes got the feeling her fellow students were studying her. Being one of the few people of color in the anthropology department could feel a little isolating. She was still thinking about going back to linguistics, which meant possibly leaving Barcelona.

Vikram was her closest friend, yet—perhaps because of the difference in their ages or countries of birth, or because his mind often seemed so faraway—there was an unspoken remove, despite everything they'd shared and their often-expressed affection for one another.

Barcelona was more cosmopolitan than most Spanish cities, more than most European cities, in general. It had had an influx of emigrants from North Africa and the Middle East and served as a crossroads in the Mediterranean. Even the Catalan language seemed to be a kind of Mediterranean stew. And the city was starting to draw tourism, despite its seedier aspects (or perhaps because of them). It was more diverse than most places in Europe, but it was still mostly white. Anna was half-white, which was the same as not-white. She remembered learning that her father had been a white man when she was a child. It meant little in Parbo, where most people were of mixed race, anyway. It meant little in Amsterdam—but for different reasons. What she learned coming of age in the Netherlands was that, in a predominantly white country—even one as tolerant as the Netherlands—whiteness was understood as a state of purity. Whiteness diluted was not-white. Being half-black, or any part black, was just another way of saying *black*. And black would never be as good as white, at least to enough people that it mattered. Even if you were white enough to pass for white, that's all you were doing—passing. Anna had never heard of anyone trying to pass for black.

As people frequently mistook her for British or American (well, she *was* American, she would point out), she knew that Europeans generally treated black folks from the U.S. better than black folks they considered to be their own problem. It wasn't something that she normally fixated on, but it did remind her that her own racial makeup was more than an academic construct. A world in which variations in skin color were given the same weight as differences in hair or eye color was the world she wanted to live in, and at times, it was nice to be able to pretend she did.

She snuggled under her comforter, cherishing her independence, enjoying the chance to sleep in, even if she was no longer asleep, until her bladder finally insisted she get up out of bed.

After flushing, she quickly washed her hands and brushed her teeth. She emerged from the loo in a refreshed, energetic mood and looked for something to do. Still in just her underwear and an oversized T-shirt, Anna walked over to the bookcase in the living room and popped a Heaven 17 cassette out of the tape deck. It was Vikram's. His taste in music was all over the place. Piled next to the boom box were cassette tapes of Billie Holiday and Dave Brubeck mixed in with The Damned, Joy Division, Indochine, Lionel Richie, and Madonna. It was as if he had just arrived on Earth and were sampling a little bit of everything. She inserted a mix tape a former boyfriend had sent her, hit PLAY, and went into the kitchen to clean up to the sound of Ray Charles singing, "Let's Go Get Stoned."

The dishes had piled up from the day before. Though Vikram was fairly fastidious for a man, his version of cleaning up involved occasionally washing one of the dishes he'd actually used and then leaving it in the dish drainer. He would dump out one of his legion of ashtrays (some of which weren't ashtrays) only after it was full to overflowing—when moving it at all precipitated a small landslide of ash and cigarette butts onto the floor. Then there were the stray hard-candy and chocolate-bar wrappers strewn randomly about. Vikram seemed to subsist on a diet of sugar and nicotine.

Coming over to the table to collect some glasses, she found a note from Vikram. It read:

Meet me downstairs when you have the time. I'd like to talk.

—*Rumbi*

It was an odd note for Vikram to leave. He could talk to her anytime he wanted, why the formal invitation? It was the first time he'd ever come across to her as the professor he used to be, and she wondered if she should be worried.

*

MEANWHILE VIKRAM waited downstairs and worried.

TIME TO GO HOME—that was the message that appeared on his hand— meaning he was now expected. It was time, but he wasn't ready. Vikram doubted he'd ever be ready, though his return was inevitable. He had postponed it for as long as he could.

But he needed to speak with Anna first. Lurking downstairs was just a way of putting it off. Maybe she'd want to take a daytrip to Girona with him, where he could explain things to her. She'd think he was crazy, naturally. He hated the thought of her feeling betrayed or, worse, her pity. He couldn't leave without saying good-bye, but mostly he couldn't leave without her.

If he didn't scare her away, he'd move on to finding out how she felt about Miles. He only needed one of them, but they were expecting one of each, so he really wanted them both. Right now he had neither. He expected she'd be down soon. He would just have to wait and see what happened.

He hadn't slept and so had showered and changed, bringing down his case and everything of importance to him in his satchel shortly after Anna had gotten in and gone to sleep. He was sucking the carcinogeny goodness from a smoke held in one hand while warming his other with a mug of heavily sweetened coffee.

Paco, who was manning the bar and the front desk on Anna's day off, came by and offered Vikram a refill on his coffee.

"*No, gracias*, Paco." Paco could be a little annoying with his over-attentive service. Anna always just left the pot on the counter for people to help themselves. This was a hostel, after all, not the Hotel Colón.

Tom sat down at the table next to Vikram's. "I liked your friend Ramón," he said. "We'll make an anarchist of you yet."

Vikram rolled his eyes and blew out a stream of smoke to punctuate his sigh.

"Oh, come on, Vik."

"Tom, anarchy does not work in the real world," he said. "No political system will ever be able to offer absolute liberty *and* equality. They eventually work against each other."

"Well, if by liberty you mean the freedom to exploit others, to exploit the Earth, then you're right, it is unworkable," said Tom. "But I think some form of anarcho-syndicalism is the only way."

Vikram shook his head. "I've only ever seen one example of that kind of system—and that was with a group of twenty or so hunter-gatherers.

It wasn't a formal system, it was just how they naturally governed themselves. It's beautiful to see in practice," he said, remembering his time with the Ndzada. Tom nodded, as if this were confirmation. "Unfortunately, some things are universal. Get more than a few dozen people together, and you have to start giving up freedoms and accept roles that are inherently unequal and often involuntary. The best systems simply limit how much you lose in the trade-off."

Tom laughed good-naturedly. "I love when you get worked up about politics, Vik," he said. He fished some prints out of his jacket pocket and waved them over his head. "Marie brought her Polaroid out with us last night. She gave me a few. A coupla good ones, too."

Vikram, disarmed, was suddenly feeling sentimental. He stubbed out his cigarette and got up to look at them with Tom. He had to laugh at the one of Tom splayed out on the stones close to where he'd landed the night before.

He turned back to his coffee, and his heart skipped a beat. His satchel was missing. He checked the bench. He checked the floor under the bench. He checked the bench again. He started for the bar—"Paco, *has visto mi*...Paco?" *Where's Paco?*

"What's the matter, mate?"

"My satchel was just here," he said, indicating the bench. *Paco.* "Did you see Paco walk by here?"

"Yeah, well, he was back and forth filling coffee and whatnot."

"Where is he now?"

"He's not in the bar?"

"No." As Vikram was saying it, he headed for the front desk where Paco was also not. He was gone, along with his satchel. *I'm an idiot*, he thought. *But how?*

"I'm sure Paco didn't take it," Tom called after him. "I can help you look if you like."

"Uh, never mind," said Vikram distractedly. "I probably left it upstairs." Vikram popped out into the stairwell but immediately headed downstairs, where on the ground floor he encountered not Paco, but four troopers of the *Mossos d'Esquadra*, the same force that had arrested him at the demonstration, minus their riot gear.

"*Hola, Señor Bhat,*" the one in front said, betraying not a little smug satisfaction.

*

WHEN MILES WAS younger, he had always wondered why grownups—and even some kids his own age—seemed to have a handle on things that eluded him so utterly. He assumed that, as he got older, he would start to understand what was going on and what was expected of him, and that his dad would let him in on the secret.

It was around the time his folks split up that Miles realized that his dad didn't have the handle on things he appeared to—and not just because his mother seemed to be pointing it out on a regular basis. He saw a man at sea, flailing around helplessly without any answers. The only thing Nate was ever likely to let him in on was an unfunny joke. It's a terrible thing to have your practical illusions dashed so early, and hard not to conclude that the man you held up as some kind of all-knowing, all-powerful authority figure was simply a big fat liar.

He'd never be able to tell his dad that he now knew that nobody knew what the hell they were doing. That he knew his father had tried his best, that he was sorry he'd judged him so harshly.

One of the things he liked best about wandering around Europe with no plan and little money was that most of the people he met on the road never made him feel like there was some secret handshake he didn't know. They made it up as they went along and never pretended they knew what the program was. Like him, they weren't trying to be professional humans. They were happy amateurs.

Now he was sitting at a table in the common room, trying to write a letter to his younger sister, Sara, one of the only people he thought might have a genuine handle on things. The late morning light was making his eyeballs ache, and Steve jumped up on the table, walked over to his pad of paper, and laid down on it with a look of pure impudence. She closed her eyes at Miles.

"What's the secret, Steve?" he asked, letting her sniff his hand and scritching her behind the ears. "You seem to have it all figured out."

45

"*Brrown*," she replied.

Steve proceeded to lean back on her haunches and begin cleaning her private parts. Miles waited until she finished and then gently began to try and nudge her off his paper. She didn't take the hint, staring at his hand as if it were a fleshy rodent. Finally, Miles used one end of the pad like a lever to upend Steve, who sprawled over and then padded lazily over to the other side of the table.

Anna walked in then, and Miles forgot all about his sister. She spied him and came over and sat down.

"*Hola*," she said. "Have you seen Vikram?"

"Nope."

A look of mild annoyance flashed across her face. "Paco is supposed to be working today, but he's not here either, and I don't want to get pulled into covering for him," she said. "Have you eaten anything?"

Miles had devoured a few hard rolls with marmalade along with some coffee and juice when he first came down. A little later, he shared some Manchego cheese, Serrano ham, almonds, and olives with Marie. "No," he said.

"I was thinking we could grab something to eat."

"Sounds great," he said. "I'm starving."

Anna took him to a dingy little hole in the wall in Barceloneta, where they went dutch on a pan of paella. After that, she suggested they go up to Tibidabo, the mountain on the northwest side of the city with an amusement park at its summit.

It was a warm, sunny, breezy fall day. After taking the funicular up the mountain, they looked down over the city, taking in the whole panorama at once. Miles could see the towers of La Sagrada Familia, the spires of the gothic Cathedral, the teeming Ramblas extending from the Plaça de Catalunya to the harbor, and the Mediterranean beyond.

"It's beautiful," he said.

"It is." The city's colors were vivid under a clear and deeply blue sky. "I was here back in spring," she remarked, ending another easy silence, "and you couldn't even see Montjuic. The whole city was blanketed with smog."

"Really?" Miles couldn't imagine that. How could this otherworldly city suffer the same indignities as its more mundane counterparts?

"On still days, the mountains hold it in over the city," she said, in answer to his unspoken question. "There are a lot of cars here."

Compared to Amsterdam, maybe. Miles didn't see any analog to the Dan Ryan Expressway here. Still, he hated to think of this place covered with a dark cloud of pollution, even temporarily. After only a couple of days, he was beginning to think of it as home.

They rode the Ferris wheel, explored the inevitable church at the top of the mountain, and strolled along the paths that wound through the park. Miles realized he knew very little about Anna and asked her about her childhood. She told him about growing up in Suriname and emigrating to the Netherlands. She said she missed the people she'd grown up with in Parbo, the food, and the tropical climate, but nevertheless felt more European than American now. He asked her how many languages she spoke and found the answer humbling, considering his mangling of French after three years of it in high school. She said she liked to travel and visited home when she could. She still had friends there and kept in regular contact with her mother. Anna could tell she was proud of her, which made her glad.

"So we both moved when we were twelve," said Miles. "You moved from South America to Europe, and, after my parents split, we moved to a smaller house across town."

Anna asked him about his family, what he wanted to do after his break ended. He told her about his sister and mother, the friends he hoped to see again when he returned. He didn't know what he wanted to do with his life when this was over. He knew he should go to college, though the prospect didn't excite him. He had been an indifferent student in high school for the most part, but his grades were probably good enough to get him into a state school. Though he didn't know what he would study if he did.

"You could study anthropology," she said. "What's more interesting than studying human beings?"

"I don't know," he said, "anything?"

"Hah," she said.

They found their way back to the funicular and funiculated down past wealthy homes and lovely manicured gardens. Once back down, they wandered the neighborhood around La Rotonda and the Plaça de John

Kennedy, heading in the general direction of the Kashmir as the shadow of Tibidabo followed on their heels and gradually overtook them.

Too far to walk all the way back, they took the Metro back to Plaça de Catalunya and drifted over to the square in front of the Cathedral to find a café and maybe a drink.

On their way through the plaza, lined with bustling cafés and packed with tourists on a Saturday evening, Anna noticed an acoustic trio playing next to the Cathedral steps. She grabbed Miles's hand and pulled him through the crowd so that they could hear the music. It was quickly getting dark as they stood and listened to the fiddler and two guitar players serenade them with something folksy and pretty, and just a little forlorn.

Miles noticed that Anna had yet to let go of his hand. Maybe she'd simply forgotten she had hold of it. Should he let go? She squeezed his hand in answer, sending a pleasant shiver up his shoulder. As the group ended the tune, Miles dropped a 100 peseta coin he could hardly afford into the hat and turned to look at Anna. He had never wanted to kiss anyone more than he did at that moment, nor had he ever been as sure he should. She smiled and turned back toward the row of cafés when he pulled her gently back toward him and leaned in to kiss her lips, softly at first, then more assuredly as she kissed him back, locked in a solitary embrace amid the bustling throng.

With his eyes shut, he felt a light come on, and his face flushed. They parted. He looked at her, she regarded him, and at the same time they turned to see that the Cathedral looked to be on fire, its façade glowing yellow-orange, as if it were lit from within.

"Ooh—I've never been here before when they turn the lights on," said Anna.

"Oh," said Miles, glad to know that she saw it too.

*

IT WAS DARK and relatively quiet up on the roof before Anna and Miles stumbled through the doorway around two A.M. The city was still brightly lit and churning with activity below. After wandering back to Plaça Reial from the Cathedral, they had met up with Krissy, Tom, a few other regulars, and some new guests of the Kashmir. From there, they trekked over to a gay bar in the Raval, after which they all grabbed supper near the Santa Maria del Pi basilica and then went dancing again at the subterranean disco off Plaça Reial. Lightheaded from alcohol and exertion, they passed the second-floor common area of the Kashmir and headed up the stairs. They were trailed by Steve, who padded up to the door in the fifth-story hall and shot them a look of betrayal as they shut it behind them and climbed the stairs to the roof.

Up on the rooftop, Anna took Miles's hand and led him over to the parapet at the rear of the building. They could see the trees of the Ramblas lit from below, extending northwest to the Plaça de Catalunya and southeast to the Monument a Colom, the boulevard still as noisy and aglow as ever.

"Look," said Anna, pointing toward the harbor. "You can just make out the top of Columbus." It was faint, but its outline could be picked out from the halfmoon-lit sky.

Miles remembered standing before it as he took in the Ramblas on his first day, Christopher Columbus pointing out to sea from atop the forty-meter-tall column. "What is he pointing at, anyway?" he asked.

"Algeria, I think," she said.

"That makes sense, I guess," he said. "He thought he was going to India."

"Or maybe he's trying to tell us, 'You'll need slaves. They're this way.'"

Miles thought that was funny but didn't think he should laugh. "Sorry," she said, "black humor." That made him laugh despite himself.

On the other side, Plaça Reial was still bustling, and above them the stars were dimly visible despite the light radiating upward from the city. After several minutes more of this crow's-nest view and necking in the open air, Anna took Miles by the hand and led him back downstairs to her apartment, Steve looking up briefly from her bath as they disappeared behind another closed door.

Once inside, Anna switched on a lamp. "It looks like Vikram's out for the night," she said, observing his unmade bed.

"I like your place," said Miles. At the age of eighteen, almost any home without parents living in it seemed nicer than it was. But Anna knew that whatever charm her apartment had came mainly from the shared rooftop deck and its location.

She asked him if he wanted something to drink. *I'm fine*, he said. They were both tired from the long day but charged with the adrenaline of lust. She led him around her red Japanese screen to a large futon made up with a billowy white down comforter and more pillows than could fit across its head. *Sit down*, she said. He did, and nearly missed the mattress for the poofy comforter. *I should really kick you out*, she said, lighting a candle on the nightstand. *I have to get up and go to work in a few hours.* She sat down on the bed and leaned into him. *But...* she added, kissing him softly on the mouth.

Although Miles was a virgin, he wasn't completely inexperienced. He'd fooled around with his last girlfriend some, had even reached third base. Or, more accurately, had been thrown out trying to stretch a double into a triple—like Bill Buckner in the 1974 World Series highlights they seemed to show during every rain delay. He'd had one other opportunity to lose his virginity but had demurred. In the end, he was a romantic and so was saving himself. Just not for marriage.

Miles returned her kisses, his hands moving from her back to her front while hers worked down to the tail of his shirt and lifted it over his head. Soon they were both down to their underwear, their smooth skin hot and tingling where their bodies touched. Miles was shaking. He wanted to make love to Anna in the worst way. Which was what he was afraid he would do.

"Don't be nervous," she said.

"Sorry," he said. "Is it that obvious?"

"It's okay. Your insecurity is actually quite charming."

Miles opened his mouth to speak, then stopped, then said, "I thought women were attracted to confidence."

"It's like cologne," she said. "A little is nice, but too much of it can reek."

She kissed his neck as they lay down on the futon, she on top, and Miles smiled, presuming her last remark referred to Anders. Then, sorry he'd invited that image into his head, returned her kisses with gusto, working his way from her clavicle to her left ear until she pulled away with a laugh.

"That tickles," she said, scrunching her nose.

"Sorry."

He was a little daunted by the difference in their age and experience, but once he gave up the pretense of knowing what he was doing and let her take the lead, they both enjoyed themselves. Of course, Miles enjoyed himself a little sooner than Anna did, but life is full of second chances, and he only needed about ten minutes for his.

A while later, after the second time, spent and now still, they remained lying tangled together, pleasantly warm and just a touch sweaty. She looked up at him, searching his eyes for the thoughts they might betray but finding them inscrutable. "What are you thinking?" she asked.

Miles seldom thought just one thought at a time, and at the moment his mind teemed with a jumble of excited and incoherent blather. "I don't know," he said, "just…happy." Anna smiled and maneuvered him into a spooning cuddle as the two quickly drifted off to sleep.

*

FOR ONCE Miles didn't dream the same dream he'd been having for the past twelve months, of his last, guilt-stricken encounter with his father followed by a half-naked standoff with the police. This time, he dreamt of a river. On the bank of the river, he lay down and drank from it while a hand massaged the back of his leg. Now the hand gently shook him, now it roused him from his dream.

Miles woke to see Anna sitting on the edge of the bed, dressed and leaning over him, her hand softly caressing the inside of his right thigh. He half-moaned, half-yawned as her hand moved up his leg. He stretched his body from fingers to toes and pulled her down into a kiss, which she returned enthusiastically but shortly had to pull away.

"I'm really sorry," she said, "but I have to go to work."

"Oh, you do? That's right, you do," he said, answering his own question.

"Yeah. See you down there later, okay?" she said, and he nodded. "Make sure the door shuts when you leave. It sticks."

"Okay."

She kissed him good-bye and left him with a throbbing hard-on, one that wouldn't subside even after a few minutes thinking unsexy thoughts.

He crossed the kitchen naked—putting pants on in that condition is like putting a shirt on with the hanger still inside—and proceeded to the bathroom to relieve his bladder, which he managed by straddling the toilet and forcing his erection down like a divining rod.

His bladder empty but his situation otherwise unchanged, Miles began to worry this was becoming a permanent condition—eighth grade all over again. Then a loud knock at the door followed by a male voice announcing the word *policia* took care of it all at once.

Miles shouted *momentito!* and raced to Anna's bedroom to find his pants, determined not to live out his nightmare. Pulling them on while walking over to the door and falling over in the process, he finally buttoned them up and opened the door to two men dressed in the light-blue uniform of the Mossos d'Esquadra.

The two officers assessed him casually, smiling inwardly at his freshly woken, shirtless appearance. His tangled mess of matted, spiky hair and bleary eyes aroused more sympathy than suspicion. The younger officer, the stockier of the two with a black bushy mustache and eyebrows, offered Miles a *buenos dias*, adding, while strolling in through the door, something that apparently made it all right for the two of them to come on in.

"Um," said Miles, his heart racing, his mind trying to figure out what they were doing here.

The older, quieter officer began nosing around the place, while the talkative one started shooting questions at Miles in rapid-fire Spanish.

"*Lo siento,*" said Miles with a shrug. "*No habla español.*"

The older officer shook his head and made his way toward the bathroom, while the other put a hand on Miles's bare shoulder and said, "*No* hablo *español.*"

"Sorry?"

"You said, '*No habl*a,' which you use for '*you*' or '*he* doesn't speak...' You should say, '*No hablo*—(I don't speak)—*español.*'"

"Oh, sorry."

"*No es problema.*" The officer stroked his mustache thoughtfully and added, "Now, in Catalan, you would say, '*No parlo espanyol.*' Of course, in that case, you'd more likely say, '*No parlo* català.'"

"Sure."

"May I ask your name?"

"Yes…Miles Townsend."

"American?"

"Yes."

"Do you live here, Miles?"

"No. I'm just a guest."

"Of who?"

Miles paused. "You should say, 'of *whom*,'" he pointed out, taking his turn being the grammar police.

The officer stared at him, unamused, with a look that reminded Miles that he was the *actual* police. The officer pulled a notebook and pen out of his jacket pocket.

"Of…Anna's," Miles said.

"Anna? This is Vikram Bhat's apartment?" the officer asked.

"No—I mean, yes, they're roommates."

"Anna and Vikram?" Miles responded with a nod. "And you're her… *friend*?"

"Yes," he said. "I mean, I'm friends with both of them."

"Oh?" The way he said it seemed to imply something. "You are a student?"

"Yes. Well, I was."

The officer didn't bother asking what that meant. "When was the last time you saw Vikram?"

"The last time was two days ago."

The officer frowned and started writing something in his notebook.

"Did something happen?" asked Miles. "Is Vikram all right?"

"As far as we know, he's fine. We're just trying to locate him." He looked over at his partner, then added, "What did you say was Anna's last name?"

"Uh, I didn't," he said. "That is, I don't know."

The other officer, having worked his way around the small flat, having rifled through Vikram's dresser and finding nothing of interest, came around the low partition and picked up an address book on the bookshelf, looked inside the front cover, said something in Spanish to his partner, and handed it to him.

"Is this her?" the officer asked Miles, pointing to a name handwritten in violet ink.

Anna de Wit, it read.

"I think so, yes," said Miles. The officer wrote it down, along with the phone number.

"*Bien*. Okay, Miles, if you do see Vikram, please call us. It's very important." The officer handed Miles a calling card, adding, "Please let your friend Anna know that we'd like to ask her some questions as well." He turned to join his partner, and the two made their exit.

As Miles examined the card, he could see that his hands were trembling. He shuffled over to the kitchen table and sat down, tossing the card aside. He didn't understand what it meant that they were "trying to locate" Vikram. *What had he done now?* He wanted to see Anna, but he dreaded trying to explain what had just happened, not to mention that the police wanted to question her. Despite his recurring dream, Miles didn't think he was afraid of the police, as such. It was more that he saw them as bearers of bad news. The last time he'd spoken to one was on the worst day of his life.

6.

ANNA'S FACE was a study in distress. She stared out the window of the common room with puffy eyes, as a solitary tear traced the curve of her cheek and fell to the tabletop with a scarcely audible *splat*. Wiping away the wet path of her tears with the heel of her hand, she observed a gaudily dressed hooker working the morning shift on the plaça and laughed ruefully to herself. *There are always jobs*, her mother liked to tell her, *for people willing to work*.

Moments before, the Kashmir's manager, Josep, had accosted her as she was opening the lounge. He rarely spoke to her, but when he did, it was usually to remind her what a douchebag he was. Josep, whose father owned the Kashmir and the apartment where Anna and Vikram lived, might have been considered attractive, in a square-jawed, hairsprayed, local TV sportscaster kind of way, if not for his personality. He had long been smitten with Anna, but had gone about expressing his interest with all the charm of a socially inept eight-year-old boy. Instead of pulling her hair or throwing clods of dirt at her, though, he did things like make awful, sexist, borderline-racist jokes or change shifts on her at the last minute. Somehow nothing he did seemed to work.

Josep had heard through the hotel grapevine of Anna's latest liaison (Miles, that is) and had come to insist that she no longer date the Kashmir's guests. She assumed it was another of his attempts at a joke. But he sincerely wanted it to stop and made clear that he thought this sort of thing fell under his purview as her manager.

Anna didn't exactly quit at this point. But she did inform Josep that whom she fucked was none of his goddamned business, and also that he should *fuck himself*, preferably with something crooked and rusty.

Even in a dingy flophouse like the Kashmir, that constituted giving notice.

Anna now began to second-guess her rash action. Perhaps she could have managed to put up with Josep a little longer, at least until she decided what to do about school. But he had to stick his nose into her personal life. *What does he care whom I sleep with? What concern is it of his?* These were questions Anna couldn't hope to answer. Certain male minds were completely impenetrable to her. Why did some men think they had a say in what she did with her body? What was there about a woman who enjoyed sex that was so threatening?

She had some savings, but not enough to pay rent for more than a couple months without a new source of income—and whether she'd be allowed to stay in her flat even if she did was now an open question. She would either need to find another job quickly or quit the program and return to Amsterdam.

Anna wondered how Josep would manage now without her or Paco, who hadn't shown up again after flaking out the day before. *Where was he?* Ahmed was the only other regular employee, and he was in Marseille until Thursday.

As she was thinking this, Josep sidled up to her table, leaving an invisible trail of slime as he did, and announced, "*Escuchar*, Anna…I really need you this week with Ahmed out and Paco god-knows-where." Anna eyed him suspiciously, awaiting his conditions. "I'm willing to forget what you said to me and let you have your job back—if you apologize. That's all I ask."

"Well, I am sorry. I shouldn't have told you to go fuck yourself—"

"—with something *crooked and rusty*," he pointed out.

"With something 'crooked and rusty,' yes," she said, working hard to suppress a grin.

"*Gracias.*"

"But," she continued, "I meant what I said before that. Who I fuck is none of your business. If I meet a guest I like, what we do is up to the two of us, and only us."

Josep shook his head. "I'm sorry, Anna, but I can't have that. It's disgusting. I'm not running a brothel here."

Anna exhaled through her nose and set her teeth, trying to compose herself. "I see," she said. "If that's the case…then I rescind my apology. Feel free to go fuck yourself anytime—it doesn't have to be with something crooked or rusty, either. Whatever's handy—an old broom handle, or maybe you can fit your own pointy head up there."

A dark cloud passed across his face, an ugly frown accentuating the lines around his mouth. "You have until the end of the month to move your things out of the upstairs flat," he snapped. "I want you out." He turned and walked away prissily.

So that's that, then, she thought. *So much for putting up with Josep a little longer.* Anna put her head down on the table and pantomimed banging her forehead against it a few more times.

"Everything all right?" she heard Tom inquire after a few seconds of this.

She picked her head off the table and peered up enough to see him standing there, looking blissfully hungover and gripping an empty mug. "Not really," she said.

"Use a cup of coffee?" he asked.

"At least."

She raised her shoulders and leaned back, following Tom with her eyes as he circled round and snaked his way over to the coffee pot. He returned with two steaming cups and set one down in front of her. He drew a few crumpled packets of sugar from his pocket, tossed them on the table, and sat down.

Anna tore open a packet and sprinkled sugar into her coffee. After swishing her mug around a few times, she took a grateful sip.

"So what's going on?" asked Tom. "Where's Miles?"

Anna managed a smile. "I let him sleep," she said. Tom wasn't being overly nosy—just curious. It had been clear from the night before that the two of them were now an item. Anna started to tell Tom what had just transpired with her manager when Krissy joined them, and she was obliged to begin again.

"What a wanker," said Krissy, after Anna had finished.

Tom looked over at Josep manning the front desk. "I'd offer to go thrash him, Anna, but he looks fairly solid....Besides, violence never solves anything."

She thought about that. "What about World War II?"

"Violence *rarely* solves anything," he allowed. "Say, are you sure he has the right to evict you like this?"

"It's his property," she said. Tom was about to say something when Anna cut him off. "Even if I had the right to remain there, I'd need a job to pay rent. I'm not sure I want to stay now, anyway."

"You mean, leave Barcelona?" Krissy asked.

Anna shrugged. "The apartment, at least. If I dropped out of university, I suppose I would leave the city, return to Amsterdam."

"What about Vikram?" asked Tom.

"Bloody hell!" exclaimed Krissy, giving the others a start. "I forgot, I heard the weirdest thing last night after you all went upstairs. Remember the Brits who came in the other night? One of them was telling me he'd seen someone out in front of the Kashmir being led away by the police yesterday. I asked him who, but he didn't know. From the way he described it, though, it could've been Vikram."

Anna put down her coffee. "Had he seen this?" she asked.

"He said he did."

"You just thought to tell her this now?" Tom asked.

"She'd already gone upstairs," Krissy protested. "It was only a few hours ago, anyway."

Tom pondered for a moment. "When did this happen?" he asked.

"Sometime yesterday."

"Morning?"

"Dunno....Why?"

Tom eyed the far wall, trying to remember the previous morning. "Vikram was kind of freaked out about losing something yesterday morning—his bag, I think. I figured he'd just misplaced it 'cause he seemed to remember where it was all of a sudden, and then took off."

Anna recalled Vikram's note. "He left me a note yesterday morning saying he wanted to talk," she said. "I remember thinking it was odd, but when I came down, he was gone." Tom and Krissy looked at Anna. "I sort of forgot about it afterward."

There was a brief lull in the conversation, and they looked up as one to see Miles standing in the archway separating reception from the common area. He came over and stood in front of them, too diffident to give Anna more than a wave hello with Tom and Krissy flanking her.

"Hey, guys—Anna," he said, pulling up a chair across from her. "You're not gonna believe what happened to me this morning after you left."

"Does it involve the police?" asked Anna.

"Um...well...yeah." He looked at the others and back at Anna. "How'd you know—did they talk to you already?"

"No. Do they want t—? Sorry. Why don't you tell us what happened?"

Miles filled them in on the police visiting Anna's apartment, their questions and searching of the rooms, and that they were trying to find Vikram.

"Anna, they told me they wanted to ask you some questions," he said. He handed her the officer's card. "This is the guy I talked to. Weird, huh?"

Anna looked the card over. Officer Amenes worked out of the main Mossos d'Esquadra station in the Raval. She wondered if she ought to go, then set the card back down. "This is a fitting addition to my day so far," she said.

"Oh."

"After I left you, I mean." Anna repeated for Miles the story she'd told the others.

Miles wasn't sure how to respond, having never been on the receiving end of that sort of treatment. He tried to imagine how he'd react in her situation. Then he remembered that no one would talk to him that way in the first place.

"Shit, I'm sorry," he said.

"Don't be, it's not your fault," she said.

"Well...not entirely," said Krissy with a laugh.

"Which one is Josep?" he asked.

"He's the one at the front desk," said Anna.

He nodded. "I suppose I should offer to go kick his ass, but he's bigger than me." Miles glanced over at the reception area and could see Josep glaring back in their direction. "He looks kind of mean too."

"Yeah," said Tom, "and violence almost never solves anything."

*

THE POLICE STATION was a monolithic beige fortress about ten minutes' away in the Raval. As they walked down Carrer Nou de la Rambla and approached the stark, block-sized building's entrance, a long, narrow

row of tinted windows reflected the typical architecture of the old city on the other side of the street—a letterboxed strip of picturesque balconies atop colorful storefronts bisecting a featureless façade.

Inside was neither quaintly colorful nor monotonous, but bustling with uniformed officers and every stripe of Barcelonan—prosperous middle-aged men in suits and scruffy young men in sandals (some of whom Miles recognized as drug dealers from the Ramblas); a Catalonian mother holding the arm of her teenage son and a mustachioed Moroccan immigrant with his brother and girlfriend; shabbily dressed young women, Iberians, and Arabs; tourists filling out robbery reports—a vibrant cross-section of the day's acquaintances with misfortune and misadventure.

Unlike Krissy, Miles and Tom had nowhere else to be and so accompanied Anna to the police station, entering the building with a mixture of apprehension and curiosity.

Tom, who was less a true anarchist than an antiauthoritarian quasi-hippie from a remote island nation with more sheep than people, didn't like or trust the police. But, if he were forced to admit it, he was secretly glad they were there. And, while Miles saw the officers in blue as dread messengers, Anna's perspective was different. Since the day she had first set foot in Europe as an adolescent, she was acutely aware of the fact that she and others who looked like her might as well have had the words USUAL SUSPECT tattooed on their foreheads as far as the police were concerned.

So it was with deep misgivings that Anna approached the main desk with officer Amenes's card. She wouldn't have come here unless she thought she had to. The officer behind the counter told her to wait, and so she sat down next to Miles and Tom in the uncomfortable, injection-molded, plastic orange chairs that were joined to each other and bolted to the floor.

A small, wiry man with disheveled brown hair and one eye swollen shut shuffled past between a male and female officer just then, his hands cuffed behind his back, as they dragged him forward impatiently.

"Anna de Wit?" called officer Amenes, who had emerged from another room and now stood in front of the row of chairs, spotting Miles sitting next to her. Anna raised her head and nodded. "*Ah, bien. Buenos dias, señorita. Habla español?*"

"*Sí, sí.*"

"*Venir por aquí, por favor,*" he said. "Come this way."

Anna got up as Amenes showed her the way and inclined his head toward Miles as they walked away. Officer Amenes showed Anna into an office and led her to a comfortable armchair next to a large metal desk. She took a seat, and he rolled his swivel-chair under him and sat down.

He began by asking Anna about her relationship with Vikram, how long she'd known him, and so on. She tried to answer frankly but without embellishment. He asked her about the demonstration two days earlier, whether she'd been there and whether she'd seen him later that same day. She answered truthfully. He asked her if Vikram had ever gone by any other names.

"No," she said, taken aback. "Definitely not."

"He ever associate with any questionable characters?"

"All the time," she said, "but what has that got to do with anything?"

"What I mean, Anna, is—any known criminals, any dangerous individuals?"

"No. What is it you think Vikram has done?" she asked.

"It's mostly what he has already done," he said. "When a suspect escapes custody not once, but twice in two days, it kind of makes us look like assholes."

Anna's eyes betrayed her shock at hearing this, but she merely gave a noncommittal shrug, unsure how to respond.

"I mean," he said, "it's embarrassing. We all like to maintain a certain level of self-respect, don't we?"

"I guess."

"And that would have been more than enough," he said. "But we had to wonder *why* he would do something so foolish. From everything you've told me so far, I gather you're just as confused about what's going on with Vikram as we are."

"That's kind of hard for me to say." She actually felt much *more* confused.

"Right." He opened the brown folder lying on the desk in front of him. "Vikram's most serious crime at this point is his habit of escaping police custody. He hadn't engaged in any violence at the demonstration as far as any of the officers on hand know. He was arrested for encouraging the protestors and not dispersing when ordered to do so."

"That's it?"

"No, not quite," he said casually. "Once we booked him on that day, we took his passport. That was when he slipped away the first time. That sort of piqued our interest, you might say."

Anna folded her arms and stared at him.

"Did you know his passport is a fake?" he asked. Anna's expression indicated clearly that she did not, but he waited for a verbal *no* before proceeding. "The local address he'd given us was false, as well. So we didn't know where he was staying. Luckily for us," he smiled, "someone provided us with a tip."

"Someone?"

"It was anonymous, but it seemed like someone who must have known him." He examined Anna's reaction carefully, but if she knew anything about who might have done it, her face didn't reveal it.

"So now he's in even bigger trouble than he was before," she said.

"True. Not that he doesn't have the grudging admiration of some of us."

"How's that?"

"We still can't figure out how he did it," he said. "It shouldn't have even been possible the second time. We were extra careful, as you would imagine. But it was as if he just disappeared—*poof!* So he's either very skilled or he had outside help. Or he's some kind of wizard."

"What do you think he's involved in?"

Officer Amenes grimaced and ran his fingers down his mustache. "Hopefully, nothing. But practically—he was arrested at a violent protest holding a fake British passport—we have to think about terrorism. ETA, communists, anarchists, Islamic Jihad—take your pick. Vikram is a Hindu name, correct?"

She nodded yes.

"Hm. In any event, we just don't want people blowing shit up...or other people. Especially people, actually. It tends to scare the more sensible ones away, especially the ones with money. And if you're going to host the Olympics in a few years, you need well-to-do tourists willing to show up."

Anna recalled hearing the other day that Barcelona had been picked for the summer games after next. She had a hard time envisioning the city she knew cleaning itself up enough for a spectacle of that sort, even if it had six years.

"Vikram would never do anything like that," she insisted. "He's a respected anthropologist, not a fanatic."

"I hope you're right," he said. "But I don't have the luxury of giving someone like Vikram the benefit of the doubt." Anna bristled at the phrase *someone like Vikram* but held her tongue. "There's clearly something going on with him, and until I know what that is, I can't afford to ignore it." He looked at her steadily for a few moments without saying anything, then asked, "Do you have any questions for me?"

She had plenty, though none she wanted to share. She shook her head.

He closed the folder and stood up. "Thanks for coming in to answer my questions. I do appreciate it. And, please, let us know if you hear from Vikram or learn anything about where he went, or anything that might help."

He extended a hand, and Anna gave it a hesitant shake.

"*Adiós,*" he said.

"*Adiós.*"

✱

WHILE ANNA was being interviewed by officer Amenes, Miles attempted to get less uncomfortable on his wavy orange chair. He threw a leg over the plastic molded armrest and tried to lean at a three-quarters angle, slightly slouched down, but he began to spill into Tom's lap. He sat up, the hard lip of the chair's back getting him right in the middle of his spine.

"You know," he said absently, "it occurs to me that Vikram wasn't the only one to go missing yesterday."

"Hm? You mean Paco?" said Tom.

"Yeah, what happened with him?"

"I dunno," said Tom. "He's a strange little guy, isn't he?"

"He seems all right."

"He looks like a swarthy Peter Lorre."

"Peter Lorre wasn't swarthy?"

They thought about it for a moment, each wondering silently whether it was racist to describe someone as *swarthy*.

"He might've been," said Tom. "I only ever remember seeing him in black-and-white movies, though."

"True." Miles tried to remember why he'd brought Paco up. "It just seems like a strange coincidence, that's all."

"The timing?"

"Yeah."

"It *was* right around the time that Vikram misplaced his bag," recalled Tom. "Vikram said, 'Have you seen Paco?' and I said, 'He's not in the bar?'—'cause he had just been in there. I think Vik thought maybe Paco'd taken it. But it was right after then that he remembered where he'd left it and took off. I don't remember seeing Paco again after that."

"You have a surprisingly good memory," Miles observed.

"What? Oh, you mean all the booze."

"Mm-hmm."

Tom laughed. "Ya cunt."

*

BY THE TIME Anna emerged from the interview with officer Amenes and the three of them were making their way back toward the Ramblas under the midday sun, Tom and Miles were both having a hard time restraining their curiosity about what had happened in there and what, if anything, Anna had learned about Vikram. On the one hand, Anna was struggling to keep the lid on some rather juicy dirt on a mutual friend— and, she had to admit, there was something undeniably cool about giving the police the slip two times in twenty-four hours. On the other hand, this was her roommate and best friend, whom the police suspected of being a terrorist.

Not that she believed any of that. But she did have to wonder how it would sound to people who perhaps didn't know Vikram as well as she did.

"Well?" said Tom. "Are you going to give us a hint?"

"Are you going to interrogate me too, Tom?" she said, trying to sound casual. "Can't we get some lunch first? Then we can talk."

At a café in the Boqueria Market, over tapas and a pitcher of sangria, Anna doled out a few morsels of what she'd learned. She told them how Vikram had escaped from the holding cell after his first arrest at the demonstration, and that he'd done it again after they'd arrested him the next day. They were impressed.

"Wow," said Miles, "he's like the Birdman of Alcatraz or something."

"The Count of Monte Cristo," said Tom.

"It was the local jail, not the Chateau d'If," she said.

Anna left out the bit about Vikram's false passport and the fact the police considered him a possible terrorist.

"But why would he try to escape in the first place?" Miles wondered aloud. "I wouldn't think he'd be in that much trouble for taking part in the demonstration. He didn't do anything violent, did he?"

"No," she said.

"How did they find him the second time?" asked Tom.

"Someone," she said, "some anonymous person informed the police."

Tom and Miles looked at each other, then at Anna with stymied expressions.

"I didn't do it," said Tom.

"Who *would* do it?" said Miles.

"I don't know," she said.

*

PACO SQUINTED in the late-morning glare as he emerged from the train station and tried to stretch his cramped, stubby legs as he walked up the street with the bag slung over his shoulder. It turned out to be heavier than it looked.

Granada was a beautiful city—before the Reconquista, the richest, most opulent city in Al Andalus. Of course, it only became that after the Moors lost Córdoba and Sevilla to the Castilians, and their rulers fled here. Its era of splendor and importance had been relatively brief, but its charm continued to flourish amid the ruin of empires.

Paco had missed Granada's white-washed buildings and red-tile roofs, its narrow, cobbled alleys. Barcelona was perhaps a little too urbane for his taste, too modern. Not content with the mother tongue, not content to be ruled. Not truly Spanish, not to Paco.

He hadn't been planning to take Vikram's bag at all. But after someone told him about Vikram's case and what it contained, it sort of became a preoccupation. But getting at it had been idle speculation up until the other day. He'd never even seen it. But when Vikram returned to the Kashmir with that story about being released by the police after a few hours, he knew he was lying. A quick phone call confirmed his suspicion. And when the fool came downstairs the next morning, carelessly dropping his bag on a table with the corner of the case peeking out, it required little in the way of deft maneuvering. Later, when he saw the police marching Vikram away in handcuffs, he couldn't believe his luck.

Now he was doubting it somewhat, as the case inside had proven impossible to crack open. Clearly, whatever was inside (jewels, he'd been assured—diamonds, he hoped), the owner had gone to extraordinary lengths to protect it. The matte black case was made of some type of unusually strong, lightweight metal, which Paco had never seen before. Unscratchable and undentable—despite his best efforts—there was no lock, just one small square of glass flush with the metal on the top of it, above the handle, the purpose of which Paco could not fathom. And it was equally unbreakable. The hinges must have been hiding on the inside, as there was no sign of them on the back of the case, where the beveled edges of the top and bottom formed a seam you couldn't fit a mosquito's dick through. Where the top half of the case met the bottom, it overlapped on the sides and front, making it that much harder to pry open, and the only hardware visible on the case was a pair of shiny metal plates on the front, holding a handle made of the same stuff as the rest of the case.

He'd hoped to return to his sister and her husband needing only a fence to move the jewels. Now he'd need their help just to get at what was inside. He didn't care for the position it put him in, but what could he do?

Paco shifted his burden and grunted as he made his way up the hill toward his sister's home on the edge of the Albaicín, where it gave way to the caves of Sacromonte. There was no direct route, as Paco trudged southeast, then south, then northeast, uphill then down, but mostly up. As he got closer, he could see the Alhambra and Generalife to the south, across the Rio Darro on the opposite ridge, in all their glory. Even the conquering Christians found them too beautiful to destroy. The infidels had to go, though.

His sister and her lummox husband lived in an apartment above the neighborhood carnicería, which they operated during the day. When he'd left a few years ago, they were dealing black-market cigarettes out of the back of the store. The butcher shop remained, just as Paco remembered it, a modest storefront you could easily walk by without noticing, if it weren't for the odor—a pungent mixture of spicy succulence and rot.

Paco entered the butcher's and immediately spotted his sister, Cecilia, behind the counter, helping a customer. They shared similar features, but where Paco's had been thrown haphazardly on a squashed face, hers were arranged pleasingly on a roundish oval. Where his brown almond eyes were beady and too close together, hers were large and bright. Where his hawk nose seemed to droop down over his mouth, hers had room to breathe and lent her face character. They were the same height, but where his squat, shapeless form seemed to droop forward, her petite yet voluptuous body, dressed in form-fitting, stylish clothes, stood ramrod straight.

There were a few others waiting, as well as an old man sitting at a table, reading the paper over an espresso.

"*Hermana*," he called, after she had handed the man his wrapped meats.

"*Francisco—Paco?*" she cried. "*Hermano! Qué estás haciendo aquí?* What are you doing here? Why didn't you call?" She made her way around the counter, calling over her shoulder, "Maria! take the next customer for me."

"I didn't have the time," he said with a shrug.

"Who doesn't have time to call?" she asked, stopping in front of him. She looked plumper than he remembered, but happy, more prosperous. She reached across, grabbed a fistful of stubbly cheek, and said, "What am I going to do with you, Paco?" She gave his face a tug and pulled him into a tight embrace.

"Things are going well?" he asked, his face full of her product-filled hair.

"Very well," she said, releasing him. "Oh, why didn't you call? Don't get me wrong, I'm happy to see you, but I could have welcomed you properly if I'd only known you were coming!"

"This is all the welcome I need," he said.

"You look so tired," she said. "And hungry, like you haven't been eating. Look how skinny you are!"

Cecilia's husband, Checho, fresh from working in the back, came out, saw his wife and Paco, and made his way around the counter to greet his brother-in-law.

"You're back," he said, sounding neither surprised nor particularly glad.

"*Sí, sí*, of course. I missed my little sister."

"So, are you back for a visit?" asked Checho. "Or back for good?"

Paco gazed up at Checho, who was a decent foot taller than him and broad—a blunt, simple man wearing a blood-and-viscera-smeared apron. "I don't know yet," said Paco. "Can I decide that later?"

"But where are my manners, Paco," said Checho, smiling, and he leaned down and gave Paco a quick hug and a kiss on each cheek, his grip firm on Paco's shoulders. "It's good to see you."

"Checho, did the deliveries come this morning?" Cecilia asked.

"Yeah."

"Better get them ready, then."

"There's time yet," he said.

"There's time now," she said. "Later on, time will be gone, and you'll be wondering where the time went to. So why not do it now?"

Checho frowned at his wife but nevertheless obeyed, nodding to Paco as he sauntered back to the room at the rear of the store, his body language making it clear this was his choice.

"So, it's a fair question, Paco," she said, motioning for him to sit down at one of the tables as she did the same. "Is this a visit, or what? It's been three years."

"I know," he said. "Look, things didn't work out in Barcelona as I'd hoped. I didn't want to just come crawling back, looking for your help again."

"You never had a plan. That was your problem, Paco."

Paco shrugged with a hangdog grin.

"Things are going well here, Paco," she said. "We've got a lot more responsibility now." It was obvious she wasn't talking about the shop, which looked as desultory and rundown as ever. "I could use you, if you're planning to stick around."

Relief washed over Paco. At the same time, he hated himself for it. This was the easy way he'd left Granada to escape. He smiled weakly at Cecilia and undid the buckles on his bag. "I was able to get hold of something before I left Barcelona," he said, lifting the black case up onto the table.

"Really?" she said. "What's inside?"

"Jewels, I think," he said.

"You *think?*"

"Well…whatever's inside must be extremely valuable."

"What makes you think so?"

"It's locked so well, I couldn't get it open. I was hoping you might help me, and we could find out together."

Cecilia examined the case, impressed. "Where did you get this?" she asked.

"I stole it."

"Who from?"

"No one important."

*

VIKRAM LISTENED to the line ring on the receiver as he stared down the main drag, a cat's-cradle of high-tension cables strung above it, an oasis of pavement and inhuman industrial architecture surrounding the petrol station about 130 kilometers north of Valencia.

There was no answer. He hung up, retrieved his fifty-peseta coin from the payphone, and made his way back to the rusty old Citroën DS, where his ride, Martin, was squeegeeing off the freshly cleaned windshield.

"*Gracias*, but they weren't in," said Vikram, handing Martin back the coins he'd given him.

"Keep it," he said.

"But I still need to pay you for the gas and the drinks when we get to Valencia," Vikram protested.

"There's no need," he said. "Think nothing of it."

Vikram smiled and shook his head. He pocketed the change and took a last look around before getting back in the car. Beyond this island of concrete, the sky was changing colors as evening approached. To the north, dark clouds were gathering. His fondness for the Spanish country-side made the ugliness of this little waystation that much more repulsive. It saddened him. If he knew how to cry, he'd have produced a tear to run down his cheek like the Indian in that old American anti-littering PSA. Of course, even if he were the genuine article, he was the wrong kind of Indian, anyway.

Vikram had had to wait a good while for anyone to pick him up on the outskirts of Barcelona—for one thing, he had no bag, which looked sus-pect. Then his first ride had only taken him as far as Tarragona. Martin picked up Vikram because he didn't look like the "typical hitchhiker," he said. He was right about that. Vikram supposed he meant it as a compli-ment. He took one-lane backroads through olive and orange groves, and had a lead foot, nearly running over a shirtless young farmer driving a pony and cart loaded with hay at one point.

"*Hijo de puta*...sonofabitch came out of nowhere," said Martin.

They stopped for a long lunch along the way, where Vikram claimed not to be hungry, but Martin bought him beer, anyway. What Vikram really had been craving was a cigarette, but he'd managed to hitch a ride from the one middle-aged man in all of Spain who didn't smoke. Vikram could see now that taking up the habit again had probably not been the best idea.

Vikram didn't have to hitchhike to get to Valencia. But he already felt like he was pressing his luck, and this seemed like the safest alternative. Besides, he never got tired of meeting new people.

Martin was an amiable fellow who loved to talk, regardless of topic. He would careen down the road with the windows open, talking about football, politics, movies—whatever came into his head—all the while tossing handfuls of sunflower seeds into his mouth. Vikram marveled that he could manage to work the seeds out of their shells between his teeth and then spit the husks out the window, even though they inevita-bly blew back into the car and landed on the floor behind them. Vikram, being a polymath of sorts, could converse on any subject Martin brought up, so Martin was happy, even when Vikram presumed to correct him.

As soon as Vikram shut the door, Martin accelerated his light-green Citroën out of the gas station like a ball being shot from a cannon. He took the AP-7 for a while but then exited to follow a more remote route, never slowing down, which on the cracked, winding roads, with the wind buffeting their heads as they bounced along, only made it feel like they were going that much faster.

Vikram nodded as Martin insisted that Valencia was the only place where one could get proper paella. "Why, did you know that in Madrid they put chorizo in it?" he asked.

"The hell you say."

"It's grotesque."

Vikram gazed out the window at the setting sun, made large and orange by atmospheric refraction, and pondered his next move.

7.

IT WAS NOT YET dawn, but Miles was awake, propped on an elbow and eyeing a vertical strip of window beyond the red screen in Anna's apartment. He could hear the rain falling softly on the square, the sound of distant thunder petering out, moving on. Clouds obscured the stars, and the only light came from the lampposts below in the plaça.

He gazed at the exposed brown skin of Anna's shoulder as she lay asleep half under the covers and recalled the feel of her body against his. He realized how desperately he craved it—the touch of her skin on his. It was a sexual urge, but it was also something else. Comfort—a kind of safety imparted through the connection. Unbidden, a memory from childhood leapt to mind, of Miles at five years old being held by his father at the public swimming pool, his arms wrapped tight around his dad's neck under the summer sun, the feel of his skin tingling from the rough hairs of his father's chest, finding warmth from the smooth skin of Nate's neck and shoulders.

He shook the memory from his head and lay back down next to Anna. He nuzzled her arm, pressing his lips against her skin and inhaling deeply.

"Mmm," she murmured and turned her head to open her bleary eyes on him. "Hey," she said.

"Hey." She turned on her side and drew him toward her, her dark brown nipples poking out, at attention. He stared for a moment, the sight still a surprising sensation, and they stared back. He looked up into her face, her eyes beckoning him with their suggestive stare, and kissed her lips, then stole a glance down at her nipples again, as if they were admonishing him, *Hey, we're down here!* He laughed, and they pressed their bodies together in the semi-conscious glow of predawn.

"I love making love when I'm half awake," she said afterward. "It's like dreaming."

Too soon it was light.

Miles had brought up his backpack, and Anna had packed a bag in preparation for the day's journey. The night before, Anna had stumbled over a clue to Vikram's whereabouts in a place she hadn't thought to look.

It had been about an hour after sunset when the sky just unloaded on the Barri Gòtic, the rain creating halos of light around streetlamps, flooding the alleys as the water rushed in rivulets over the cracks in the paving stones, and generally drenching anyone without umbrellas or raingear, which seemed to be everyone. The five of them—Anna, Miles, Tom, Krissy, and Marie—had ducked into a bar to get out of the downpour, soaking wet and laughing from the surprise and chill of the rain. Only when they stopped giggling did they realize it was quiet as a church in there, and Miles recognized it immediately from his first night in Barcelona. A man and woman were sharing a bottle of wine at a corner table but were otherwise ignoring each other. A grizzled man was sitting on a barstool grimly strangling a bottle of beer. Once oriented, Anna remembered the place too—she'd been taken here by Vikram, who knew the owner, Pau. It had been a favorite of his for some reason. She recognized Pau, who was behind the counter having an intense conversation with a young patron sitting at the bar.

The skinny college kid, wearing round, metal-framed glasses and long dark hair, was laughing good-naturedly while shaking his head. Pau, a fiftyish, stocky man with wispy dark-blond hair retreating across his head, an island of tuft left behind in the middle of his mottled pate, had a paperback book open and was pointing at a passage of text with a gnarled middle finger.

Tom led the group toward a table in the far corner next to a bookcase while Anna wandered over toward the bar with Miles in tow. The college kid was talking to Pau now as the older man rolled his eyes dismissively. Anna could hear they were arguing about books—Pau extolling the virtues of Catalonian verse and magical realism, while the kid insisted that literature was irrelevant and that only history, biography, and philosophy mattered.

"Literature reveals deeper truths than history can ever tell," said Pau.

"Maybe," said the kid. "I just think that truths, deep or not, ought to at least be true."

"Listen to this," said Pau. "A poem can make history live." And he proceeded to read from the book, a poem called "An Old Soldier" by Ferran Dolorada. Anna wasn't able to understand all of it, as her knowledge of Catalan was limited. The kid nodded when Pau was done reading.

"*Que era encantador*," she said. "Beautiful. Though I admit I didn't understand all of it."

Pau eagerly translated the verse into Spanish for her, pointing out the correct pronunciation and meaning of each unfamiliar word. The poem was about a Spanish soldier who'd taken part in the sixteenth-century sack of Rome, which all but destroyed the city. Decades later, as an old man, he returned to tour a Rome rebuilt but still just a shadow of its former glory. As the old soldier revisited the scenes of his atrocities, he began to see the ghosts of his victims everywhere.

After Pau translated the poem for Anna, she translated for Miles, from Spanish to English, the last stanza of the poem:

> *The faces of the dead followed him*
> *Through the rubble of the ancient Forum.*
> *Ghosts and ruins:*
> *Created by men—starving and insane—*
> *Who, in orgies of destruction, remade Rome once again.*

Miles nodded. "I don't know why," he said, "but that really makes me want to go to Rome."

"I know what you mean," she said.

Pau raised an eyebrow at the kid.

The kid shrugged and said, "*Esta bien*. I guess. Maybe when I'm old, I'll like poetry more, too."

"*Hmph.*" The man throttling his beer made a noise, reminding the others he was there. The man—he could have been forty-five or seventy-five, it was impossible to tell—wore a black wool pea coat and a Greek fisherman's cap pulled down over his forehead. His weary eyes never wavered from staring straight ahead as he pulled the bottle to his cracked, sunburnt lips.

Tom sidled up to the bar, leaving the others back at the table. Krissy was still trying to untangle her wet hair and Marie dabbed at her face and neck with a cocktail napkin. "Are we having a class?" he asked.

Anna summarized the literary discussion going on at the bar.

"'You keep all your smart modern writers,'" said Tom, "'give me William Shakespeare.'"

"Ugh," said Miles. "I had to read *Merchant of Venice* in high school."

"'Hath not a Jew eyes?'" said Tom, who was apparently speaking only in quotations now.

"You don't like Shakespeare?" asked Anna.

Miles shrugged.

"Not even *Romeo and Juliet*?" she said.

"I liked the movie," he said.

Pau had put his book away behind the bar and turned back to Anna.

"*Tu es Anna?*" he said.

"*Sí,*" she said, surprised he remembered her. "I'm Vikram's friend. His flatmate. You're Pau, right? I was going to ask if you'd seen him recently."

"Hold on." He held up a palm and walked over to the other end of the bar, where a small drawer was tucked under the counter, and rifled through its contents.

"Are we ever going to order something to drink?" asked Tom, getting a little impatient.

Pau returned with a folded sheet of paper with "Anna" scrawled across the front.

"Vikram left this for you," said Pau. "I wasn't sure if you'd ever come in."

Shocked, she thanked him and opened the note. It was a green bar receipt and carried simply the address of an apartment in Valencia printed neatly in Vikram's hand, with the signature "Rumbi."

"Huh." Anna assumed Vikram meant he was staying at the address in Valencia, but why she had no clue.

"What is it?" asked Miles, who, along with Tom, was craning to see.

"A note from Vikram," she said and handed it to Miles.

He held it for him and Tom to read, then flipped it over a couple times, expecting maybe to find an explanation for the cryptic message. "It's an address," he said. "That's it?"

"That's it."

"Who's 'Rumbi'?" asked Tom.

"Vikram," said Anna and Miles together.

The hoary mariner looked up at the mention of the name. Anna asked Pau when Vikram had given him the note. "It was late last night," he said. "Vikram came in around midnight and seemed preoccupied, moreso than usual. He asked me if he could have something to write on, so I ripped off a sheet for him. Then he asked me for a pen. As I say, he seemed preoccupied, even a bit flustered...not his usual self. Anyway, he gave me the note and said he was going out of town for a while and asked if I could make sure you got this if you came in. You did, and so I have."

Anna thanked him and asked how long he was there.

"Not long," said Pau. "He tried to tell me he didn't even have time for a drink, but I poured him a glass of Port. I knew he couldn't resist *that*—though I didn't ask him to pay. He seemed embarrassed, and I got the feeling he couldn't have, anyway."

"Oh."

"Then he told me, 'If I don't see you again, Pau, it was good knowing you.' And he left." Pau stroked his chin. "I didn't even know he was leaving."

"Neither did I." Anna paused to absorb this latest shred of information, then translated for Miles and Tom what Pau had told her.

"Well," said Miles, "it makes sense he was preoccupied."

"Yes," she said, "and that he'd leave town. But why Valencia? I suppose he can't leave the country without his passport."

"I hadn't thought of that."

Anna examined the corner of the ceiling, as if distracted.

"So what are we going to do?" asked Tom.

Good question, she thought. "I'm not sure," she said. "I suppose I should try to contact him."

"No," said Tom, "I mean, what should we order? I'm parched."

KRISSY AND MARIE were telling the others about the places they'd visited that day. La Pedrera, the Palau de la Música Catalana, the Picasso Museum, the zoo—they had made a circuit around the Gothic Quarter and returned to the Ramblas via Barceloneta, passing by the government buildings by the harbor.

"It was a little disturbing seeing guards out on the street armed with automatic weapons," said Marie. "Seems a bit reactionary."

"That's thanks to ETA," said Anna.

"*Eta?*"

"Basque separatists," she said. "They've blown up several car bombs over the last couple years, here in Barcelona and Madrid."

"Oh."

They were all well aware of the recent terrorist attacks by various Arab factions in Berlin and Paris, but ETA was new to everyone but Anna.

"There was a bomb scare at the Paris train station when I was there," said Miles. "Someone left a suitcase unattended. The police blew a hole through it."

"Wouldn't that detonate any bomb inside?" asked Marie.

"I was thinking that right after they did it," he said. "But, apparently, it was just a case someone left behind, so I guess we'll never know." He shrugged. "My mother tried to talk me out of even stopping in Paris. Can you imagine?" Five bombs had been set off in the streets of Paris that September, killing nine bystanders, injuring more than a hundred others, and instilling fear into anyone with any sense, which was the point.

All Anna could think about was what officer Amenes had told her. She took a sip of wine and waited for the inevitable turn in the conversation to Vikram's arrest.

"So what happened to Vikram?" asked Marie. "I heard he was arrested."

"Indeed he was," said Tom. "The police questioned Anna today, as it seems he's *at large*." That piqued Marie's interest, to whom this was fresh news.

"Oh," she said. "How is he 'at large' if the police arrested him?"

"He escaped." Tom looked at Anna, unsure what she did or didn't want to share, as Marie didn't know about this, though Krissy knew some of it.

"Twice," Anna said. "He escaped the first time he was arrested after the demonstration, and then again after they picked him up yesterday in the plaça."

"Wicked," gasped Krissy. "What is he, then, some sorta Houdini?"

Anna shrugged as if to say, *For all I know.*

Krissy laughed and made a silent toast to Vikram before taking a drink. "Did they tell you if this had anything to do with what was in his bag?" she asked.

"No," said Anna. Which was true.

"What bag?" asked Marie. So Tom told her what he'd seen the day before, when Vikram lost his bag and Paco disappeared.

"And Paco's been missing since then, hasn't he?" she said. "Weird."

"I wonder," said Tom, "if Vikram knew that Paco had stolen his bag."

Anna turned to him, surprised. "I thought Vikram said he'd remembered where he left it."

"I thought that's what he meant," he said. "But maybe he just figured it out. It wouldn't make sense to keep looking around for it if he knew who took it."

"But we don't know that Paco stole anything," said Krissy.

"True," said Tom. "Still, the timing's a bit suspicious."

Anna was glad when the topic of discussion finally moved on to something else.

At a lull, she leaned over to Miles and pointed out the jukebox sitting against the back wall. "Help me pick out some songs," she said. They walked over and found an old Rock-ola filled with forty-fives of 1960s-era Afro-Cuban dance music. If Pau's place had a vibe, it was definitely cool jazz, or perhaps the sort of acoustic delta blues found on scratchy old seventy-eights recorded during the Depression—but not Tito Puente.

"Three plays for fifty potatoes," said Anna. Some of the English-speaking guests had taken to referring to the currency that way. "Do you have fifty potatoes?"

He searched his pockets and found a fifty-peseta coin. She took it and, after blowing dust off the top panel, inserted it into the coin slot. She seemed to know what she was doing as she scanned the song titles.

"Officer Amenes told me something else I didn't want to tell Tom and the others," she said, punching a button on the console.

"What?"

"He told me that Vikram's passport was a fake." An infectiously happy salsa tune started up, making the bar seem like a wake in the middle of Carnaval. Anna tried to gauge Miles's response to what she'd told him and pressed another number.

"Why would he have a fake passport?" he said.

"I have no idea, but the police take that sort of thing seriously." Miles let out a nervous chuckle at her understatement. "That, and breaking out of jail, of course."

"So he's in big trouble, basically," he said.

"They think he might be a *terrorist*, Miles."

"*What?*" he said, taken aback. "Vikram's not a terrorist. That's... crazy."

"So is everything that's happened with him since the day he was arrested at the demonstration," she said.

"But he only came along to the demonstration that day after you told us about it," he said. "He just got caught up in it."

"Yes," she said, wincing at the reminder of her role in Vikram's undoing, "but if you combine that with the passport and his escapes—how would someone even do that?—it looks very bad."

He thought for a moment about what he knew of Vikram. "I know," he said. "But it doesn't make sense. I mean, there's something up with him, but I'm sure it's not that. Vikram isn't violent."

"And he's been my closest friend since I moved here."

Miles sighed sympathetically. "What are you going to do?" he asked.

"I think I ought to go to Valencia," she said. "And I know I shouldn't ask this of you, but I was hoping you'd come with?"

Miles nodded his head. "No problem, I want to go with you."

"Miles," she said, "you realize the police know who you are now."

"I'm not scared. I'm from Chicago, the most dangerous city on earth."

"You grew up in the suburbs."

"Still deadly."

Later, after leaving Pau a healthy tip, Anna and the rest of them filed out of the bar into the alley, where the rain was reduced to spitting. She and Miles hung back from the group and passed by a darkened doorway a short distance on. In the shadow of the archway, the man was almost invisible, dressed all in black and shrouded in mist. As Anna passed him by, he spoke in a low rasp: "*El hindú.*"

Anna had trouble placing the source of the voice at first, was surprised to see the ageless sailor standing outside the bar. Miles stopped a few paces in front of her and turned around. "Who?" she said.

"The Hindu," he repeated. "Your friend."

"What about him?"

"He's not what he seems."

"Well, few of us are," she said and turned to rejoin Miles on their way back to the hotel.

*

THE MEDITERRANEAN sparkled in the distance, seeming to follow them, as olive groves, cypress trees, and scrub brush rushed by their compartment window. The train rolled south toward Valencia, its back-and-forth motion rocking Anna to sleep against Miles's shoulder, while he tried to bury himself in his book.

Miles was finding it difficult to focus on the story, though, having read the same sentence three times now. In between lines of dialogue he would mentally attempt to quantify or categorize his feelings for Anna. Was he in love with her? He wasn't sure. He liked her a lot, he knew. He liked being with her. Even, or especially, at times like this, when they could each just be, with no pressure to say something interesting or smart. Not that she had to be asleep for that, though he did enjoy watching over her catlike repose. Most of all, he liked who he was when he was with her, which was not usually the case. Was *she* doing that? Was it Barcelona?

It all seemed academic, anyway. He certainly didn't think she was in love with him. She was way too sophisticated and cosmopolitan for that, wasn't she? And, even if she were, what were they going to do about it? This was her real life. To him, this was an escape from it.

A sideways jolt jerked Anna awake. She looked around, startled. "Was I sleeping?" she asked rhetorically, screening a tired yawn with the back of her hand. "What are you reading?"

"A novel," he said. "Science fiction," he clarified with a shrug.

"*Skygarden…?*" she read off the cover. A buxom alien with blue feathers stared back at her from a dense green forest. Over its shoulder a gray-brown planet glowed in the night sky. "Any good?"

"Yeah," he said.

"What's it about?"

Miles began to describe the plot of the book to her, or at least the part he'd read so far. The story was set on an Earth-like planet inhabited by a race of intelligent avian hermaphrodites.

"So how do they have sex?" Anna asked. "I mean, how do they decide who's the man or woman?"

"It depends," said Miles. "Some might prefer the female or male role, or they might enjoy both and take turns."

"So do they also take turns having babies?"

"Yeah, or just one would take on that role if they wanted to," he said.

"Could a person get pregnant all by herself...or, uh, *their*self?"

"Yes, though that's frowned on, for the same reason incest is taboo," he said. "And apparently not that easy, anyway. But pregnancy is of less significance because the raising of children is mainly handled by professionals."

"Oh," she said. "Are couples monogamous?"

"Most definitely not."

"Huh."

In the various languages the bird-people used, he told her, they called their home "Our World," as opposed to their word for *earth* or *soil*, as humans refer to their planet. This was because, he said, Our World possessed a sister planet, a nearby heavenly body of more or less equal size, closer in to their star, which completed an orbit in about half the time that Our World did. Skygarden—the name they gave the sister planet—was, unlike Earth's moon, a lush planet covered with massive oceans, rainforests, grasslands, and snow-capped mountains. It had a visible atmosphere and long, streaky white cloud formations. Though it harbored abundant plant life, no large land animals had yet evolved. So the bird-people of Our World had always seen Skygarden as a kind of Eden, an unspoiled paradise rising and setting over their world, a prominent fixture in the heavens for half of every year.

"So does anything happen?" Anna asked.

"Well, when the story begins," he said, "Our World is dying. The bird-people polluted their planet, overpopulated it, just generally destroyed their ecosystem. They know what they have to do to stop it, but they just can't bring themselves to do it."

"So, kind of like Earth," said Anna.

"But much worse," he said. "Their planet starts to overheat. The oceans rise and swallow up the coastal areas, and drought causes widespread famine."

"Because of the greenhouse effect?"

"Right," he said. "They put too much carbon pollution into the atmosphere, and the temperatures kept rising until the polar ice-caps melted. It caused all sorts of other problems.

"Millions of bird-people die because so many of them live on the coasts, which get flooded by the rising seas. Clean drinking water becomes scarce. Bigger, harder-to-predict storms hit with more and more frequency. Species die off at an accelerating rate. Their planet starts to become uninhabitable, and so they decide to colonize Skygarden."

"Rather than fix their own planet," said Anna.

"Exactly."

Miles went on. The main character in the story was a science officer called Artaxa who goes on the first large-scale emigration. Having explored the planet during their own Space Age, the bird-people knew it was habitable. What Artaxa realizes fairly quickly is that the ecosystem on Skygarden is far more delicate than that of Our World, and that what they'd begun there—mining operations, burning fossil fuels, dumping waste into rivers and seas—was having a much more immediate and dramatic effect on Skygarden. He thinks it will soon be as bad or worse than the condition of Our World.

When Artaxa informs his fellow settlers of what he's learned, a contentious split develops, pitting those who reject his conclusions against those who believe him. After a few years on Skygarden, they witness the environment collapse in a much shorter timespan than it took on Our World, while one faction refuses to accept the facts and the other worries and argues about what can be done about it. At the next Alignment—the time of year when Skygarden and Our World are closest to one another—Artaxa returns to Our World to warn the people there, on his way passing hundreds of spacecraft headed toward Skygarden. In the time since he left Our World, millions of colonists have emigrated to settlements on the planet. Back on Our World, while trying to convince the leaders in his city-state of Danevesu of what's happening up there, Skygarden travels on its orbit to the other side of their sun, no longer visible and out of contact with the people on Our World for an octat, or an eighth of a year.

"Why an eighth?" she asked.

"Oh, because the bird-people all have eight fingers and eight toes," Miles explained. "So their math is all base-8."

"All right."

When Skygarden finally reemerges, it appears changed from its blue-green appearance to have a drastically reddish-brown cast with scarcely any clouds. When the bird-people of Our World try to communicate with the colonists on Skygarden, they receive no answer.

And that's as far as Miles had read.

"So the bird-people on Skygarden all died?" asked Anna.

"It looks that way," he said. "I think that's what the author wants us to think, at least. I'm only about halfway through."

"Sounds interesting."

"It is. His writing isn't the greatest, but he's a pretty interesting author." Miles filled Anna in on Tor Bass's story, gleaned from his bio on the back cover—how he had lived in New Mexico and wrote a number of unsuccessful sci-fi novels in the 1940s and '50s, before being found dead in a Santa Fe bus station men's room in 1962. He'd gained a short-lived following a few years after he died, discovered by college students who were also discovering weed and hallucinogenic mushrooms.

"In a bus station loo?" she asked. "What had he died of?"

"It doesn't say," he said. "When I first met Vikram on the train in France, we got to talking because he'd read Bass too."

"Ah."

The train slowed as it approached Valencia, arriving at the Estacio del Nord in the heart of the city. Moments after exiting the train, Anna and Miles found a kiosk beside the tracks with city maps, bought one, unfolded it, and entered the building. The Valencia station is a grand modernista masterpiece with intricate woodwork, stained glass, and cracked ceramic tile covering the ceiling and columns in vibrant color. All of which Anna and Miles would no doubt have appreciated had they bothered to look up from their map between entering the station and exiting it on the Carrer de Xàtiva, next to the Plaza de Toro, a miniature

Colosseum and Valencia's bullring. The address Vikram had left Anna was only a short walk north, on a side alley off the Plaça de la Mercè.

The apartment building was in the middle of a shabby-looking side street much like the side streets of the Barri Gòtic, with a bit more graffiti. The front door had a buzzer, and the label for Vikram's apartment on the third floor was blank. Anna pressed the button but got no answer. Miles tried the door, but it was locked. He buzzed other apartments, just in case, but to no avail. It was the start of siesta, so a lot of people were out and about, on their way home or out to eat. In a few minutes, a small, portly man stepped up to the entrance and unlocked the door. He paused to pocket his keys and turned back to Anna and Miles, who were waiting with wide, innocent eyes. He apparently found the pair pathetic enough to hold the door for them while they gratefully followed him in.

After climbing the three flights of stairs, they found the door to Vikram's apartment. Anna knocked. No answer.

After a pregnant pause. "Now what?" said Miles.

"I don't know." She knocked again, more forcefully.

"You don't have a key?"

"I didn't even know this place existed until last night," she said.

"Right."

They stared at the door for a minute. Then Miles thought to try the knob and found it unlocked.

"Oh," she said.

They walked into a small one-bedroom flat with dilapidated old furniture and fixtures; painted-over, cracked molding that was once probably pretty nice. Vikram wasn't in the main room, so they checked the bedroom. A rusty iron frame held a ratty, unmade, but comfortable-looking bed.

"He's not here," she said, "but it looks like he slept here recently."

"Yeah," he said. "Unless he always just leaves it that way."

"Mm."

The room had the one double bed, a small dresser under a window, and just enough room between it and the bed to open the drawers halfway. Out the window was a view of more sad apartment windows facing the dark, cramped courtyard. On the dressertop was a broken-off corner of a brick holding down a folded-up piece of paper with an *A* written on it. Anna stopped and pulled the paper from under the rubble and nudged Miles's arm. She unfolded the letter so they both could read it.

Anna—

Since you're reading this note, I take it you got my message from Pau. I tried to call you more than once, but you were always out. (In retrospect, an answering machine would have been a good idea.) I apologize for not waiting for you, but I had to leave for Granada as soon as I could. I'm trying to find Paco. He has my bag and a very important case which was inside. I learned from his landlady that his sister owns a bakery in the Albaicín. That's where I'm headed. I don't know where I'm going exactly, but if you decide to come, I'll leave word at the youth hostel where to find me. I may have to leave Spain on a permanent basis, but I would very much like to see you before then.

—Rumbi

P.S. I had some money and other necessaries squirreled away here, which is why the detour. Could you lock the door when you leave? I left a key in the drawer.

P.P.S. If you've never seen the Alhambra, it's worth the trip.

"Ah, shit."

*

ASIDE FROM THE architectural grandeur of the building, the other thing Anna and Miles might have noticed had they stopped to look around the train station when they arrived was Vikram himself, buying a carton of smokes and some chocolates at the tobacconist's.

Vikram didn't see them, either. Having gone without a cigarette for more than twenty-four hours had given him the jitters so severe his teeth rattled. As a result, he only had eyes for the tobacco on the shelves, which looked more like candy than the candy he was also buying. They didn't have his preferred Chinese brand (extra tar), but he could always smoke two at a time.

After inhaling half a pack of unfiltered Camels, he boarded his train and found an empty compartment. He itched to get moving again. He always did.

Slumping down in his seat, he relaxed as the nicotine coursed through his veins, idly staring out the window and willing the outside world to start moving past him. He dug his fresh passport out of the breast pocket of his sportcoat and opened it up to look it over once more. He was now Dinesh Patel to anyone who might want to check. Like the last one, this one would only hold up to casual scrutiny. So no getting arrested again before reclaiming his case.

*

ANNA AND MILES returned to the train station as Vikram's train was rolling away from the platform, unaware they'd managed to just miss Vikram for the second time in an hour, as if some invisible hand were making them miss each other for a larf. The next train for Granada didn't leave till evening, so after buying tickets for the overnight trip, they had time to kill. They left the station again and wandered the old downtown. Coming across a long park, they were thinking that it was an oddly shaped garden, almost as if a meandering dry riverbed had been converted into a public green space, until they realized that's in fact what it was, the Riu Túria having been diverted west and south after flooding the city for the last time in the 1940s.

"I don't know where he thinks he's going to go once he gets his case back," said Anna, in reference to Vikram's note. "He hasn't got a passport. It's a little difficult to leave the country without one."

"Maybe that's what he meant by 'necessaries,'" said Miles.

"You mean...another passport?" she said. "How could he have *another?*"

"How could he have had a fake passport to begin with?"

"I see your point," she conceded.

It was another warm sunny day in Spain, and the two found an empty park bench. Anna lay her head on Miles's lap, and they held hands while they gazed on the parkway that snaked its way through the center of town.

After a while, Miles said, "What do you suppose is in Vikram's case?"

Anna shook her head, looked up at Miles. "Something valuable to him, I guess." She hadn't even known about the case, if she were being honest. Vikram had carried his shoulder bag around with him all the time. But Anna had never seen any case tucked inside of it. She assumed he was just another untethered academic scraping by like the rest of them. The idea of his having something valuable enough to chase someone all over Spain for had never occurred to her.

"This is nice," she said. "But should we head back toward Vikram's flat?"

"Are you getting hungry?" It was getting late for lunch.

"In a sense," she said, raising a suggestive eyebrow.

"Oh," he said.

They walked back to the apartment at a purposeful pace and climbed the stairs to Vikram's safehouse. Falling into bed already sweaty from exertion, they tore off each other's clothes. Miles was still afraid of breaking Anna, but she managed to coax him into enjoying the reckless abandon of angry lovemaking. And he was glad she did. Especially the second time. At this point in their relationship, the first round was usually a mulligan. A waste pitch. The first pancake cooked on a too-cool griddle.

After, they grabbed some dinner at a felafel stand and lazed the afternoon away till it was time to catch their train.

*

"I WAS TOLD," said Paco, "by someone who ought to know, that there is a fortune in precious stones, possibly even diamonds, inside."

Checho held an industrial-looking drill in his beefy, bloodstained right hand and eyed the case up and down. He dragged the cord over and positioned the drill tip against the front of the case and gave Paco and Cecilia a nod that said he'd take care of this. They were in the back room of the butcher shop, behind the open area where the carcasses were carved, beside the meat locker. Vikram's case lay atop a steel prep table.

"Just be careful with that," said Cecilia.

Checho hesitated involuntarily and eyed his wife impatiently, lifting the heavy tool for her to see. "This isn't going to break any diamonds," he protested.

Cecilia just glared at him. "No, but it might destroy whatever else is in there."

Checho sighed and returned the drill into position, switching it on with a squeeze of his finger. The drill was loud, and after a minute or so of its high-pitched racket, smoke began to rise from the spot he was drilling. The problem was the smoke was coming from the half-inch-thick drill bit, not the front of the case. He stared in disbelief at the now-blunt, smoldering bit, then at the case. The place he'd been drilling didn't show a mark.

His jaw muscles clenched, and he put the drill down on the table. He grabbed a tire iron from a lower shelf and hefted it in his right hand. Then, abruptly, he brought the elbow of the tire iron down square on the handle of the seemingly impregnable case. One end of the handle broke off, but the case's seal remained unaltered. He repeated his first attempt and broke off the other end of the handle, but clearly the handle's hinges were made of softer stuff than the rest of the thing. Annoyed now, Checho just started wailing on the case like the shaved gorilla he was. The case bounced around but never opened a hair, dented, scratched, or changed appearance in the slightest.

They could almost hear the case laughing at them over Checho's exasperated panting.

"Fuck this," he said, a vein bulging from the side of his sweaty forehead. He dropped the tire iron with a clank and stormed over to the heavy gray safe in the corner. Unlocking it, he retrieved the Czechoslovakian-made CZ-75 from a shelf inside. It was a suitably scary, black 9mm handgun, just big and phallic enough to frighten any troublemaker into meek compliance. Checho marched back toward the case, released the safety, and aimed the barrel straight at the place where the case would open if it were ever going to open.

"Wait!" Cecilia shouted. But not in time to stop Checho from squeezing the trigger, letting loose an earsplitting *blam!* that reverberated around the small room. At the same time that the noise started echoing off the walls, the bullet slammed into the edge of the case, nudging it back ever so slightly, while the 9mm brass-clad lead projectile, now badly deformed from its collision but still traveling at close to the speed of sound, ricocheted off the case at a predictable angle for anyone who had paid attention in geometry class or ever played Pong, hitting about three feet in front of where Paco was standing. After hitting the concrete floor at a 45-degree angle, the bullet bounced up and headed straight for Paco, who, at the sound of the shot, had reflexively brought his hands up to his face. The bullet tore through Paco's right pinky exactly like a mangled hunk of metal traveling at the speed of sound would through a man's little finger.

It took a few moments for Cecilia and Checho to distinguish the sound of Paco's screams from the high-pitched ringing in their ears, but when they did, they could see him gripping his right hand, the last knuckle of his pinky finger dangling from it by a frayed strip of skin, a Jackson Pollock spatter of atomized blood sprayed across the white wall behind him.

Cecilia immediately went to him, examined the gore where his formerly intact finger had been, and led Paco to the swivel chair in front of the cheap metal desk and had him sit down. Meanwhile, Checho was staring stupidly at the gun, still trying to figure out what had happened. Remembering his reason for firing it in the first place, he looked down at the case. Not a dent or a smudge on it. He scratched the side of his forehead with the CZ-75's smoking barrel, then yanked it away when he realized it was still hot. "*Ay,*" he murmured sheepishly.

Cecilia tore a strip of cloth off a stray rag and tied it tightly around the base of Paco's pinky, which he was cradling gingerly in his other hand. She rolled him over to the wood-block countertop against the far wall, placed his injured hand on it, and pulled the meat cleaver that had been sticking out of it free.

"Look over there," she ordered him, holding his hand down with an iron grip.

"Can we talk about this?" he said, starting to hyperventilate.

"Suit yourself," she said and lifted the gleaming steel implement, lining it up with the remaining knuckle. Paco quickly turned away, met Checho's eyes as he was turning that goddamn case over in his hands, then looked down at the floor.

Thwack!

He wasn't sure which it was—the sensation of having his finger severed for the second time in as many minutes or the sickening sound the cleaver made chopping through his flesh and bone, but before another scream could escape his lips, Paco lost consciousness.

"Get the first-aid kit, dummy," Cecilia said to Checho with an irritated sigh.

When Paco came to, he was lying down with his bandaged hand resting above him on an icepack atop a stack of waxed cardboard boxes. His finger stump was numbed by the ice, and he was alone in a large storage closet off the back room. The boxes, which surrounded him, were stacked near to the ceiling on one side. From an opened one, he could see they were stuffed with Moroccan cigarettes. Still good money in that, apparently. There were wooden crates along the other side, covered with straw, containing god-knows-what sort of contraband.

After a few moments of consciousness, his head began to clear and the pain in his stump returned with equal clarity. There was a half-empty bottle of Amontillado sitting next to him on the floor, and Paco grabbed for it, pulling the cork out with his teeth and spitting it onto the straw. He took a long pull from the bottle and winced as it went down. He'd never cared for sherry and wished, if Cecilia were going to leave him something he didn't like, she could have made it something stronger. The hand still throbbed, and he downed another gulp, the amber wine spilling over his chin and onto his collar.

Just then, Maria, one of his sister's employees, opened the door to check on Paco. She gave a brief gasp at seeing him awake and covered in sherry, and left to fetch Cecilia.

His sister returned, and after some brief ministrations and negotiations, she allowed him to get up and sit down again in the back room. She mentioned something about a doctor, who it turned out was actually a local mortician, who could come over later to stitch up his wound. Paco kept his hand iced, and his bottle close.

"Well, you convinced us," she said.

"Convinced you of what?" he asked.

"Whatever is in that bastard case must be worth an awful lot," she said, "because I've never seen anything like that. And if it's only to protect what's inside..." She left the rest unsaid.

"But we can't open it."

"No, but presumably your friend can," she pointed out.

"What friend?"

"The friend you stole it from."

"Oh, him." Paco thought of Vikram being led away by the police the last time he saw him.

"There's a glass panel on the top—"

"Yes, I know."

"Checho tried smashing it with the crowbar after you passed out," she said. "It didn't crack it. Not even a scratch."

"Strong glass." Paco took another swig of Amontillado.

"If that's what it is," she said. "You know, there's not a lock or keyhole or hinge anywhere on that thing. I think the glass part must have some way of unlocking it."

"You may be right," he said. "But I can't see how."

"That's why you need to talk to your friend," she said. He looked at her like she was crazy, or just cruel. "Look, make him a deal. Right now, neither of us can get at what's inside. Maybe we can both get *something*."

"I don't know," he said, shaking his head.

"We could try explosives," she said. "Checho knows a guy. Even that probably won't work, though. Besides, even out on *las llanuras*, someone might notice us blowing shit up."

"Okay, okay, I'll think about it," he said.

"Only *think?*"

Paco looked up at his younger sister with a resigned grimace. "You win. Just get me something stronger to drink, will you?"

After discussing Cecilia's plan for Paco to return to Barcelona to find Vikram and what kind of offer to make him, she left to pick up Paco some hard liquor. Cecilia was well known among the neighborhood's small proprietors. After dabbling for years selling illicit tobacco out the back of their carnicería, she and Checho had been recruited by the Galician mafia to be the local distributor of hashish from Turkey and cocaine from Colombia. They used "independent contractors" for their salesforce, most of whom were under the age of fourteen and could be counted on to keep their mouths shut if they got pinched. The Galicians dropped off the drugs in back with the meat deliveries. Even a small slice of the drug trade in Granada had meant a good deal more money than before for Cecilia and Checho, not to mention increased respect from the other shop owners. Or fear, at least. To their mob contacts, Checho was the face of the operation, but everyone in the neighborhood knew who the brains behind it all was.

So, although Cecilia would normally have picked up the least expensive rotgut she could find for her brother (who clearly didn't appreciate the good stuff), the owner of the liquor store came around the counter and presented her with his finest bottle of aged *oruja*, a kind of Spanish grappa—strong but not without subtlety—and was glad to receive her profuse thanks, and even gladder to see the back of her.

The mortician came later that afternoon and used something to numb Paco's hand before sewing up the finger. Cecilia had cleanly removed the pinky down to the first knuckle with the cleaver, but "Doctor de la Muerte" (the nickname bestowed upon him by his still-living clients) had to remove more bone in order to stitch the flaps of skin together. Luckily, between the local anesthetic and the oruja, Paco was pretty well out of it for the duration.

Three hours later, hungover, his newly rebandaged hand in worse pain than before but with a pocketful of prescription opiates, Paco boarded a train for Barcelona to find Vikram.

8.

"CAN I JUST GET an *iced tea?*" the man asked, a map spread out on the table. The café waiter didn't speak English and couldn't tell if he was trying to order something or maybe ask directions.

Vikram had been staring at the cobblestones, enjoying a little espresso with his sugar while sitting outside in the shade of a large Cinzano umbrella. He smiled. "I don't think they have that," he said to the American.

"What *do* they have?"

"Coffee." It was a little after ten in the morning.

"*Sí, café,*" said the waiter.

"Anything cold?" he asked of both of them, or neither, as if this were just what you did when the waiter couldn't be bothered to learn English. "It's hotter'n hell out here."

Vikram asked the waiter in Spanish what kind of soft drinks they had, and he told him. "They've got Coca-Cola…or water," he said.

"Tell him I'll have a Coke," he told Vikram, though the waiter understood that. After the waiter left, the man leaned toward Vikram from the next table, "They serve it cold, don't they?"

"More or less."

The waiter returned and set an opened 300-milliliter bottle of Coke down on the table in front of the man followed by a Collins tumbler. He walked back inside as the man examined the bottle, made miniature in his largish hands. "Even the pop bottles here are smaller," he said, shaking his head and taking a swig. He had oversized features—ears, nose, lips, eyebrows—and wore thick, black-framed glasses and close-cropped gray hair on a large, rectangular head. "You English?" he asked.

"Not originally, no," said Vikram. "I lived there for a while, though." The man nodded. "You're from the Midwest, I take it."

The man looked himself over, as if his baby-blue, short-sleeve dress shirt, ankle-length plaid slacks, or brown dress shoes and black socks had given him away. "What makes you say that?"

"You said 'pop' instead of 'soda,'" he said.

"Well, that's what it's called," he said matter-of-factly. "Soda pop."

Vikram nodded, like he'd just learned something.

"From Missouri," the man said, "just outside of Kansas City."

"On holiday?"

"A bus tour of the Mediterranean—Italy, France, and Spain," he said. "The wife's idea."

"Oh, where's she?"

"My wife and the rest of the group are up at the Alhambra," he said, pronouncing it "Al-*ham*-bera."

"You've already seen it?"

"Nah, just seen enough."

Vikram nodded, like he could relate.

"How 'bout you," he said, "on holiday too?"

"Visiting a friend," Vikram said. Which was more or less true, or would be once he found his friend. "I just arrived late yesterday on the train."

"You're lucky then. Our tour guide told us they went on strike last night," the man said, shaking his head. "Second time in a *week*."

"Really?" said Vikram, surprised. "I hadn't heard that."

"What can you expect with socialists running everything?" He finished the lukewarm remains of his Coke and grimaced. "At least with Franco, the trains ran on time—isn't that what they say?"

"I've always heard that adage with Mussolini, but I suppose it works just as well with Franco."

"Well, I wouldn't say that about Mussolini," the man said. "He was the man in charge the first time I came to Italy...then he wasn't. Then he was again, for a while."

"You served in the war."

"Fifth Army, Thirty-fourth Infantry. North Africa, then Italy for nearly three years." He paused, and Vikram popped a cigarette half out of his pack, offered him one. He waved it off while Vikram pulled it out with his lips and lit it. "I lost a lot of friends then." He paused again, not sure why he was confiding in this stranger. "It was a lot more fun the second time around. My wife just loved Florence." He laughed.

Vikram nodded again.

"You know the thing I remember most?" the man asked.

Vikram shook his head, blew a stream of smoke out of the side of his mouth.

"When we entered Naples, early on," he said. "Before they retreated, the Germans burned down the university there. Now, I never went past high school. When I was young, only rich kids or eggheads went to college. But I could never understand that." He wiggled his empty bottle of Coke, clinked it against the glass. The waiter seemed to have disappeared. "You know, they wouldn't let the Italian firefighters put out the fires. The Germans just made 'em watch. Three days, they told us, that's how long it burned. S'like…they wanted to burn everything good in the world they couldn't have."

Vikram nodded, understanding very well.

"I saw a lot worse things," he said. "But for whatever reason, that sticks out."

They talked a little while longer, the man telling him about an Indian division he'd fought alongside. *They called 'em Red Eagles, and they were at Monte Cassino like the rest of us. There was another colored outfit from New Zealand, if I recall.* Whatever it was, people just felt comfortable dumping the contents of their brains out to Vikram. He had that effect on people.

Vikram finished his cigarette, settled his bill, and bidding the man *adiós*, set off on his way. There were only so many bakeries in the Albaicín, and being bakeries they opened early, so Vikram had already investigated three before stopping for espresso. There were *panaderías* (bread shops) and *pastelerías* (pastry shops), some that sold both. Paco's landlady had told him it was *una fleca*, which was Catalan for bread shop, but Vikram figured it best to check both. None so far seemed to be owned by a sister of Paco's. Not that Vikram was necessarily convinced his straightforward approach would work. But he knew they'd never be able to open his case, and that made him think that maybe they'd be ready to discuss some type of arrangement.

Still, he had a few more bakeries to visit before he'd have to consider rethinking his strategy.

*

MILES NEVER WOULD have considered hitchhiking in the United States. It was the stuff of cautionary made-for-TV movies and horror flicks—the driver offering a ride would invariably turn out to be a serial killer, or if not, the ones hitching would be Satanists or vampires or some shit.

But he'd hitchhiked through Ireland and found the people friendly, talkative, generous. So far, his experience of the people in Spain was similar, and so hitching with Anna seemed like a perfectly reasonable idea. It never occurred to him to suppose that Americans would be just as affable and benevolent if he'd ever traveled around and spent time with strangers in his own country, depending upon their goodwill the way he did here.

Anna's only concern was if they'd get a ride before the strike ended. In the hierarchy of hitchhiking, the most likely to be picked up were the least threatening, in order: one woman; two women; one man; a man and a woman; two men; and finally, any combination of three or more people, which was just wishful thinking. So they weren't the worst case, but they were hardly the best.

After passing a night on the hard, uncomfortable floor of the beautiful train station hoping a train for Granada would materialize, a short bus ride had deposited them at a large roundabout on the southern edge of the city. Not sure how long they'd be there, they stood up their backpacks—Miles's large one and Anna's little one, as if they were Papa and Mama Bear—on the sidewalk next to the road. Anna stood and waved her hand out to signal passing cars, while Miles sat down on the ground with his pack propping him up and fished a wedge of cheese out of an outer pocket.

Anna looked back at him sitting there, unwrapping his cheese. "Are you going to help?" she asked.

"Come and sit down," he said. Of the two of them, Miles was the more experienced hitchhiker, and he had a method. "Have some Edam."

Anna watched the cars passing by and shrugged, sat down cross-legged next to Miles, and took the proffered hunk he'd cut with his pocketknife. "In the Netherlands, we grate this over our Corn Flakes."

"Really?"

"No."

Miles laughed. "I realized when I was hitchhiking in Ireland that drivers were more likely to pull over if you didn't look too eager."

The cars were still passing them by. "But what if they can't see us?" she said. "Or don't realize we're looking for a ride?"

"They know," he said, annoyingly sure of himself. "What else would we be doing out here, taking our luggage for a walk? Besides, this way is more relaxing." He bit off a piece of cheese and patted a side pocket of his backpack, where a bottleneck was sticking out. "Should I open the wine?"

Before Anna could answer, an old orange Datsun compact pulled over and stopped in front of them. The driver, a thirtysomething woman with dark brown hair pulled back in a ponytail, leaned over to crank down the passenger window and said, "*Hola! Necesitáis un paseo?*"

"*Hola,*" Anna answered. "*Sí, sí.*"

"*A dónde vais?*"

"*Vamos a Granada.*"

"*Bien,* hop in," the woman said. "I'm going to Sevilla and can drop you on the way. I could use the company."

Miles tried not to look too pleased with himself as he schlepped their bags to the car and insisted on taking the backseat. With a nod and a *gracias* to the driver, he tossed the backpacks in and then crammed himself headlong through the narrow opening between the door and the folded-over front seat. There was just enough room back there for him and their stuff, and perhaps a few styrofoam packing peanuts.

Anna got in, and they headed off toward the A-7 and Granada.

*

IN ADDITION to being angry at Checho for shooting off his finger, Paco felt traumatized at having narrowly escaped death's icy embrace. In the split second before the bullet took his pinky, Paco had instinctively brought up his hands to protect his face, deflecting the shot with a non-essential but cherished appendage. If not for this dumb bit of luck, the bullet probably would have opened a new hole in his face. He'd had a vision, during a drug-induced nightmare on the train, of Cecilia holding his bloody braincase down on the chopping block, lining the cleaver up with his neck while he pleaded with her to reconsider.

None of the thoughts preoccupying his mind, however, could stop his finger stump from hurting like a mother. The pills helped dull the pain somewhat, but mainly just induced a general fogginess that caused him to care less about the pain that remained. This, combined with his feeling of living on borrowed time, caused him to feel a distinct unease, as if something bad were waiting for him around a corner.

He'd made it as far as Madrid before being forced off the train in the middle of the night and left to fend for himself in Atocha Station. It was the second strike in a week, which was not normal. Typically, the labor union announced the strike far in advance (like the one last week) and scheduled it for a day or a few hours, so you knew how to plan around it, unless you were an absolutely clueless tourist.

Now it was morning, no one was overly concerned, just more irritated, more put out than usual, which was probably the point. Unlike the other stranded travelers who were anxious to get to where they were headed, Paco dreaded the resumption of his journey, destined for nothing good as he was convinced it was.

He was sitting on the floor of the high-vaulted, steel-and-glass terminal, propped against a column he had all to himself.

"*Exactamente el hombre*," said a familiar voice from behind him. "Just the man I've been looking for."

Paco turned around to see the massive chest, then craned his neck up to see Anders standing there with that annoying smirk on his chiseled face.

"When I arrived back in Barcelona," Anders continued, "you were gone." Paco shrugged, a little disconcerted but trying to conceal it. "Someone told me you had disappeared just before Vikram was arrested. And that Vikram's bag had gone missing at the same time. They also told me that Vikram escaped from jail. *Twice*. Amazing, right?" Paco couldn't hide his surprise at that. "Tom said Vikram skipped town and left an address in Valencia for Anna—though I wasn't supposed to tell anyone that. You won't tell, will you?"

Paco thought about what Cecilia would want him to do. "Who would I tell?"

"I don't know, the police?" said Anders, "You must have done so once already." Anders shook his head as at a naughty child. "But I thought, Vikram isn't going to Valencia. He's going to Granada to find you. I assume you have his case?"

"For all the good it's done me," said Paco, "I should have let you take it."

"Yes, but Vikram would never have been so careless while I was around. He knows what I am, or thinks he knows. Why do you think I told you about it?"

Paco had never really given it much thought. "A favor?"

Anders laughed. "So what on earth are you doing in Madrid? Stuck here like me, I suppose? But where are you headed, and where *is* the case?"

"In Granada, safe," said Paco. "Very safe. It can't be opened. Not that we didn't try." He held up his bandaged hand.

"Ouch." Anders sat down beside Paco. "So you were on your way to Barcelona to try and make a deal with Vikram?"

Paco nodded reluctantly.

"But Vikram must have known you'd never open it," said Anders, making a show of thinking out loud. "He's probably in Granada right now...looking for *you*."

Paco sighed, wondering why he'd ever even bothered.

*

VIKRAM'S FACE rarely betrayed anything like worry or despair, though as he rose from the squishy mattress in his dimly lit room in the *pensióne*, he indeed felt desperate, and worried that his carelessness had cost him incalculably this time.

He was no closer to finding Paco than when he'd arrived in Granada two nights ago. He'd methodically worked his way through the business listings of bakeries in the Albaicín. This morning, he'd decided to simply walk the neighborhood in hopes of seeing a bread shop, pastisseria, or mercado he hadn't already infiltrated.

But he didn't have high hopes.

By eleven, with the sun beating down on him, he had exhausted his possibilities in the Albaicín and was now on the neighborhood's outskirts.

He stood at an intersection just below the hillside that rose up eastward into the whitewashed caves of Sacromonte, the traditional Roma enclave in Granada. He'd consumed nothing but sweets, espresso, and nicotine all morning, so he stopped into a rundown-looking carnicería for something substantial to put in his belly.

The butcher shop sold bocadillos, in addition to a selection of meats and cheeses in a large glass case, the serrano and Ibérico hams hung prominently from the ceiling behind the counter in between various types of sausage. Vikram ordered a *jamón y queso* from the young female clerk, who took his money and rubbed the bread with a tomato half while an older woman who appeared to be the boss cut the ham cradled in its *jamonera*. She made razor-thin slices from the exposed shank with a long knife and laid the translucent crimson-and-cream strips on a square of wax paper.

Vikram watched her as she worked. Though he could only see her face from the side, she looked familiar. When she was done, she turned and handed the pile to Maria.

"*Gracias, señora,*" she said and arranged the cheese and meat slices on the baguette. Wrapping it in paper, she handed it to Vikram.

He accepted it graciously but never took his eyes off the owner. He recognized her features, but it was her mannerisms, the way she moved and nodded her head, first to Maria, then to him, that convinced him.

The man was looking at her oddly, Cecilia thought. He could have been one of her *gitano* cousins, though he was dressed a little too conservatively. Like "gypsy," *gitano* was a corruption of "Egyptian," reflecting the general ignorance about the origins of the Roma, Hindi speakers who migrated out of northwestern India around the sixth century. Cecilia did not take him for a more recent Indian migrant until he spoke to her in his lightly English-accented Spanish.

"*Con permiso,*" he said, "may I ask you a question?"

"Of course," she said.

"Do you know a man named Francisco, by any chance…called Paco?"

She paused, taken by surprise. "Yes, Paco is the name of my brother," she said with an innocent shrug. It was a common enough nickname.

"I've been looking for him," he said. "My name's Vikram, and I'm a friend of his from Barcelona. I needed to talk with him before he left so suddenly. I wasn't sure where he'd gone, but I thought he might have returned home. And I was told his sister owned a...carnicería. I noticed your resemblance," he added, oblivious to the fact that that might be an insult.

"He did return," she said, not dignifying the last comment. "But he had to go out of town for a few days. Perhaps I can give him a message?"

Vikram's smile vanished as his face became still and the only feature that seemed to remain relevant were his eyes. "Do you have the case?" he asked evenly.

"It's...nearby."

"He didn't take it with him."

"No," she said, though he'd said it more as a statement, as if he knew she wouldn't lie to him while he was staring at her like that. She broke away from his gaze and came around the meat case to talk to him privately. "He left it with me," she said. "Not here, but in a safe place. I didn't know where he got it."

"Of course," he said. "Paco naturally wanted what was inside the case. But it's much more valuable to me than it would be to him. I'm willing to compensate him, though. He knows I can't go to the police. I know he can't open the case without me. What's inside isn't worth ten million pesetas to you or Paco, but that's what I'm willing to pay for its return. You see, it is worth that much to me. So, if you can get me the case, I could get you the money. We could arrange a place and a time to meet for an exchange. Does that sound reasonable?"

Cecilia was about to say she had to wait until Paco returned, but Vikram was offering her more than $60,000 for an inert slab of black metal. What the fuck was there to think about? "We close at eight. Be here at 8:30," she said. "Come around the back entrance and knock."

*

ANNA AND MILES looked out at the Albaicín across the valley from their perch on the Alhambra mount. Beyond Granada to the north were more mountains, to the west the Andalusian plain.

They'd more or less given up trying to find Vikram. Having arrived at the youth hostel the night before and discovering he'd left no word for them there, they were at a dead end. Might as well enjoy Granada.

At the hostel, they had had to sleep in separate dorms, their second night in a row of forced celibacy. All day, as a result, they couldn't keep their hands off each other. Moments earlier, Miles and Anna had been awkwardly interrupted by a group of German tourists in one of the old harem rooms of the palace—their lips locked, one of his hands under her shirt, one of hers on the front of his pants. There was no use trying to play it off as anything other than what it was, so they simply left for some fresh air with as much dignity as they could muster.

They'd checked out of the youth hostel that morning and found an inexpensive pension closer to the Alhambra that had a double available. Unable to occupy the room until later, they'd dropped their bags and walked up the hill to the old Moorish fortress and pleasure garden. They'd been exploring the Alhambra and Generalife complex for hours, and the shadows were finally starting to lengthen as the sun began its descent over the western flats. In this light, the hilltop looked stunning, yet neither had thought to bring a camera.

Miles did have an old Argus stuffed in the bottom of his backpack, but he seldom brought it out. There was a roll of film he'd snapped in Ireland, and half a roll taken in Paris. He'd forgotten to take any in Barcelona, though, and didn't have even one of Anna. He figured there'd be plenty of time. It was a young way to think.

"I should have brought my camera," he said. They were walking through another manicured garden and stopped in front of a large archway cut into a long, tall hedgerow. "Hold on," he said, holding a pretend camera to his eye, "I'll take your picture." Anna posed against the opening to a different section of the garden, and Miles gazed at her smiling face, lingering a second before clicking his imaginary shutter.

"That's a keeper," he said. She smirked and turned, leading him through the arched opening.

They followed a shallow rill, which fed a rectangular pool at the other end of the enclosure. A few palms stood out here and there among the poplar, cypress, almond, and fruit trees.

"When I was a kid, I discovered some snapshots my dad had saved from Vietnam," said Miles. "He and his buddies standing around in front of palm trees. It looked so exotic. I didn't realize till later on what he was doing there."

"He fought in the war?"

"Not really. He was stationed in Saigon during the war, but he never saw any action. This was before I was born—I was actually conceived while he was on leave."

"Sounds like he saw *some* action," she said.

They passed under another archway carved out of the shrubbery. "I suppose he might've seen some disturbing things over there. He never really liked to talk about it much. The thing I remember from those old photos, though, was how much I wanted to go to someplace like that—a strange place with jungles and mountains."

"Suriname has plenty of jungles and mountains," she said. "Of course, it was mostly flat along the coast where I grew up—kind of like the Netherlands, actually, only poorer and much hotter."

"Hm. That's the one thing my dad would talk about—the heat. In Chicago, our summers tend to get pretty hot and humid, and there's always a couple weeks in July or August when it's just unbearable"— Anna wondered what Miles considered unbearable—"and he'd always say, 'Damn, feels like I'm back in Vietnam.'"

"You never told me," she said, "how did he die?"

"Um, well, it was about a year ago, last summer. He died in a car accident." Miles hesitated, knowing that wasn't exactly true. "He died crossing the street, actually. A truck hit him in the crosswalk."

"Oh, my God." Anna shook her head at the thought of it.

"Apparently, the driver was trying to make a yellow light. That's what he said, anyway. There weren't any witnesses, so....Some people thought he was lying and ran the red. But if he wasn't, you have to wonder why my dad was crossing against the light with a truck coming toward him."

"Oh."

"I don't know. He'd been living in the city since the divorce, and I hadn't seen him much..." Miles trailed off, both wanting and not wanting to talk about what he considered his part in it. "I mean, I still saw him every other weekend, mostly. But the weekend before he died, we had this big fight."

Anna nodded like she knew somehow or at least understood.

"It was over something stupid, too," he said, shaking his head. "He wouldn't let me borrow his car to drive to a party in the suburbs. So I told him I didn't see why we bothered visiting him anymore."

"Mm."

"Then I told him to fuck off and left."

Anna looked at Miles. "We all say dumb things to our parents," she said. "It doesn't mean what happened was your fault."

He nodded.

They had stopped by the big rectangular pool and stared into it for a few moments.

"What about your dad?" he asked.

"What about him?"

"I dunno, what's his story?"

"I don't know much about him," she said. "I don't think he ever even knew about me. He was white, I know that."

"Hm."

"My mother knew him beforehand, but after, she didn't have any contact with him. Supposedly, he left the country before I was born."

"Why didn't she tell him?"

"Mmm...I don't think it was consensual."

"Oh....Wait, what?" said Miles.

Anna shrugged, letting him work it out. He opened his mouth partway, then closed it, unsure how to respond.

"She never told me that, of course, but when I was a kid I'd occasionally overhear her say something to one of her friends or my grandmother. Hints I only understood later. But mainly her hatred of him never seemed like what you feel for an ex."

"Oh," he said. "I guess you must hate him too."

"I can't hate him too much," she said. "If he hadn't done it, I wouldn't be here."

That seemed a grim yet apt analogy for something, though Miles couldn't think what.

They were working their way back to the entrance along a gravel path beside a square vermillion tower when they both saw him. He looked the same. Same disheveled black hair, same linen sportcoat, same bag slung over his shoulder, same cigarette dangling petulantly from the same crooked mouth. He was leaning against the low brick wall looking out at the trees with an air of such casual insouciance, it made Anna want to laugh despite herself.

Before either one of them could yell his name, Vikram looked up to see them standing about twenty feet away with somewhat incredulous expressions on their faces. "Oh, there you are," he said, as if he'd just left them by the Court of the Lions a few minutes ago.

Anna and Vikram quickly closed the distance between one another, with Miles close behind, unsure if Anna was going to hug Vikram or punch him. She wrapped him in a tight embrace and held him for several seconds before pushing him away forcefully. "Rumbi!" she said, "what the hell have you been up to?"

"I missed you," he said. He pivoted toward Miles and gave him a quick hug. "You too, Miles."

"Nuh-uh," she said, "you're not getting out of it that easily. We got interrogated by the police, chased you halfway across Spain following your trail of breadcrumbs, slept at a train station, hitchhiked our way here, and then found out you didn't even leave word at the hostel like you said you would. All because you broke out of jail after giving the cops a fake passport and are now a fugitive from the law. You've got some explaining to do."

Vikram looked around him, searching for a reply. "You would have missed all this," he said, indicating the surrounding gardens and city.

"This *is* nice," Miles agreed.

"You're not helping, Miles," she said.

Vikram held his palms up in submission. "Let's go grab some food and something to drink. It's closing now, anyway," he said, referring to the Alhambra.

They took a leisurely and mostly silent walk down the hill and across the bridge over the Río Darro, Anna refusing to draw Vikram out, Vikram blithely keeping mum, and Miles feeling the awkwardness like an ill-fitting suit. Once across the river and in the Albaicín, Vikram finally broke the silence by suggesting they walk to a café he liked in the neighborhood, which he now knew like the palm of his hand.

"I can see how the fake passport would look suspicious," he said as they strolled up a winding alley. "I got it in Manchester a few years ago so I wouldn't have to return to India. It was stupid, I admit."

If the explanation didn't satisfy Anna, at least the attempt at one did.

They arrived at an unassuming corner establishment with a few empty café tables scattered out front. A waiter came out to seat them and handed Vikram a menu. He ordered them a pitcher of sangria and some small plates to share.

Notes plucked on a guitar echoed from around a corner, and a tubby calico cat was cleaning himself against a nearby wall. When he turned over on his side, he looked like a football slowly rolling away.

"That is one fat cat," said Anna.

Miles nodded. "The food here must be good." When that didn't elicit even a polite smile, Miles decided to keep quiet. He was between Anna and Vikram, who were sitting across from each other. The waiter brought out the sangria, a dish of olives, and three glasses.

"I don't know what to think of all this, Vikram," she said. "You're taking it all rather lightly, but you're wanted"—she lowered her voice—"*wanted* by the police. They think you must be involved with some terrorist group."

"Really?" he asked. "Which one?"

"Does it matter? I don't think there are any good ones."

"You know me, Anna," he said. "I'm not political. I'm only interested in people—and the things they do. I'm an academic. I would never hurt anyone unless a tenureship were at stake." He shook a cigarette loose from his pack and pulled it out with his lips, quickly lighting it. "Mainly, I didn't want to leave Barcelona the way I did, without talking to you first."

"I still have questions, Rumbi."

"Okay."

"For one," she said, "why were you keeping an apartment in Valencia?"

"I'd had the apartment there before coming to Barcelona," he said, which was true. Vikram wanted badly to come clean with her then and there, but the same fear stopped him. "It was so cheap," he said, "I thought it would be handy to hold onto."

"And you kept a horde of cash there?" He shrugged. "And what else? Another passport?"

"Well...yeah. The guy who made them offered me a really good deal on two. So..."

Anna shook her head. "So what's your plan now? Where are you headed?"

"I'm going back home," he said. "Once I get what I came here for."

"Your case?" asked Miles.

Vikram nodded.

"You mean it's not in there?" she said, indicating his satchel.

"In this? No, I picked this up in Valencia."

"Oh. So what's in the case?" asked Anna. "I never even knew you had it."

"A lot of valuable research, for one thing," he said. "It took me years to gather what's in there."

Anna looked dubious. "Anthropological research?"

"Mmm, not exactly."

"Fine. What else?"

"Some diamonds," he admitted.

Anna raised an eyebrow. "You have a briefcase full of diamonds?"

"No, not 'full of.'" He took a gulp of wine. "A small legacy. Just enough to finance my travels while I've been between jobs."

This was news to her, though it explained some aspects of his lifestyle. "So have you found Paco?"

"No, but I found his sister," he said. "Cecilia. She owns a butcher shop, it turns out, not a bakery. Not far from here, near Sacromonte."

"So does she know where Paco is?" asked Anna.

"Not at the moment," he conceded. "But he was here and apparently left the case in her care."

"Paco *did* steal it," she said. "I can't believe he did that. He was always so sweet."

"The two things aren't mutually exclusive, you know," he said. "Anyway, I'm going back there tonight."

"She's going to get you the case back?"

"Well, I'm going to buy it back," he said. "We agreed on a price."

"But it's *your* case."

"I know that, Anna. But they *are* thieves. You don't expect them to just give it up for nothing, do you?"

Anna leaned back in her chair. She'd never really been a party to any criminal transaction she knew of. So few things in the Netherlands were even illegal. "So why didn't they just take the diamonds?" she asked.

"They're unable to open the case, as I knew they would be."

That sounded ridiculous. Anna didn't think much of criminals who couldn't even manage to open a locked briefcase.

"The case is impervious," he continued, "and it has a very sophisticated locking mechanism."

"And you have the key?"

Vikram held up his right hand. "In a manner of speaking."

Anna shook her head again, clueless as to what that meant, and sighed. She sipped at her sweetened wine, and probed the ham croquette on her dish with a small fork. "Speaking of locking mechanisms," she said, "how did you manage to escape from jail?"

Vikram shrugged, knowing he was only digging himself in deeper. "You wouldn't believe how porous the security is at the Barcelona lockup. It didn't take much."

That seemed to satisfy Anna as much as anything else he told her, which is to say it didn't. They resumed eating, piling more olives on their plates, soaking up more white bean dip and oil with crusty bread, pouring themselves more sangria from the pitcher. They had the outdoor café almost to themselves and seemed to have all the time in the world.

"This is all I wanted," said Vikram, a propos of nothing. "A little more time with friends and then...well, who knows?"

Anna gave him a half-smile, realizing herself how sad it would be if he really did leave.

The meal done, it was almost completely dark, and Vikram asked for the check.

"This exchange is when?" she asked him.

"Eight-thirty," he said. "In about fifteen minutes. I'd still like to talk with you about something—both of you, actually—but it'll have to wait until I get back."

"We're going with you," she said.

"We are?" said Miles.

*

"*QUIÉNES DEMONIOS son ellos?*" Cecilia asked after opening the back door to the shop. "Who the hell are they?"

"Just friends," said Vikram. They were speaking Spanish, so Miles could only understand a little of what was going on.

"Fine," she said. "Did you bring the money?"

"Yes." He patted his satchel. "Do you have the case?"

"Yeah, it's here. Come on in, all of you."

They entered the back room of the butcher shop and saw a thick slab of Spaniard leaning against a steel table, where Vikram's case lay, its handle missing. Checho held Vikram's eyes with a menacing stare, ignoring Miles and Anna after throwing them a perfunctory glance.

"As you can see," said Cecilia, "the case is there. We'll need to see the money now."

Vikram opened his satchel and showed them the ten stacks of one hundred 10,000 peseta notes stashed in a crumpled paper shopping bag. "Ten million pesetas," he said.

Anna formed an O with her mouth. Miles leaned in next to her and whispered, "*Diez millones?* Does that mean ten *million?*" She nodded yes.

Checho picked up the case and stepped over beside Cecilia. Vikram pulled out the shopping bag full of cash and held it, waiting for Checho to hand over the case, aware that they were waiting for him to do the same. Before either party could figure a way through this impasse, the knob of the door behind them jiggled, and from the hall off the meat locker came the thud of someone walking headfirst into the other side of the door, followed by a muffled *Mierda!*

"What the hell?" said Checho.

Cecilia threw up her hands and rolled her eyes. "It can only be Paco," she said. "May as well let him in, Checho."

He glared at her for a second but then put the case back down on the table. As Vikram held the bag protectively to his chest and watched, Checho walked over to the door and opened it. Paco shuffled through,

his eyes wary taking in the larger-than-expected crowd. More blood had
soaked through the bandage on his right hand, and his left was buried in
his coat pocket. He looked pale and a little dazed.

Behind Paco walked in Anders. Being a good head taller than Paco—a
sort of Scandinavian version of Checho—he was hard to miss.

"Anders?" said Anna incredulously. "What are *you* doing here?"

"I could ask you the same thing," he said, raking Miles with his eyes
before returning her glare. "I guess we all share an unusual interest in
what your flatmate's been up to." He looked over at Vikram and then at
the case sitting on the table, where Checho had left it. "Ah. There it is."

Vikram's expression changed almost imperceptibly when Anders
spoke. Ever calm, if more serious than usual, what passed over Vikram's
countenance was difficult to discern if you weren't paying attention. It
was initially recognition, as if he'd suddenly realized who Anders was,
then simply fear—an emotion Vikram's face had never betrayed, as far
and Anna and Miles knew.

"Paco accomplished what I couldn't," Anders continued. "He had no
way of knowing, of course, that he'd never be able to open that thing."

"Just open it now," said Paco, pulling Checho's black Czechoslova-
kian handgun out of his pocket and motioning with it to Vikram.

"Hey…" objected Checho, more to Paco's having stolen his gun than
anything. One drug-addled look from his recently maimed brother-in-
law quashed any more complaint.

"We'll take the diamonds *and* the cash," said Paco. "Anders can have
whatever else is in there. That's the deal."

Cecilia didn't like this. She was a drug dealer and black marketeer,
ran a small numbers racket, and occasionally had to use muscle to protect
their modest share of the local criminal pie. But she wasn't a monster.
Her arrangement had been fair, she thought. Neither side would walk
away completely satisfied—but wasn't that the sign of a good deal? Her
way, Vikram walks away feeling lucky to get his stuff back for the price
of a little (okay, a lot of) money. Paco's way, they've made enemies, a
move that might haunt them later. Plus, there was no guarantee Vikram
was going to open that case. He might call Paco's bluff. Then what would
he do? What would Anders do?

Vikram stared at Paco's gun. Paco had it cocked with the safety on and now flicked the safety off. He glanced at Anna and Miles, who were both terrified, having never been menaced with a deadly weapon before. He looked back at Paco and flashed a crooked smile. "All right," he said. "It isn't worth dying over." He walked over to the case, everyone's eyes glued to him as he touched the black glass panel on the top side of the case twice with the print of his right thumb. Cecilia, Checho, and Paco all watched him closely, wondering if he'd actually be able to open the thing. Anders looked on with a smirk, knowing he would.

Vikram continued tapping the combination into the glass panel by touching the tips of the fingers of his right hand—index, ring, ring, middle, index—and the case seemed to exhale as it unlocked.

"Open it, Checho," said Paco.

Checho pushed Vikram aside, grasped the lid of the case, and easily lifted it up. A glimpse of the interior, with its various compartments, was all they got before the alarm went off.

The siren that Vikram had triggered with his thumbprints was more like a booby trap, though, intended to disable its victims, not simply warn others of a breach. Immediately, everyone in the room but Vikram and Anders doubled over in excruciating pain. Anders wouldn't get the chance to try anything, however, as Paco immediately dropped the cocked and loaded gun butt-first on the concrete floor, causing it to fire—a shot that no one heard over the din. The bullet didn't ricochet this time but sailed backward and up right into the meaty part of Anders's left thigh, stopping just before hitting his femur.

The next sequence of events took only a few seconds. Once Vikram saw Anders crumple to the floor with the rest of them, he made a kind of sign with the fingers of his right hand above the palm of his left. Just as it had five nights ago in the Barri Gòtic, the palm of his left hand lit up with a bluish light. Vikram, his right hand held above his glowing left, rubbed his right thumb and forefinger together as if playing a miniature violin, and what looked like a little black asterisk appeared in midair about a meter in front of him. He stretched his thumb and forefinger apart and the ragged little hole floating in front of him grew from a few millimeters to about two meters in diameter. He shut the case, and the siren ceased, allowing his victims sweet relief. He threw the case into his satchel, along with the shopping bag filled with cash, closed it, and slung it over his shoulder. Roughly grabbing Anna and Miles by their upper arms like two mischievous children, he dragged them both stumbling into the center of the black hole, where the three of them disappeared into nothingness.

The hole and its black corona clinched shut, and they were gone.

9.

CECILIA TRIED TO follow what was happening, but her eyeballs were vibrating so violently, it was all a blur until Vikram closed that godforsaken case. When her vision returned to normal, she saw Vikram lead his two friends into a floating Rorschach inkblot that swallowed them and then closed, disappearing as if it had never been there.

Impossible, she thought.

Sitting up, but still on the floor, Checho rubbed his throbbing temple and looked around. "They're gone? She told you we'd worked it out," he spat at his brother-in-law. "Why did you do that?"

Paco shook his head, knowing it hadn't been his idea.

Anders was grimacing as he dug his middle finger into the hole in his thigh. Cecilia watched with a blend of awe and disgust as Anders pulled the mangled bullet from out of his leg, which was now pumping out blood in a steady stream. Dropping the bullet to the floor with a *tink*, he grabbed a dish towel from a side table and tied it tightly around his wounded thigh, stanching the flow.

"You people and your guns," he said, shaking his head and pulling something that resembled a stiff black playing card from his shirt pocket. "Let me just apologize in advance for what I'm about to do," he said while rubbing a finger across the face of the card. It emitted a similarly ear-splitting tone to what Vikram had just subjected them to, in a slightly higher register. As Cecilia, Paco, and Checho covered their ears and writhed in pain once again—their eyes rattling in their heads, their bowels opening up—Anders knitted his brow and sighed, wondering if this was truly necessary and concluding that it probably was. After about forty-five seconds of that—their internal organs had burst, their brains turned to mush—they were dead and someone else's problem, as far as Anders was concerned.

He tapped his card, stopping the noise and causing its face to light up. After a few moments dragging his finger around the card some more, he soon had his own ragged, two-meter-wide portal in front of him. He climbed in and was off before the smell of evacuation and death could reach his nose.

*

THEIR HEADS THROBBED, but the pain was quickly subsiding as the sounds of the ocean soothed their traumatized ears. They had fallen. Somehow, they had fallen in the back of a butcher shop and landed on the soft sand of a beach. Vikram had led them here somehow. Their eyes had stopped vibrating, and now they could see where they were, next to the ocean—some ocean—on a white sand beach at night.

The moon provided enough light to make out faces. Anna blinked her eyes from her prone position and stared at Vikram, who was sitting in the sand staring back at her anxiously. Her heart began racing, her breaths coming in short bursts. "What just happened?" she asked.

"Well…" he began.

On the other side of Vikram, Miles stood up unsteadily and started shuffling toward the shore.

"Where are you going?" asked Anna.

Miles looked back over his shoulder. "It's a little embarrassing," he said, kicking off his shoes and pulling off his socks as he made his way. He walked with a slow, awkward gait, as if he had a load in his pants, which he did. He unbuttoned his pants, taking them off carefully and tossing them clear of the incoming tide. With only his boxers on, he entered the surf.

"Oh," said Vikram. "Yeah…it'll do that."

"Do what?" asked Anna, still perplexed.

"The alarm I set off back there can cause your bowels to loosen," he said apologetically. "It can actually be fatal with long enough exposure."

Anna stared at him now as if he were from another planet, which, she was beginning to suspect, he was.

"It's a good thing we wound up here, eh?" he said, digressing. "Right on the Atlantic—or is this still the Mediterranean?"

"I don't even know where *here* is," Anna pointed out.

"The Algarve," said Vikram. "Southern Portugal. I think it's actually the Atlantic, though it doesn't really matter, I suppose."

"We're in Portugal now," she said, evidently a plausible statement.

Miles was waist-deep in the waves now, removing his befouled shorts and muttering something neither of his companions could hear.

"Can you believe it's still this warm out?" Vikram said. "Going for a swim looks nice."

"I'll pass," she said.

After flinging his laden boxers as far away from himself as he could, Miles did his best to clean himself in the salty sea, eventually resorting to scraping his ass along the sandy bottom. He emerged from the water concealing his nakedness, not so much out of modesty but because the Atlantic was quite cold. He hurriedly pulled on his pants and shirt and made his way back to his friends.

He lay down next to them, wet and drained, and felt the salt sting in his eyes. "This isn't Granada, is it," he said.

"We're in Portugal now," Anna informed him.

Miles looked at her, looked around, nodded, and lay his head back down, staring straight up.

"Uh...how is this possible, Vikram?" she asked. "If we're in Portugal...and that's clearly the ocean, so...what did you do...beam us here from Granada?"

"'Beam' us?"

"I don't know," she said. "*Beamed*, like on *Star Trek*."

"Teleported?" Miles put in helpfully.

"No, teleportation isn't feasible, I'm afraid," said Vikram. "We used a spacetime portal to get here."

"A spacetime portal?" asked Anna.

"Yes," he said. "It's funny—loosely translated from my language, we refer to them as 'arseholes'."

"A wormhole, you mean?" Miles said. Anna turned her bemused stare on him now.

"Yes. Same idea," said Vikram, nodding. "I mean, I never really understood why '*worm*hole,' as opposed to—"

"*What* is a wormhole?" asked Anna.

Miles looked at Vikram, who seemed hesitant to answer, and offered, "It's a theoretical shortcut through spacetime."

Vikram looked impressed, and added, "Not theoretical, in fact."

"Right."

"A shortcut through spacetime?" said Anna.

Vikram nodded at Miles, encouraging him to go on. "Yeah," he said, "the idea of a wormhole is that, with relativity, space can warp in unexpected ways, the way light bends around an object with really strong gravity, like a star or a black hole."

"How do you know this?" she asked.

He shrugged. "I read a lot of sci-fi," he said, shifting uncomfortably as his wet nether regions soaked through his pants.

"Is he right?" she asked Vikram.

"I don't know," said Vikram, "sounds right to me."

"What do you mean, *you don't know?*" she said.

"I'm a biologist, not a physicist," he said.

"Wha— I thought you were an anthropologist."

"That too."

"But, then...how did you create a wormhole for us to travel through?"

"With this." Vikram held up his left hand, still glowing blue. "We call it 'smartskin'—it goes on like a tattoo, but it's a powerful quantum computer."

"I knew I saw your hand glowing the other night," said Miles.

"And you have no idea how it works?" asked Anna, exasperated.

Vikram laughed nervously. "Do *you* know how your television works?"

Anna was about to say, *Of course I do*, when it occurred to her that she had no idea. "Not...as such," she said.

"My understanding," he said, "is that there are subatomic wormholes everywhere. All around us in every corner of the universe, on every planet. Just literally *everywhere*. After the smartskin scans a few billion subatomic wormholes, it finds one we can use—that will take us somewhere we tell it we want to go—and creates a cocoon of dark matter, making the opening large enough for us to enter and carrying us through to the other side. Since we can't travel faster than the speed of light, we need to find a shortcut between distant points, an arsehole—sorry, *wormhole*—and that's what this smartskin does."

"About that—smart skin—on your hand," she said. "Just where does one get that?"

"Where I'm from," he said. "A place that you'd need this to get to."

"Okay. So, you're saying…outer space?" she said.

"No, not outer space," he said with a chuckle. "Just another planet like Earth. In my language—in most of the languages where I'm from, in fact—we simply call it 'Our World.'"

Miles tried to think. This was too familiar. "You mean like in *Sky-garden*?" He said it with a sort of implied *aha*, as if he'd just proven Vikram was crazy. Which didn't explain what they were suddenly doing in Portugal.

Anna turned to him. "You mean that novel you were reading?"

"Exactly as in *Skygarden*," Vikram said.

"Wait…*what*?" said Anna.

"You're saying you come from a planet in a novel?" said Miles.

"No, I'm saying that novel is about my planet. This isn't my first time here," he said.

Anna shook her head like she'd just knocked it against something heavy. "Do you remember…" she began, "…earlier? When I said you had some explaining to do?" Vikram nodded. "You have…a lot more explaining to do now."

"I know," he said with a sigh and stood up, throwing his satchel over his shoulder. "I don't want to rush you, but there is a small chance that Anders might show up here at some point. So perhaps we should get going."

Anna tried to speak, but only managed to form a circle with her lips.

"How would Anders find us here?" asked Miles, sitting up.

"The same way we got here," he said. "I admit it's unlikely, but better to run and not need to than the other way round. If we find the road and follow it west for a kilometer or so, we should run into the town."

The beach was a small crescent of sand surrounded by steep rock formations, which curved out into the sea in irregular clumps, beautiful in the light of the moon and stars. But it meant they had to scramble up the rocks with only that dim light to guide them to the road.

After a few scrapes, bruises, and Anna nearly spraining an ankle, they found themselves on more or less level ground, a cracked ribbon of pavement before them, the lights of the town visible off in the distance.

After twenty more minutes of walking the winding path into town, they found themselves in the central square of a picturesque old fishing village, now a tourist spot for sun-loving Brits and Germans. With the season approaching its end, the town was relatively quiet but still lively. A number of bars and restaurants around the square hummed with activity, and the odors they sent into the night air would normally have made Anna and Miles salivate, if they weren't still in shock.

"Could anyone besides me use a drink?" asked Vikram.

Anna shrugged noncommittally.

"Mm-kay," Miles mumbled.

Vikram sighed to himself. This wasn't going quite as he had planned. But perhaps that was a good thing. Coming here the way they did, they may have been rattled, but they were also less likely to think him crazy or full of shit.

He led them to the first place that looked likely to provide decent food and drink, a busy-looking pizzeria with an open table under a canopy. Vikram ordered a pizza for the table, a glass of wine for himself, water for Miles and Anna. He propped his bag up in the chair next to him, where he could keep an eye on it. Anna and Miles stared at it, then looked at Vikram.

"What's in it?" Anna asked.

"A gene bank," said Vikram.

"Come again?"

"A gene bank."

Anna didn't know what that was, but it didn't sound like something worth risking your life over. "A gene bank?" she repeated.

"Yes," he said. "If you read *Skygarden*, you know a little about what happened to my world."

Anna looked at Miles.

"I only read half of it," said Miles. "And it's back in Granada, along with the rest of our stuff."

"Okay," said Vikram. "Well, Our World went through an ecological cataclysm, made worse when we tried to colonize our sister planet, Skygarden. You know this part?"

Miles and Anna nodded.

"We wasted precious resources sending people there and then bringing back as many survivors as we could when its ecosystem collapsed. Ninety-nine percent of all species on our planet went extinct over the course of a century. At the beginning of the crisis, there were about twenty billion people on Our World. Now, five centuries later, there are about five or six million. The country I come from, a city-state you'd call it,—"

"Danevesu?" Miles said.

"Yes. Danevesu adapted and continued to make scientific and technological advances. Other countries didn't fare as well. As I mentioned, I'm a biologist by training. That's my specialty—anthropology is merely my avocation. I came here to find biological samples, seeds, anything I thought we could use on Our World to bring back the genetic diversity that was lost."

The waiter brought out a piping hot pizza topped with ham, salty fish, and black olives. It smelled delicious, but Miles and Anna just glanced at it idly while Vikram lit up a smoke.

"So why does Anders want it?" asked Miles.

"I'm not sure," said Vikram. "I have some theories. But if he is what I think he is, his motive is simply profit. There are others on Our World determined to stop any kind of research along these lines. Others wanting it for their own uses—all willing to pay."

"Wait, back up," said Anna. "What do you think Anders is?"

"Someone like me," said Vikram, "only not as nice."

Anna looked vaguely ill.

"You think he wants to steal your gene bank to sell to someone else?" asked Miles.

"I honestly don't know," Vikram admitted. "But I've spent the last fifteen years gathering and experimenting on the samples contained in that case. Our World used to be a green planet. We'd built many seed and gene banks over time, of course. But in the end everything had been consolidated into one large, secure facility. It contained all the biodiversity of our planet, but it was destroyed during one of the wars following the fall of Skygarden. That was hundreds of years ago. Since that time, our planet has been reduced to a desert, but life has held on somehow.

I'm convinced that there are at least a dozen genetic samples that could help return my world to something like what it used to be, in time."

Miles and Anna nodded mutely, unsure what to say in response.

"About the book," said Vikram. "I told you on the beach this wasn't my first time here?"

They nodded again, uncertainly.

"The last time I visited Earth," he said, "I took the name Victor Bass—*Tor* Bass. I lived in New Mexico and settled into the fabric of life there, collecting information on human cultures, languages, technology, and history, but mostly trying to understand people. I even wrote a number of science fiction novels."

"So you didn't die in a bus station toilet?" asked Miles.

"I'm not sure how that rumor got started," he said, taking a sip of his wine. "My mission then had been simply to gain knowledge about Earth and its human inhabitants, to learn as much as I could. When I was sent back this time, I chose the name Vikram along with this body and endeavored to explore more of your world. I had a different mission—in addition to gathering the gene bank, that is—a mission of selection. The ultimate goal has always been to make contact. And...select someone to bring back to Our World. A sort of foreign exchange, if you will."

"You want to bring back one of us?" said Anna.

Miles was suddenly aware that Anna might go off without him.

"I've been hoping that you might want to come back with me," said Vikram. "I had intended to ask you for some time now—both of you, actually, just more recently with you, Miles—when the time was right. I didn't plan on the trouble with Anders, though."

Anna shook her head, confused. "I don't understand," she said. "You look human."

"This body was created with DNA collected surreptitiously—hair, dead skin, fingernails—many decades ago, before my time. It was grown and assembled in a lab, an organic mechanism capable of storing consciousness."

Miles let out a breath. "A cyborg?" he said.

"We call them flesh puppets," said Vikram. "Fluppets, for short."

Anna looked like she'd just tasted something sour.

"Fluppets?" said Miles.

ANY OTHER WORLD WILL DO

"A fluppet behaves more or less like a clone of the organism—with a few important differences."

"Like…?" asked Anna.

"A lack of sentience, for one thing. You have to migrate someone's consciousness into it before it can perform any kind of autonomous behavior. It ages at a much slower rate. It's not susceptible to most disease. It's impervious to extremes of hot and cold, radiation, or the kind of dangerous decibel levels you recently experienced. On the outside, I'm indistinguishable from the Indian man whose DNA was used to make this body. But if a surgeon were to open me up, he'd soon find out something was very wrong." He paused, noticing that Anna and Miles were both staring at him blankly. "I'm not losing you, am I?"

"Anna?" a man's voice shouted at them from a few tables away. "Vikram! is that you?"

Anna and Miles slowly turned their heads in the direction of the man's voice in stunned silence, while Vikram rolled his eyes in annoyance.

"Derek?" said Anna, finally recognizing him.

Who the hell is this? thought Miles.

Derek bounded over, leaned in, and gave Anna a hug, shook Vikram's hand, and extended a hand to Miles. "Derek," he said.

"Miles," said Miles, like he wasn't quite sure of it.

"When'd you guys get in? Isn't this place great? Have you checked out the beaches? Damn, it's good to see you. Where're you staying?" Derek delivered this litany in a rapid-fire patter, leaving no room for replies. He was standing with his hand resting on the back of Vikram's chair, a disarmingly handsome American in torn jeans and a faded T-shirt. His wavy dark brown hair hung almost to his eyes, and his deep tan betrayed a life spent in the sun. He had a lithe, athletic build. Miles disliked him immediately.

"We just got in," said Anna.

Derek went right on, filling them in on the local beaches, the food, and whatnot. Miles learned that he had met Anna and Vikram a couple months ago at the Hotel Kashmir and had been following the Iberian coast south and west since leaving Barcelona. He and his friends—another guy and two young women—were staying in a couple rooms rented by an older local lady. "She's got a third bedroom free, if you want to check it out."

"Yeah, okay," said Anna.

Finally, even Derek couldn't help notice he'd interrupted something, so he excused himself to return to his friends at the other table, giving Anna another quick hug.

"Hmm. Funny running into Derek like that," said Vikram.

"Yes, that really is odd," said Anna sarcastically.

Miles cleared his throat. "So…you and he…?"

"Yes," she said.

"Oh."

"That can't be your primary concern at this point," she said.

Miles tried to look contrite. It wasn't his primary concern. It just played into his overall feeling of things spinning out of control at the moment.

"So you call this body a 'flesh puppet,'" she said to Vikram. "Making you the puppeteer?"

"There's no perfect analogy," he said. "Maybe a better one is the concept of an avatar…"

"You mean, like, you're a deity," she said.

"I was thinking more how the term is used in computer games than in Hindu mysticism," he said. "Though I'm real, not virtual, so I see your point. But no, I am not a god as far as I know."

Anna didn't know how to feel at the moment. Part of her mind had just been blown away. Part of her was annoyed at Vikram for lying to her all this time, even though she couldn't really blame him. Part of her was just trying to cope with the unreality of it all. And Miles, why was he taking this so calmly? *Wormholes!*

They picked at their pizza in silence for a while longer, and when the time came, they paid their bill and followed Derek and his friends to their apartment.

"Hey, guys, where's your stuff?" he asked them.

Anna just shook her head, like, *Don't ask.*

"Uh, okay," he said. "Travel light, that's my motto, man."

When they arrived at the apartment, the owner greeted them and seemed pleased to take on the additional guests. Vikram gave her a 5,000 peseta note in payment for the next few days, since he didn't have the local currency, but he did have a lot of potatoes.

Miles was grateful to be able to use the shower and basked in the soothing hot spray. As he was drying himself, he inventoried his belongings laid out in front of him: a pair of army-surplus cargo pants, one pair of white socks, tennis shoes, a white short-sleeve undershirt and dark blue long-sleeve T-shirt, his wallet with about six thousand pesetas and an Illinois driver's license, his lanyard passport holder with passport and travelers cheques, a few Spanish and French coins, and his Swiss Army knife. He realized he had nothing to wear to bed. After dressing, he asked Derek if he had any boxers he could borrow—or *have*, he would have said if he were being honest. Derek laughed, dug into his backpack, and tossed him a pair of red bikini briefs.

"No boxers, man. Hope these'll do," he said with a laugh.

Miles held up what there was of them to appraise. "Thanks," he said, wanting to mean it.

Miles, Anna, and Vikram shared a room, Miles and Anna taking the double bed with Vikram content to occupy the floor. Anna made a comment about the briefs, and Miles grumbled something under his breath before getting into bed.

"What? Oh, right...." she said, suddenly remembering what had happened to his boxers. "Where'd you get those, then?"

"You mean you don't recognize them?" he said, regretting it immediately.

"What, did you get them from Derek? Oh, grow up, Miles."

"We had to jump into a spacetime *asshole* to escape your last boyfriend," he said, unable to stop himself. "I would've thought the chances of running into another one out here would have been more remote."

Anna laughed without finding it funny. "We can't *all* be virgins, Miles," she said. Then added, "If only I'd known earlier of your existence, I could have saved myself for you." With that, she rolled over, showing him the back of her head.

With Vikram lying there on the floor beside them listening to all this, there was really no prospect of makeup sex—something Miles had only ever heard of. Thus there was no rush to make up. And so a third straight night of celibacy loomed. Despite their being both angry and horny, they drifted off to sleep with surprising ease.

Running into backpackers you'd met earlier in other hostels in other cities and countries was not so unusual. Miles had done it himself, bumping into two Canadian girls in Paris he'd met weeks before at a hostel on the southern coast of Ireland. Vikram had also had the experience many times in his travels. But it unnerved him this time. He believed in coincidences, but he also knew that, at the heart of the quantum mechanics that guided his smartskin, there was a synchronicity of people and events he couldn't pretend to control or even understand.

Vikram's circadian rhythms had never completely adjusted to the twenty-four-hour cycle of Earth, and so he stayed up, looking out the window at the stars, his own out there somewhere, much too distant to see.

Though Miles and Anna were quickly unconscious, their sleep was fitful, beset by dreams.

Miles found himself in the hallway of his high school. For no reason he could fathom, the abrasive waitress from *Cheers*, Carla, was herding the other students around as though she worked there. When she saw Miles, she said, "Come on," and dragged him into a classroom, where he sat down to take a test he was late starting. Anna was sitting in the aisle across from him, working away on her paper, and looked up at him when he sat down. It was a short-essay test, but it was all in Spanish, so Miles only understood a few words. Somehow, the scene changed from a classroom to up in the air, where Miles was flying his desk over the open ocean. He was flying it by pedaling his desk like a bicycle. If he slowed down, he started falling and had to pedal faster.

In the dream Anna would remember the next morning, she sat aboard a moving train car with rows of seats—an old-fashioned American train of the type found in westerns she'd seen on TV as a child—and saw the back of Vikram's head in the seat in front of her. When she touched his shoulder to get him to turn around, he refused to face her. He wouldn't let her see his face as he stood to walk away down the aisle. She followed and pleaded with him, yanking him roughly by the arm, all to no avail.

When Anna finally woke it was light. Miles was already dressed and looking at her.

"Hey, Anna."

She stretched and looked around the room for Vikram, but he wasn't there.

"Where's Vikram?" she asked.

"He was talking to the landlady," he said.

She nodded, rubbed the sleep out of her eyes, and sat up.

"About last night..." he began, "...I'm sorry. About what I said. I don't know why I—I mean I know *why*, I just—"

"Miles," she said, "don't feel bad. We can't be held responsible right now."

"Yeah. So did you have weird dreams last night?"

"Yes."

They told each other about their dreams, and Miles asked her, "Have you ever had a good dream right before waking, and when you wake up, for a second you think whatever was in the dream is still true?"

Anna nodded.

"Usually, after a few seconds, you remember it was just a dream. And it's kind of a letdown, even if what you dreamed was obviously ridiculous—like, you're suddenly rich and famous for no reason. When I woke up this morning, I felt like that. But then I remembered we were actually in Portugal. I remembered how we got here. And then I wasn't sure how to feel."

She looked at him and said, "I don't know, either. But at least we're not alone in it."

Bleary-eyed and dimpled in a black tank top, her bare legs half-concealed by the bed clothes, Miles marveled at how beautiful Anna was. Sitting on the side of the bed, he leaned over and kissed her. She returned his kiss and drew him closer, tangling their arms and legs together for a few moments, until they separated at the sound of Vikram outside the door.

*

ANDERS HAD STARTED his search on a rocky beach in the South of France. It was an inexact science, to say the least. His computer never told him anything definitive. But it did suggest probabilities, which tended to narrow down the possibilities. It couldn't equal the power of

ALEX LUBERTOZZI

Vikram's device, but it was still state of the art where he came from. And it made the most advanced technology on this planet look like a stick a chimpanzee uses to eat ants off a log.

But the signs all over the beach he'd just come from—not to mention the sandy footprints on the side of the road—were like a map leading him inexorably to his quarry. It was like the idiots weren't even trying to cover their tracks.

Once he got into town, he felt quite conspicuous. Bad enough he was platinum blond and about a foot taller than most of the locals—the only ones up at this hour of the morning—but his left pant leg had a neat round hole in it and was covered with dried blood. If he really wanted to draw attention to himself, all he had to do was start asking around about Vikram and the others. So instead he hung back and tried to get the lay of the downtown area, figuring if they were here, they'd have to come out to eat at some point, and there were only so many restaurants.

Having spent the night going in and out of arseholes and dreading the inevitable glitch (his mentor had liked to say there were two kinds of arsehole-riders—those who had experienced the sheer terror of a destination glitch, and those who would), he'd had time to think about what he'd do when he caught up with Vikram. He knew he wouldn't have a chance if Vikram saw him coming, so the best strategy was to lie in wait someplace where he was likely to show up. Which sounded sensible but posed the potential drawback of stranding him futilely in a place Vikram would never appear.

He found a café where he could sit in a corner and look out on the square while he nursed a drink and read the local paper. Portuguese. He didn't really know it, but once you knew one or two Romance languages, others were pretty easy to pick up. He wondered if there'd be any news of Paco and the others. Poor bastards. But no, that news was too recent for the papers, if it was known at all. The noise had probably drawn someone to investigate last night. If not, surely an employee had found them by this morning. Maybe it would be on the TV news? But there was no TV in the café, so he could only surmise. A waitress brought him a hot chocolate and a plate of *pastéis de nata*, sweet custard-filled pastries.

"*Obrigado*," he said.

"*De nada*."

Anders emptied four sugar packets into his cup and stirred the dissolving granules gently, folding them in deliberately with the thick chocolate. He cast his eyes over the square and prepared to wait.

*

"I WAS JUST talking with the owner, Octávia," Vikram was saying as Anna and Miles sat on the bed, flustered and frustrated. "She recommended a spot for breakfast, if you're hungry."

"Okay," said Miles, who had regained his usual appetite.

"I need to shower and then get dressed," said Anna.

"Why don't Miles and I get some pastries while you shower," he said, "and we'll bring them back here? Then we can talk."

"Fine."

Vikram slung his bag over his shoulder as Miles kissed Anna good-bye.

"Are you sure that's a good idea?" Miles asked, meaning the bag.

"I can't afford to let this out of my sight again," said Vikram.

Miles and Vikram walked outside into the narrow alley and started down the gradual slope of the hill. A small coffee shop sat right on the corner of the block where they were staying, but the café Octávia mentioned was downtown, and they felt like stretching their legs anyway, so they continued down toward the central square.

They passed more whitewashed, red-tile-roofed buildings, a neon green cross signaling the *farmácia*, a smallish church, and heard the occasional high-pitched whine of motorbikes making their way up and down the cobblestone streets. Finally, they could see the clearing of the central square, lined with palm trees, the harbor visible not far beyond.

Passing a small grocery, they heard a radio playing, an announcer reading the news in Portuguese. It was all Greek to Miles, but Vikram was fluent, at least in the Brazilian dialect, which was near enough. He stopped suddenly, and Miles wondered why. *What is it?* Vikram held up a finger. *Hold on.*

"Three local people were found dead this morning in a butcher shop in Granada," he said, translating the news. "The police don't know the causes of death, but they're treating it as a crime scene."

"Paco and his sister, and…"

"The big guy, yes."

"Jesus." Miles could feel his heart pounding in his chest, while his surroundings seemed to slow down and close in on him.

Vikram turned to face Miles and grasped him by the shoulders. "Anders is dangerous," he said. "I knew him before he was Anders, and he's fairly ruthless."

Miles had puzzled out that much for himself. "You knew him?"

"I did, yes."

"Last night you said he might be able to follow us here," said Miles.

"Theoretically," said Vikram. "I would think it would take weeks, if not years, to follow someone that way. But I've never even tried, so I have no way of knowing. I think we should pick up some rolls and return to the apartment straightaway." Vikram nodded in the direction of a café on the square, buzzing with people dressed for a day at the beach. They took a few steps toward it and suddenly froze. Miles had no idea what was going on, but he was paralyzed, unable to move either his legs or arms to break his fall as he tilted forward, his face headed for the polished smooth stones of the square.

Unlike Miles, Vikram knew at once what was happening and only had to wait a moment before his smartskin's automatic defenses kicked in, releasing him from the paralysis and allowing him to grab Miles's arm before he fell on his face. He quickly used his smartskin to interrupt the signal to Miles's nervous system and enable him to stand on his own. Then he turned to see Anders, about twenty feet away and headed straight for them, pointing his credit card–sized device in their direction.

With a start, Miles now saw Anders and turned to see Vikram moving his hands, his left palm already glowing blue, his fingers twirling while he pulled his hands apart, as if he were making Chinese noodles. He heard a gasp from an onlooker and then saw Anders's large body being lifted up into the air as if it were a plastic shopping bag borne on a gust of wind. At the peak of his trajectory, Anders's body contorted as it folded in on itself like a rope being tied into a knot, then fell to the square in a heap. Someone screamed, and now there were several bystanders looking at Vikram, who was standing with his hands in some kung fu–looking pose, making it clear, in case there was any doubt, that he had just practiced this sorcery. They all had looks on their faces like this was the craziest shit they'd ever seen.

For a few moments, with Anders lying on the ground twitching, no one seemed to know what to do. Vikram turned to Miles, and a crooked smile formed on his lips, as if he were both embarrassed by and proud of what he'd just done.

Miles laughed nervously despite himself. This probably only made the situation worse as people concluded that these were indeed a couple of black-magic-practicing psychopaths. Miles and Vikram, noticing this and sharing the same thought, turned and began to run back toward the maze of alleys that led them here. Though he didn't understand Portuguese, Miles could hear a few people yelling out what he assumed was something along the lines of "Get them!" As they approached the corner of their street, a short but thick-bodied man stepped in front of Vikram, and without thinking, Miles darted in front of Vikram and lowered his shoulder into the man's barrel chest, sending him sprawling to the ground.

"Ow!" Miles yelled, rubbing his bruised shoulder as they continued up the hill to safety.

"Thanks," said Vikram.

Whether anyone was still chasing them or if anyone saw them enter the apartment building, they couldn't tell, because they never looked back. Taking the stairs two at a time up to the third-floor flat, they entered with the key Octávia had given Vikram.

Miles opened the door to their bedroom and saw Anna, mostly dressed, with a towel in her hands as she squeezed the last drops of water out of her hair. "Sorry I'm not ready, but it took me a while to find some natural shampoo. Fortunately, someone had left some in the vanity drawer." Miles and Vikram were standing beside each other, out of breath and looking on with a mixture of apprehension and guilt. Anna stopped and regarded them. "Where's breakfast?" she said.

Vikram and Miles quickly explained to Anna what had just happened, including the news that Anders had likely murdered Paco, his sister, and brother-in-law.

Anna sat down, a far-off look in her eyes. "So no pastries then."

"I could take you both back to Granada or Barcelona or any other place you want," said Vikram. "It might be safer than coming with me, but…"

"But…?" she asked.

"Well, Anders can't follow us to Danevesu," said Vikram. "Besides, I think you both want to go with me."

"I'll go wherever you do," Miles said to Anna.

Anna sighed. "So it's up to me?"

They could hear people milling around in the street outside, loud talking, and some excited yelling.

"What do you want to do?" she asked Miles.

"I want us to go with Vikram," he said. Any other option seemed crazy. How could they not follow him now, after what they'd experienced?

"So do I," she decided.

Anna threw on her shirt, and she and Miles looked around to make sure they had everything they came with. Since they were wearing everything they had, there was really nothing left to gather. Which was good, because while they'd been talking, a group of people had climbed the stairs and were now banging on the front door of the flat as Octávia responded with an irritated shout to hold on.

Vikram activated his smartskin, revealing the blue monitor on his palm with strange icons and inscrutable writing. "Ready?" he asked. They each nodded, and Vikram used the glowing tattoo on his hand to open up a microscopic portal right in front of them to a size they could easily walk into.

Down the hall, Octávia opened the door to a small agitated crowd, two of whom quickly informed her what had happened in the square. She let them in and pointed to the closed bedroom door, close on their heels as they made their way through the apartment.

Anna approached the portal first—the closer she inched, the stronger the pull became—and disappeared into it. Miles was close behind, trying to see into it, its black interior obscured by the ragged edges that distorted the light coming from the other side of the room. Then he disappeared. Vikram followed, nonchalantly hopping in.

And the floating black asterisk shrank until it winked out of existence, leaving nothing for the pursuers who burst into the room a moment later to find but a damp towel, the only evidence they'd ever been there.

Danevesu

Deep down, what really would appear to
be a diabolical invention is what we call life,
that chronic, degenerative, and necessarily
fatal sexually transmitted disease.

—*Narcís Comadira*

10.

IF MILES HAD KNOWN that Vikram was recording the moment Anna and he stepped into the portal on their way to Our World, he might have thought of something smarter to say than *Oh, shit!* as he was pulled into it and rather inelegantly dumped out the other side. From his hands and knees, Miles looked out to see they were now on a raised round platform. A kind of translucent curtain surrounded them on the dais, and the room beyond to their right had a long, curved wall of what Miles took for windows. Beside Miles stood Vikram, casually eyeing the smartskin on his hand like someone waiting at a bus stop. On the other side of him Anna had landed on her rear end and was staring at the intricate ceiling inlaid entirely with colorful shards of luminescent glass.

Their journey through the wormhole had been instantaneous, which made what they now saw more than a little disorienting. It was a bit like waking up from a dreamless slumber—one in which someone moved you from your bed to a teeming coral reef while you were sleeping.

Anna and Miles stood, feeling heavy and out of breath, and looked around. Danevesu—if that's what this was—did not appear as they expected. Far from sleekly modern and space-age, the room they found themselves in seemed to be carved out of some veined, blue stone and trimmed with exotic woods. The curved walls were echoed by the ramped floors and the undulating glass-tiled ceiling. Even the large windows—which they soon saw were actually video monitors—had no right angles to them. It seemed the room was designed purely for aesthetic pleasure rather than as a functional station implementing the most advanced technology Anna and Miles had ever heard of.

"Wow," was all Miles could think to say. Anna nodded in agreement.

They almost didn't see the two aliens sitting about five yards in front of them. It was the feathers, bright red on one, light blue on the other, that allowed them to stand out enough for Anna to recognize them with a surprised "Oh." They were working at a console sunk below the floor and were each wearing a pair of goggles, the dark lenses obscuring their eyes. Although they were facing the new arrivals, they didn't appear to notice them. They seemed to be laughing about something they were watching on their headsets.

Vikram cleared his throat loudly.

The red alien made a subtle motion with his hand, and the glass of his goggles turned transparent, revealing large green eyes that opened wide upon seeing three human beings suddenly standing in the portal room. He stood up immediately and smacked his blue colleague in the head with the back of his hand. The blue one turned on the red one in annoyance until he realized they had just received visitors—the purpose of the portal room, after all—and stood up to face Vikram.

"They've been expecting us," said Vikram.

While Vikram and the red alien exchanged a few words in their native tongue, Anna and Miles got their first good look at a couple of honest-to-God extraterrestrials. They were each about five and a half feet tall and slender, their limbs long and lithe. The feathers swept back from the bridge of their rather large, beaklike noses, covering their heads down to the napes of their necks. The beaks converged with the flesh of their firm upper lips, and they had reddish-brown skin.

Miles and Anna were both struck immediately by how beautiful they were. They had not expected that, as the cover art of *Skygarden* didn't really do them justice. Vikram introduced them—Daka with the red feathers trimmed neatly, Sibu with the downy blue feathers flowing past his shoulders. Sibu sat down immediately and started moving his eight dexterous fingers furiously, as if he was typing a message on an invisible keyboard, which he was.

"So this is Danevesu?" asked Miles.

"Yes," said Vikram. "A part of it, anyway."

"On Our World," said Miles.

"Yes. In the Danevesan language, we call it *Tonshu*."

Tonshu. Anna mouthed the word.

Daka and Sibu stared at Anna and Miles, clearly as taken with them as they were with Daka and Sibu. "They've never seen natural-born humans before," said Vikram. "They're checking you out."

"And these are the birdmen?" said Anna.

"Birdpeople," corrected Miles.

"In Danevesan, we refer to our kind as *yishi*," said Vikram.

After a few awkward moments of silence, the door at the far end of the room slid down into the floor and three more aliens entered. One with dark blue feathers stepped forward, accompanied by one with orange feathers, and stood behind the partition separating them from the platform. Dark blue began to speak to Vikram in Danevesan. "You're back," he said, nodding.

He looked at Anna and Miles wordlessly for a moment, then said something, which his orange interpreter translated as "Hello" and made another birdlike bob of his head. Anna and Miles nodded, as the other yishi did now. "You both speak English?" the translator asked.

"Yes, we do," said Anna. "Um, I'm Anna," she said and turned to Miles.

"Oh, and I'm Miles," he said. "Uh...how's it goin'?"

The interpreter nodded and said, "This is Elusia," motioning to the yishi with dark blue feathers, "and I'm Geresh, his interpreter." He looked around anxiously. "Oh, and that's Kerak."

Geresh then relayed the Earthlings' names to the others, and they all made the same curious O shape with their mouths in response.

To Anna and Miles's confused expressions, Vikram explained, "They're smiling."

Vikram began to speak to the others in Danevesan. It was a surprisingly harsh language, with its whistles, clicks, and guttural consonants. Anna watched them entranced, her head cocked slightly to better pick up any discrete words or phrases she could.

Finally, Elusia spoke directly to Anna and Miles, as Geresh translated. "We trust you had a safe journey....We are so happy that you're here." Elusia and Geresh both seemed somewhat at a loss for words now that they were actually face to face with their human visitors.

The thought that their hosts might be disappointed upon meeting them suddenly occurred to Anna. She felt decidedly underdressed for the occasion, and a glance at Miles in his scruffy cargo pants and ripped T-shirt did nothing to reassure her that they looked the part of ambassadors for the human race. She tried to think of something to say.

Miles coughed, and he and Anna looked to Vikram for help.

"Kerak has reminded us," said Geresh, before that was necessary, "that you all need to be cleared medically before you can enter the city proper. Kerak…"

With that, Kerak, with unruly yellow-and-gray feathers and clearly older than the others, stepped forward while donning a clear, flexible breathing mask. The translucent curtain surrounding Vikram and the two humans disappeared, revealing another partition of the same stuff separating the other half of the room from them. Kerak stepped through the curtain and approached the platform. The three of them climbed down, and Kerak led them through a door to another room.

It was a medical facility, but even it seemed too fanciful for its purpose—colorful, cluttered, and whimsical rather than the spare, antiseptic, white room they would've expected.

The thought did occur to Miles that he and Anna were perhaps about to get probed. However, it also occurred to him that, if this were the case, Vikram had gone to an awful lot of trouble just for that.

But Kerak didn't probe them, exactly. He did draw their blood, took hair, dead skin, and saliva samples, and examined them minutely without having to shove anything up their asses.

Kerak had never seen a human female before—natural or otherwise—so he was fascinated by Anna's body and kept shaking his head and making an O with his mouth. Of course, Kerak and the other yishi actually resembled Anna much more than Miles or Vikram. Kerak was a little shorter than Anna, had larger breasts concealed by a loose-fitting tunic, and possessed womanly hips and legs shown off by form-fitting leggings.

Once finished with Miles and Anna, Kerak explained to Vikram that he needed to run some tests on their bodily fluids and skin samples and would return shortly.

"He's just going to run some tests," said Vikram.

Kerak disappeared through an ornate stained-glass door, and Miles felt himself relax now they were alone. He turned to Vikram. "Did you say *he* rather than *she*?" he asked.

Vikram nodded. "It's an artifact of English," he said. "No neutral pronoun."

"Then why not say *she?*" asked Miles.

"It's a fair question," said Anna.

"Well, it's mostly thanks to a misunderstanding on my predecessor's part," said Vikram. "In English—and all Earth languages, for that matter—we use the masculine pronoun to refer to ourselves."

"You mean other yishi speak English?" asked Miles.

"Oh, many," he said. "All children in Danevesu learn at least one human language."

"What misunderstanding?" asked Anna. "And what predecessor?"

"Arak," he said. "He was the first yishi to explore Earth. He's greatly admired in Danevesu—a kind of national hero, actually. He brought back data on the history, languages, and cultures of Earth, as well as human DNA. And he had to do it all without being detected."

"You mean he visited Earth as a yishi?"

"Of course," said Vikram. "He had to."

"When was this?" she asked.

"In the 1890s. About fifty years ago—in Our World years, I mean."

"So what was his misunderstanding?"

"It was the same one I had when I first arrived in New Mexico in the 1940s as Victor Bass," said Vikram. "On Tonshu, even when there was much greater biodiversity, all organisms were genderless. That is, they're like yishi, they carry both male and female reproductive organs. So Arak assumed, as I did, that human females were some type of... sub-species."

"Excuse me?" said Anna.

Miles looked at Vikram and just shook his head.

"You have to remember, Arak never had any direct contact with humans," said Vikram. "So his understanding of people came from observing them at a distance, examining their artifacts and artwork, or reading what they'd written—there were no movies, TV, or radio then. What he observed was that, except for not being able to give birth, human males were like yishi in status and role. Females, on the other hand, held a clearly subservient position. They appeared to be weaker physically, were less educated, and were often treated as irrational, or mentally deficient."

Anna was staring at Vikram with her mouth slightly agape, as Miles kept his shut. Finally, she asked him, "Wouldn't the ability to grow a person inside you make you *super*human, not *sub*human?"

"Well, yes," he conceded. "But you have to understand that everyone here can do that—so no one regards it as any kind of special gift or privilege, in fact quite the opposite."

Anna narrowed her eyes at Vikram, begrudgingly accepting his point. "I see."

"During Arak's visit, women weren't allowed to vote or hold office," he continued. "There were no female heads of companies, virtually no female doctors or scientists or philosophers. Mostly what they were allowed to do was care for or instruct young children. And—unfairly, no doubt—those jobs tend to be viewed as among the lowest-status roles on Our World."

Anna could see this was less a flaw in yishi logic than an indictment of human civilization.

"When I first came to New Mexico in human form, it seemed to me that Arak had been right," said Vikram. "But fairly soon I had reason to question it. And then I met Grace."

"Who was Grace?" asked Anna.

"She was the first woman I ever knew…intimately," he said. "She was an instructor in astronomy at the university where I had managed to get a job. She'd had to be twice as smart as the men in her field to make it half as far." Vikram paused. "She was really the most remarkable person I ever knew. You remind me of her, actually."

Anna stared at Vikram differently now. "You were in love with her," she said.

"We were lovers, yes."

"Did she know what you were?"

"Oh, no," he said with a sad smile.

"What happened?"

"We had several years together before she died," he said.

"I'm sorry, Vikram."

"It was after she died that I started writing," he said. "She was the one who'd introduced me to science fiction—H.G. Wells and Jules Verne and the sci-fi magazines I later sold stories to. Anyway, when I wrote

Skygarden, I invented neutral personal pronouns to describe yishi the way we do in our language—*e, em, ey, es*—it just confused my editor, though. We had a big argument over it, which I lost. Anyway, here on Tonshu they still use *he*, but at least now they know that females aren't subhuman."

"Yes, that's good to know," said Anna.

Kerak returned and nodded to Vikram, saying something in Danevesan. "He says we're all clear," said Vikram. "But we need to go in there now."

Anna and Miles followed the two into a brightly lit room with what looked like two giant salon hair dryers sitting sideways opposite each other. Kerak guided them to a raised seating area on the other side of the room. There was a row of what looked like injection-molded plastic orange chairs, so Anna and Miles sat down while Kerak turned on a partition screen around them. Vikram nodded at them from the other side as Kerak led him over to one of the hair dryers.

"Where'd you pick up these assholes?" asked Kerak in Danevesan, glancing over at Anna and Miles.

"They're friends of mine," said Vikram. "And Spain, since you ask."

"They're Spanish?"

"No," he said, "just tourists like me."

"I'd hardly call you that, Viku," said Kerak.

"Call me Vikram. I've become accustomed to it."

"You never asked me to call you 'Tor' last time," he said.

"I left Tor back on Earth, Kerak."

"The hell you did," he said. "I transplanted you then too, don't you remember?"

"You know what I mean."

Kerak smiled at his old friend. "I haven't asked you what's in the bag," he said. "Did you fill the case?"

Vikram hesitated, his eyes exploring the corners of the room.

"It's all right," said Kerak. "No recording can take place in here unless I authorize it."

Vikram nodded. "I did," he said.

Kerak sighed. "I figured as much, but I was kind of hoping you'd come to your senses."

"You can still turn me in," said Vikram.

"Fuck you," he said. "If I examined your case, would it be brimming with Type 2 organisms?"

"Among other things."

Kerak twitched his head side to side and made a low whistle. It was a yishi way of expressing disapproval.

"What's your plan?" he said.

"Take it to Berejian," said Vikram. "He has the facilities and the expertise."

"If they find out you brought them in," he said, "they'll know I helped you."

"Probably," said Vikram. "But if Berejian fails, it won't matter. And if he succeeds, it will have been worth it."

"Even if it means war?"

"We've always been at war," said Vikram.

Kerak seemed to be asking Vikram a lot of questions, Anna thought. She also wondered why she and Miles needed to be separated from him this way. Finally, Vikram stood and began to strip down to his underwear. Kerak waved a device down Vikram's back and, after running a sponge dipped in some liquid solution down Vikram's spine, inserted a long, flexible needle into it. Vikram lay down on his stomach, placed his face in the cradle, and remained still. After Kerak had Vikram in position, he spoke aloud to no one in particular, and the screen of the console in between the two machines lit up. It responded to him, and he nodded, speaking more instructions. A door slid open, and a tallish yishi with dull red and gray feathers and olive skin entered the room. The yishi was naked to the waist and carried a device that was attached by a cord to his spine.

"Is that...Vikram?" Anna whispered.

"What do you mean? Vikram's th—" Miles started, before realizing. "Oh, that's *Vikram*."

Vikram's androgynous avian face wore a dull, glassy expression, as though he'd been lobotomized. Of course, he had been, in a way. His eyes were large and orange, the black pupils thin vertical slits in the bright light of the room. His skin was slightly crepey, with laugh lines around his mouth and crow's feet around his eyes. His feathers ran down the back of his long thin neck, ending at his narrow, pointed shoulders.

"If it's him," Miles asked, "how is he walking around?"

Anna just shrugged.

When the half-naked yishi turned away, Miles and Anna could clearly see his vestigial wings. Tucked neatly behind his forearms were limb extensions concealing the loose skin of his folded wings, the webbing of which was attached along a line going from his shoulders to the small of his back. The feathers covering his wings were completely gray, and his bare feet sported gray feathery fuzz on top, the three toes in front and one in back ending in thick hard nails. Though he was quite thin, he looked healthy—sinewy and fit, if not exactly youthful. He had to be fairly old. It was Vikram's body, but emptied of the essential stuff that made him Vikram. Making his way toward the empty machine, he handed Kerak the device he'd been holding and lay mechanically, facedown on the bench, same as the other Vikram.

Now Kerak sat down in front of the console and motioned with a finger above the screen. He began to move his hands as if he were miming playing an instrument, as they'd seen Vikram do with his smartskin on Earth. Both Vikrams were slowly conveyed into the giant hair dryers on their benches. The machines whirred, and Kerak continued playing his instrument, manipulating the machines through the computer he controlled with the subtle movements of his hovering four-fingered hands.

Then it was done. Both Vikrams emerged from the dryers. The Vikram Miles and Anna had known turned over and sat up with a dull, affectless expression. Kerak hurried over to the yishi who, moments earlier, had looked like a mindless zombie. The yishi sat up and nodded at Kerak, who asked him a series of questions and had him perform some simple motor skills.

Then new Vikram looked over at Anna and Miles and smiled his old crooked smile.

*

IT TOOK ANNA and Miles and Vikram himself a while to get used to what was to them his new body, and to him his old body. His expressions and way of talking were the same (though his voice was higher), as were some of his gestures. But his physicality was otherwise completely different. Apart from his appearance, his gait and movements were now more graceful but also more deliberate as he got accustomed to navigating in his original skin.

Kerak greeted Vikram by pressing his beak against his old friend's cheek and nuzzling. After Kerak removed the IV from Vikram's spine, he took Vikram's slender hand in his and held it for a moment before turning off the partition keeping Anna and Miles at bay. Once he did, Anna and Miles stood and approached the new Vikram.

New Vikram tapped the thumb and middle finger of his right hand above his left hand twice, and a screen appeared on the palm of his hand. Kerak swiped and tapped one corner of the screen, and it turned dark, looking now like a dark blue tattoo on Vikram's hand. Kerak positioned the nozzle of a crane-like machine's arm over Vikram's hand and switched it on. The nozzle emitted a laser that removed the tattoo from Vikram's hand. When it finished, it doubled back and etched a new blue tattoo across Vikram's palm, then did the same on a smaller area on the back of his hand.

"Done," said Kerak. Vikram tapped his fingers above the tattoo, and a new screen appeared with different images and colors. "The latest hardware and software," Kerak added. "Though a bit pedestrian compared to what you're used to, I'm afraid."

While Anna and Miles hung back, hovering a few feet away as Kerak operated, new Vikram beckoned them to come closer. Holding up his hand, he said, "Smartskin. See? I told you it was like a tattoo." He closed his other hand above it, and the screen seemed to disappear, camouflaging itself by blending into the skin of his hand. "One that goes away when you don't need it."

Meanwhile, old Vikram just sat on the other bench like a heavily sedated mental patient while Kerak removed his smartskin with the laser. New Vikram stood and embraced Anna and then Miles, touching cheeks the way yishi do and as Vikram and Anna always had. Miles was surprised to discover that the feel of Vikram's skin was no different than his own. And with Vikram being naked to just below where the curve of his hips began, his pendulous breasts drooping down to just above his navel, Miles was privy to a lot of it.

"Miles," said Vikram, "my eyes are up here."

"Well, Viku," interrupted Kerak, now speaking English with an odd accent, "I hope you took better care of this one," referring to his former human body.

"Well," Vikram said with a shrug, "it may have acquired a fairly serious nicotine dependence."

Kerak sighed. "Goddamnit, you know how smoking fucks with their maintenance," he said.

"I know," he said, "but I really missed it."

"Asshole."

Anna and Miles didn't know what to make of Kerak's sudden ability to speak English—or his casual use of profanity.

"I'm Kerak, by the way," he said by way of introduction. "Araviku tells me he met you two cunts in Spain."

"Um…" said Miles.

"Don't mind Kerak," said Vikram. "He likes to give everyone a hard time."

"Araviku?" said Anna.

"My Danevesan name," he said with a shrug. "You can still call me Vikram."

Anna stared into Vikram's large orange eyes. With short red feathers extending in a V up his forehead and a blade-like nose dipping down below the line of his mouth, he looked a little like a medieval plague doctor or a masked Venetian at carnevale. "Why did we need to have a screen around us?" she asked.

"You were being decontaminated," said Kerak. "And inoculated."

"Decontaminated?" asked Miles, a little offended.

"Type 1 organisms," said Vikram. "Infectious agents—bacteria, viruses, other parasites. Fortunately, our bodies are naturally immune to most of the bugs you could bring in, but still."

"You said, 'Type 1,'" said Anna. "Is there a Type 2?"

"Yes, you and Miles, for one," said Vikram. "Any potentially invasive species."

Miles and Anna both unconsciously eyed Vikram's satchel.

"What about your gene bank?" asked Miles.

Kerak looked over at Vikram in surprise. "You told them?"

"It's a long story," replied Vikram dismissively. Then to Anna and Miles: "Kerak tells me we can speak privately here. But you should know that, anywhere else, everything we say is public. I can't really talk about the gene bank while we're in the city."

"What do you mean?" said Anna. "Why the hell not?"

"I think the less you know about why the better," he said.

Before Anna could respond, they were interrupted by a lilting, yet insistent electronic whistle, and Vikram and Kerak both checked their smartskin. "You should get dressed," Kerak said to Vikram. "They're ready to meet the ambassadors."

Miles looked around like there might be somebody else in the room.

"I think he means us," said Anna.

"Listen, I'll explain everything as soon as I can," said Vikram, pulling on an odd-looking brassiere. "Until then, you'll just have to trust me."

22.

VIKRAM, ANNA, AND MILES followed Kerak, who led them into a winding corridor off of the medical facility. The curving hallway was lined with colored tiles, made cozy by a low planked ceiling and soft recessed lighting—and the walls seemed to get progressively closer as they neared the opening to the room where Kerak was taking them.

By the time they reached the end of the passage, the opening was wide enough to allow only Anna, Miles, and Vikram to look out into the amphitheater beyond. It was a massive space, and made clear the two rooms that had come before it were strictly functional in comparison. They looked down into the bowl of the auditorium from the side—the main entrance was off to their right—and saw several hundred yishi standing on terraced steps leading down to the semicircular stage, which ended at huge windows bowing out over the city's harbor. The ceiling was domed, giving the space the shape of an enormous globe. From the apex of the great dome hung an inverted mini-dome covered in red, turquoise, violet, and gold glass tiles, lit from within—a big, glowing, psychedelic teat. Long colorful columns lined the circular walkway leading Anna, Miles, Vikram, and Kerak around to the main vestibule.

Once there, the audience turned to look at them, a sea of yishi between them and the stage below. Kerak dove straight ahead, heedless of the crowd, and the yishi parted, moving in concert the way a school of fish or flock of birds might, clearing a path for their guests. As Kerak, the humans, and Vikram descended the steps single file, the yishi reformed silently behind them.

About a dozen yishi were gathered on the stage to receive them. Two of them, Elusia and Geresh, Anna and Miles recognized. The yishi greeted them with nuzzles, which was an odd sensation but also made them feel instantly closer to these strange feathered creatures. Aliens. Looking around, however, Anna and Miles realized they weren't in an auditorium filled with aliens. They *were* the aliens. Which explained why everyone was staring at them with a mixture of fascination and awe.

Anna and Miles, on display at the focal point of the amphitheater, shuffled down the line in a fog, overwhelmed by the spectacle around them. On three sides, the yishi appeared in all their diversity of color and style of dress and in all their similarity, as well. They all looked beautiful and thin. They were all within a few inches in height of each other, and their skin tone ranged from dark tan to light brown. Outside a black ocean rippled under an orange sun, as gray clouds streamed past it, modulating the light in the amphitheater in intermittent pulses.

The last yishi on the reception committee, slightly taller than the others with orange feathers and green eyes, nuzzled each of them and then shook their hands. He began to speak in Danevesan, the acoustics of the auditorium amplifying his voice to the farthest corners of the room, while another interpreter stepped forward to translate.

"On behalf of all yishi, welcome to Our World," he said, and the crowd broke out in melodic whistling, nodding their heads as they did so and holding up their hands to record the moment on their smartskin. "This is Tchuvu," said the translator, "and I am Okiva, his interpreter. We would like you to know how honored and thrilled we are to receive you here today. To welcome ambassadors from Earth for the first time on Our World is a significant and historic occasion for all of us. And, as Danevesans, we would also like to welcome you to our city." With that, Tchuvu motioned toward the large windows in front of them. The small reception group parted to let Anna and Miles follow him to an observation area. The huge windows were set into irregular honeycombed frames of stone, and when Anna and Miles looked out of them, they each gasped.

The amphitheater—the entire city, in fact—was built into the side of a mountain, its sheer rock cliffs forming the city's façade. Thousands of other irregularly shaped windows reflected the orange sunlight like facets of an enormous jewel several hundred meters above and below them and following the contours of the cliff face as far as they could see to their left and ending at a rocky promontory a mile or so to their right.

The city ended well above the ocean below them, but they could see in the harbor what at first appeared to be underwater rock formations breaking the surface. They were in fact the tops of mostly submerged buildings—spires, cupolas, domes, pitched and tiled roofs, some windows still remaining intact, most broken. The colors that had clearly once adorned everything were now badly faded to pastels and shades of gray, many coated with some kind of reddish-orange scum.

Miles pointed, as if Anna might miss it. The city under water went on for miles—disappearing in spots, only to resurface in farther reaches where the buildings soared higher or the ground swelled beneath the waves.

"Old Danevesu," said Vikram, who had sidled up behind them.

"So this is…New Danevesu?" asked Miles.

"Just Danevesu now," he said.

Beyond the remains of Old Danevesu, Miles could make out several black fins protruding out from under the surface of the harbor, the sleek bridges of what he correctly took to be submersible watercraft. One after another began to submerge until only a few still floated in the distance.

Miles wished they could have spent more time looking out at the city and harbor, but they had an audience. He and Anna turned around to see Elusia and Tchuvu standing next to each other on the stage, flanked by Geresh and Okiva. It was clear that Elusia was not as good at this sort of thing as the outgoing Tchuvu, who strode to the center of the stage. He spoke up, his voice echoing throughout the hall, and Okiva translated: "If you'll permit us, we would like to show you a program that gives a brief introduction to Our World and the yishi, as well as Danevesan history."

Miles and Anna nodded agreeably, as they didn't exactly have other plans. From either side, two black round discs flew straight at them and stopped, hovering a few feet above the floor behind them. They looked like cushions. Then four telescoping legs projected down to the floor from each seat while a curved back extended upward. They were chairs. Miles and Anna sat down, impressed and a little bemused by the technological overkill, while everyone else remained standing.

Another, smaller device flew up and hovered in front of Tchuvu, who, with a slight gesture in its direction dimmed the lights, darkened the windows, and caused a large hologram to be projected out of the inverse dome above the crowd. It first appeared as an opaque black cloud holding bright, twinkling lights in its midst. As the three-dimensional image zoomed in on one of the lights, it became clear this was a star system—Our World's system. Soon planets became visible, orbiting a large orange sun. Two in particular stood out in their blue-and-green vibrance. Our World was one of them, Skygarden the other. Our World could be distinguished by the lights that appeared on its dark side. It was a time-lapse movie, covering who knew how many years. In a few seconds, Skygarden turned brown and dry, the few lights that appeared only a second earlier winking out forever.

The hologram of Our World became larger, until it filled the space above them. It was mostly covered by white clouds and deep blue oceans with ice-covered poles and one huge, ragged continent that ringed the planet's middle. Large and small islands dotted the seas between the continuous landmass and the north-south poles. Gradually, the poles turned as blue as the oceans, and many of the islands disappeared, along with the edges of the central continent, turned from dark green to pale brown and finally orangish-red. Then the oceans inundated the landmass until all that remained of it were scattered islands separated from each other by increasingly murky gray-brown water.

Tchuvu had been narrating all the while. Most of this Miles and Anna knew already and so listened to Okiva's translation with one ear. But seeing it happen in front of them made an impression. Our World hovered above them, spinning leftward on its axis, looking like a drowned, lifeless husk of its former self.

Why, wondered Anna, *does Vikram not want to even mention the gene bank he risked our lives bringing back to Our World?* She would have thought they'd be desperate for the potential it held. Miles wondered when they might get something to eat.

Now the image zoomed down to Danevesu after the cataclysm, a flooded city with a fledgling colony of survivors carving out of the mountain a new city that overlooked the old. "Technological progress slowed, but never stopped in Danevesu," said Tchuvu. Anna and Miles watched as the city grew into the marvel they'd glimpsed out of the windows earlier. They were then treated to what could most accurately be described as a promotional tourism video, but in three-dimensional holographic technicolor splendor.

By the time it was over, Miles and Anna were both ready to purchase timeshares in Danevesu, whatever their reservations about the endless wasteland surrounding it.

Tchuvu concluded the show, bringing up the lights and sending the flying remote control on its way. He said some words now to the audience, which Okiva didn't bother translating, and the yishi, who were still standing, whistled their applause one last time and then began filing out of the amphitheater with spooky orderliness.

Now the windows undarkened, revealing a raging storm outside—rain flew sideways, blown by violent gusts of wind, while lightning flashed across the horizon and dark clouds blanketed a roiling sky—of which they heard nothing through the thick glass and stone of the city's outer wall. No one but Anna and Miles paid it the least mind.

Tchuvu approached Anna and Miles, followed closely by Okiva. "If you'll accompany Elusia," he said, "he can take you on a tour of our city—with Araviku and Kerak, of course." Vikram and Kerak were standing beside Elusia and Geresh, while the other members of the yishi reception committee congregated by the edge of the stage.

Miles and Anna nodded. "That would be nice," said Anna.

"After your tour," said Tchuvu, "I hope we will have the chance to talk more and answer any questions you may have."

"I do have a question," said Anna. Tchuvu nodded politely after Okiva relayed her words. "Why make contact in this way?" she asked. "I'm just curious. But why not send ambassadors to Earth, instead of bringing us here?"

"Control," Tchuvu said simply. "We don't know what the reaction would be on Earth to the knowledge that an alien intelligence not only exists but has the ability to make physical contact. By the same rationale, we're reluctant to contact any particular power—the leadership of one or several powerful nations, for example—as we assume their response would be prejudiced by self-interest or, worse, fear. Just as Araviku and Arak before him gathered information about Earth, now we are giving you that opportunity, but in a controlled way. You aren't meant to bring any message back to Earth. But it's our hope that you will be the first of many to visit Danevesu and learn about us—a way of laying the foundation for future contact, ultimately out in the open."

Anna nodded, accepting the explanation, while her expression betrayed the fact that she still found it counterintuitive.

"You are our guests here," said Tchuvu. "We ask nothing of you but to enjoy your time with us."

Tchuvu made a slight bow, nuzzling their human guests once again, and took his leave with Okiva following behind as they climbed the steps to the main entrance.

Anna and Miles were left with Vikram, Kerak, and the rest of the reception committee. They soon learned that they were members of the Danevesu's governing council, and that Tchuvu and Elusia were the council designates, or co-executives of the government. Though it seemed clear from the deferent and anxious way they all handled Tchuvu that he was the more powerful of the two.

Although the councilors were a bit standoffish, they congregated near Anna and Miles, clearly excited to be in close proximity to their human guests. Miles, who towered over everyone, seemed to cow all but the boldest councilors. Meanwhile Anna, who was the first female human the yishi had ever seen in the flesh (there were no female fluppets) and was closer in height, body type, and skin tone with her hosts, drew the yishi to her like a magnet. As some of the councilors spoke Spanish or German or one of the other languages Anna knew, she could converse with them without needing Geresh to translate.

Most of the councilors treated them with a nervous reverence and made only small talk of greetings and well wishes. When Geresh was no longer being used to translate for Miles, he turned to Miles as they stood next to the windows and said, "Forgive me. I've never had a chance to use my English with a native speaker. I hope you're able to understand me."

"Oh, not at all," said Miles, absently looking out at the harbor. "I mean, your English is really good. Much better than my Danevesan."

"You speak Danevesan?" asked Geresh, a look of surprised delight in his eyes.

"Um, well, no," he said. "I don't....That was sort of a joke."

"Oh," said Geresh.

The storm had passed already, though gray clouds continued to streak across the sun, now about midway to being directly overhead. Rain beaded up on the windows and ran down in streaks.

"Well, English has always been my favorite," said Geresh. "I'm fascinated by some of your colloquial expressions."

Miles nodded, adding, "Like what?" as it seemed Geresh needed prompting.

"Well, for instance, 'piehole' means *mouth*, and 'cornhole' means *anus*," he said. "Yet never the other way around. Why is that? You'd think they'd be interchangeable. The terms, I mean."

Normally Miles would have laughed at that, but the horizon line of the ocean was visible now and did not look right. It seemed to be roiling and swelling in the distance, as the water below them appeared to be receding.

Geresh began again, "Because, it's my understanding that pie and corn are both edible, so—"

"No, I get it, Geresh," said Miles. "I just...I don't know why."

All of the subs Miles noticed before were nowhere to be seen now, submerged or gone off somewhere, and a bright light on a building above the harbor pier had turned from red to yellow.

"Is it a sexual reference?" Geresh asked.

"I—I don't think so," Miles said distractedly.

The thing that was distracting Miles's attention turned out to be an enormous wall of water heading straight for the city, gathering speed as it approached. Over a quarter-mile tall and stretching wider than his field of vision, it looked prepared to wash everything and everyone away with it.

"What is *that*?" asked Anna.

The councilors, mindful of their guests' obvious discomfort, looked around and at each other in mild confusion.

"It's a tsunami," said Vikram. "They're fairly common here."

Miles stepped away from the windows to Anna's side, and they tensed in expectation of the impact. The wave's crest looked to be beneath the level where they were standing. Still, it crossed from the outermost spires of the old city to the face of the new in almost no time. Unlike the storm earlier, they heard and felt the shockwave this time, a sudden explosion below followed by the spray of water shooting up past the windows in front of them and drenching the city's glittering façade.

Miles and Anna looked around to see many of the councilors still talking among themselves or smiling benignly in their direction.

"That's not something you see every day," said Miles, his heart thumping, Anna's hand attached to his forearm with a vice-like grip.

"It is here," said Vikram.

Anna and Miles turned to face Vikram, who just shrugged. "Ever since the cataclysm," he said, "seismic activity on Our World has increased in regularity and destructiveness. On many of the smaller islands, it's been disastrous. But Danevesu has never been damaged by the quakes or tsunamis. It's been engineered too well."

Miles let out a sigh of relief. "I mean," he said, "that *was* kind of cool."

As the swell of water gradually receded, Miles and Anna gazed out at the harbor under a temporary reprieve of sunshine. With the sea level dropping, the rocky headland that supported the docks revealed clumps of abandoned buildings along the side, covered in reddish scum, windows broken out, roofs crumbling, walls caved in. Above these and directly over the docks stood a group of newer buildings hugging a terrace of rock. Amid what looked like homes was a lifthouse now displaying its bright yellow light, two large capsules hanging over the side of the precipice, a half mile or so above the waterline. The capsules, suspended by large cables, were set into two channels carved into the rock and heading straight down to the docks.

The bridges of the submersibles began to reappear on the surface outside the harbor, a few chugging in to dock. From the windows in the amphitheater, they could see the little community above the pier come to life. The light on the lifthouse turned from yellow to blue, and the capsules began to descend to platforms beside the docks, ant-sized yishi getting in and out, going to and fro. One of the submersibles had docked and now extended a walkway to convey yishi off and on.

Beside the lifthouse, Anna and Miles could see one of the yishi strip to the waist and stretch his arms out wide, unhinging the two hidden forelimbs attached to his wrists. When unfurled, the wings revealed the webbing that extended from the ends of his arms to his sides. With a slight knee bend, he launched himself over the side and glided down slowly, landing roughly on one of the dockside platforms. It caused a little bit of commotion, as some of the yishi waiting there seemed annoyed and started lecturing him.

Vikram just smiled and shook his head. "Kids," he said.

*

AFTER ANOTHER ROUND of nuzzling—it seemed odd to Anna that these yishi, who otherwise seemed so shy, were so readily affectionate in their greetings and sendoffs—the councilors dispersed, leaving Miles and Anna alone with Vikram, Kerak, Elusia, and Geresh.

"Would it be all right if we began your tour now?" asked Geresh, translating for Elusia, their nominal guide. Anna and Miles said yes, and they soon fell in formation with the others and made their orderly way up to the main entrance.

A short corridor led them into a large vaulted space with a long, main hallway running parallel with the cliff's face and dozens of arterial side halls leading off in every direction. The main hall on this level followed along the cliff's curving face, and the intersecting passages meandered off on crooked paths. It seemed impossible that the maze of winding corridors around them could comprise a functioning city, let alone one that was constrained by being carved out of the rock of the mountain. There was no logical grid in evidence in this place. The floor of the main hall sloped down gently at certain points and up in others, as did the height of the ceiling, making Anna and Miles wonder how these variations were handled on the floors below and above.

The main hall was swarming with briskly walking yishi, most of whom either wore the same goggles as Daka and Sibu or were occupied with something on their smartskin. When they did look up to see Anna and Miles, they slowed down to gaze diffidently at the humans in their midst. Above them all flew countless remotely controlled devices, little black gewgaws going back and forth over their heads or hovering over certain individuals, as if delivering something. They came in various shapes and sizes—mostly much smaller than the chairs that had flown up to Anna and Miles in the amphitheater—and seemed to perform a range of tasks, though most of them were used as delivery vehicles. Vikram said they referred to the flying devices as *zhinks*, their word for a long-extinct flying insect, similar to a bumblebee.

In the main hall on the walls closest to the harbor, long horizontal screens showed a continuous strip of live video from the harbor, mimicking the view from the windows facing the ocean. On the other side of the hall, video screens showed movies of what seemed to Miles and Anna to be news or public affairs—talking heads interspersed with pre-recorded or live segments. Often the video would switch to something that seemed more promotional, usually featuring what on Earth would be considered pornography. The first time an explicit scene came on, it momentarily stopped Anna in her tracks, bringing an uncharacteristic flush to her cheeks. Miles just stared unabashedly at the open displays of twosomes and threesomes engaging in what he assumed were typical yishi sex acts. The yishi put their sexual versatility to good use, as well as their large proboscises. If nothing else, the spots provided a good primer for the uninitiated in yishi reproductive anatomy.

The halls were extravagantly furnished, like everywhere else, and structural columns and beams dressed the corridors, dramatically exposing some of the engineering required to keep the city from collapsing. Other pieces of public art—sculpture and mixed media both still and moving—filled every available space. Elusia led them too quickly through this visual wonderland, where the yishi themselves finished a close second to their architecture.

They turned down a side hall and arrived at a vaulted vestibule where a transport awaited them. It was a sort of elevator that could move in any direction the shaft did, as well as veer off into intersecting shafts at will. The hatch slid open, and they all piled into the car—an orb that traveled on a cushion of air. Not expecting it to move sideways, Miles and Anna nearly fell over as it started to wind its way through the shaft and away from the harbor, into the heart of the mountain and upward to the plateau above. The sensation of moving in this way was more like an airplane or roller-coaster than an elevator. The floor of the car remained level as the car rotated and they inclined steeply up toward the end of their journey, the top-level facilities of the farm.

The agricultural laboratory, or farm, was a vast complex at the farthest end of the city from the harbor. The upper rooms held the greenhouses, which were covered by a wide canopy of skylights. Since it was raining again, everything was illuminated by artificial orange grow lights. It was entirely indoors and there was no soil—the roots of the rows upon rows of plants floated in some type of organic aqueous solution that one of the yishi workers had explained to them through Geresh's translation,

which Miles and Anna didn't totally grasp but did gather involved recy-
cled sewage.

After seeing where the few crops the yishi cultivated were grown,
they moved on to the processing centers where freshly harvested raw
materials were converted into a wide range of edibles by technicians. All
of their food came from what they grew here and the few edible species of
gelatinous zooplankton they could harvest from the sea. Growing crops
outdoors had become impossible, in part due to the extreme weather, but
now mainly because of the redscale.

"Redscale?" asked Anna.

"You may have noticed it growing on some of the rocky outcrop-
pings around the harbor, or on the tops of the submerged buildings,"
said Geresh. "It infests the soil and kills anything we've tried to grow.
And nothing seems to kill it."

"Oh." That sounded bad.

"Fortunately, the technicians are able to do a great deal with the limited number of crops they grow here."

Miles flinched as a zhink suddenly appeared at his elbow, carrying a few
refreshments—tumblers full of a brown liquid and a bowl of what looked
like large green Cheez Balls resting in orange foam. Geresh and their hosts
at the farm encouraged them to try some with big smiles on, while Vikram
shrugged as if to say, *It won't kill you.* Miles picked up one of the glasses,
wondering if it was anything like coffee. He took a sip and winced from its
cloying sweetness—like maple syrup cut with Dr. Pepper. Anna's reaction
was about the same, but she managed to smile as she put her glass down
and made a curious gesture to her hosts about the globular food.

Their host made a yummy smacking noise and rubbed his tummy.

So she picked up one of the green blobs dripping orange slime and
bit into it, shards of it breaking off and shattering in her mouth like glass
before dissolving on her tongue, the puffy ball a crunchy variation of
cotton candy with its sugary blandness, while the foam was a lighter but
more pungent version of fermented fish sauce.

"Mmm, good," she lied. Miles raised an eyebrow and popped one
into his mouth, instantly regretting it as Anna hid a laugh with the back
of her hand. "Mmm," he repeated in mock agreement, as their hosts
looked on approvingly.

They offered them more samples of food and drink, but whatever wasn't simply too sweet was sweet with the aftertaste of rotting seafood. Miles, who was starting to get hungry, idly wondered if anything they grew and transformed into something else there was even remotely palatable.

Anna asked a lot of questions and usually tried to learn the Danevesan words for basic things like *water*, *light*, *plants*, and *sweet*, which gratified her hosts, Geresh in particular, to no end.

The city-state of Danevesu was completely self-contained and self-sufficient, housed in one continuous complex, a kind of mixed-use apartment building that was its own country. As a result, their yishi hosts never once ventured outside as they led Anna and Miles through the various levels and departments concealed within.

The Danevesans they met and passed along their way tended to vary widely in feather and eye color, hardly at all in skin tone, and shared a similar height and build. Also, if the snatches of yishi pornography that flashed across the ubiquitous video screens could be taken as representative, the yishi were generally more well-endowed than both Anna and Miles.

At the nearby bioengineering labs, they met with the head of the program, a former underling of Vikram's, as it turned out. He and Vikram tried valiantly to explain to Anna and Miles how their forbears had managed to identify and separate consciousness from the brain—thus paving the way for migrating consciousness from one individual to another—and how they were able to create a hybrid synthetic-organic fluppet from an individual genome, but without much success.

Their questions only seemed to confuse things further.

"So, in a fetus, the consciousness develops after the brain?" asked Miles.

"In a way, yes," said Vikram. "Think of the brain as the hardware and the consciousness as the software in a computer." Miles and Anna nodded, pretending they understood the difference. "Only the brain writes its own software, creates the consciousness as it grows larger and more complex, and stores the memories that become part of the conscious mind."

"Uh-huh. And this works the same in human brains as in yishi?" Miles asked.

"Yes."

"How did you know that?"

"We didn't."

"So you experimented on human…DNA?"

"Sort of, yeah."

"Sort of?" Miles repeated.

"Cloned embryos, actually."

"Okay." Miles found Vikram's nonchalance a little disconcerting. "So after you figured out how to separate the consciousness from the mind—"

"—the brain," Vikram clarified.

"Sorry, the brain—then you figured out how to grow a clone without a consciousness?"

"We figured out how to deny the developing brain's ability to create consciousness," said Vikram. "Without killing the host," he added.

"And then transplant a consciousness later?"

"I think you've got it," said Vikram.

Miles didn't feel like he got it.

"The mind?" Anna put in. "Does that just mean the brain and consciousness combined?"

"More or less."

"Well, how does that work when you transfer your consciousness to another brain in another body—a *human* brain in a *human* body?"

"Well, you're never exactly the same going from one brain to another," Vikram admitted. "It's always important to find a good match. But the human and yishi brains are remarkably similar. It's one of the great mysteries, really—how that happened."

"How so?" said Anna.

"Well, I mean, look at us," said Vikram, meaning the two of them.

All Anna could see were the differences.

"We're practically the same," he said, to her visible surprise. "Our ancestors couldn't be more different. You evolved from apes, and before them, small furry mammals. We evolved from large winged creatures akin to pterosaurs on Earth. And yet we both evolved to a similar size and shape, to be upright, to have almost the same physical features, despite some trivial cosmetic differences."

Other than the wings, feathers, beaks, and dual genitalia, Anna had to concede this was true.

"And if you examine the structure of our brains, they're almost identical," said Vikram. "How is it that that happened? And what are the chances that the one intelligent species we discovered across millions of light-years of space are so like us? It's mind-boggling."

"So you think other intelligent species are like us?" said Miles.

"It's one of the things we're dying to find out," said Vikram. "But we may never know."

"And that's how you could transfer your consciousness into a human brain?" asked Anna.

"Yes. But even so, there are always individual differences in abilities, personality, temperament. It's like playing a violin your whole life and then switching to the cello."

"Okay."

It was easier to explain the genetic engineering they were doing at the embryonic level among the yishi of Danevesu. Selecting genes for intelligence, strength, longevity, and of course, beauty—and selecting out genes that carried hereditary diseases, disorders, and other "undesirable" traits—the yishi of Danevesu had been trying to evolve the species on a local level for twenty generations, as natural selection couldn't be relied upon to do the job, or at least not do it quickly enough. This was simple enough to grasp for Miles and Anna, even if the specifics were beyond them and the ethical implications troubling.

From bioengineering they took the same transport line down toward the amphitheater, pausing midway to turn left and then further down to the menagerie. Miles and Anna tended to be unprepared for how impossibly big and expansive some of the areas inside the city could be. Approaching the menagerie on foot through a typically tight side corridor, their mouths fell open like a couple of tourists as it let them out in an eight-story atrium the width and breadth of a football pitch. Arrayed in front of them were various natural-looking hillocks, walls, pits, ponds, and fake foliage, as well the electronic partitions that screened the separate habitats off from each other and the animals inside from escape.

"This is a zoo?" said Miles.

"This is *the* zoo," said Vikram. "The only one I know of left on Our World."

One of the keepers came out to meet them—Veylan, a large, gregarious yishi almost as tall as Anna but twice as wide, with green feathers and piercing yellow eyes. He spoke some English and was more than eager to use it on Anna and Miles. He took them around the displays and artificial habitats for the creatures they housed. It was obvious that Veylan was proud of his zoo and loved the animals in his care. The menagerie had begun as a zoological garden in Old Danevesu. It had been restored in the new city, its mission changed since the mass extinctions following the cataclysm.

"Most large animals died out during this period," he said. "They tried to save the ones who could not live outside, which inevitably was all of them. To be honest, they had trouble keeping them alive in captivity. The ones you see here were cloned from the last surviving descendants born in the menagerie."

Veylan led them over to one of the larger habitats. There was a group of winged creatures occupying the crotch of the large tree in the center of the enclosure.

"These birds we once kept as pets," said Veylan.

They didn't look much like birds to Anna and Miles. Or pets. They were small and they flew, but they looked more like little dragons with feathers. About the size of cats, they were called *sordies*. A few young flaplings were fighting over a piece of what looked like bright green Play-Doh while others hunted more green bits suspended from the ceiling with wire.

"They liked to hunt insects and other small flying animals," said Veylan. He explained that insects were practically nonexistent, and the few other prey animals in the menagerie were too valuable to feed to the sordies. But the green blobs dangling from strings seemed to satisfy them.

"Can they reproduce?" asked Anna.

"No," said Veylan. "We alter their genes to make them sterile."

"Why?"

"It would be inbreeding," he said. "They all have the DNA of siblings. Cloning is safer. Less chance of congenital defects."

There were other exhibits with clones of other Our World species—some cuddly, a few ugly, others ferocious-looking. But not many in all. They completed their tour in the natural history wing, where stuffed specimens of extinct species were posed against large murals of bygone nature scenes in realistic dioramas while interactive screens looped educational videos.

At the end, Miles and Anna caught a glimpse of the first yishi children they'd seen, a school group up for a field trip. Laying eyes on the first human visitors ever to set foot on Tonshu eclipsed any other thrill the young yishi were likely to experience that day.

*

ON THE TRANSPORT en route to their next stop on the tour—a relatively dull journey straight up—the car carrying them stopped unexpectedly, without turning down another branch or opening up at a drop-off point. The large video screen on the curved wall of the car showed a yishi newsreader standing in a studio. The same video appeared simultaneously on every yishi's smartskin with a musical whistle to alert them.

"What is it?" asked Anna.

"A bit of news," said Vikram, following the newsreader's words. "They've paused all the transports and blocked off a sub-sector of the city temporarily for a possible security breach. It's just precautionary, I think."

"Fucking Bandarians," muttered Kerak.

"What are Bandarians?" asked Miles.

"Terrorists," said Kerak. "From the big island west of here, a shithole called Bandary, all that's left of what was once a great power on Our World."

The newsreader was still speaking, but now video came on the screen of a corridor somewhere in Danevesu.

"That looks like a seven-hundred-red level," said Kerak, "near where we got on."

"Someone left a case unattended, that's all," said Vikram. "See there? It's probably nothing."

The newsreader continued to speak, occasionally letting the reporter on the scene, who was also shooting the video from his smartskin camera, interject something. "The civil guards have cordoned off the area," said Vikram, translating for Miles and Anna. "They're trying to scan the case's contents." They could see some young-looking yishi in green uniforms, masks, and protective gear were swarming around the area on screen. At the center of the activity, a small, oblong case with a smooth but worn metallic top sat on the floor of the hall. Next to it knelt a heavily armored guard with a special screen painted on the back of the armor over his wrist showing ghostlike images of the inside of the case.

Now the guards started to push the reporter away from the case. "They're saying the reporter needs to move back now," said Vikram, less sure of his previous assessment. "I'm not sure what tha—"

Before Vikram could finish wondering aloud what that meant, the lights went dark and the air pressure dropped noticeably just before the transport followed suit. It fell straight down the shaft toward Danevesu's nether regions, a thousand stories down. For anyone who'd ever ridden a roller coaster or a spacecraft into low Earth orbit, or who had dived out into Danevesu harbor as a youngster before spreading his wings, the sensation of freefall was nothing new. But hurtling down a tube of rock in a metal ball to an uncertain end was less familiar.

In an instant, they were all tumbling around the transport as if weightless, too scared to really enjoy the rare opportunity of experiencing a virtual zero-gravity environment. Also, Elusia had regurgitated his breakfast, and the blob of vomit that was hanging in midair only added to the general sense of alarm.

The car was in disarray, with Miles, Anna, and their yishi hosts floating haphazardly at various attitudes, while the transport's glass control panel started to blink brightly in alarm—a flashing yellow hexagon surrounding a red squiggle. It seemed to Miles to be calling out for someone to press it, though he couldn't reach it himself. His feet, however, were above his head, brushing against the upper curve of the transport. So he pushed off slightly, and now his face was hovering before the blinking console. He reached his hand toward the hexagonal icon on the screen, then hesitated.

"Should I press this?!" he shouted.

"Sure!" Vikram yelled back, much calmer than circumstances seemed to warrant.

Miles pressed the yellow hexagon, turning it blue and causing a loud *whoosh* to sound all around them. Everyone immediately fell on top of him for his trouble. The spherical car slowed to a safe stop on a cushion of air, but there was still some bruising and a few sprains, not to mention the puddle of puke that had splashed just about everyone after it hit the floor.

The lights had come back on, and Kerak was attempting to make sure everyone was all right. Geresh was fussing over Elusia, while Elusia brushed him off, already embarrassed about having thrown up. Miles and Anna, for their part, were a little more shaken than their yishi counterparts, being unaccustomed to suddenly plummeting down a vertical shaft at escape velocity and floating around as if they were aboard a space shuttle, when a short elevator ride was what they were expecting.

The video screen had come back on, and Vikram relayed what the newsreader was now saying. The civil guards had decided to set off a small electromagnetic pulse to deactivate any potential detonator within the abandoned case. The pulse had inadvertently knocked out the adjacent transport shaft and a car with six passengers, Vikram told them the newsreader said. "Us, he means," Vikram added. The newsreader reported that the transport's failsafes had kicked in.

"Well, Miles kicked them in," said Anna.

Geresh explained that each transport tunnel was designed to end in a gently sloping trough, as a failsafe so that if one were to fall, it would be prevented from crashing to the bottom of the shaft.

"Oh," said Miles.

"But thank you, anyway," said Geresh.

"Think nothing of it."

"All right."

The news cut back to the reporter on the scene, describing what had happened with the suspected bomb. The yishi in the car looked up at one point and seemed rather annoyed, almost disappointed.

"It looks like the case only contained clothes and personal effects," said Vikram.

"But that's good, isn't it?" said Anna.

Vikram shrugged. "It's better than the alternative."

"There have just been a lot of these false alarms lately," said Kerak. "People are getting a little irritated with the civil guards' overreacting to everything."

As he said this, a message flashed on the control panel, and the doors of the car opened. Two frowning yishi dressed like alien repairmen hovered just outside, one holding what might have been a tool or possibly a swizzle stick, the other a roll of bright red tape with writing on it. They stopped upon seeing Anna and Miles, temporarily stunned. "I think we need to get off here," said Vikram.

"Where are we now?" asked Anna.

"One of the orange twelve-hundred levels," said Vikram.

The six sectors of the city were denoted by colors of the visible spectrum, orange being toward the left end facing the harbor, between red and yellow. Each sector comprised a more or less comparably sized section of the city. Level twelve hundred was actually the six hundred and fortieth (converting to base-10) down from the top floor, or level one. The lower, outer sections of the city tended to house the least prestigious members of Danevesu's egalitarian society—maintenance and janitorial staff, teachers, childcare providers, nurses, as well as dormitories for the children who scored lowest on the aptitude tests.

In all of the previously visited sections of the city, natural light from harbor-facing windows or video screens simulating a view outside could be seen. But not here. It was dark and claustrophobic, and the looks the surprised local denizens gave them were a strange mixture of wonder and resentment. Elusia led them all out of the car while Geresh fiddled with his smartskin to figure out where to go next.

Passing through the off-tour depths of the city on their way to the yellow sector, they saw lights burnt out or blinking, video screens either not working or covered in graffiti, and scraps of paper and plastic littering the dim corridor. Anna, no stranger to urban blight, looked around, fascinated. Miles had a strangely comforting sense of recognition—the scene could've been from a State Street subway station or a West Side alleyway. A setting that normally might have put him on alert in regard to his personal safety now made him feel homesick.

At the nearest yellow sector transport, they stopped, and Vikram suggested they take a break to rest and change before heading up to the network control center. "It would be nice to wash the barf out of my hair," said Anna. Geresh coughed and translated that very loosely for Elusia, who smiled and nodded.

After they exited the transport on Kerak's floor, they made their way to his spacious apartment. It had no view, per se, but its large video screen on the far wall was showing the view they would have had through the window had they been a in a cliffside flat.

Kerak found them some yishi clothing to change into and showed Anna the loo, where she washed her hair and changed. Though the sleeves were long and the pants short, the clothes were soft and comfortable and cut more or less for a woman's curves, with more room in the shoulders and the front of the pants than she was used to.

Miles found the clothes oddly shaped for his lanky frame, but at least cushy and elastic, a little like wearing his little sister's sweats (he presumed). Yishi clothing didn't have buttons, snaps, or zippers but fasteners that were a sort of hybrid of Velcro and plastic zipper bags.

After everyone had changed and Anna emerged from the washroom, Miles asked about getting something to eat, as he and Anna were famished. Kerak brought them over to what looked like a dining nook, with a series of built-in drawers against one wall. The drawers were color coded in shades of blue to red. "Feel like something hot or cold?" Kerak asked.

"Do you have anything that isn't sickeningly sweet or fishy?"

Kerak thought for a moment, opened a yellowish drawer, and drew out a tub of something red. "This isn't *terribly* sweet," he said.

Miles tried to unscrew the tub's lid and then pry it off to no avail. Kerak tapped the top of it twice, and the lid disappeared. With a long spoon Miles sampled the reddish paste. It tasted like creamy peanut butter mixed with honey and a hint of some spice he didn't recognize. It was so good he wanted to faint. He forced himself to share the spoon with Anna, who tried a bit and then dug in for a much bigger dollop. Miles found another spoon, and they both gorged on the red slop like starving street urchins.

Vikram got them to sit down at the table, both still clinging to the tub of gastronomic orgasm, and got them some water. They were hungry and dehydrated, not to mention tired from the oxygen-thin atmosphere in the city. Miles and Anna were also struggling to emerge from their deer-caught-in-the-headlights stupor, taking every new thing in like newborns.

When they couldn't eat any more, they set down their spoons and realized they were both panting, which caused them to laugh at themselves, which, in turn, caused more panting and finally coughing and watery eyes.

After a drink of water, Miles asked Kerak about the bomb scare. "You said there have been a lot of false alarms lately," he said, just above a whisper. "Have there been any real alarms? Actual bombings?"

Kerak and Vikram looked at one another. "It's okay to talk about, Miles," said Vikram.

"There have," said Kerak. "Not for some time. But once they were pretty common."

"You mentioned terrorists—from Bandary?" said Anna.

"A wasteland," said Kerak. "It's just a big desert, on the last large island of Our World."

Miles's and Anna's grasp of Our World geography was hazy, limited to what they could remember of the hologram Tchuvu had shown them in the amphitheater. Vikram explained to them that Bandary was the largest island—about the size of Madagascar—on what was left of the once-contiguous continent ringing the tropic zone of the planet, west of the Danevesan archipelago. Bandary's former capital, Baradel, had been swallowed by the sea, and most Bandarians now lived in the ancient city of Lagaredel.

"Anyway, Lagaredel is little more than a ruin," said Kerak. "People still live in it, if you can call it living. Most of them have to eat their own shit to survive." Miles and Anna raised their eyebrows, not sure if he was exaggerating. Kerak just shrugged.

"It's not like *our* drinking water doesn't come from our own sewage, you know," Vikram pointed out.

"Yes, but it's been purified," said Kerak.

"Well…" said Vikram, who trailed off.

"The water comes from where now?" asked Miles.

Vikram laughed, but Miles really wanted to know.

"So the Bandarians are terrorists?" asked Anna, putting down the cup of water she'd just been drinking.

"Well, not all of them," said Kerak. "But Bandarian terrorist groups have plagued Danevesu for generations."

"What do they want?" she asked.

"Who knows?" said Kerak.

"For centuries now the Bandarians have blamed technology—and, by extension, Danevesu—for causing the cataclysm," Vikram added. "We fought two major wars with them, the last over a century ago. But since then, our technology advanced to the point they couldn't make war on us. Terrorism is the only tool they have left with which to hurt us. Their government is careful not to associate formally with any terrorist groups, but they support them all. They used to shun all modern technology because it led to Our World's downfall. But the most extreme terrorist groups now fear technology because they think it could be used to *reverse* the effects of the ecological collapse."

"But wouldn't they want that?" said Miles. "It doesn't seem to make any sense."

"Exactly," said Kerak.

"Are the Bandarians aware of us?" asked Anna.

"They have their spies like everyone else," said Kerak. "So it's possible."

Anna wanted to ask about Anders. Was he a Bandarian terrorist? She wanted to know how the gene bank fit in with all of this new information. But the look Vikram gave her discouraged further conversation.

"There's a whole history you know nothing about," said Vikram. "But given time, it'll become clearer."

"It's complicated," said Kerak.

*

MILES WASN'T EXACTLY sure what he expected to see in Danevesu's network control center, but he was certain there'd be a room full of electronic hardware humming and beeping away, like the big computer setups he'd seen on TV of NASA or the phone company. But the room was nearly silent, and there was no computer equipment in evidence

anywhere, except for the ubiquitous monitors that seemed to be painted
on the surface of the walls and desktops, in addition to tattooed on the
hands of the four or five computer technicians who ran the place.

Although Anna did have some experience with computers—she'd
used a database program for a senior thesis and had a local network
email account for one of her graduate courses—she'd never used a computer outside of university. Miles had had one computer science class
in high school, where one of the math teachers tried to teach the students BASIC on three-year-old Commodore 64s. The only skill Miles
actually learned, however, was using a 20 GOTO 10 command to get the
classroom's dot-matrix printer to spit out the following exchange in an
endless loop:

> KNOCK KNOCK.
> WHO'S THERE?
> KNOCK.
> KNOCK WHO?
> KNOCK KNOCK....

He also recalled playing something called Hunt the Wumpus. It was
difficult to envision from his limited experience how computers might
become even remotely important to him at some point in the future.

Unlike the menagerie or the farm or even the bio lab, the network
control offices were modest in size, tucked into a remote suite of rooms
toward the upper reaches of the city. Miles and Anna soon learned that
it was just the main hub of many similar stations distributed across the
city. The manager responsible for showing them around, Fippa, was a
slight fellow with grayish-blue feathers and pale brown skin who tended
to avoid eye contact and mutter into his chest, making Anna and Miles
wonder if the words Geresh used were really what Fippa was saying.

Fippa showed them some of the consoles—just screens with no guts
as far as they could see, same as everywhere else—and Geresh explained
how the city was networked via cables and also wirelessly through some
type of broadcast signal that had boosters throughout the city, as the sig-
nals had trouble traveling through stone. It was all fascinating but utterly
foreign to Anna and Miles.

"This center stores all of the data in the entire network," said Geresh, "which anyone can access at any time through their smartskin or goggles, or any other networked device. New data from users in Danevesu are constantly being added to the network and backed up through mirror sites around the city."

"Uh-huh," said Miles.

"Sure," said Anna.

Geresh had been filling in a little for Fippa, who started speaking his native Danevesan again. "As the main computing center," translated Geresh, "this is also a communications hub, linking all of Danevesu with dozens of offsite locations around the archipelago and the planet." Fippa waved his finger slightly and expanded a small icon on the screen on the desktop in front of them. "This is applied quantum mechanics, located in the old particle accelerator on an island not far from the city. There are other scientific outposts doing theoretical and experimental work scattered around the islands, like the dark energy lab and the observatory. We coordinate with a number of specialized biology labs across the archipelago, as well as other remote sites controlled from Danevesu, like oceanic monitoring stations and field gauges measuring seismic activity and weather."

Fippa warmed to his subject as Miles and Anna began to look more interested. "Here," he said motioning to them both to come over to the desktop's flat screen. "Place your hand here," he said to Anna, indicating a metallic plate next to the screen. "Either hand." Anna placed her right hand on the plate while Fippa made a few quick gestures above the screen. The plate lit up briefly, illuminating the blood flowing through the veins of her fingers. "Now," he said, "like this." Fippa closed the window open on the screen and demonstrated a basic gesture to open another—showing her in an exaggerated motion how she could manipulate the images on the monitor by opening apart or pinching together her thumb and forefinger.

She tried it with her hand hovering above the screen and laughed in surprise when she found she could do it. Soon she realized her hand was in control of everything she saw on the screen, and the movements she needed to move things around, open, scroll, or collapse the contents of the windows were completely intuitive.

"Wow," she said, bringing a slight smile from Fippa. A heady experience for Anna, she felt a rush of power flowing through her fingers. In a matter of minutes she had gone from witnessing technology sufficiently advanced to appear as magic to becoming the wizard who wielded it.

While Miles watched Anna with a mix of envy and awe, Fippa fitted him with a pair of goggles—not an ideal fit, as Miles's nose was much smaller and his ears much bigger than the average yishi, but close enough for demonstration purposes. The glasses and integrated earphones glowed silently for a few seconds while they scanned Miles. Fippa had him raise his arms, then slowly open and close his hands. Once paired with their user, the goggles could be controlled much as the smartskin or desktop computers were, with added control from the user's eye movement. Fippa showed Miles how the goggles could be used in one of two modes—one completely immersive, in which the outside world was essentially shut out to everything but a knock upside the head; the other a hybrid mode that allowed Miles to see and hear everything around him, while computer-generated imagery and textual information (all Greek to him) appeared in front of him as translucent, ghostlike, animated images superimposed on the real world.

After Anna and Miles played with their electronic devices for a while, Fippa hinted at his purpose in showing them all this. "Our World had been completely networked before the cataclysm," he told them, "which destroyed much of our existing infrastructure. So we're limited in our ability to communicate with people in other parts of the world."

Miles and Anna nodded.

"Araviku tells us that your world, Earth, has the infrastructure already in place for networking the entire planet."

"It does?" said Miles.

"I didn't know that," said Anna. "When did Vikram tell you this?"

"Araviku downloaded all of his records shortly after you arrived," said Geresh, answering for Fippa, as if the implications of that ought to be obvious.

"Araviku says that you're at a pivotal point in developing your computer technology," said Fippa. "That soon he expects computers will become much more important in everyone's lives."

"God, I hope not," said Anna.

"I guess it's easy for me to see," said Vikram. "But quantum computing is still only theoretical on Earth," he added, speaking to Fippa so that Geresh could translate. "Human understanding of physics is still just emerging, with no unified field theory, and the computer chips they've developed so far are pretty pathetic."

While Fippa was trying to explain to them some of the basic quantum mechanical concepts like uncertainty and entanglement, Miles and Anna began to feel lightheaded and had to sit down.

Anna asked Vikram and their hosts if they could break for the day, and they all agreed, as this was the end of the tour in any case. They all thanked Fippa, and Geresh said something about reconvening the next morning for a celebratory feast. Apparently, breakfast was the main meal of the day, the other meals consisting of numerous light snacks throughout the day and night. Elusia and Geresh led them away, and after a short and uneventful transport ride, left the four others at the door to Kerak's flat.

*

KERAK SHOWED Anna and Miles the sleeping arrangements. There were just the two bedrooms, and it was then that it dawned on Miles that Vikram and Kerak were more than just friends. The bed for Anna and Miles was raised on a perch in a large, shallow bowl that resembled a larger version of one of the sordie nests in the menagerie. Loops of silky cloth were bunched together, arranged like the bristles of a very soft brush, lining a sort of cocoon. It looked heavenly. And it had been a very long day.

Vikram noticed the longing in their eyes. "Day's not over yet. And if you go to sleep now, you'll just be jet-lagged," he warned.

They threw Vikram a petulant glare but begrudgingly obeyed.

"Have some *gelum*," he said. "You'll feel better, and then we can go out."

"What's gelum?" asked Anna.

"That red goo you liked so much."

"Mmm..." said Miles, remembering the red goo.

While Miles and Anna reenergized themselves with a snack, Vikram and Kerak changed into evening dress, outfits both more colorful and revealing than the conservative, practical clothing they'd seen so far on their tour.

"We want to take you out," said Vikram. "This time somewhere we can relax, and where you can see Danevesans at play instead of just at work."

"Sounds nice," said Anna, surprised by the sudden display of cleavage. "Where are we going?"

"Wherever the four air-conditioning vents take us, Anna," said Vikram, drawing an odd look from Kerak. "Probably a bar."

Centrally located several floors below the amphitheater, amid a row of watering holes and eateries with real harbor views, the nightclub was loud and teeming with yishi. Through a soft haze, they could see the atmosphere was lively, dark, and beautiful, a mix of sleek, flashing technology and the typically organic, sculptural architecture. After the cave-like entrance, the club opened up to a spacious two-story loft with a balcony hugging the contours of the curving walls. Against the far wall were windows overlooking the harbor, illuminated by the city lights and the occasional flash of lightning, as a fine, misting rain condensed on the glass. Inside, a bluish haze muted the brighter colors while spreading the glow of hanging lamps and the light from everyone's smartskin. Walking further into the club, Anna and Miles saw a huge video screen—a circular band suspended over the middle of the room playing 360-degree videos on either side simultaneously. They were mainly pornographic scenes that made the ones they'd seen earlier look tame by comparison. In one, a naked yishi had smartskin running the length of his rather large, erect member, which was playing its own widescreen pornographic movie. Then the scene cut to a penis's-eye view of that same member entering his partner, a perspective akin to that of a colonoscopy monitor.

The horrified looks on Anna's and Miles's faces caused Kerak to laugh out loud.

"Oh, grow up, you two," said Vikram, shaking his head.

Soon a zhink host hovered over to them, led them to an open table with a view of the dance floor and the harbor, and flew away. Anna and Miles looked around for the bar but saw none. There were no waiters either, just more zhinks flying around carrying trays of drinks and food.

Kerak was fiddling with the smartskin on the back of his hand, finished up, and said, "I ordered us something to drink."

"Oh," they said, knowing better by now than to question how.

As Miles and Anna sat there rubbernecking, a zhink waiter buzzed over carrying a large glass beaker to the table next to them. The beaker was filled with a translucent pink liquid, and in the center of it floated a deep blue sphere. The three yishi sitting at the table stuck long straws into the indigo ball and began to suck up its contents as if it were a contest, the sphere shrinking in size until it disappeared entirely. With that, the yishi gave a few satisfied laughs and sent the pink remnants of the beaker back to wherever it came from.

Around the club, Anna and Miles noticed many zhinks flying to and fro and hovering over tables with improbable displays of culinary ingenuity—food stretched and twisted into shapes impressive more as feats of engineering and design than gastronomic appeal. Frozen food, boiling food, food in the form of a gas encased in a bubble, powdered food that arced and flashed when an electrical current passed through it, putting itself out as the powder transformed into a billowing foam.

Despite the outlandish presentation of many dishes, the yishi's relationship to food was actually less complicated than it was for humans. The extremes of texture, structure, color, and shape that distinguished Danevesan cuisine masked a profoundly limited selection of ingredients. If Vikram was any indication—he who'd lived on a steady diet of hard candy, chocolate, and cigarettes—the yishi palate was just as limited. The fantastical look and feel of much of their food seemed designed mainly to create interest in a dull routine that otherwise held little fascination for them.

Their relationship to sex seemed similarly uncomplicated, at least in Danevesu. Having just the one gender, yishi had no concept of gender politics or the vicissitudes of sexual orientation and identity. They were all, by definition, homosexual. Some preferred the "female" role behind closed doors, some the "male," others liked both. Some were into group sex, or oral, or anal, or nasal—none of their preferences caused consternation or were perceived as a threat to anyone, weren't closely guarded secrets nor even regarded as especially private. Nor was privacy particularly valued in Danevesu. As such, the expression of sexuality was more or less uncontroversial as public entertainment.

The drinks arrived, four tallish clear bottles with six layers of colored liquid inside. Anna noticed that everyone drank with some kind of glass straw or curved tube, as their beaks made drinking straight from the vessels precarious. The glasses their drinks came in had six tubes protruding from the rims, each tube accessing a different layer of the drink so you could drink it from the bottom up or in any order you chose.

"Is it alcoholic?" Anna asked.

"Oh, yes," said Vikram. "All except the bottom layer. That's a mild stimulant."

"You have alcohol on Our World?" asked Miles.

"Sure," said Vikram. "It's just carbon, oxygen, and hydrogen. Ethanol is a fairly common compound that occurs naturally throughout the universe. Though the stuff we're drinking was cooked up in one of the labs we went through earlier today. The critters that used to cause fermentation—our version of yeast—are all gone. Or were." Vikram smiled at the furtive reference to his gene bank. "It's another strange coincidence in human-yishi evolution. Our pterosaur ancestors evolved an enzyme necessary to more efficiently digest ethanol just as your ape ancestors did. And alcohol would eventually play an important role in the evolution of both our civilizations."

Miles was sorry he asked. He felt like if anyone tried to cram one more bit of information into his head, his brain was going to try to escape through his ears.

"Interesting," he said.

Anna took a tentative sip of the top layer of the drink. Not having had the best experience with food and drink outside of the gelum, she braced herself for the worst. "Hmm," she said. "Not too strong, not terribly sweet. A little bland, actually."

Miles looked at her, dubious, but tried it anyway. She wasn't kidding this time, fortunately. The second layer was slightly stronger and a little peppery, which mitigated the sweetness. "Will this get us drunk?" he asked.

"Probably not," said Vikram. "Probably less than the hallucinogen in the mist in any case."

"The what?"

"There's a mild hallucinogenic compound in the blue fog they pump in," he said. "It's like smoking a joint...or three."

"They pump drugs in to get everyone high?" said Anna.

"A long time ago, they found that it drastically cut down on violence," explained Kerak. "Also, it gives people an appetite. So it more than justifies the expense."

"What if you don't want to get high?" she said.

"Don't fucking come in," he replied. Vikram shot Kerak a look. Kerak shot back a look as if to say, *What?*

At one point an old friend of Vikram's stopped by their table and greeted Vikram and Kerak with effusive nuzzles. Vikram stood and introduced his friend, Erestu, to the human ambassadors from Earth, Anna and Miles.

Anna nodded and repeated the traditional Danevesan greeting she'd learned from Geresh, which greatly impressed Erestu, who gave her a warm nuzzle.

"Hey," said Miles, who got a nuzzle anyway.

Erestu had long auburn feathers and green eyes. Like many of the other yishi in the club, he wore a form-fitting, off-the-shoulders top that showed off his cleavage and allowed his wings free rein. He and Vikram spoke for a few seconds in Danevesan about something or other before Erestu had to leave and nodded good-bye to everyone.

"Vikram," said Anna, "does everyone in Danevesu go by just one name?"

The Danevesans did generally all go by mononyms, the sort of thing only famous people like Sting or Madonna could pull off on Earth. Vikram explained Danevesan naming conventions to Anna and Miles. Every child is given the names of his parents at the age of viability (birth, more or less)—the name of the egg donor (mother), followed by the name of the sperm donor (father)—but at some point in his formative years, the child receives a kind of official nickname that becomes his de facto name and the name that will get passed down to his children.

"So my name at birth was Arak-Temal," he said, "but I was later called Araviku, which means essentially, 'Arak's shadow,' or more appropriately now, 'Arak's ghost.' Of course, a lot of people shorten it further to Viku."

"Wait a minute," said Miles. "You mean *the* Arak? You're the son of the guy who first explored Earth?"

Vikram nodded. "I resembled him when I was younger," he said. "I worshipped him too. He took an interest in me at an early age, after his first trip to Earth. I excelled in the physical sciences as a youngster, especially biology, and he encouraged that. Though his field was not biology, it was anthropology—and linguistics, which is one of the reasons they sent him."

Anna, surprised by the revelation, smiled at that.

"What about Temal?" asked Miles.

"I never knew him," Vikram said matter-of-factly.

"You say, 'They sent him,'" said Anna, "but we don't know anything about your government or political institutions. Or...if we're even allowed to talk about it," she added this last part under her breath.

"It's okay to talk about," said Vikram. "Freedom of speech is a right protected by long tradition and law. But surveillance is everywhere, and everything is recorded. Your notions of privacy don't really exist here."

"Oh."

Vikram leaned back and took a slow sip of one of the blue middle layers of his drink. "I suppose," he said, "after the cataclysm, our system evolved as we did. By the time Old Danevesu was abandoned, our old government had collapsed and we were still at war with Bandary the first time, even though the fighting had more or less ended. For a time, we had both exhausted our supply of weapons, as well as our ability to get at one another. This was when the people started to tunnel into the mountain, creating the first settlements that would become the current Danevesu. The population was at its lowest point, and the people who were left had no use for government. So they set up a loose sort of collective, dividing the governance of the city into professional guilds, with representatives chosen by consensus, but no central authority. Everything was shared, everyone was equal. There were no laws or private property, no religion, so people policed themselves—relying mainly on the desire to conform, and the need to survive.

"As the new city grew up next to the old, the system became less tenable. People exploited the power inherent in their positions, there was corruption, crimes went unpunished. But, much like other survivors around Our World, the people here had no desire to return to the way things had been done in the past. At the same time, too many were dissatisfied with the way things were for the status quo to remain.

"Old Danevesu had been home to many of the oldest and greatest universities in Our World. They had attracted yishi from every nation, every city on Tonshu. When the cataclysm came, most of Our World's capitals and major cities were drowned, along with their accumulated knowledge. But Danevesu, and its learning, survived. Many of the most influential yishi in Danevesu had either come from one of the universities or were their protégés. They tended to populate the most powerful guilds—those comprised of engineers, physicists, biologists, and various technical fields. Everyone was supposed to be equal, and within guilds they generally were. But different guilds commanded resources differently—sometimes according to the yishi's needs, sometimes their own, not always equitably.

"Many of the more educated citizens had come to the conclusion that no form of government, no matter how rational or idealistic, could function effectively without a more evolved population. Natural selection took too long, might even be countered by a society that cherished and prolonged life, or by individuals likely to pass down undesirable traits. We'd domesticated countless crops and animals, transforming species to suit our needs in a matter of a few generations, why not domesticate ourselves?"

"*Domesticate* yourselves?" said Anna.

"Maybe that's not the right word, but you get the idea. Anyway, we'd long ago taken over the machinery of reproduction from nature—when everyone can become pregnant, bodily autonomy tends to trump any religious debate over when life begins. We hadn't yet discovered how the consciousness develops, but, in Danevesu at least, we didn't believe in a 'soul' separate from the consciousness. Even among the various belief systems on Our World, the soul was thought to be endowed at birth, not conception. Which is convenient, if you're unwilling to give up control over your own body.

"The point is, we knew a lot about genetics, and it wasn't long before we were able to select the hereditary traits we wanted to promote. Intelligence, physical fitness—"

"Large breasts and penises," Miles put in.

"Those too," Vikram admitted with a crooked grin.

"How did the scientists get everyone to agree to this?" asked Anna.

"Well, that's when the government began to *evolve*," said Vikram. "Not everyone was keen on the idea of being domesticated. But the scientific guilds gradually established some laws regarding reproduction, eventually creating an enforcement arm in the civil guards—a quasi-military police force made up of young conscripts. Everyone serves a stint in either the civil guard or a remote posting when they come of age. Within a few generations, every yishi in Danevesu had been conceived with preselected traits and gestated under laboratory conditions."

"But how can they enforce laws regarding reproduction?" asked Anna.

"Well, to create a child, you first need to obtain a permit," said Vikram.

"So how are babies conceived?" said Miles.

"Well, Miles," said Vikram, "when a mommy and a daddy yishi love each other very much—"

"Ha ha," said Miles.

"After they provide sperm and egg samples, a reengineered, fertilized egg is grown up to the point when it's viable outside the lab and can be reared," said Vikram.

"And unauthorized pregnancies?" asked Anna.

"Are soon discovered and ended pharmaceutically," said Vikram. "Not that I've ever known anyone to object."

"Uh-huh. I thought evolution could only happen when mutations occur in reproduction. You seem to be eliminating any possibility of that. To say nothing of the unintended consequences of this type of eugenics program."

Vikram leaned forward. "This was all begun many generations before any of us were born," he said. "But you're right. Genetic diversity, among other things, has been sacrificed. On the other hand, I can't blame them for what they started—they did it to survive."

"Okay," she said, dropping it for now and taking a sip of her drink. "So what form of government does Danevesu have now? I take it that anarchy is a thing of the past."

"I'd describe it as a form of socialist-democratic republic. The guilds still function more or less as always, but a central authority was set up with a council and the two executive designates," said Vikram. "In theory, a representative from any guild could be elected designate, but in practice, the scientific guilds maintain a death grip on the office and have a say in who in the other guilds sits on the council. But everyone still gets to vote, even children," he added. "Not only within guilds for their representatives, but directly and en masse for periodic referenda."

"You said that there's no privacy," said Miles, "that everything is recorded. But by whom?"

"By us, by and large," he said, much to Miles's and Anna's surprise. "All of us, basically, anyone who uses smartskin. Beyond that, every screen you see is a two-way monitor connected to the surveillance apparatus. Additional cameras and microphones are essentially invisible and can be anywhere."

The thought was more than a little chilling.

"Yet you still have freedom of expression?" said Anna.

"There's no censorship," said Vikram. "But they can always use what you've said against you."

Anna and Miles shuddered inwardly. Miles absently sucked up the last, bottom layer of his drink, and the instant it hit his gullet he felt an overwhelming rush in his head, as though his brain really were trying to escape out his ears. Then, as though a wave had crashed in his mind, relief swept over him, and he burst out laughing—hysterical, uncontrollable laughter, tears streaming down his eyes.

"Are you all right?" asked Anna, genuinely concerned.

Miles nodded and tried to speak, but could only emit falsetto squeaks.

"He'll be fine," said Kerak. "It's just the stimulant. Only lasts a short while."

Once his hysteria subsided to giggles, Miles assured Anna he was fine. He was flushed and breathing hard, but seemed to have rather enjoyed the experience. Anna noticed that when Kerak and Vikram drank their liquid rush, they just sat back and smiled, the pupils of their eyes transforming into large black pools. Anna decided to leave hers at the bottom of her glass.

The oddly syncopated music started to pick up, and the yishi down on the dance floor and up on the balconies grooved to it—that or some combination of it and the hallucinogenic ether, synthetic alcohol, or other recreational drugs.

Vikram sat back and smiled, feeling high.

On the outside of the large circular video screen suspended above the floor, X-rated fare had given way to something less explicit, more purely visual, nonlinear, and edited in time to the music. The video intercut moving images from nature—rainforests, beaches of sparkling black sand beside impossibly clear blue water, tropical mountain ranges topped with snow, herds of alien herbivores running over grasslands—with what Miles and Anna assumed were other long-gone urban scenes of green parks filled with masses of cavorting yishi. Another kind of porn in its way, the hyper-realistic, computer-animated imagery was an inventory of all that Our World had lost.

The yishi danced. If the images that danced on the screen above them made them at all bittersweet, they didn't show it.

*

ANNA, A LIGHT SLEEPER under normal circumstances, awoke later that night as if a switch had been flipped. It was completely dark but for the glowing lights of various electronic devices lying around or in panels on walls and tabletops. She sat up next to Miles, who was still dead to the world. She could hear him breathing heavily as he lay on his back on the butter-soft mattress. The shortness of breath came less frequently for her as she acclimated to the thin air. She felt heavier here too, not bloated or full, but denser, as if her bones were made of iron.

She tried to read her watch but couldn't without better light. Finding her purse lying on the floor beside their cocoon, she dug out a lighter she kept in there mainly to light Vikram's cigarettes when he forgot his matches. She flicked it on. Her watch read half past three, but she didn't know if that was morning or afternoon. Letting the lighter flicker out, she felt for her blister pack of Levlen and could tell she was on her last week of pills. She took one then, swallowing it dry, not sure how much longer than twenty-four hours it had been. Then she remembered these were the placebos, anyway. Her period hadn't started yet, and she'd only bothered to throw one pad in her purse, the rest nestled safely in her backpack in Granada.

Damn. Did yishi menstruate? If so, what kind of products did they have for feminine hygiene? *They probably just call it "hygiene,"* she thought. She relaxed after thinking about it. They must have something she could use when the time came, she reasoned.

She looked over at Miles, who hadn't moved since she woke up. From the dim light her eyes were beginning to adjust to, she could see his mouth was slightly open. She pushed aside a layer of blankets and touched his chest. No reaction. She gently grabbed his shoulder and tried shaking him. He stirred a bit, then lay still. She moved her hand down past his stomach. He must have been having a good dream, she thought. Carefully pulling down the red briefs he'd resented having to wear so much, she removed her own and slid on top of him. She was ready, having waited three days. And he was ready, even if he didn't know it.

He awoke just as she shuddered at consummating the deed. At first he assumed he was having an unusually vivid dream and just went with it, continuing to go along well after he realized he wasn't. For once, they finished together and collapsed in a heap, breathing hard from the exertion and oxygen deprivation.

"I think you just had your way with me," he said, panting.

"I guess I did," she admitted. She wondered if she'd have done that back home, since she'd never done it before. Maybe it was Danevesu.

"Do you think they saw us?" he asked.

"Who?"

"*They*," he said, meaning the Big Brother-y state of Danevesu.

"I doubt we could have shocked them," she said.

"True," he said. "Still, it would be novel for them."

Anna didn't like the thought of being recorded doing anything, much less that. But she took solace in how dark it was in the room.

"I can't sleep," she said.

"Me either."

"Let's get dressed and go explore," she said.

"Can we do that?"

"I suppose we'll find out," she said.

*

THEIR OWN CLOTHES had been cleaned, folded, and laid out for them by house zhinks, so they quickly dressed and made for the front door. As they were trying to figure out how to unlock it, the door slid open with a low hum. They were in the empty corridor now, lit only by the glow of the video screens, which apparently never shut off.

"Since we know we're being watched at all times," Anna said, glancing at the monitors lining the long hallway, "the important thing, it seems to me, is to not act suspicious."

"I can do that," said Miles, looking around him suspiciously.

They walked toward where they remembered a transport stop was and soon ran into one of the blue-uniformed civil guards standing in the vestibule next to the transport doors. He eyed them with evident surprise, either simply because they were human or because they were out and about when no one else was.

Anna greeted him in Danevesan, and he returned the greeting.

"Do you speak English?" she said.

He stared, uncomprehending.

"*Sprechen sie Deutsch?*"

Nothing.

"*Habla español?*"

"*Oh, sí,*" he replied. "*Un poco.*"

"*Mi amigo y me,*" we would like to go outside," she said.

You could tell he wasn't expecting that, as it took him a beat before he repeated, "Outside?"

"Yes, if it's possible," she asked as sweetly as she could.

He started playing with the smartskin on the back of his hand. Was he checking the weather, getting clearance from his higher-ups, watching porn? They didn't know, but in a few moments, he seemed satisfied. "All right," he said. "But I'll have to go with you."

"*Sí, sí,*" she said, nodding. "He's going to take us up top," she told Miles. "Outside."

Miles was impressed. "It's amazing how handy your language skills come in here, of all places," he said.

"You're welcome," she said.

They rode the transport to its upper terminus and were led into a glass-ceilinged room where two more civil guards stood behind a counter. Nodding to his fellows casually, Anna's and Miles's guard brought them over to a line of turnstiles with sliding gates. Each gate was flanked by consoles with small video screens. It conformed to Miles's vision of what a Japanese subway station would look like. The guard waved his hand in front of one of the screens and motioned for Miles to approach. A mechanical arm extended from the console, and the guard showed Miles where to put his hand. Miles held his hand out, while the mechanical arm hovered just above it and laser-inked a red symbol with Danevesan writing on it onto the back of his hand. Then it did the same for Anna. She looked at it curiously.

"What is this for?" she asked their guard in Spanish.

"So you can come back in again," he said.

"Oh."

Going through the turnstiles, they all made their way to a bank of transports screened by one of the transparent partitions they'd seen upon arriving the morning before. Their guard led them through that, and Miles reached backward after coming through, confirming that the partition was one-way, barring entry from the other direction.

Once at the top of the underground city but still enclosed in a glass-and-metal structure, they crossed over another partition and finally through a last set of sliding doors to the outside.

Before the sliding doors were open an inch, they felt it. The heat saturated every pore and made their nostrils burn the moment they stepped out onto the ground beyond the threshold that separated Danevesu from Our World. Miles and Anna had to fight the urge to turn around and go back inside (even though the way they'd come was strictly an exit). Moving slowly now, while their guard strolled nonchalantly on ahead, they conserved their energy so as to minimize the flow of sweat, which was already beading up on their foreheads and running down the small of their backs.

The exit of the vestibule was slightly below ground, so they ascended to the top level up a gradually sloped ramp. On the roof of the city, they could see a vast plain of glass and stone much like the curved façade of the city, with its honeycomb pattern covering the rooms of the apartments, labs, and offices below. Winding walkways with railings ran where corridors lay underneath, and a low parapet followed the curving line of the city's leading edge. Over Danevesu's harbor the predawn sky was lightening, turning from black to a deep reddish orange. No rain fell at the moment, but clouds continued to stream overhead as if drawn by an invisible conveyor. The nights were much longer on Our World, and it seemed the city was truly asleep now, scattered lights showing intermittent signs of life. Inland, the city reached halfway to the line of foothills on the horizon, marked by the now dark skylights of the farm. It wasn't far, in fact, as New Danevesu was tall and wide, but not very deep. The land beyond the city was barren, and even in the halflight they could see the redscale that seemed to grow over everything.

Hanging low over the foothills was what looked to Anna and Miles like a moon. Though it was larger and appeared browner and hazier than the Moon, its glowing presence in the nighttime sky brought it readily to mind. Until they remembered.

"Skygarden," said Miles, pleased with himself for realizing what it was. Anna nodded, having come to the same conclusion. Its name was an ironic joke now, or a poignant reminder of the paradise it once was.

"What do you call it?" she asked their guard in Spanish, pointing to Skygarden. He told her the Danevesan name for it. She repeated it to him, trying to get the pronunciation right, and he nodded appreciatively.

They stared at it for some time, as if it were what they had come up there for.

Eventually their eyes drifted to the stars above, visible between the clouds over the dark city. *Are any of these stars the same ones we see from Earth?* Anna thought. She wondered, too, what constellations the yishi must have created from the patterns the stars made in their sky. She tried to ask their guard, now their guide, about it, but his Spanish was not as good as hers.

Miles wandered toward the city's edge, and Anna followed, the sweat now soaking through her clothes. The parapet came up just to his waist, as Miles looked out on the harbor. A breeze would have felt nice, but all the same, he was glad none blew up just then, as the view down was terrifying.

"Oh, my," said Anna, as she walked up beside him. The view from inside the city the previous day didn't do what they now saw justice. With the sky over the harbor starting to glow brighter, the stars above began to fade as the features of the clifftop and surrounding mountains came into relief. The curving façade of Danevesu below reflected the red-orange sky, its windows catching the light.

Miles staggered back as he saw it now, its silhouette huge against the predawn sky. Off to their left was an enormous statue, rising ten meters above them, perched on the very edge of the city. As they moved closer to inspect it, Miles and Anna could see that it was carved out of the gray stone of the cliff—an anomalous outcropping on this spot transformed into a monument of some kind. The statue was of a yishi, and he was pointing up at the sky, his arm stretched at a forty-five-degree angle, with an expression on his face not of grim nobility or steely-eyed determination, but of wide-eyed wonder.

"Wow," said Miles.

"Who is it?" Anna asked their guard.

"It's Arak, of course," he said.

"So this is where we find you," came a fourth voice from some distance behind them, causing the three of them to turn abruptly. It was Vikram, walking toward them with Kerak just behind him. Anna and Miles still weren't quite accustomed to his voice, so they were relieved when they saw them. Relieved, but still surprised.

Vikram greeted them and their guard, looked up at the monument to his late parent. "What do you think of my mother?" he asked.

"He's big," said Miles.

In the gloaming, they could just make out the statue's face, and despite its rendering in stone, it did resemble Araviku, Arak's ghost.

"You were right," said Anna. "You do look like him."

"Is he pointing toward Earth?" asked Miles.

"Not at the moment, no," said Vikram. "Not ever, actually. Earth is more or less on a line with Our World's south pole—not that you'd be able to see it or even the Sun from here, it's too far away for even the old orbital telescopes. But I guess they thought it made more sense to have Arak pointing to the sky, rather than at his feet."

"Ah."

"We were looking for you," said Kerak. "We wanted to show you around the harbor village and the docks."

"Before dawn?" asked Anna. Kerak glanced at Vikram.

"We thought, what better place to see your first sunrise than from the wharf?" said Vikram. "The sun rises in the west, you know."

"How do we get there?" said Miles, who had no idea which direction west was. He also didn't seeing any trams or other forms of transit up there.

"We walk, mostly," said Vikram.

"It's a little hot for that, isn't it?" said Anna.

Vikram had his old satchel slung behind his back, and he pulled from it a pair of hooded cloaks. "Put these on," he said.

"Thanks, we're hot enough as it is," she said.

"Trust me," he said.

They were heavier than they looked, as Anna and Miles took them from Vikram grudgingly. Once they slipped them on, however, they felt the welcome chill hit their upper bodies. "Oh," they said.

Vikram laughed and shrugged at their guard, who had been wearing something similar the whole time.

Miles pulled his hood over his head, and the relief was even more dramatic. "You've got to try it with the hood," he said to Anna.

Vikram began speaking to their guard in Danevesan, apparently negotiating something, as the guard didn't want to let them go off on their own. But somehow Vikram and Kerak convinced him, and they were soon on their way across the top of the city toward the harbor community and then down a ramped switchback before arriving at a stepped path carved into the side of the rock that led down to the cluster of buildings that constituted the village.

Down among the modest sleepy buildings, they found the lifthouse, its red light aglow, and watched as Our World's sun rose above the sea, red and huge above the horizon. When the doors to the lift opened, Vikram, instead of boarding with the others, removed his satchel, cloak, and tunic and handed them to Kerak. Extending his arms like a conductor, he unfurled his veined, wrinkled wings and stood over the edge of the platform, naked to the waist.

"Um, Vikram, do you thi—" started Anna just as he jumped.

He floated—or fell slowly—down and out beyond the lower-level platform. He was angling for the center of the platform as best he could, his arms flapping once or twice in an attempt to both steer and slow his descent. He managed to land on the platform, but hit it hard, skidding and then rolling to a stop just before going over the far side.

He popped up, a little wobbly. "I'm okay!" he yelled up to the others, who were peering at him over the railing next to the lift.

"I think he's been holding that in for a while," said Kerak.

"I think you're right," said Miles, as they got on the lift and rode it down to meet him.

They met Vikram below, where he looked sweaty but happy. Retrieving his clothes from Kerak, he dressed while Anna and Miles looked around. There were a few black submersible fins sticking out of the water, but only one seemed to have any activity surrounding it. Beyond the platform, on the dock, a handful of yishi in hoods were busily carrying boxes up the ramp to their sub and running back and forth to the dwindling stacks, loading supplies and cargo, presumably. They were the only ones on the dock as Vikram led the others over to take a look.

"So what are we doing here?" asked Miles.

Vikram was slinging his satchel over his shoulder and then raised his hood. "Well…" he said.

He wasn't able to finish his thought before one of the sailors threw a cloth sack over his head while three others did the same to Anna, Miles, and Kerak. The sailors quickly bound their arms and legs with some kind of self-sealing bands, making it impossible for them to fight back. Anna and Miles yelled out, though their voices were muffled by the bags over their heads. The other sailors joined in to help carry them away, whispering instructions while their abductees writhed and shouted in protest. In a matter of seconds, they had carried them up the ramp and into the bowels of the sub.

Anna and Miles, having given up yelling, could tell they were inside the craft from the echoing sounds of the hull. Their heads inside the cloth sacks, they could see nothing, nor could they move. Next they heard the sound of the hatch closing, and Vikram whispered urgently to them, "Everything will be fine—don't worry!"

Terrified and confused, Anna and Miles lay on their backs next to each other, struggling against the bands that held them and wondering if they should say something.

One of the kidnappers leaned down close to them and whispered in English, "You okay? All right? Not hurt?"

"Yes," said Miles, responding to the first two questions. "No," said Anna, responding to the last.

The kidnapper paused. "Okay."

Now they heard the electric motor quietly whine and hum, and they were moving through the water, then under it, out of the harbor and into open ocean. The last thing they heard before the sacks came off their heads was the sound of muffled laughter.

12.

ANDERS EMERGED from the operating room about a foot-and-a-half shorter than when he entered. He still had the same confident strut and superior sneer as he led his companion out the door and onto the gallery overlooking a large, dilapidated atrium.

"So," said the doctor, which in Bandary also made him a priest, "did you enjoy your time on Earth?"

"Of course I did," said Anders, trying to forget the recent events in Portugal. The doctor-priest raised an orange eyebrow at him. "I enjoyed being big, for one thing," Anders said and turned, continuing down a hallway of the pyramid-like fortress that was Lagar Temu palace, the doctor falling in beside him. "Such a wonderful feeling, looking down on everyone. I definitely enjoyed that. And human sex is oddly enjoyable. Each partner having just the one set of genitalia feels almost transgressive…exciting in a way."

"Oh, my."

"I also enjoyed not having to eat my own shit for a change."

"The sensory pleasures, yes," said the doctor. "You've always had a weakness for those."

"Everyone does," said Anders. He stopped to adjust his brassiere, which because of the yishi's winged anatomy was more like a sling secured around his neck. "I did miss having breasts, I have to admit. So strange walking around flat-chested."

"What about the planet itself? The culture? The people?"

"Overpopulated, gaudy, violent," said Anders, who resumed walking. "Much like Our World used to be, I imagine."

"The culture is gaudy and the people are violent?" the doctor asked. "Or the other way round?"

"Either works."

"You know, we understand so little about Earth compared to your brethren in Danevesu," the doctor said. "I hope you at least gathered records while you were there."

"They're not my brethren. Besides, I wasn't there to do anthropological fieldwork," said Anders sarcastically.

"Neither was Araviku," the other replied. "It would seem one of you failed in your mission."

Anders stopped and tried to look down at the doctor, despite his being half a head shorter. "The chances of successfully making off with Viku's gene bank were always slim," he began. "It took me years just to find him. The theft was worth the attempt, though, and I almost made it."

"Almost," the doctor sniffed.

"But it doesn't change anything," said Anders. "Did you think I would rely on such a long shot as my only strategy?"

"You have a secondary plan?"

"Stealing the case *was* the secondary plan," he said and continued on.

The doctor hated the way Danevesans spoke in riddles and allusions, always concealing their meaning. Why couldn't he just say what he meant?

Anders slowed as their corridor came to an end at a crossing hall. "This way," said the doctor, motioning to the right with a patronizing smile. They were in the heart of the palace, in the maze of long hallways that seemed to go on forever. Coming out the other side about halfway up the pyramid—the higher you went, the more powerful the office— they entered a vaulted tunnel leading into one of the small domes that sprouted up along each of the palace's three sides. Anders followed the doctor-priest until they came to a colored-glass screen blocking their way, with two draped entrances on either side. Turning left, Anders went ahead of his companion and pushed aside the mouse-turd brown drape and entered the spacious circular room under the cupola.

It was a once-grand space, still impressive in its size and as a reminder of how thoroughly things had deteriorated. The stepped platforms leading to the center were warped and uneven, the finish long gone, and large cracks and treacherous holes exposing conduit created a sort of mine field for visitors. Reddish-brown dust hung in the air, illuminated by beams of sunlight peeking through the narrow band of windows at the base of the dome. An ornately carved round bed sat in the middle of a raised circular platform in the center of the room. Even more sumptuous than the cocoons in Kerak's flat, the bed also featured eight posts supporting colorful curtains and gauzy fabric screens. From each post hung a gaslamp fixture, unilluminated, as there was precious little gas left on Our World. On top of the bed lay a soft, overfed, sickly pale yishi, the minister Salas, whispering with an underling.

Several others were huddled together at a table next to the huge bed, poring over their handheld screens and talking quietly in the musical Bandarian dialect of the capital. The minister's back was propped up and a glass monitor positioned to his left side, the underling to his right now whispering in his ear as Anders and the doctor approached up the steps.

The minister's rheumy eyes lit up as Anders and the doctor-priest came into view. "Dar Telesu," said Salas, addressing Anders with the honorific before his given Danevesan nickname. "You've returned safely to us. Thank Gee."

"Yes, thank you, Dar Salas," said Anders.

"My lord," said the doctor, bowing.

"You may leave us, Oliph," said the minister, addressing the doctor by his familiar name.

Oliph hesitated, then bowed again, backing away obsequiously from the minister before turning to step down off the platform and leaving the hall.

Salas looked at Anders, his aide standing officiously to his right. "Did I hear correctly, Telesu, that you failed to retrieve the alien gene bank?"

"You did," said Anders.

"Should I be concerned?" he asked.

"Not at all."

"So you know where it is now?"

"I think so," said Anders.

"You think—" he began. "And you have a plan for recovering it, I assume?"

"Of course," he said. "I only require—"

"I don't need to know," said Salas, interrupting. "In fact, it's better if I don't. I am trusting you, Telesu. I know you are not among the faithful. But I also know that you hate Araviku and the Danevesans even more than I do." That wasn't precisely true. Anders hated *all* yishi, including the Bandarians, and what Our World was reduced to, even more than Salas. "Dar Peleg here," Salas now pointed to one of the yishi standing around the table away from the others, "is authorized to get you whatever you need. Go with him. Report back once you've succeeded. Bring me the gene bank. I want to see it with my own eyes before I destroy it." Turning to Peleg, he added, "You'll be in charge of the guards under you, but remember, Telesu is in command of the mission."

Peleg bowed in assent. It seemed Salas didn't trust anyone fully.

He dismissed them both, and Peleg led Anders out through a hidden rear exit and down a stairway that led to a gallery overlooking the city's old main square. Through thin vertical strips of glass on one of the sloped sides of the palace, they could see yishi in rags crowding the filthy square, agitated and angry about something. A three-deep line of Revolutionary Guards formed a barrier around Lagar Temu's main entrance at one corner of the three-sided pyramid's base. The palace and several of the buildings around it were the few structures left in the capital with dependable electricity or indoor plumbing, or that didn't blow away in a windstorm.

"We need soldiers," said Anders, looking down at the guards in their body armor. "And then we'll need to travel to the port of Ashedel and commandeer a submersible."

Peleg shuddered at the thought of an ocean voyage, even as the sun was temporarily blotted out of the sky by windblown dust and sand. "Are you sure that's necessary?"

The sun reappeared, then quickly disappeared as a massive dust cloud descended on the crowd in the square, dispersing the protesters as the guards looked on behind the darkened face-masks of their helmets.

From where Anders and Peleg stood, it was quiet, even as dirt and debris blasted the windows overlooking the scene below, now obscured completely by the swirling dust storm.

Anders laughed. "Yes, it's necessary," he said. "We can't drive to where we need to go to. And we certainly can't fly. I take it you've never left this island?"

"No," Peleg admitted. "Will we be going far?"

"Not as far as I've just come," said Anders. Which wasn't really an answer.

23.

THE MUFFLED LAUGHTER had grown louder with the addition of another voice, one Miles recognized as belonging to Kerak. This didn't strike him as a particularly good sign. Miles had heard of Stockholm Syndrome, of course, but he assumed it usually took longer than a few minutes to take hold.

And then the bags were lifted from their heads, and they could see that only three of the kidnappers had stayed on board the craft. One of them sat up front, at the helm, while the other two helped remove the bands from around their arms and legs.

Vikram was sitting up on the floor across from them, next to Kerak. "First off, sorry about that," he said.

"Huh?" said Anna, speaking for her and Miles, as they looked around the cramped space.

"It was the only way I could figure to get us out of Danevesu without being branded an outlaw."

"It's against the law to leave?" asked Anna, rubbing her legs and eyeing her erstwhile captors suspiciously.

"For what we're doing, yes," he said. "And I couldn't just leave you there. These are friends of ours—Shikar, Dinev," Vikram indicated the two with them, who waved sheepishly in turn. "And that's Erestu up front, driving."

"Hello again," said Erestu, turning his head around and giving a wave.

They recognized him from the club the night before. "So..." Miles said, shaking his head, "this was a fake kidnapping?"

"You sound disappointed," said Vikram.

"No, not exactly," he said. "But you could have asked us beforehand."

"You forget the surveillance," said Vikram. "It follows us everywhere in the city." Vikram held up his left hand.

"Right. I did forget. So who are we trying to fool?"

"Tchuvu and the council, mainly," said Vikram.

"And who is supposed to have kidnapped us?"

"Bandarian terrorists—or at least that's what I assume they'll think," he said. "It's the sort of thing they might do."

"It is?"

"Them or the Revolutionary Guard—Bandary military," he explained.

"Oh."

"How many groups want to abduct us?" asked Anna.

"Probably just the two," said Vikram.

"Why?" Anna asked.

"To secure a *casus belli*," he said.

"A what?" said Miles.

"A justification for war," said Anna.

"To prove that we'd brought humans to Our World, violating the treaty," said Vikram.

"I see," said Anna. "So when you said you'd explain everything in time, you meant after you kidnapped us?"

"Yes," he said. "We're safely out of range and can speak freely now."

"Good," she said. "Then you can explain the secrecy around the gene bank and why the council seems to think your only mission was to bring us back from Earth."

"That was supposed to be the only mission," he said. "That and collecting more data, exploring, and observing. The gene bank was *my* mission. But if they knew I'd brought back a case full of Type 2 organisms, they'd have locked me up or exiled me."

"Why?"

Kerak spoke up. "Aside from the threat of contagion, it's against international law. When we signed the treaty with Bandary and Cardevise, Arak had already been to Earth and retrieved human DNA. When they found out, we had to promise not to bring back any more potentially invasive species, and to keep the human fluppets confined to the city."

"But wait," she said, "if the council wanted you to bring back ambassadors, isn't that just as illegal as the gene bank?"

"Yes, but your arrival is a state secret," said Kerak. "No one outside Danevesu is supposed to know. Beyond that, however, the gene bank has implications for all of Our World. You two were never meant to stay on Our World, just facilitate our…departure."

Miles and Anna stared at Kerak and then at Vikram. "Sorry," she finally said, "your what?"

One of the kidnappers, Dinev, spoke up. "Maybe I can show you," he said cheerfully, intently fiddling with his smartskin.

"Good idea," said Vikram.

Just like that, Dinev projected a hologram into the middle of the rear section of the sub, while Shikar dimmed the lights. Zooming past a large yellow sun, a small red rock, and a cloudy pink ball, a blue-green planet came into view.

"Earth," said Miles snarkily. "We're familiar with it."

Earth spun around as the image zoomed into the surface, the western hemisphere now filling up the room, close enough for Miles and Anna to touch. Now the west coast of South America was enlarged. On the northwest corner of a small cape, a city could be made out.

"Where is this?" Miles asked Anna.

"Looks like Ecuador," she said.

The image kept zooming in until the city took up their entire field of vision, and then the point of view tilted ninety degrees to afford a perspective that floated above the streets and around the buildings and landscaped gardens of the metropolis. It was like no city Miles and Anna had ever seen. Or, rather, it was very reminiscent of the city they had just recently glimpsed under water in the harbor. Old Danevesu, only clean and above sea level.

"Maybe not Ecuador," said Anna.

"It is Ecuador," said Vikram. "The city isn't real, though. Just a speculative model superimposed over Ecuador's sparsely populated Emerald Coast."

In the imaginary city, Yishi and human figures strolled side by side down tree-lined streets. An outdoor café staffed by hovering zhinks served human and yishi guests, laughing and conversing with one another in exaggerated gestures of friendship and goodwill.

As it began to dawn on Anna and Miles what this presentation was meant to suggest, the Sun in the hologram set over the Pacific and lights twinkled on across the skyline. Danevesan writing appeared, superimposed over the image of the twilit city, and remained as the vista faded to black. "*That's* New Danevesu," said Vikram.

"They want to colonize Earth?" said Miles.

Vikram shrugged, looked to Kerak and Dinev, who clearly knew more about it than he did. "They don't think we can last much longer on Our World," said Kerak.

"When were they planning on springing this on us?" asked Anna.

"Well, they weren't," said Kerak. "You're just the first phase of a multi-step plan."

"Tchuvu is running a long con," said Vikram. Kerak and Anna stared at him blankly, while Miles looked surprised, understanding the term's meaning. "He's trying to gain your confidence. So that by the time some other event or emergency takes place on Our World, it won't even be his idea. Some future ambassador will suggest it for him."

"Ahh," said Miles, impressed. "That's sneaky."

"Some of us are still interested in saving Our World," said Dinev. "I believe in reaching out to humans as much as anyone. But what Tchuvu's planning is dangerous and misguided."

Miles considered it, shaking his head. "Americans go apeshit when people cross over into our country from Mexico," he said. "I have a hard time believing they'd be okay with immigrants from another planet—even if they were confined to Ecuador."

"Yes," said Anna. "Humans don't have the best track record when it comes to accepting refugees."

"Well, Tchuvu is a short-sighted twat," said Kerak. "And he's desperate. He sees this as a transaction, rather than a free exchange. In payment for allowing Danevesans to settle on Earth, humans would receive access to our technology—advanced medicine, computers, bioengineering, a unified field theory."

"So, just Danevesans?" asked Miles.

"As I say," said Kerak, "a transaction."

"But why is he desperate?" asked Anna. "I would think with your technology, you could find other habitable planets easily."

All the yishi but Shikar, who didn't speak English, chuckled at that. "You would have no way of knowing this, I know," said Dinev, "but do you know how many star systems our ancestors investigated before finding intelligent life? Or any life at all? More than eight-and-a-half billion. Starting with our own galaxy, then branching out to neighboring galaxies, and finally searching at random before finding a world with even rudimentary life. The planets that had life on them made up less than one-ten-thousandth of one percent of the ones we looked at. We knew our system, having had two life-supporting planets, was unusual. But we had no idea. After searching through more billions of systems, we finally came across your world about sixty years ago."

"Over a hundred Earth years," said Vikram.

"Why's that?" asked Anna.

"Our years are about twice as long," he explained.

"Anyway," said Dinev, "that's why Tchuvu's desperate. Earth is the only planet we've ever come across with anything like intelligent life, and we've been continuing to search ever since."

Anna and Miles weren't sure what Dinev meant by "*like* intelligent life," but let it go.

"What makes Tchuvu's strategy dangerous," said Vikram, "is that this may be the only opportunity yishi ever get to make contact with other intelligent life…and likewise for humankind."

"I never thought about it like that," said Anna.

"I'm glad that Tchuvu at least agreed to make contact the way we did," said Vikram. "But if we reveal ourselves to the whole of humankind before we're ready, when we're in a desperate position—or before humans are ready—it won't end well for anyone."

*

SHIKAR BROUGHT UP the lights in the cabin, which helped make the conversation seem a little less ominous. The four "captives" were still sitting on the floor and Dinev helped them find more comfortable seats.

"So can I ask where we're heading?" said Anna.

"East, to an island in the Edrisian Archipelago," said Vikram. "Twenty-six."

"As in, the island is called 'Twenty-six'?" she said.

"When so many new islands were created by the cataclysm," said Vikram, "we got a little lazy about naming them."

"Okay," she said. "What's on Twenty-six?"

"There's a research station there. It's run by a former colleague of mine called Berejian. He's a botanist and geneticist, and he's quite brilliant. The farm at Danevesu is only able to feed the city because of the technology he developed. He's also been able to successfully splice DNA from animals and microorganisms into plants, but he can only work with what little genetic diversity we have left. I'm hoping the samples I've gathered on Earth might provide the raw materials he needs."

"To do what exactly?" she asked.

"Develop crops that will grow outdoors," he said. "You've seen the redscale. It keeps any plant life from growing. We've tried everything to eradicate it, but nothing will. If Berejian can develop a plant that's resistant, that can grow in that, it would be a real reason for hope."

"How long before we get there?" asked Miles

"About a day and a half," he said.

"And what happens when we return to Danevesu?" asked Anna.

"We'll have been miraculously rescued," said Vikram.

"What if someone else, like Bandarian terrorists, really do kidnap us before then?" she asked.

"They'd have to find us first," Vikram pointed out.

"What about Anders?" she said. "He found us once."

Vikram shook his head. "Anders doesn't know about Berejian. And I don't think he's working with the Bandarians. He's a mercenary, and I doubt their fanaticism would appeal to him."

"You said you knew him, didn't you?" said Miles.

This was news to Anna.

"Yes, I did," said Vikram. "He's a Danevesan, like us. He worked with me in the biology labs years ago. His name was Telesu. I mentored him, or tried to. He was quite brilliant, but he sold our technology to the Cardevisi—the technology that allowed us to migrate consciousness."

"That's not all," said Kerak.

"No," said Vikram, clearly discomfited. "Before he was caught, he committed murder in his attempt to cover up what he'd done."

Kerak almost added something, then decided against it.

"Hold on," said Anna. "I was dating a murderer, and you *knew*?"

"No, of course I didn't know," he said. "Suspected *something*, maybe, but not that. Something about Anders did seem off to me, I grant....But I never—I didn't think it was possible anybody from Our World could track me down, but the idea of that happening *and* its being Telesu—Anders, I mean—I would have never imagined it."

"When did you know?" asked Miles. "In Granada?"

"Yes," said Vikram. "When he appeared in the butcher shop. His manner had changed, it was so...familiar."

"So who are the Cardevisi?" asked Miles.

"Cardevise used to be a large country east of Edrisia. Now it's an island chain on what's left of its old central mountain range," he said. "They were once our allies, a democratic republic, but they've since devolved into a sort of cartel, a loose confederation of anarcho-capitalist states. My guess is Anders is still working for one or more of the Cardevisi oligarchs, who'll sell the gene bank to the highest bidder."

"If Anders had been caught, how did he escape Danevesu?" asked Anna.

"He didn't escape," said Vikram. "There are only a few prison cells in Danevesu, and no death penalty. For really serious crimes, the worst thing they can do is exile you, which is practically a death sentence—usually. But apparently Anders had friends to help him."

DINEV SHOWED their guests to their berths, hammock-like bunks stretched two up and two across in each of the two sleeping quarters. Miles could see they were clearly not built for six-foot-tall humans.

Although there was no such title on either civilian or military subs, Erestu was the de facto captain of the boat, the one with the most knowledge and experience and the one the others looked to when in doubt. Shikar functioned as the sub's navigator and engineer, while Dinev, whose job was everything else, showed them around the sub. Erestu sat at the front console with a large concave screen showing the sea directly in front of them. Large screens along the sides showed the view outside, making it look like the sub was covered with large, curved windows. There wasn't much to see, though. They were about a hundred meters below the surface, so it was fairly dark. But there was no marine life, other than the occasional gray gelatinous blob that floated by, sometimes a scattered group of them, their feathery filaments dangling below, emanating a subtle bioluminescent glow.

Dinev sat Anna and Miles down at a console along the port side and showed them some of the features of the sub's computer, superimposing another "window" on top of the image of the mostly featureless seascape outside. Text appeared onscreen, which Anna and Miles recognized as the hieroglyphic-looking Danevesan language they'd seen everywhere in the city.

"Does Danevesan use a logographic alphabet?" Anna asked.

"That?" said Dinev. "Oh, that's not Danevesan. That's Script. It is logographic, but Script is exclusively a written language. It doesn't correspond to any spoken one."

"So you don't speak it, just read it?" said Anna.

"Well, I tend to hear it in Danevesan," said Dinev. "But it can be read aloud as any language. It's universal."

This was interesting to Anna, so Dinev showed them how it worked. Reading Script from bottom to top in columns that go from left to right, subjects are placed at the bottom, with verbs above them. Modifiers float to their left, while objects go to the right of the verbs. Logograms that formed a sentence were all connected, and a break indicated a new one. As a written language, it was incredibly economical, taking up much less space than the equivalent text written in English or Spanish. And the logograms were surprisingly sophisticated. Subtle differences in their construction could signal wildly different meanings. Even though the "alphabet" of logograms was huge, there were basic forms upon which you could build, and Dinev showed them how this was accomplished with deft finger movements that seemed like another kind of sign language.

"Have yishi always used Script?" asked Anna.

"No, it's actually fairly recent," he said. "Danevesan still has its own phonographic written language, which was used for thousands of years.

So does everyone else. But no one uses them anymore. Script was developed sometime before the cataclysm," he said. "Before smartskin, they had other handheld communication devices. At some point, a developer put out a set of small icons that could replace simple words or phrases, to make it easier to key in long messages. A group of linguists started to play with this original set, simplifying the icons and expanding the vocabulary, developing a syntax and grammar. Soon, everyone was using this new Script and just stopped typing messages in their traditional written languages. Devices started coming out with Script key sets and eventually dropped the letters of the older spoken languages altogether."

"That's amazing," said Anna. "It's like Esperanto, only successful."

She had to explain to Dinev what Esperanto was, and things quickly degenerated into the kind of inside-baseball discussion only a linguist could appreciate. Dinev pulled up examples of old texts in Danevesan and Edrisian, which segued into more primers in learning spoken Danevesan and basic Script, much to Anna's delight.

It didn't take long for Miles's eyes to glaze over, so he looked for something to do. He found Erestu at the helm, moving windows on the desktop screen by wiggling his fingers, and said, "Hey."

"Hello," said Erestu.

"You speak English?" asked Miles.

"Of course," he said.

Miles thought of his mother, worried that he wouldn't be able to communicate with anyone in Europe. *They don't speak English everywhere, you know*, she'd said. If only she knew.

Erestu explained to Miles how the sub was normally steered by the computer, its present course preset. He switched the autopilot off and showed Miles how to control the boat manually with the joystick-like lever. It was fairly intuitive, like a videogame, and since they weren't close enough to anything to be in danger, Erestu let Miles take the helm for a while. Though the view was monotonous, Miles found that he liked the sensation of steering the twenty-five-meter, hundred-tonne boat through the water. He made a game of spotting and then running down any of the alien jellyfish they came across.

By the time Vikram suggested they get some breakfast, Anna and Miles were already famished. Fortunately for them, the galley was well stocked with tubs of red goo. "Dinev was trying to explain your written language to me," Anna said to Vikram as they sat down to scarf down the sweet gelum. They talked for a while about Script's massive character set, its simplified grammar, and other interesting facets of the universal text that sailed far above Miles's head.

"I got to drive the sub," he muttered to no one in particular.

*

LATER, MILES REJOINED Anna as Dinev tried to teach them a few words and phrases of spoken Danevesan and their Script equivalents. Miles managed to learn a little bit. But he could see his remedial language skills were holding Anna back. Shikar seemed nice enough, but Miles soon realized the navigator's English was as limited as Miles's Danevesan. Vikram and Kerak were off again somewhere canoodling, so Miles sought out Erestu again.

Erestu was as fascinated with Miles as Miles was with the controls of the sub. Surrounding the joystick, mounted on the front edge and to the right on the large glass console, were various color-coded displays, which Erestu could manipulate by gesture. Erestu explained what some of the instruments were. One showed a three-dimensional relief map of the seafloor in front of them. Others displayed their rate of speed, depth, reactor level, air, et cetera. Miles had no idea how fast they were going, as speed was measured in an alien unit of distance per some other alien unit of time. Regardless, Erestu let Miles take the helm again. Practiced at it by now, he steered the boat casually with one eye on the hi-res sonar and another on Erestu, who gazed at Miles with uninhibited curiosity. Like most yishi Miles had met, Erestu had the characteristic high cheekbones and pointed, bird-like beak. But his face was softer, more inviting perhaps than the cold beauty of the other yishi. He, like his fellow crew members, dressed in an all-black version of Danevesan business casual: long-sleeved baggy tunic, ankle-length leggings, and feathery bare feet.

While Miles was furtively observing Erestu observe him, a shudder rippled through the entire sub, as if some aquatic giant had shoved against their starboard flank, causing the craft to roll sharply to port and then back again.

"What'd I do?" said Miles, a little panicked, scanning the monitors for a cause of the turbulence.

"Nothing," said Erestu. "Look there." He indicated a screen that showed a blinking orange light in the middle of a 3D map of a long ridge on the seafloor ahead of them.

"What is it?" asked Miles.

"Seismic activity," said Erestu. "The light shows the quake's epicenter. Not terribly strong—probably just be a minor tsunami."

"How far away is it?" asked Miles.

"About twenty or so scela," he said. A scela was about a half-mile, though Erestu didn't know what a mile was. "That's about, uh…well, not very far. We should pass by it soon."

As the boat stopped rocking, Miles calmed down but was still happy to let Erestu take back control of the ship. Soon the sea in front of them began to turn cloudy, and the light that had penetrated the depths they navigated began to be blotted out by the combination of steam, sediment, and smoke they were heading into.

"There might have been some volcanic activity," Erestu mused, unperturbed.

According to the sonar map, they were passing within a few scela of the source of the eruption, and were soon past it. In a few moments the ocean in front of them began to lighten in an odd way. Instead of diffuse sunlight illuminating the brownish water above them, the water seemed to be roiling with light gray orbs all around them.

It was a zooplankton bloom.

Just as they had made their way out of the gray cloud created by the gash in the seafloor behind them, they had blundered into a massive cloud of zooplankton—jellies—a common marine hazard on Our World. With these types of blooms, millions or even billions of adult jellies could clog twenty or thirty cubic scela worth of ocean. These jellyfish were remarkably large, about two meters across with masses of long, angel-hair tentacles streaming down and billowing around.

"Let's try this," said Erestu, confidently pressing a switch that caused the immediate area outside the sub to strobe with bright white light—an electric shock, as if the boat were a giant cattle prod. Unfortunately, instead of dispersing the jellies, it only seemed to draw them in closer and tighter.

"Damn." Erestu clearly hadn't expected that.

Now the sub was completely surrounded, the boulder-sized jellies blocking out all light but that emanating from themselves and reflected by the boat's running lights, trapping the craft in a dense swarm of undulating gelatinous slime. Gradually, and with sickening inevitability, the sub slowed to a stop.

"What's happening?" asked Anna, who had come forward with the others.

"The propulsion system won't work with those things blocking the intakes and exhaust vents," said Erestu.

"What can we do?" asked Miles.

"We could wait and see if they disperse on their own," Erestu said, thinking out loud.

"So they'll just move on?" she said.

"Well…I don't really know," he said. "Their behavior's hard to predict, and I've never come across this species before."

"Oh." That didn't sound encouraging.

"Another option is to try ascending to the surface," said Erestu.

"Will that get us out of this swarm?" asked Miles.

"It might," he said. "With recent quakes, though, it's usually a good idea to stay well below the surface. There are usually aftershocks, which can cause more tsunamis. Of course, we could also dive down."

"Well, why don't we do that?"

"That could present other problems," said Erestu, stroking his feathers nervously. "We can only go so deep before we reach a point of no return, and we can't gauge our depth with any accuracy inside this swarm."

"Oh," said Miles. "And by 'point of no return,' you mean…"

"Implosion. We'd get squished."

Before Miles could respond, Shikar wedged in between them and began talking animatedly to Erestu in Danevesan. Vikram joined in, and suddenly everyone was at the front of the sub looking out at the over-sized monitors in equal parts disgust and dread.

After a little more conversation, Vikram turned to Anna and Miles and said in English, "It doesn't make sense to try and do anything at the moment. We're going to wait a while and see what happens."

Erestu nodded and then shook his head. "I can't understand why the electric shock seemed to stimulate them," he said. "It's one of the few defense systems we have, and it usually works with these types of swarms."

"I know of at least one variety of jelly that feeds off of electrical current," said Vikram. "But you could fit four of that species in the palm of your hand. Nothing like these."

"Man, these things are weird," said Miles.

"In most other respects, they behave pretty much like jellyfish on Earth," said Vikram.

"Oh," said Miles

"That doesn't really help much," said Anna.

Vikram tried to explain. "Mature jellyfish like these come from polyps—immature jellies that attach to some hard surface, kind of like coral do—same as jellyfish on Earth. When they're ready to become adults, they detach from the seafloor or wherever and float away. For some reason, sometimes they seem to do it en masse and create these giant blooms. That also occurs on Earth, just with much less frequency. We still don't really understand why it happens."

"So their behavior's a mystery on Our World just as it is on Earth," said Anna.

Vikram nodded. "When I first saw images of them as a child, I thought they looked like some sort of alien creature," he said. "I remember thinking how ironic it was when I found out you had them as well."

Anna and Miles looked around at the monitors, covered completely by the creatures.

"Some of the species are edible, of course," said Vikram. "But mostly they're just a nuisance."

Now they sat and waited inside the jellyfish bloom.

Being close to the quake's epicenter, they felt a number of aftershocks, none nearly as violent as the first, though it could be the jellies were absorbing some of the shockwaves, as they wrapped the sub in a kind of living bubble-wrap.

On Our World, the passage of time was measured by a combination of natural and artificial units, just as on Earth. A Tonshu year—the time it took the planet to orbit its sun—lasted 412.6723 days, so the typical year was 413 days, but every third year skipped a day to account for the cumulative remainder. Each day, which was about twice as long as an Earth day, was divided into thirty-two dibs (40, counting in base-8), which were each subdivided into sixty-four dibels, which were further subdivided into 256 mims. After a couple of dibs, or a about three hours, the sub was still encased in the swarm of jellyfish.

Knowing they couldn't wait indefinitely, the crew discussed their options with Vikram and Kerak, with Anna and Miles looking on, uncertain how concerned they should be. Erestu finally decided they would make a limited, timed dive, giving themselves a safe buffer before reaching collapse depth. Vikram, filling in Anna and Miles, explained that jellyfish blooms tended to migrate to the surface, so going down was the logical first move.

In tense silence, Erestu took the controls and began the slow descent. With the instruments unable to guide them, Shikar kept track of the time, hoping his estimate of their rate of descent was accurate. With the naked eye, it was at first impossible to even tell they were descending, as the enormous jellies clung to the side of the boat with some tenacity before gradually sliding up, only to be replaced by more gray, mucousy blobs. Soon, however, the auditory evidence of their dive began to impress itself on the ears of those aboard. The creaks and groans of the sub's hull confirmed they were indeed going down, but provided scant comfort. After about ten dibels, the sub's quarters seemed to visibly contract, and the air pressure increased to the point of causing acute headaches. Aside from the upward movement of jellyfish, the scene outside hadn't altered. The jellies still surrounded them. Erestu decided they had to stop.

A submarine doesn't stop on a dime (or whatever the equivalent unit of currency on Our World is). Thus there were some tense moments as Erestu manipulated the controls to reverse their dive and begin their ascent, while the sub continued to move inexorably downward. Finally, their descent came to a halt, and gradually, to the great relief of all, the sub began to lift toward the surface.

Miles exhaled audibly. He hadn't realized he'd been holding his breath. He wasn't the only one. "Let's not do that again," said Anna, whose knuckles were almost white from gripping the edge of her seat.

Nothing, however, had changed with respect to their original problem. The jellyfish didn't seem to be going anywhere, and surfacing could invite other complications, as the aftershocks from the quake continued to intermittently remind them.

"If we can surface," said Erestu, "we should at least be able to get proper readings from our instruments again."

"But we'll be more exposed to wave fluctuations," said Vikram.

"Another tsunami, you mean?" asked Anna.

"Yes, but we're oriented away from the quake's source," said Erestu. "In the event, I think we'd be unlikely to roll."

"Rolling would be bad," Vikram agreed.

"First rule of piloting a sub," Erestu said. "Don't turn the boat upside-down."

Perhaps it was Erestu's cavalier attitude, or simply fatigue, or maybe getting carried away by a tsunami paled in comparison with the idea of being crushed under a thousand meters of ocean, but the tension Anna and Miles had felt during the dive lifted with the sub, and the two fell asleep where they sat before they even reached the surface.

If anyone aboard was the least bit surprised when, upon the sub's bridge breaking above the waves, they found themselves still firmly ensconced within the jellyfish bloom, they didn't show it. Erestu looked at his instruments and enlarged the image of the most troubling one.

"The hell," he said and brought up another image on the desktop, the perspective of the bridge's-eye camera. "Hmm." With a shake of his head, he got up and moved aft to access the bridge. Climbing the narrow ladder, he opened the hatch to the bridge with a press of his thumb. While the others watched him with a mixture of curiosity and resignation, Erestu looked through the only analog instrument on the sub. A simple periscope that allowed him to see with, more or less, his own eyes what they were in the middle of.

Erestu sighed and climbed back down, the hatch closing automatically above him. He sat back down at the helm and brought up the first sonar image that hadn't looked right to him. "This is right," he said. The image showed an enormous blob covering dozens of square kilometers (or scela) of ocean. It wasn't a static or solid shape, but a fluid, oscillating thing. "We don't show up anywhere within this mass, but I think we're about here," he said pointing to a spot somewhere between the middle of it and its right-hand edge.

"How do you know?" asked Vikram.

"Because that's the only direction in which I could see ocean," he said, meaning to the right.

"What's that?" said Vikram, pointing to a much more distinct, unnatural shape about ten scela from the amorphous giant goober they were hidden inside, moving across the upper-right corner of the sonar display.

"Another sub," said Erestu with obvious surprise. He examined its profile and quickly tried to gauge its speed. "It's military from the looks of it—probably Bandarian, moving fast, though I don't know what they'd be doing out here."

"We can see them," said Anna. "That means they can see us."

"I don't think so," he said.

"Why?" she asked. "They have sonar too, don't they?"

"Yes, but we can't see ourselves—look." Erestu showed Anna and the others the situation according to the sonar. They were invisible, at least according to their own instruments, wrapped in the slimy embrace of millions of giant jellyfish.

"We've stopped, so there's no noise from our propulsion," he explained, "and we've only been using passive sonar since we surfaced. They can't see us here."

Anna nodded, feeling reassured.

"Just, you know…try not to make any loud noises for a while," he added.

That was less reassuring. Anna sat back down silently.

Shikar and Vikram hovered over Erestu, as they kept an eye on the other sub and the instruments, peppering Erestu with the occasional whispered question or observation. Miles and Anna sat across from Kerak, who tucked one leg under the other and looked on unconcerned. Dinev hunched over his terminal, working on something presumably related to their current predicament.

Once again, all they could do was wait—this time, until the Bandarian sub moved far enough away to be safely out of its sonar range—and now hoping that the jellyfish bloom didn't disperse before that happened. The Bandarians were apparently in a hurry, and as suddenly as they had appeared on screen, they disappeared, out of range and on a heading east-southeast, near enough to their own.

Then, as if they had merely been protecting them from the Bandarians all along, the jellyfish slowly loosened their grip on the sub and began to disperse. On the sonar screen, the blob grew larger but more diffuse, and less coherent as a single mass, now morphing into many loose affiliations. It took a long time before the sub could move, but after it dove down to a normal cruising depth with its instruments still functioning, its electric motor could once again propel it through the water.

IT WAS LATE at night. Or, at least, that's what he assumed. Between the seemingly endless Tonshu days and the eternal darkness under water, Miles felt appropriately at sea. He wondered what time it was back home. He imagined being back on land and having a telescope powerful enough to see Earth. Of course, he knew from having watched *Cosmos* that any image they could conceivably see would be millions of years old. But as mindblowing as that thought was, he really just wanted to know what they were doing back in Barcelona now, or even in Chicago.

Miles had awoken after sleeping fitfully on his child-sized hammock. Anna was curled unconscious in the berth above him, while Vikram and Kerak made whistling noises as they slept. He couldn't get back to sleep and now he had to pee.

Miles entered the darkened corridor to find the head. Shikar helmed the sub alone while Erestu and Dinev slept. If Miles had known anything about submarines, he would have been impressed by the fact that three people could fully operate an eighty-foot sub, or that one could control it alone. In truth, on a typical run the sub drove itself and rarely required a yishi to do more than observe.

The door to the facilities had a small sign with the silhouette of a yishi in profile squatting over what looked like the top swirl of a soft-serve ice cream cone. This struck Miles as crass, though the silhouette of a yishi just standing there wouldn't have meant much to anyone in a genderless world. The toilet inside was a simple pit with a perch in front of it, not too different from how he'd heard his fellow travelers describe, with distaste, public facilities in Turkey, a place that had seemed too strange and chaotic to Miles at the time, his only exposure to the country being the film *Midnight Express*.

When he was done, Miles exited the head and saw Erestu standing there, softly lit by the glowing strands lining the corridor, naked but for a black thong and a sling-like bra which his large, firm breasts were struggling against. She looked—*he* looked, that is, undeniably sexy, his hips and thighs shapely and toned, his stomach flat and trim, his youthful skin smooth and soft. If not for Erestu's round face, Miles wouldn't have recognized him.

"I was just, ah…using the little yishis' room," said Miles.

Erestu looked at the restroom door, confused.

"To pee," he added. Miles, who was standing there in his underwear and a T-shirt, pulled reflexively at his red briefs, which were always riding up his ass, and tried not to stare at Erestu's body.

Erestu looked Miles up and down appraisingly and smiled. "Little yishi room?"

Miles shrugged, and Erestu squeezed past him with an amused expression on his way into the head, as Miles lingered over the image of his naked posterior. It was going to be hard to think of the captain in the same way from now on.

In a few hours, they would be on Twenty-six.

*

ANNA WASN'T SURE what she expected Twenty-six to be. From a distance, the contours of the island appeared rocky and denuded. Only within close range could she see that it was covered by crumbling structures and cracked pavement, all made dull and monochromatic by age and redscale. Like Danevesu, the ruins of a once-teeming city could be seen below the waves. Here, more of the old urban landscape came popping up out of the ocean. Whereas Old Danevesu had rested at a safe remove, this ghost town angled up out of the water to greet them, the waves lapping against the sides of buildings, rushing in and out of broken-out windows that once had dramatic views of the city.

The metropolis used to be the sixth-largest in Edrisia, home to more than twelve million yishi. What Anna could see above the waterline were the outskirts of the city's urban sprawl—apartment buildings, convenience stores, banks, dry cleaners, fast-food places, and useless power and communication lines still strung like spider webs above the abandoned streets.

A long floating pier extended from the main road and reached out into the small bay where the sub was docked. Instead of Danevesu's sheer cliffs bracketing the harbor, rolling hills rose gently away from the water, centuries of wind and water having worn down the concrete and brick buildings, leaving the glass and steel to poke up intermittently like unruly hair.

They deboarded, and after a tense day and a half on the sub, Anna had never looked forward more to seeing dry land, even if it was hotter than the bejeezus out, mitigated somewhat by the driving winds that howled off of the bay and blew dust everywhere. She donned her cooler, which was quickly becoming her favorite alien technology, and covered her head with its hood as she walked up the pier beside Miles.

Just in front of them, Dinev and Shikar had unloaded about a dozen large bins carrying food and supplies for the Edrisian outpost and were walking behind them as the bins hovered above the pier on zhink pallets.

Vikram, with his satchel thrown over his shoulder, walked on ahead with Kerak, while Erestu remained with the sub.

"I guess the captain has to stay with the ship," said Anna, looking over her shoulder as they made their way on.

"Yeah," said Miles, "she has to take it out of the harbor in case of a tsunami."

"Oh, y—wait, did you say *she?*" she said.

"Hm? Oh—I meant *he*," he said dismissively. It didn't really matter, did it? They were only using masculine pronouns out of convention, because the yishi themselves did.

Anna shook her head and smiled. "Do you have a *crush* on Erestu?" she teased.

"*No*," he shot back defensively. "What do you mean?—I…no."

She looked at him and laughed. "Relax, I was only fucking with you."

*

VIKRAM'S DEMEANOR had always exuded insouciance, a devil-may-care attitude that only increased the longer he lived, regardless of which body he was living in. But he was anxious as they climbed the road to meet Berejian at his research facility.

Earlier, as they were approaching the harbor, Vikram had sent Berejian a message from the sub that they would be arriving soon. It was a rather long, rambling message that he spoke into his smartskin, which transcribed it to Script before transmitting.

"Can't you just call him on that?" asked Miles.

Vikram shrugged. He knew Miles found it odd, but they rarely used their devices for voice or video calls. Berejian's only response was a set of detailed instructions on how to get to the facility, which hardly seemed necessary as it was beyond the ruins and the only inhabited structure on the small island. Berejian's impersonal reply nagged at Vikram. *Have I been around humans too long?* he wondered. Humans were constantly reading imagined subtext into even the most straightforward communications. Perhaps the tendency had rubbed off on him.

Still he worried now. He thought that bringing Berejian the gene bank had always been a worthwhile risk. But it was a big risk nonetheless. There was no telling the havoc that could be wreaked if his briefcase full of live alien biological agents fell into the wrong hands. Even in the right hands, the unintended consequences of Berejian's best efforts could still be catastrophic. And, although Vikram trusted Berejian completely, he hadn't seen him since before he left Our World. He'd been in communication with his old friend since he'd returned to Danevesu, of course, limited to coded messages that, on the surface, were innocuous enough. But Berejian was even older than Vikram. What if he'd lost his senses, or his acute intelligence had simply dulled over the intervening years? What if the messages were only coded from Vikram's perspective and were really just banal small-talk as far as Berejian was concerned?

In any case, there was not much he could do about it now.

Vikram was starting to feel markedly older himself. Maybe it was because he was still adjusting to his former body, or maybe it was the strain of the uphill climb in the swirling wind, but he moved slower and felt more bent and bowed in the heat and stronger gravitational pull of Our World.

The road flattened out as they came upon a broad intersection. On one corner was an old refueling station, a very ancient yet futuristic-looking vehicle parked out front, covered in redscale. Kitty corner stood an oddly cartoonish statue next to a low-slung building. It was a caricature of a yishi in yellow overalls, breasts exposed, wings out, his right arm reaching up to hold aloft a platter of what could have been food.

"Fast-food chain," said Vikram, noticing them staring. "They used to be everywhere. Walk through any old ruin, and you'll see one." The colors of the corporate mascot were faded, the end of its prominent beak broken off, and like everything else it was covered in splotchy patches of redscale. But they could still see its huge O-shaped smile and bug eyes staring creepily back at them.

As they moved past the crossroads and further into the hills, the ruins became less dense, until there were only scattered houses set back from the road, some of them big, sprawling places where wealthy yishi once lived. After clearing one last rise, they came upon a plateau, a barren field but for a large, one-story, octagonal building in the center with a tall metal tower reaching up out of one end. This had to be the place, as it was the only building on the island not falling down and covered in redscale.

An entranceway on one of the sides facing them slid open, and a remote figure riding a little hover-scooter emerged from within and started gliding over to them. As he came into view, they stopped to let him approach. He was wearing a light blue cooler over a white tunic and baggy white tights. His feathers were nearly as white as his clothes, and his beak hung down low over his wide mouth. Despite his brown skin, he had a gray pallor that spoke of little time spent outdoors. He came to a stop and looked at them with twinkling orange eyes partially obscured behind tinted goggles.

"Viku!" Berejian beamed at Vikram and held out his hands.

Vikram approached, took his hands, and they nuzzled cheek to cheek. "It's good to see you, my friend," said Vikram, still holding hands.

"You have it?" Berejian asked, smiling, almost vibrating with anticipation.

Vikram was relieved at his old colleague's warm reception, as well as his evident enthusiasm. "It's here," he said, motioning to the satchel on his back.

Berejian nodded to the others and then gazed up at Anna and Miles with obvious reverence. "And these must be your human friends," he said.

"What gave them away?" said Vikram.

Berejian aimed an Edrisian expletive Vikram's way and laughed. "I'm glad to see you haven't changed."

Vikram smiled and silently shared the same sentiment.

*

THE FACILITY INDOORS was much larger than it appeared from outside. There were at least three levels visible from the central atrium, only one of which was above ground. It reminded Miles of the agricultural facility in Danevesu with its grow rooms and skylights. But there was little machinery for production, as the agricultural work being done here was strictly experimental.

Berejian and his staff of four other geneticist/botanists were searching for a solution to Our World's horticultural holocaust. Nothing green grew in nature—not crops, not trees, not a nice shrubbery, not even weeds. But, despite making advances in the production and manipulation of indoor hydroponic crops, their efforts at overcoming the central problem of developing new plants that could survive outdoors had so far amounted to nothing. The limited biodiversity on their planet had made progress unattainable. Genetically speaking, they needed more raw material. That's what Vikram had brought.

Once the formalities and introductions were dispensed with, Berejian wasted no time getting himself and Vikram scrubbed and dressed for the clean-room environment of the lab. While the newcomers dealt with the necessary details with one of his subordinates, Berejian got down to work with Vikram and his gene bank in one of the subterranean genetics labs.

With their expedition's leader off with Berejian, no one was sure what to do with themselves now. One of Berejian's underlings, a rather gifted geneticist called Raldinian, found them sleeping quarters and showed them where the kitchen and bathroom facilities were. He peppered Anna and Miles with questions about Earth through Kerak, who acted as their reluctant interpreter. Another island, another tour, but with a sense of unease weighing down on them while Vikram and Berejian barricaded themselves off behind closed doors.

*

CENTURIES HAD PASSED while scientists before Berejian searched for solutions to the problem of horticultural sustainability on Our World. It would take Berejian only two days to come up with what he was looking for.

In the lab, he and Vikram sat across from each other at a long white table, dressed for surgery in white smocks, masks, goggles, and gloves—the impervious black case laid on the table between them. Even behind his surgical mask, Berejian's expression was plainly excited, his eyes lighting up as Vikram removed a glove and tapped in the combination on the glass panel of the case. The case, which he had programmed to recognize both his human and yishi fingerprints, opened with a soft hiss. Vikram took Berejian through its contents, pulling out small compartments that housed different categories of plant life and other critters. First were the seeds of common Earth crops—subdivided into grains, vegetables, fruits, nuts, and so on. Many of these had familiar analogues in Our World's agricultural history, though none of them Vikram thought could be grown outside a greenhouse on Our World now. Then he identified some of the commoner and hardier plant species he thought had intriguing characteristics—grasses, mosses, heathers, clovers, ivies, vines, as well as some more unusual weeds and several strains of cannabis. Another compartment was devoted to algae. Next Vikram explained his collection of spores from various fungi, molds, and yeasts, some of which were edible to humans, others which were inert, and others that produced medicinal compounds or toxins. Berejian made it clear this was where he wanted to focus his attention. It was *traits* he was looking for, he stressed to Vikram, not organisms—which, of course, Vikram knew well.

Any plant that hoped to grow in Our World's compromised soil would have to be able to not only withstand extreme heat and drought but resist the redscale that infiltrated everything.

Although the scourge of redscale appeared more like a mold or a fungus, the species was closer to what would be classified on Earth as an insect. While its biology was distinct from either, it did share a similarity with ants and bees and termites—a linked neural network, or hive mind. But redscale colonies had no queen, no specialized members. The colony could function with or without any one individual or group, at any size, over any area. How distinct colonies formed and sometimes split off or combined was a mystery. They could reproduce sexually or asexually, and when their offspring hatched, their immature bodies were equipped with lace-like wings that would catch the wind and deposit the larvae as far away as the air would carry them. Their only limiting factors were the availability of food and effective predators. The larger flying insects and small pterosaur-like birds that used to feed on them were long gone. As for food, the redscale needed only moisture and sunlight. And, since they fed off their own dead, which formed in layers beneath their surface, at a certain point light was all they really required.

As if this weren't already depressing enough, redscale came in two varieties—the kind you saw everywhere, layered on top of the ground, on rocks and buildings, and the other kind, which didn't need sunlight but fed off of moisture and the scant nutrients in the soil. That kind was much, much worse. It was this subspecies of redscale that bored underground and had rendered almost all of the soil on Our World unfit for agriculture or practically any other kind of vegetation.

Both types of redscale were individually tiny—flat and less than a few hundred microns in length—but colonies constituted trillions or quadrillions of individuals, not counting the desiccated exoskeletons left behind that often grew into coral reef–like formations on the land. As the *coup de grâce*, the redscale, like yishi and humans but unlike plants, took in oxygen and excreted carbon dioxide.

For decades, the yishi had tried to combat the plague with insecticides (some of which actually seemed to nourish the redscale) or other chemicals that damaged everything in the habitat but the redscale; they introduced potential predators and erected physical barriers, tried irradiating the redscale, then genetically altering the species—all in a drawn-out war they just kept losing.

Berejian explained to Vikram his hopes for finding a mold that could either produce compounds toxic to the redscale or retard its growth, which he could splice into the DNA of a surviving crop species. Molds and fungi had virtually disappeared on Our World, so Vikram's case was a gold mine, fungus-wise.

"They've often been the bane of agriculture," Berejian said, referring to the microorganisms. "But they're extremely useful at keeping weedier species in check."

"Weedy species—like redscale?" said Vikram.

"Redscale is a perfect example," he nodded. "Most living things benefit from a healthy ecosystem, but these 'weeds' thrive in compromised habitats. They're adaptable, opportunistic, fast-growing, hardy, can consume almost anything. They push out other, less-adaptable species. Where most life forms depend on biodiversity for survival, they thrive on monopoly. And they have few natural predators—or, in some cases, have had their predators removed for them. The jellies are a good example in aquaculture....We're another."

"Yishi, you mean," said Vikram.

Berejian shrugged matter-of-factly.

Vikram proceeded to educate Berejian on the properties of some of the hundreds of spore varieties he'd collected over the years. Some were very common on Earth, others relatively rare. Some had intriguing properties, such as tolerance for extreme heat and drought or frigid cold, the ability to consume hydrocarbons and excrete oxygen, et cetera.

Though Vikram and Berejian were both fluent in English, Danevesan, and Edrisian, the names of all the species were in Latin. "What's this, '*Spinellus fusiger*'?" Berejian asked.

"It's also called bonnet mold," he said. "It's a parasitic pin mold that grows on mushrooms, a category of fungi that usually look something like an open umbrella."

"I know what a mushroom is." Berejian looked intrigued nonetheless. He was taking notes on everything Vikram showed him, using the

ANY OTHER WORLD WILL DO

familiar sign language in front of his computer's scanning monitor that

familiar sign language in front of his computer's scanning monitor that transcribed it into a specialized form of Script used by biologists and geneticists. Vikram went on running down the aspects of various types of *Aspergillus, Penicillium, Stachybotrys,* as well as a healthy number of mushrooms and yeasts until Berejian was satisfied and attempted to send Vikram away.

"Berejian, I'd like to stay, if it's all right," Vikram said.

"I work better alone," he said, "you know that, Viku. We've already spent half the morning together, and I need to run about a dozen organisms through the sequencer just to start with." A large blue machine with a 3D display sat softly humming next to the long white table with its monitors, microscopes, burners, vials, and flasks. "You'd be bored, and I'd get irritated. I'll call you when I need you again."

"Oh."

Vikram slunk out of the lab in a funk. Berejian could have that effect on him, he now recalled, though he was also trying to contain an excess of undirected energy. He had some consolation in Kerak's company, but after a quick shag found himself not only bored but frustrated at being excluded from potentially seeing the fruits of his years of work spent trying to save this miserable planet. Plus, he desperately wanted a smoke. Unfortunately, the only cigarettes he knew of were a few million light-years away, and his access to spacetime portals had been taken away with his fluppet's smartskin.

✳

TWO LONG DAYS passed with Berejian holed up in the lab, keeping Vikram at a distance. Raldinian and Berejian's two other assistants, Gildeshian and Carneg, seemed more involved with whatever Berejian was doing than Vikram, which only aggravated an already testy situation, making Araviku very un-Vikram-like. Which, in turn, only made Kerak even more Kerak-like.

On the second day, Anna and Miles—on an alien planet in an uncharted corner of the universe—grew bored. But a break in the hurricane-force winds and violent lightning storms that had set in shortly after they arrived allowed them to venture outside. And so they set off to explore the island of Twenty-six with Dinev. Dinev acted as their de facto guide, despite his never having been there before either. Bundled in their air-conditioned coolers, they made their way down the other side of the plateau, where a wide valley lay before a lone mountain, red and rocky as it jut into an orange sky. Away from the sound of the surf, it was eerily quiet. No birds or frogs chirped, no insects buzzed. No breezes blew through the leaves of trees. It was dead silent but for the sounds of their own footsteps.

They were wending their way across a dry riverbed that came down from the mountain, where snowmelt once flowed, to a depopulated town, presumably a suburb of the drowned city. Cracked and crumbling roadways and a gnarled, desiccated tree poking up through the collapsed roof of a one-story house were the only visible signs that vegetation had briefly taken back the ghost town—a temporary interlude before it too was defeated by an inhospitable climate and the insidious redscale.

The three of them walked through the former suburban outpost with its alien architecture, so different yet familiar, and came upon a tall, multi-domed structure at the town's heart. Except for its faded, red-tinged exterior and doorless entryway, it seemed to be in pristine condition.

"Can we take a look inside?" Anna asked Dinev, as if the permission were his to give. She was already a little out of breath, and she and Miles both felt light-headed and heavy-limbed after the exertion.

"It might not be safe," Dinev said uncertainly. But boredom and the urge to impress his guests trumped discretion. "Of course, it *is* still standing. I suppose a quick look inside would be okay."

Once inside this outwardly impressive edifice, their anticipation quickly turned to disappointment. The interior space resembled a large abandoned supermarket, with row after row of empty shelves and counters, debris scattered all over the curled and peeling plastic floor. Their hope of seeing the underside of the four massive domes was dashed by a white-tiled drop-ceiling that made the space dark and claustrophobic.

"Umm…" was all Miles could think to say. Anna and Dinev nodded in agreement.

Feeling vaguely cheated, they searched for a staircase or doorway to another room. Finding a doorway behind a bank of shelves toward a rear corner of the room, Dinev felt around the door's edges, applying pressure to see if there was any give. He finally put his shoulder into it hard, trying to force it open, but no luck.

"Let me," said Miles. He leaned back and kicked the right side of the door with the bottom of his heel as hard as he could. Other than the tingling sensation it left in his foot, it had no effect.

Anna reached up to the top of the jamb and pressed a button next to the defunct motion sensor. The door clicked open a crack, and she slid it the rest of the way with her finger.

Dinev watched as Anna walked through the opening.

"We loosened it up for you," said Miles, following close behind.

The small room was a stairwell with steps leading to the second floor. The staircase looked solid, so they carefully proceeded up the stairs, which led them to a long corridor with a number of archways each spaced a few meters apart. They walked through one of the arches into a vast space that at last resembled the outer structure they'd been drawn to. The four domes towered above them, each a different height and diameter and arranged asymmetrically, though not at random. Yet this voluminous upper story looked totally unfinished, as if they had framed the building but ran out of funds before they could complete it. Or as though a formerly grand public temple had been systematically stripped of all its decoration and ornament, down to the trim and walls them- selves, before being repurposed for something strictly utilitarian.

The dusty uneven floor rippled beneath them, and the studs framing the walls and the beams overhead looked rotten, porous. They didn't resemble wood or steel to Anna and Miles, and even if they had asked Dinev, he wouldn't have known what kind of outdated composite mate- rial they were made of, the building having been constructed centuries before his time. They were saturated with the redscale, the corners of the room stained wine red with legions of the critters.

The light streaming in through the windows at the base of the domes and dotting the walls created marvelous shadows inside the unfinished space, though. Anna, Miles, and Dinev were inexorably drawn to the center of the floor, where they could stare straight up and best admire the room's charms, such as they were.

It was while they were looking up as a group in the middle of the room that the floor moved. Minutely, almost imperceptibly, at first. Then more noticeably. The section of floor beneath their feet moved down, then slightly to the right, and then fell open as if it were on a giant hinge, turning the horizontal surface on which they'd been standing into a snowless ski run. Though they couldn't appreciate it as they skittered helplessly down the rough incline, they were lucky in one respect. If not for the drop-ceiling and all of the shelves on the first floor to catch the second floor, their angle of descent would have been much steeper. As they slid on their butts toward the upper half of one of the open doorways at the front of the building, Miles grabbed Anna's arm while Dinev, on the other side, grabbed the other. There was nothing else to hold onto, so the three of them pressed their feet against the floor, trying to create enough friction to slow their fall. Miles tore the palm of his left hand trying to gain some kind of purchase. But it was Dinev's taloned heels that managed to stop them before meeting the top of the arched entrance or the ground outside with violent force.

They had stopped before the edge of the collapsed floor, above a row of noisily crushed shelving units, several feet from the open doorway. Miles's feet dangled over the edge, the fingernails of his left hand clinging desperately to the blood-and-dust-covered floor. Dinev was already starting to stand up, and Miles let go of Anna's hand as Dinev made sure she was all right. Miles gingerly felt with his foot for a shelf steady enough to stand on. Back on a level surface, he helped Anna and Dinev down, and they all jumped down to the first floor and then out the front entrance as quickly as they could.

"Son of a bitch," said Miles, examining his bloody hand. He showed the others, and they each shared their worst cuts and bruises to impressed nods and expressions of mild disgust. Not to be outdone, the old building creaked and groaned in not-so-subtle warning. The three of them started jogging away nonchalantly, as if they were just out for a bit of exercise. When they heard the low rumbling—like thunder, but angrier—they broke into a sprint.

The domes behind them started to crash down slowly, the sight of the building imploding and sinking into a sea of rubble and dust at once horrible and beautiful. Unfortunately, Anna, Miles, and Dinev missed this memorable sight, as all around them was dust, billowing outward as if blown by an enormous bellows. They didn't stop running until the noise abated, and then collapsed, themselves, in the middle of the road, their eyes, mouths, and nostrils caked with dust and grime.

As the haze cleared, they faintly made out a row of others approaching them from the way they had first come. There were six of them, the four in front arrayed with military precision, wearing identical cloaks over light body armor, and sporting small devices on their wrists that seemed to be pointed in their direction. Anna, Miles, and Dinev stood to greet them and, once upright, realized they could no longer move. The four soldiers stopped, and one of the two in the rear stepped forward between them. Even for a yishi, he was a scrawny little homunculus. He stood there with a self-satisfied smirk, his head both too big for his body and too small for his long, crooked nose.

He looked from one to the other and back again and started to laugh. The three of them—their eyes streaming tears, covered from head to toe in a layer of fine gray dust—were almost unrecognizable.

"I almost didn't know you," he said. "Which is funny, considering."

Anna, Miles, and Dinev stared straight ahead, their eyeballs unable to move enough to see him.

"Cat got your tongues?" he asked. He looked over at the soldiers. "Oh, right. That." He said something to them in a language only Dinev recognized, and they released their captives from the field that had immobilized them.

Anna relaxed momentarily, brushing dust off her face and hair. She looked at the speaker closely now and said, "Who are you?"

"Is that any way to greet an old boyfriend?"

"Oh...*shit.*"

Miles did a double-take and let out a snort. "Really? *You?*" He looked at Anna. "That's *Anders?*"

"It's not funny."

"It's...a little funny."

"Would one of you mind telling me what the fuck is going on?" said Dinev.

*

RALDINIAN, SENT BY Berejian to fetch Vikram, knocked on the door of his sleeping chamber and called through in a loud voice. Vikram, whose head was buried between Kerak's thighs, couldn't quite hear him on the other side of the partition.

"Lmmrphg?" he said.

"Thanks!" Kerak yelled, breathlessly. Then to Vikram—"It's nothing. I'll tell you later."

After several more minutes, Vikram collapsed next to Kerak, exhausted, and tried to cough up a feather stuck in the back of his throat.

"Oh, that was Raldinian earlier, by the way," said Kerak.

"What did he want?" asked Vikram.

"He said Berejian wanted to see you."

"What? Why didn't you tell me?"

"Why do you think?" Kerak said with a laugh. "Why didn't he message you?"

Vikram was out of the habit of checking his palm for messages and had turned off his alerts, which he considered a nuisance. He checked his smartskin, and, sure enough, there was a message from Berejian:

Come see me in the lab right away. New development to report.

Vikram was soon dressed, rehydrated, and standing outside the door to Berejian's lab. The door slid open, and Berejian stood before a large visualizer, staring into the eyepiece of the powerful microscope and 3D modeler.

"Ah, Viku," he said, noticing Vikram in the doorway, "come in, come in."

"You said you had a development?" said Vikram.

"Oh, yes," Berejian said, shaking his head. "Quite so. Although… it's something of a mixed bag. That is to say, I have good news, but I also have some bad news."

"Okay. Tell me the bad news first then."

"The good news is I've finished what I set out to do," said Berejian. Vikram cocked his head at this. "The bad news is I don't think you're going to like it. Better have a seat."

Vikram sat down across from Berejian and let out a nervous laugh. "I don't understand," he said. "What am I not going to like?"

"Do you remember our discussion of weeds?" Berejian asked.

Vikram nodded.

"I said then that we were like a weed—but the analogy wasn't entirely apt. Being able to adapt to harsh environments is the hallmark of a weedy species," he said, a bit pedantically. "But yishi-kind stopped adapting to their environment long ago, and began making their environment adapt to them."

"True."

"There have been climatological periods in which various weedy species have dominated—when the oceans were nothing but jellies like they are now, when the land was baked, arid desert, almost devoid of life. But nature always returned things to balance, always remedied a sick planet."

"But not now," said Vikram, finishing Berejian's thought.

"No," he nodded. "And why is that?"

"I have a feeling we're getting to the part I'm not going to like."

"Because at the end of the evolutionary string is a weed with sentient intelligence. A weed that can't help its nature, yet can act in unnatural ways—alter its environment, fiddle with its own DNA, create new life forms."

"So being sentient is unnatural?" said Vikram. "I have to say, as the only one of the two of us who's actually spent time on another world, sentience strikes me as an inevitable milestone in the evolution of life."

"I don't know if sentience is inevitable or just an evolutionary mistake—"

"Evolution doesn't make 'mistakes,' Berejian," Vikram insisted.

"That's ridiculous, Viku," he said. "Natural selection is based entirely on selecting which *mistakes*—which genetic mutations—will best equip species to adapt, survive, and evolve."

"You're arguing semantics now," said Vikram angrily. "Obviously, mutations are small-scale mistakes in replication, but the selection process isn't subject to error. Traits that survive are by definition better suited for survival than traits that die out."

"Now who's arguing semantics?" said Berejian. "The point is, we add nothing. As a species, we're a plague."

Vikram was stopped short, the worst dawning on him. "What have you done?"

"The logical thing. A hybrid biological agent. Infectious, airborne, fast-acting, easily spread...lethal." Berejian looked at his old friend compassionately. "I'm sorry I lied to you. I didn't play fair."

Vikram sputtered, temporarily unable to speak. Finally, he said, "So your solution to all our problems is worldwide genocide?"

Berejian appeared to think about this for a moment. "Yes," he said. "Although I believe the correct term would be *speciocide*."

"The end of yishi civilization. The end of Our World."

"The world will still be here, Viku," he said. "I'm trying to save it. I'm looking out for the other life forms—the few we haven't already wiped out. And the many that will hopefully come after we're gone."

Vikram stood up and began to pace aimlessly. "What if your hybrid pathogen sends the world past its tipping point?" he asked, throwing his arms up. "You have no idea what kind of unintended consequences might come from your creation. You could render Our World permanently uninhabitable."

"It's possible," he said with a what-are-you-gonna-do? shrug.

"And you're comfortable making this decision for everyone," said Vikram. "No one else gets a say in it?"

"I wasn't planning on putting it to a vote, if that's what you mean," he said.

"This is worse than my worst fears about you," said Vikram. "I don't know who you are."

"I'm not the same person I was," he said. "I would hope you're not the same person, either. I know you've been away for many years, Viku. I don't know if you noticed during your short stay in Danevesu, but things aren't exactly improving here. I don't do this lightly—"

"Oh, good," said Vikram. "I was worried you hadn't thought this through."

"I don't expect you to accept what I've done. But I did want to at least explain myself to you. I owe you that."

"Thanks."

"Look what we did to Skygarden, Viku. No biological agent was needed to devastate our sister planet. Just yishi going up there and doing what we do. Imagine what could have evolved on Skygarden if we hadn't interfered. Imagine what life might evolve on Our World with us out of the way."

"And in a hundred million years," said Vikram, "if another sentient species evolves to take our place, will they be any better?"

"They couldn't be any worse."

"No. They'll be the same," said Vikram. "But they won't have the benefit of the accumulated knowledge we've earned over a hundred millennia of trial and error. You'll make sure of that." Vikram stalked over to Berejian. "I can't just let you do this."

"It's done, Viku." Berejian switched on his smartskin and twirled his fingers. "Telesu and his Bandarian soldiers are already in the building, on their way here." Vikram's horrified expression summed up the enormity of Berejian's betrayal. He tried to hurriedly send a message to Kerak and the others, but his own smartskin was suddenly disconnected from the network. "You'll find that doesn't work for much of anything now," said Berejian. "You won't be able to message each other—or call anyone off of Twenty-six, either."

Shhhhuuf. Vikram whirled around at the sound of the door sliding open.

Anna, Miles, and Dinev filed in through the entry, covered in dust, bruised, and bleeding, their arms pinned to their sides by some invisible force. Anders and five yishi in Bandarian military uniforms followed in closely behind.

"What did you do to them?" Vikram demanded of Anders.

Anders laughed. "It wasn't me," he said. "They did that to themselves."

Miles tried to turn to face Vikram but lost his balance and, unable to right himself, knocked over several trays of glass vials on a cart behind him, before landing on the cold floor of the lab himself. "This is *really* annoying," he muttered, looking down at his useless arms, broken glass and various liquids splattered all around him.

"Well…doesn't matter now," Berejian said with a wave of his hand.

Anna and Dinev couldn't help Miles up and, not knowing what else to do, plopped down on the floor next to him, careful to avoid the glass shards and pools of viscous liquid.

Kerak and Shikar walked in just then, followed by Raldinian, Gildeshian, and Carneg. "What the fuck?" said Kerak, as he noticed the Bandarian troops on either side of the door, Dinev and the humans on the floor, the diminutive yishi he knew as Telesu standing in the middle of it all. "Oh." Kerak nodded as he and Shikar were directed to sit down on the floor next to their cohorts, which they did, still in somewhat of a fog.

Vikram stared hard at Anders and said, "So you're behind this."

"Sorry, wrong again. This was Berejian's idea," said Anders. "He reached out to me before I ever departed Our World. I guess he'd figured out why I'd left Cardevise for Bandary. I might never have gone—I mean, there was really no need to—but I sure as hell didn't want to wait around in Bandary, and I really wanted to see Earth. You'd told me so much about it."

"I remember," said Vikram.

"Plus, I'd worked hard building my own fluppet," he said. "It would have been a shame not to use it."

"You always were a talented engineer," said Vikram.

"Gee, thanks, Dad."

Anna and Miles looked at each other to make sure they'd heard right.

"I can't say I'm grateful to you for bringing me into this world," he continued, "but I do have to thank you for showing me how to get to another. Sorry you're going to die on this one."

Berejian approached Anders and said, "We discussed this."

"Don't worry, I'm not going to kill them," he said, shaking his head. "You have a soft spot for your old friend here, but you'd murder all of yishi-kind without a scruple."

"I'll let you do that," said Berejian, lifting two black cases off the counter and showing them to Anders. He handed him the squat, boxy one first. "There are twenty canisters filled with the pathogen in a liquid medium. Each one will release the medium in an atomized spray." He handed Anders the gene bank, as well. "I thought you might want this, too."

"Aw, that was thoughtful of you."

It was clear Berejian didn't care much for Anders. He let go of the case and turned away.

Anders handed the cases to Peleg, who couldn't follow what was being said but understood they had what they'd come for. Anders looked over at Anna and Miles, quietly seething on the floor with their arms pinned. "We had to blow up your sub, by the way," he said. They all looked up in shock at that, except Shikar, who did once Dinev translated for him. "So, unless the fellows decide to take you along with us—no?—I think this is good-bye. I'll miss seeing you back on Earth…well, one of you."

"Asshole," muttered Miles.

"I really did enjoy our time together, Anna. So I hope you'll consider some friendly advice: keep your eye on that one," Anders said, meaning Miles. "He'll say anything to get what he wants."

Anna stared up at Anders, who standing wasn't much taller than her sitting, and could not recognize anything of her onetime lover. She looked away. Miles grit his teeth and glared, recognizing Anders in the person of Telesu without much difficulty.

"The cases are unlocked," said Berejian. "So you'll want to set up your own access codes."

"Yes, you wouldn't want to accidentally expose yourselves to the pathogen," said Vikram. "Then you wouldn't be able to infect the people of Danevesu…and Bandary, I assume?" Vikram looked from Anders to Berejian, who gave each other meaningful glances. "I mean, that is your plan, isn't it? Do *they* know that?"

Anders gave Peleg and his troops a patronizing smile. Then to Vikram he said, "As a matter of fact, no. Fortunately, none of them speaks English."

Before Vikram could say anything else, Anders trained his own device on him and paralyzed just his head above his neck, rendering him wide-eyed and speechless, his arms and legs still moving about, weirdly disconnected from the shocked expression on his frozen face. For good measure and because it amused him, Anders nodded to the soldiers to do the same to the others.

"The Bandarian leaders want to destroy all the non-believers," said Anders. "And pretty much all the believers who don't believe quite the same way they do, for that matter. Which is *almost* everyone." Then he added, under his breath, "I just plan to do them one better, that's all. Then I leave this dismal hellhole for good." He smiled and waved a finger at them as if they were mischievous children. "Let's not spoil the surprise, now. *Ciao!*"

With that, Anders turned on his heel and led Peleg with his case full of liquid death, Vikram's gene bank, and the soldiers out the door and back the way they'd come. The six prisoners—Vikram, Kerak, Anna, Miles, Dinev, and Shikar—were free to move their lips and limbs now, but still confined to Berejian's lab and the desolate island of Twenty-six.

Carneg, whom Miles had taken to calling "the Mecknificent" in a joke only he got or at least found funny, trained his own immobilizing device on them, but didn't zap them with it yet. "Carneg and the others will walk you back to your rooms," said Berejian. "I'm sorry about the humans, I really am," he said to Vikram in Danevesan. "But I believe what I'm doing is right."

"How long?" was all Vikram asked.

"Maybe an octat, maybe less." An eighth of a year, or about fifty-two long days, was as long as the supplies would last. "The facility was designed to be self-sufficient. But we obviously had to destroy those capabilities. There won't be anyone out there soon, anyway. Everyone will be gone."

"Even the Edrisians—your own people?" Vikram asked.

"They're part of everyone, last I checked."

14.

IT WAS A LONG NIGHT for the three sets of roommates locked in their respective cells. The nights were long, anyway, but this one really dragged. In their room, Shikar and Dinev silently mourned the death of Erestu. Kerak was too angry to speak to Vikram, who, not taking the hint, went on in dismay about Berejian's betrayal and his descent into madness. It was madness, wasn't it?

Miles and Anna were as confused as they were frightened, having only understood some of what they'd heard in the lab. Miles paced while Anna sat up on the edge of her nest-like bed. "So Berejian created a virus or something for Anders to use on the yishi of Danevesu and Bandary," said Miles.

"I think he means to use it on everyone," Anna said.

"It's insane," he said. "And why didn't Vikram tell us that Anders was his...offspring?"

"Does it matter?"

"I guess not," he said. "It's just...weird."

A momentary uncomfortable silence intervened.

"So what did Anders mean when he said you'd say anything to get what you want?" she asked.

"Uh..." Miles started then stopped. "Is that really important right now?"

"Well, I don't know, do I?"

Miles sighed. "It's really stupid, but....You know the night he cheated on you with Tawny?" She nodded. "It was earlier that night. I was kind of drunk, and I might have told her that I thought you and Anders were already broken up."

"Oh." Anna shook her head. "Why would you do that?"

"I don't know. I really liked you, and...Anders *is* a psychotic alien."

"You didn't know that then!"

"Well, I knew he was kind of a prick."

Anna laughed, a loud staccato *hah* that made it clear she didn't think it was funny. "Did you even think about how doing that might affect me?"

Miles had nothing clever to say to that.

*

THE NEXT DAY, around the time they were starting to wonder if they'd ever be released, the doors of their three rooms slid open without warning. The captives emerged in pairs from their quarters into a shared corridor and looked at one another for the first time since being locked up.

After debating for a minute what to do, they decided to head to the control center, which they assumed also held the communications equipment. They were still unable to use their smartskin for sending or receiving messages to the outside world or even to each other unless they were in the same room. They didn't know if Berejian and the others were still there, or if they had left the facility or the island altogether.

Berejian and his staff weren't in the control center, but someone had been in there and done a number on the computer equipment. "I guess they weren't fucking around," said Kerak, looking about. Somehow, the sight of all the smashed consoles and screens did more to convey the seriousness of their situation than anything else that had happened in the past day.

The control room was at the center of the facility, with corridors, offices, and living quarters surrounding it on the main floor in concentric circles. Berejian's lab was on one of the several levels below ground, where the other labs and growing facilities were housed. They headed down there now. They saw more deliberate destruction through the curved glass separating them from one of the grow rooms, where formerly green plants suspended in air now hung there wilted and brown in the blue haze of some deadly herbicide.

They found the others lying on the floor in Berejian's lab. The bodies of Berejian, Raldinian, Gildeshian, and Carneg the Mecknificent were contorted mid-spasm, their faces frozen in expressions of agony. Whatever their minds thought of committing suicide, their bodies clearly disagreed. A blue plastic pillbox sat on the counter above where they lay, with a flat, card-sized computer sitting on top, with its screen pulsating slowly. Vikram slid a finger over the screen to reveal a message.

"What does it say?" asked Kerak.

"Help yourselves," he said.

Miles shook his head. "What a *dick*."

Vikram tossed the card computer aside carelessly. He picked up the box of poison capsules and took it over to the incinerator chute.

"Wait!" said Kerak.

Vikram looked at Kerak in wide-eyed surprise. "None of us is taking one of these!" he declared, looking at each of his companions in turn.

"The time may come when it's our best option," said Kerak calmly. "There's only so much food. Have you ever seen someone starve to death?"

"Have *you*?" Vikram said.

"Well, not as such, no," he admitted. "But I've read enough accounts of what happens. I *am* a physician. And I'm not interested in being driven to gnaw off my own fingers, or...eat one of you."

Miles laughed nervously just then, and the others turned to glare at him. The thought of whether the yishi would taste like chicken had just popped into his head, though he could hardly say that. "Sorry," he said.

They were all in various stages of shock and having trouble thinking clearly.

"What should we do with them?" said Dinev, reverting to Danevesan.

"Who cares about *them*?" said Shikar. "What are *we* going to do?"

"We have to get them out of here first," said Kerak. "Then we can figure out a plan."

"Incinerator?" suggested Shikar.

"Not big enough," said Kerak.

"Bury them?" said Dinev.

"I'm thinking outside on the ground," said Vikram. "Either way, the redscale will have them."

Dinev and Shikar found a large wheeled cart from one of the storerooms, and the others lifted the bodies of Berejian and his colleagues onto it. Their bodies were still warm, as they hadn't been dead for long, but they were stiff. It wasn't rigor mortis but the effect the poison had of contracting the bodies' large muscles. It was eerie, and it made them harder to stack on the cart, though it did make them easier to pick up. Once outside, they deposited them on the ground beside a path at the rear of the facility.

A strong wind blew hot air and dust into the faces of the amateur undertakers, causing their eyes to water. Those tears would be the only ones shed for Berejian and his colleagues. Anna and Miles stole a backward glance at the bodies as they all hurried back inside.

*

IT HAD BEEN at least a full day, or about forty-eight hours, since they last ate, and so Kerak insisted they go up to the kitchen to refuel.

Miles, like everyone else, was starving. But he didn't dare eat too much of the savory-sweet red gelum, as he had no idea how long the food would last. Plus he hadn't had one solid bowel movement since arriving on Our World.

Kerak was not speaking to Vikram, and Anna made a point of sitting with Dinev and Shikar as they ate in relative silence. They didn't linger over their spartan meal. At Dinev's suggestion, they decided to return to the computer room to catalogue the damage and find out if anything was spared, or at least salvageable.

Among the debris were several intact high-tech devices. Some were purpose-specific sensors or gauges. There were a few more card-sized computers that functioned similarly to smartskin. None of which were capable of communications, as the central network console had been dismantled and the pieces crushed with a heavy dull implement. Anna picked up a gray metallic device about the size of a *National Geographic* and about as thick as a clipboard off the floor. Its glass screen was blank, and she couldn't figure out how to turn it on.

She showed it to Dinev, who turned it over in his hands. "It's old." He tried to turn it on. "It's dead, but I think it might be light-sensitive." He held it under a lamp for a few seconds, and it whirred to life, then blinked on. "It's an old electronic library," he said, tapping an image on the screen. "This might be a helpful reference. Its networking functions are down like everything else, though."

The mini-library had manuals for every system in the facility, a redundant resource in case of a catastrophic breakdown of the computer network or power supply. Dinev quickly found the information on the communications network and what backup systems there were, if any.

"Look at this," he said. "There's a communications tower on the east side of the island, here. It's on the far side of the mountain we saw from the old town."

"Could we transmit a message from there?" Anna asked.

"Unfortunately, probably not," he said. "According to this, it's just a big antenna controlled from this room. Or it was."

"Oh."

"Our problem is we have many computers, but no way to connect them to the communications network," said Dinev. "And even if we could, I'm not sure how we'd send a message out. If only we had a universal transmitter."

"What's that?" she asked.

"Well, since we don't have one, it doesn't really matter."

Shikar was looking over Dinev's shoulder and pointed to an icon on the screen. Dinev handed the library to Shikar, who started browsing the contents. "He figures there ought to be a separate server room, which could at least get us a computer we could use to tap into the network."

Vikram interjected, "If there's a chance the tower has a computer terminal, shouldn't one or two of us go check it out?" No one answered right away.

"Fine with me," said Dinev.

"Does anyone want to go with me?" asked Vikram.

"I'll go," said Miles.

*

VIKRAM AND MILES started out, wrapped in their coolers, hoods up and goggles on to protect their faces from windblown particles. They were frankly relieved to get a break from the others. Vikram hadn't eaten much and was moving sluggishly as he stared out at the desiccated landscape, a cloud of dust sailing up and into his nose.

Miles walked beside him, not saying much of anything for a good half hour.

"I'm sorry about Berejian," he said finally.

Vikram seemed startled when Miles spoke and turned to notice him. "Don't be," he said. "He deserved worse than what he did to himself."

"No, I know. I meant…" Miles fumbled for words. "I meant I was sorry about how he betrayed you."

"Oh." Vikram sighed. "Don't feel sorry for me, either. *I* did this to us." He grimaced, stopped to look around and scratch his beak. "Maybe I really am an avatar of Vishnu—destroyer of worlds. One, anyway," he said, referring to the crack Anna had made back on Earth. He tried to shrug it off, as he could see he'd lost Miles. "I thought I could trust Berejian. I thought I knew him. Now…I don't think I ever knew anything."

"You know more than I do," Miles said.

"Thinking we know things just makes us dangerous."

"You think Anders will go through with it?"

"I don't know. I hope not."

They began making their way up the dry riverbed, toward the base of the gently sloped mountain.

Miles couldn't think of any better way to ask and finally said, "So Anders—Telesu, I mean—was your child?"

"Still is," he replied. "I can understand why so many Danevesans choose not to know their offspring at all. It seems being disappointed by your children is universal."

"Did you raise him?"

"Oh, no," he said. "I wasn't even on Our World when he became viable—born, that is. My partner at the time thought it was our duty. Anyway, he wanted a child, and so we conceived Telesu. We designed his genome with intellect in mind, as we're obligated to do, with an emphasis on scientific, logical intelligence. We didn't worry much about his physical traits and wanted to leave those to chance—rebelling in our small way. Everyone was starting to design their children with the same standard of beauty in mind—what was fashionable. But then I heard later that Telesu had a rough time as a child with his small stature and… appearance. He was precocious, though. By the time I got to know him, he was almost grown."

"What about your own parents?"

"I remember Arak from an early age, though I never met Temal," said Vikram. "Arak didn't raise me, exactly. He left the messy, quotidian stuff to professionals. But he would show up unexpectedly and take me with him places young yishi weren't usually supposed to go."

"My dad took us to the racetrack a couple times," said Miles. "My mom said he was acting more like a bachelor uncle."

"Arak was idolized," Vikram continued, "so the rules didn't really apply to him. Nobody else could have gotten away with the things he did. I guess he must have liked spending time with me, too. It never occurred to me to try to do the same for Telesu."

Miles shook his head. "My dad helped raise me, even did some of the messy stuff," he said. "I never really gave him credit for that."

"You loved him."

"Not as far as he knew," said Miles. He shrugged. "We weren't on the best of terms when he died."

"That doesn't mean he didn't know," said Vikram.

"At his funeral, I think half the people there were still mad at him," he said. "I know I was."

"Well, you're handling your anger better than my son did," said Vikram.

Miles laughed. They looked up at the nearing peak as a gust of wind blew up a cloud of dust that temporarily blocked out the sun.

"I miss Earth already," said Vikram.

"Me too," said Miles.

"The thing is," said Vikram, stopping to take a breath, "I didn't want to come back here. I was enjoying myself too much."

"So why did you?"

"I had to," he said. "These are my people." He shook his head and looked at Miles. "But I feel like you and Anna are my people, too, maybe moreso. And then I lied to you both, anyway."

"Well, it would have been hard to tell us the truth under normal circumstances," said Miles.

"The telling would have been hard, at first," he admitted. "But it would have been very easy to show you. I just didn't want to upset my new reality—your reality."

Miles looked around at the reality of Twenty-six and sighed. "So is this what Earth is going to look like in five hundred years?" he asked.

"I hope not," said Vikram. "But...yes."

They walked on in silence as they turned away from the riverbed to ascend the summit.

"Did I ever tell you about my time living with the Ndzada in east Africa?" Vikram asked, a propos of nothing.

"Um, Anna mentioned it to me once."

"They lived around the central Rift Valley near Lake Eyasi—bush country, hard land to live off of. One night, the men took me out on a baboon hunt," he said.

"They hunted baboon?"

Vikram nodded. "They're kind of a delicacy, actually. Anyway, when we surprised the baboons up in their tree, one of them jumped down and mauled a boy from the camp. Killed him. On the way back, his father and I carried him while two others carried the dead baboon. Back at the camp, the boy's mother collapsed and wailed over his dead body, along with the other women of the tribe who'd helped raise him. The men butchered the baboon and set it on the fire to roast, and soon the women joined in the feast, though it was more subdued than usual. After eating, everyone started telling stories about Sotze, the boy who was killed. It was sort of an impromptu wake. The next morning, Sotze's parents and siblings took his body far from the camp and gently laid it out for the hyenas and vultures, and then walked back."

Miles grimaced. "Sounds familiar."

"By the time they returned to camp, everything was back to normal."

"Like it never happened?"

Vikram paused and checked the map on his smartskin. "It was more like everything that wasn't in front of them now was part of the same big nothing," he said. He pointed back at the riverbed. "If you or I live near a stream, we think of the water in it as being the same water. We may even give the stream a name. But they know the water is never the same. Yesterday's stream is gone. Each day brings a new river."

Miles knew Vikram well enough by now not to bother asking what this had to do with leaving a dead boy out to be eaten by hyenas. "It just sounds cruel to me," he said, "if they loved him."

"It seemed cruel to me at first too. But these weren't malicious people, and everyone had loved Sotze before he died. They were just happy, not bothered by the past or worried about the future. If you asked them what happened to them after they died, they had no idea and didn't care. You know, their language actually lacked a past or future tense—they literally had no words for what *was* or *will be*....What might've been," he added, correcting himself. "I used to think they must have known something the rest of us had forgotten."

"You don't anymore?"

"No. I don't know." Vikram shook his head and started climbing again. Miles followed. "You have to understand the deep impression they made on me. There's no people like them on Our World, haven't been for thousands of years. They didn't know war, had no need for religion or formal rituals or class. They were the freest, most egalitarian people I'd ever known. I would've stayed with them if I could, but—"

"The bugs?"

"Well, yes, the flies were insane. And the thorns—I swear every goddamn bush out there had big old thorns on it, and they'd stick you as you walked by. But it wasn't that. You can't un-know certain things. They lived in innocence, with no way of accumulating or building on the knowledge of their ancestors. So each generation knew more or less what the one before it did. Even if I still believed their way of life held some profound secret, I always knew their way was closed to me."

Miles shook his head. "I always figured there was some secret that other people knew that I didn't, and I was too embarrassed to ask."

"You're not alone," said Vikram.

Winded from climbing and talking, they found a place to sit and have a drink of water. Miles was starting to get used to the thin atmosphere and more intense gravity. Vikram was starting to look his age. They could see the summit clearly now.

"Shouldn't the antenna be visible from here?" said Miles.

"Not necessarily," said Vikram. He showed Miles the map on his hand. Miles loved looking at the smartskin displays. He wanted one. "The tower is supposed to be here on the other side of the peak. It can't show us where we are now, but I think we're about here."

It had been a few hours since they left the others, but the sun was still high in the sky. "How much farther, do you think?" asked Miles.

"Shouldn't take us long," Vikram said, getting up slowly.

"Are you okay?" said Miles.

"I'm just pacing myself," he said.

It took them less than an hour to mount the summit. The transmitter station was directly below them, and it was now clear why they hadn't seen any sign of it from the other side. The tower was gone. The antenna lay on the ground in several mangled pieces, while the small building that had stood next to it was a blackened crater.

"Shit." Vikram sat down on a rock.

Miles's heart sank. This was not good. His mind had been doing a good job convincing itself that they would find a way out of their predicament. Now his mind was telling him things he didn't want to hear, brutally honest things. He scanned the horizon below, the coffee-dark sea in the distance swallowing up more suburban sprawl, a cracked and winding road leading out of the foothills in between. In this state, it was hard to trust his eyes.

"What is that?" he asked, pointing down at the road.

Beyond a field of boulders, on the old highway that once connected cities and towns, was the ghostlike figure of someone shambling toward them.

15.

"**HOW DID YOU** survive?" asked Dinev.

In the control room back at the facility, Dinev, Anna, Kerak, and Shikar gathered around Erestu, all wondering the same thing. Miles and Vikram hung back, having already heard the story.

"Someone warned me," said Erestu. "I had just enough time to gather one or two things and evacuate in the escape pod before the explosion. I hid in my life-bubble down among the ruins until I thought it was safe to venture out, and then made my way to shore."

"What do you mean, someone warned you?" asked Kerak.

"Their sub was cloaked, so the passive sonar didn't pick it up," Erestu explained. "But before they attacked, someone on board sent out a signal to let me know they were there. It was a small Bandarian attack sub, well within weapons range. I don't know who alerted me or why, but he saved my life."

"Show them what you showed us," said Vikram.

Erestu drew a slim black device out of his fanny pack. "I only had time to take a survival kit and this with me," he said, holding it up for all to see.

Dinev's and Shikar's mouths went round in expressions of relieved joy.

Kerak looked at it closely and said, "Is that——?"

"Of course," said Erestu.

"Is it *what?*" Anna demanded, the only one who didn't know.

"It's a universal transmitter," said Erestu simply. "It can send messages to any fixed communications device, digital or analog, anywhere on Our World."

"That's convenient," she said.

"The technology has been around for a long time," explained Dinev, "but they only became useful again after the satellites failed and the communications networks broke down. They can only receive messages if they stay exactly where they transmit from, so they're a transmitter of last resort. Few yishi have them, which is good since they use gamma rays."

"That's bad?" said Anna.

"I don't know how it is with humans," said Dinev, "but too much gamma radiation tends to kill yishi."

They wasted no more time before sending a message directly to Danevesu's governing council, warning them of Anders's imminent biological attack. It sort of glossed over what Vikram, Kerak, and the human ambassadors were doing on island Twenty-six in the Edrisian Archipelago in the first place, and simply requested emergency transport back to Danevesu.

Several minutes passed while they waited in anxious anticipation for a response. After several minutes more, they were ready to transmit the message again when they received a response, which Erestu read to them:

> The Civil Guard disrupted the attempted attack earlier today. Two guards died in the operation, as well as the four Bandarian terrorists. It was not a bioterror attack, but a conventional explosive. The city has been secured. We have contacted one of the military subs already looking for you to collect you as soon as possible. Estimated time of arrival to follow. We are greatly relieved to hear that you and the ambassadors are alive and well. Our best reports indicated that you had all been kidnapped by terrorists. Just what the hell is going on, anyway?
>
> Tchuvu

Vikram sent back a quick response that took the long way around to not answering Tchuvu's question, but thanked him effusively in a vain attempt to distract him from that fact. Which only made it less credible when Vikram warned Tchuvu again to be on guard against an attack with an airborne pathogen.

After more back and forth, Kerak stated the obvious. "He doesn't believe you, Viku," he said.

"Maybe they failed to get the agent into Danevesu," said Vikram.

"You need to tell him the truth."

So Vikram confessed everything to Tchuvu, explaining in painful detail just what he'd done and why, and how it had all blown up in his face with Berejian's betrayal and now endangered Danevesu's existence and, really, all of Our World.

This time they waited an even longer time and in more suspense for a reply. Finally, Tchuvu sent his response:

> I appreciate your candor and the warning. Still, we are certain Danevesu is secure now. We will convene a trial upon your return to deal with your and Kerak's crimes against the state.
>
> Best regards.

Vikram turned to Kerak with a look of exasperated recrimination. "Well, fuck me," said Kerak.

*

THE DANEVESAN military sub was much bigger but considerably more cramped and less luxurious than the craft they'd come in on. Of course, that one was in several pieces at the bottom of the sea off the coast of Twenty-six. So Anna couldn't really complain.

But her period had started just prior to their discovery of Berejian's plot to wreak a biological holocaust on Our World. So she wasn't exactly in a good mood, either. Luckily, yishi did menstruate—every twelve days. Vikram, being her former roommate and well-acquainted with the differences and similarities of her cycle to yishis', had been prepared and was able to help her out. She'd told Miles, of course, but despite that, or perhaps because of it, he was being a little clingy and possessive. And it was starting to strain an already frayed bond. But she didn't want to have to have that conversation with him just yet.

So she and Miles and Dinev were hanging out in the mess of the boat. Anna was attempting to explain two cornerstones of human civilization to Dinev—racism and sexism. She had a lot to say about both, too much really to do more than scratch the surface. In listening, Dinev expressed amazement and outrage, but also seemed enthralled, as if he were enjoying a really good yarn. He understood intuitively how splitting gender roles would lead to oppression. "It seems inescapable," he said, shaking his head. "One sex saddled with pregnancy and child-rearing, the other sex physically bigger and untied to domestic duties. That's a blueprint for misery."

But he struggled to understand prejudice based on skin color. "What about hair color? Do humans discriminate based on hair? or eyes?"

"No, not really," said Anna.

"Why not?"

Dinev had learned about slavery in his survey course of Earth history back in school. In reality, slavery was just as much a part of Our World's history. But Dinev didn't really grasp the significance of the racial component on the evolution of the institution on Earth. Or the concept of cosmetic and cultural differences constituting distinct races within the human species. Anna tried to explain it, but to Dinev it all boiled down to a fetishistic preoccupation with skin tone.

Miles could understand why Anna was so drawn to the yishi. She had never experienced the lack of otherness he'd enjoyed his entire life, until she arrived on Our World, despite her obvious otherness. Although she had no wings or feathers, Anna resembled the yishi to a surprising degree—much more than Miles, at any rate—certainly in complexion and stature, and in the fact she had breasts and hips.

For her part, Anna was curious to learn more about yishi religious beliefs.

"With the exception of the Bandarians, most yishi aren't religious," he said.

"Yes, but what about the Bandarians?" she asked.

"They practice Bahgee," he said. "'Submission to Gee,' it means literally. We call them 'Geeists,' after their supreme being, Gee. The religion was founded in Bandary thousands of years ago and eventually spread to the city of Lagaredel, which became the center of the faith and the old Bandarian Empire."

"Was the religion always limited to the Bandarians?" Anna asked.

"Oh, no. At one time it had the most followers on Our World, even in Danevesu. There was always a diversity of faiths, of course, but Bahgee was the only one that sought converts. Most other religions were more limited by geography, or culture. That was before our first space age, though, before most yishi stopped believing in those things. After the oceans rose, and so much of Bandary remained dry, of course, a lot of Geeists took that as a sign of their god's favor."

"Even though the ocean swallowed their capital, Baradel?" asked Miles.

Dinev shrugged.

"Were the Geeists the ones who colonized Skygarden?" he asked.

"A lot of yishi wanted to go there," said Dinev, "at least according to the histories. The Geeists were just a little more resistant to the facts once things started to deteriorate. Of course, modern Geeists consider them all to be heretics, as bad as the Danevesans—the atheists. Skygarden was supposed to be the paradise good Geeists went to after they died. So when they dared to go up there on their own, Gee destroyed it to punish their hubris."

"Tell me about Bahgee itself," said Anna. "What's the story, its creation myth?"

"You sound like an anthropologist," said Dinev. "Okay, let's see—I have to think back to school....Gee has always existed. He created the universe, the stars and Our World and Skygarden. I don't remember if he always lived on Skygarden, but that's supposed to be where he made his home. Gee is like us, but bigger, all-powerful, immortal, et cetera. He was lonely, so he impregnated himself and bore twins, the gods Gar and Dan."

"Dan?" Miles said with a smirk. Anna gave him a side-eyed glance.

"Yes. Anyway, Gar was noble and beloved of Gee. Dan was stunted and deformed—an impish trickster who was spurned by his father. Once, Dan flew to Our World and had his way with some of the animals who lived there, sort of like big sordies, if you know what those are. When his father found out, he vowed to kill Dan for his crime, for defiling the creatures Gee created. But Gar interceded on his brother's behalf. Gee relented and instead exiled Dan to Our World as punishment."

"Wait," said Miles, "he exiled Dan to the place where he'd raped all those animals?"

"I know, it doesn't make sense," Dinev admitted. "But he also exiled his favored son, Gar, to Our World. As punishment for taking Dan's side or to keep watch over his brother, I'm not sure which. But once Gar came to Our World, he fell in love with one of the big sordies and mated with him."

"So the children of Gar and this sordie are yishi?" said Anna.

"Yes, but so were the children of Dan and the other sordies," he said. "And, plainly, there have always been more descendants of Dan than of Gar—more wicked ones, that is, than righteous."

"I see."

"Gee is the god they worship, but he never involves himself in the affairs of yishi," said Dinev. "Gar and Dan are both immortal and are still on Our World, apparently, though they stopped living among yishi long ago. Gar, being benevolent, will sometimes help deserving yishi. But Dan is a mischievous god and will often interfere to frustrate the ambitions of bad yishi. Though he's just as likely to mess with good yishi, just for the hell of it."

"Is there a Hell in Bahgee?" asked Anna.

"Not exactly. It's a little like reincarnation in Hindu or Buddhist traditions, if I understand those correctly. Except that someone who is evil in life will come back as an inanimate object, like a stone or lump of iron or a drop of water—and the cycle ends there. A pious yishi, on the other hand, their consciousness will ascend to paradise, which used to be Skygarden, but now…"

"Now…?"

"Well, it's hard for me to say because Danevesans so rarely come into contact with actual Bandarians," he explained. "But some of them believe that paradise will only return for the faithful once Our World is destroyed."

"So that explains Telesu's involvement with the Bandarians," said Anna.

"Well, I'm not so sure," said Dinev. "Bandary always sponsored various terror groups over the years—their way of striking at Danevesu while claiming no involvement. But they've refused to support the Hopmoul."

"The Hopmoul?" she said.

"Sounds like something they'd serve at Oktoberfest," said Miles.

Anna turned on him, annoyed. "It's not really funny, all things considered." Miles, she reflected, was acting his age. She turned back to Dinev. "Who are the Hopmoul?"

"They're a popular splinter group of an extreme cult of Bahgee," he said. "Fundamentalist, nihilistic, apocalyptic—in love with death. They try to create as much chaos as they can, as much destruction as possible, and have no loyalties outside their own organization. Once they started assassinating Bandarian ministers, the government had to cut all ties. Officially, at least."

"So you think it was the Hopmoul helping Telesu?" she said.

"It's possible," he said. "It seemed like Telesu and Berejian were being careful to keep the others in the dark to some extent."

"But they failed, anyway," Miles put in. "Didn't they?"

Dinev and Anna each nodded, hoping more than anything that this was true.

Anna shook her head and frowned. "It's fascinating," she said. "I have so many questions. But I have a feeling it would take a lifetime just to scratch the surface—it's overwhelming."

"I would think you'd be anxious to return home now," said Dinev.

Anna's wide-eyed expression said otherwise. "Oh, no," she replied. "I need more time."

Dinev laughed. "Your world seems like a paradise to me," he said. "I suppose it's all in your perspective."

It seemed like a paradise to Miles, as well, just then.

Dinev excused himself. Like the others, he had a backlog of messages from friends and colleagues in Danevesu and elsewhere, as he had been incommunicado for more than three days. Anna looked lost in thought, and Miles could feel her drifting away.

"Doesn't it scare you?" he asked.

"Of course it does," she said absently. "I mean, well....Doesn't *what* scare me?"

"All of it, I don't know," he said. "I was amazed by Danevesu and the yishi and all their technology at first. But this world is a post-apocalyptic ...desert. And they're trying to destroy what's left of it."

"All worlds are dangerous," she said. "Apparently. And beautiful too."

He nodded and looked her in the eyes. "I think you're beautiful," he said and touched her hand. It was clumsy but sincere.

She clutched his hand and said, "I want you to know I care about you, Miles."

"I care about you too," he said.

She could see she was going to have to be less subtle. "Friends have always been more important to me than lovers, anyway," she said. "And I hope you'll always be my friend."

"Wha...are you breaking up with me?" he asked, a little shocked.

"Miles—"

"I'm the only—" he said, raising his voice, before lowering it to just above a whisper in such an enclosed space—"I am *literally* the only human male on this entire planet."

"Well, it sounds worse when you put it that way."

Miles frowned, tried to make sense of his jumble of thoughts. "It's just, I've never been in love before," he said. "I thought...I thought maybe you felt the same way."

Anna's shoulders slumped, and she wore a pained expression. "We've been through a lot together in a short time, Miles. But let's not confuse whatever this is with love."

"I'm not confused," he said. "At least not about 'whatever this is.'"

She squeezed his hand. "I'm sorry, Miles. Coming here has clarified things for me in a way. I understand now why Vikram wanted to bring me here."

Miles nodded his head slowly, the truth of it dawning on him.

*

VIKRAM AND KERAK had their heads buried in their smartskin, worriedly communicating back and forth with friends and colleagues back in Danevesu. Miles sat across from them, feeling like a fly on the wall—if there were flies on Our World, that is.

They'd learned more about the foiled attack. All of the dead conspirators had been positively identified as Bandarian.

"How can they tell?" asked Miles.

"They were all circumcised," said Kerak.

"Oh."

Anders wasn't among them, apparently. "Aside from that," said Vikram, "he stands out physically. Someone would have recognized him."

"You told Tchuvu it wasn't a bomb, though, right?" said Miles.

"Well, it could've been," he said. "They could have tried to use an explosive device to disperse the toxin. Or it could have been a diversion. But then there was no secondary attack."

Erestu joined them. He had been in the medical bay taking intravenous fluids and had finally regained his color and vigor.

Miles had been surprised back on Twenty-six by his elation at finding Erestu alive. Part of it was relief that the apparition they'd seen in the heat and dust wasn't another Bandarian sent to finish them off. But mainly it was genuine pleasure at seeing the face of someone he considered a friend. The captain had gone out of his way to be kind and show an interest in Miles, so Miles naturally felt closer to Erestu than any other yishi except Vikram. But he was ashamed to admit that Anna had been right, as well, that he was attracted to Erestu. Even ensconced in relatively modest attire, there was something different about the way Erestu's body moved against his clothing, something earthly and alluring. His luminous green eyes scanned their faces and settled on Vikram.

"I'm sorry I got you involved in this, Erestu," said Vikram.

Erestu brushed it aside. "I would have been insulted if you hadn't," he said, taking a seat.

Vikram laughed. "I know, but first I nearly got you killed. Lost you your sub. And now they're probably going to try you along with me for my crimes," Vikram said.

"They are?" Erestu thought about that. "Well, fuck you then. Better?"

"That's all I ask."

They filled Erestu in on what little they'd learned en route, which wasn't much more than what Tchuvu had told them.

"Is it possible they released the pathogen, but it just didn't work?" said Erestu.

"That would be the best possible scenario," said Vikram. "But I doubt that's the case. Berejian may have been insane, but he wasn't stupid. Honestly, I'll feel better when we get back to the city, trial or no."

There was little to nothing they could do but wait until morning, when they would reach Danevesu. Vikram had told Elusia everything he could think of about what Anders might be planning. Kerak had talked to his colleagues in the medical guild. After the attack, the city was on high alert. But, honestly, the foiled bombing was no different from a dozen other failed attempts.

After more idle conversation, Vikram and Kerak retired to their cabin for a midday nap, leaving Miles alone with Erestu.

"I don't suppose they'll let me drive the sub this time?" said Miles.

"Probably not," said Erestu.

"Are you going to be in trouble when we get back?" asked Miles.

Erestu tilted his head back and forth, which Miles took for a shrug.

"Are Anna and I in trouble?" he asked.

"Of course not," said Erestu. "We kidnapped you, remember? Besides, I don't know how it is on Earth, but it's never a good idea to arrest ambassadors from someplace you don't want to piss off."

"But nobody else on Earth even knows about Our World," Miles pointed out.

"You don't understand how revered you and Anna are here," said Erestu. "Danevesans have been dreaming about meeting a human from Earth since the day your planet was discovered. We've studied your history, culture, and languages for generations. There are dozens of clubs for terraphiles in the city—English clubs, Spanish, Russian, Chinese, Hindi, even Latin. Yishi are endlessly fascinated by Earth and humans, and with your culture, really everything to do with your world. You've no idea how we all look at you and Anna. You're like gods walking among us."

"I don't feel like a god," said Miles. "Not even a demigod, really."

Erestu smiled in that odd yishi way. "I wish you could see yourself through my eyes."

Miles felt his cheeks warm. He could have said the same about Erestu.

*

MILES HAD ALMOST nothing to call his own on Our World and so had clung to Anna like a toddler to a mother's hand. Now she had declared her independence, he felt naked. As night "fell"—evening aboard the sub was indicated by the gradual dimming of the lights—Erestu offered Miles a berth in his cabin, which he accepted gratefully.

The cabin was cozy and moodily lit by recessed bluish lights. Whether it was his late afternoon nap or the gelum, Miles felt wide awake and sat on the edge of his bunk across from Erestu.

"How did you know Vikram—Araviku, I mean?" Miles asked him.

"We're cousins," said Erestu.

"Oh," he said, surprised.

"It's not unusual," said Erestu. "At this point, most of the inhabitants of Danevesu are related. Viku's egg donor, Arak, was a sibling of my sperm donor, though Viku is much older than I am."

"So you're family?"

"Technically, yes," he said. "Though the concept of 'family' is a little different in Danevesu. We tend to think of a family as the group of friends and colleagues we choose to socialize with. And lovers... sometimes. Of course, we know who our genetic relatives are. But we don't necessarily consider them family."

"So...how do you know Viku, then?"

"Oh, right," he said and smiled. "I first met Araviku when I took him out to a research station on one of the Danevesan islands. He was already pretty famous after he returned from Earth the first time. I wanted to talk to him, as I'd always been keen on all things Earth-related. So I mentioned the familial connection, asked him all about his adventures, and we ended up becoming good friends. Really, I'd do anything for him."

"I think you have," said Miles.

Erestu shrugged. "How did you get to know Araviku then?"

Miles told Erestu about how they met on a train in France and eventually wound up on Our World. He realized as he did so that no one else in Danevesu would know the story.

"So that's how you became an Earth ambassador?" Erestu said and laughed. "That is quintessential Viku."

"I think he always meant to just bring Anna here," Miles said. "I just sort of tagged along."

Erestu wasn't familiar with the phrase, but he understood what Miles meant. "That makes it more impressive, if you ask me."

"I guess," Miles said, though he couldn't really see how. "In any case, I think my tagging-along-with-Anna days are behind me."

Erestu arched one side of his feathered brow, so Miles explained the situation.

"I'm sorry," Erestu said.

"Thanks," he said. Miles threw his legs up on the bunk and lay back. "The days are so long here, it seems like it happened yesterday." He wasn't sleepy yet, just tired of talking. In the low light, Erestu could see him staring up at the ceiling.

After several minutes of listening to the hum of the sub's electric motor, Erestu started undressing. Miles glanced over, innocently at first, then intentionally. By now, of course, he had seen plenty of yishi genitalia on screens of every kind, in every setting. Regardless, the sight of a feathery cock and balls bracketed by womanly hips below a pair of breasts always caused a mental hiccup in him. If he focused on Erestu's breasts—which he could manage—it was all right. Except then he was staring at Erestu's breasts. Erestu turned his round, firm backside to Miles as he stowed his folded tunic and cloak in a bunkside cubby. Then he strolled back across the room and sat down next to Miles, crossing his legs to hide his masculinity, which he correctly intuited Miles found intimidating.

Erestu leaned over and kissed Miles on the mouth. It was an odd sensation, with Erestu's upper lip forming the base of his beak-like nose, but not unpleasant. Erestu then helped Miles remove his shirt, his eyes locked on Miles the whole time.

"So...we're really going to do this, aren't we?" said Miles.

"Only if you want to."

Part of Miles, the part that was pushed way down below the surface by his raging libido, screamed that this was a bad idea. But, in addition to his heedless sex drive, a more rational part of his mind dismissed his qualms as simple fear, fear that made no sense in this world.

So Erestu helped Miles off with the rest of his clothes, and after exploring each other's alien bodies, they made love. For Miles, the breaking of taboos only made the whole experience more arousing, as did Erestu's carnal skills. Miles soon overcame his initial hesitation and proved an enthusiastic and considerate partner.

Afterward, as they lay on his bunk spooning, Miles's arm thrown over Erestu, his chest blanketed by Erestu's downy wings, Miles wondered if this made him gay. He realized he would probably never be in a place where that mattered less. He thought of Anna and wondered if she was what he had really been afraid of.

＊

VIKRAM'S HAND VIBRATED and an insistent whistle echoed in his small cabin, waking him from a fitful sleep. A message from Geresh had come in on his smartskin:

> Elusia woke suddenly in the night coughing and wheezing uncontrollably. He's now sedated but still in some pain. I started experiencing similar symptoms soon after, and I've taken the same antitussives / depressants but am doing a little better. No signs of a second attack, but others are reporting symptoms. Any idea what's going on?

Vikram dashed a quick note off to Geresh and then roused Kerak. After filling him in, Vikram left their cabin to find the sub's "captain," whom he found already up, standing behind the pilot, his eyes surfing the numerous monitors and screens arrayed around the bridge of the boat.

The captain nodded to Vikram. "Something's going on," he said. "I don't suppose you know anything I don't?"

"I might," he said. "What do you know?"

"They're closing the harbor," said the captain. "When I asked the sea traffic controller what was happening, he told us to continue on into port and don breathing apparatus before disembarking. I tried asking if it was chemical or biological, accidental or intentional, but he either didn't know or wouldn't say."

"It could be either," conceded Vikram. "But I would prepare for an intentionally released biological agent if I were you."

"Outstanding," he said. "Any idea why they'd want us to proceed if the port is closed due to a bioterror attack?"

"Blame that on me," said Vikram.

"Don't worry, I will." The captain checked on four or five monitors and then turned to Vikram. "We only have enough full-body suits for the crew. The rest we can fit with simple breathing filters. I hope that will do."

"And if it doesn't?"

"Tough titties."

Of the refugees from Twenty-six, only he and Kerak had any inkling of what was happening in Danevesu. The others were all asleep. Vikram dreaded the inevitability of their waking to hear the news.

He should have stayed on Earth. He could see that now.

Or, better yet, he should never have amassed the gene bank. And then Anders would have had to spend years combing the Earth himself, gathering biological samples one at a time. And, ultimately, the result would be the same—except that he and poor Anna and Miles would be safely back on Earth. A bit fatalistic and self-centered, but probably true.

Vikram shook his head, knowing there was nothing he could change about any of that now. He thought about what he would say to the others to prepare them for their landing in Danevesu. And then about what he would say to Tchuvu and the other councilors, depending upon what they said to him.

*

"OUR NUMBER ONE priority," said Tchuvu, "has to be ensuring the safety of our ambassadors from Earth."

Miles agreed with that, nodding his head until he realized how it looked. His and everyone else's faces were covered by some form of mask. The marine civil guards, who had arrived wearing the equivalent of hazmat suits, had handed Vikram and the others off to local guards wearing the same simple breathing filters they had—transparent flexible masks that covered the eyes, nose, and mouth. Those already infected wore them to try and prevent spreading the pathogen, while the few uninfected wore them to stay that way.

The new arrivals stood on the stage of the amphitheater, which was also the council's regular meeting place—where they deliberated policy and met dignitaries, sometimes in private and sometimes with an audience. Tchuvu, seated like the other stewards, looked wan and feeble, as if all the vitality had been drained from his body over the last few hours.

Geresh, translating for the incapacitated Okiva, looked even worse. Elusia was too sick to leave his bed, as were several of the stewards who were also absent. Only four could make it to this hearing, and all were infected.

"Our guests have seen more of Our World and suffered more as a result than any of us would have wished." Tchuvu aimed this comment at Vikram. Then he spoke directly to Anna and Miles: "I can't speak for all yishi, but I think most of us would want to express how sorry we are for what you've been put through."

"What are you going to do to Araviku?" asked Anna.

Tchuvu nodded his head as Geresh translated. "Ultimately, it's not up to me," he said, "at least not me alone. In the short term, I would ask him to help us figure out what it is we're dealing with."

"Of course, I will," said Vikram.

"If the pathogen is as lethal as you say," said Tchuvu, "those who survive will have to worry about how to deal with you. They might judge you as no worse than us, since we had our suspicions and did nothing." Tchuvu turned back to Anna and said, "For now, we need to get you and Miles back to Earth while we still can."

Anna shook her head. "No," she said, a little more forcefully than she intended. "I mean, I want to stay."

Miles couldn't hide his disappointment, nor Tchuvu his shock. "Be that as it may..." he began, before being interrupted by Dinev, who argued for the humans remaining, even though it was only Anna who actually wanted to. It touched off a debate joined by Vikram, Kerak, Erestu, and the councilors until Tchuvu ended it. "Enough," he said, starting to cough. "This isn't up for debate. They have to return. What would we tell future delegations if we allowed anything to happen to them?" He coughed again into his mask, the effort to stop bringing tears to his eyes. "No, we have to send them back home—today."

It had less to do with Anna and more to do with the council's long-term plan. Her and Miles's importance was mostly symbolic. Since before Arak's first secretive mission to Earth, councils had been trying to form a strategy for making contact with the humans. And Miles's and Anna's visit served as a trial run—the first of more to come. At least that was the plan, and Tchuvu was determined to stick to it, despite the uncertainty of everything now that Berejian's deadly pathogen had been unleashed on Danevesu.

Anna and Miles made the reverse trek from the one they took upon first arriving in the city, now with a larger entourage in tow. Outside Kerak's medical lab and quarantine area, they awkwardly began to say their good-byes.

Miles quickly hugged Erestu, who seemed more broken up than he did. Miles probably should have known by then that in most relationships, an imbalance of affection existed, but he was too caught up in his own angst to see that clearly. Then Miles locked Vikram in a tight embrace. "Thank you, Vikram," he said, "for everything. I'm going to miss you....I hope we get to see each other again someday." He didn't need to add that that was pretty unlikely.

After saying farewell to the others, Anna took Vikram aside and could get out only, "Rumbi," before throwing her arms around him and breaking down in tears.

"It's all right, Anna," he said, though of course it wasn't. He held her close while she struggled to speak.

"Will I ever see you again?" she finally asked.

"I don't know."

"I don't want to leave like this," she whispered.

"I know."

Kerak managed to pry them apart and took them inside to begin the decontamination process prior to departure. Once done, they emerged in the room they'd first found themselves in, now with Vikram and the others standing on the other side of the partition.

The wormhole—Miles preferred not to think of it as a six-foot-wide asshole—hung there like a strangely inviting splash of ink, the black hole at its center surrounded by an undulating black corona. Another technician, presumably one who was uninfected, worked the controls. Anna and Miles would return to Granada, since that's where they'd left their stuff. From there, Barcelona for Anna. For Miles, wherever the four winds took him.

There was a one-way partition in front of the portal to prevent a clumsy tech or zhink from just falling into it and emerging into some random destination on the other side. It dissolved, and the technician signaled to Vikram, who told Anna and Miles that it was ready to go. "*Via con dios*," he said.

Miles turned with a wave to Vikram and the others, lifted a foot to dip into the wormhole, and then was swallowed by it.

Anna gave one last look at Vikram but couldn't hold his gaze and maintain her composure. She turned to the spacetime portal and began to step toward it when a muffled *thump* sounded off to her right, the harbor side, followed by a loud boom, causing the floor to wobble perceptibly. The lights in the room blacked out, and the portal puckered, shrinking to nothing before flashing a bright pinprick of light, like an old black-and-white TV being shut off. The portal was gone, and Anna overheard the technician and Vikram talking anxiously while the tech fussed with the computer console. Anna now noticed that the translucent partitions had fallen away as well. The room was dark but for the emergency lights around the entrance and the rebooting computer screen.

Anna looked back at where the portal had been.

"Was it a tsunami?" she asked.

"No, it couldn't be," said Vikram, who whispered something to the tech. "We're not sure what happened."

"Miles!" she gasped. "Vikram, what happened to Miles?"

"Miles is fine," he said. "He's in Granada now...I think."

After another few moments of confusion, with Anna left standing on the darkened platform, a more insistent *thump* landed much closer this time, demanding everyone's attention more forcefully, as the entire room shook with a deafening boom. The shockwave brought them to their knees as glass tiles and pulverized stone sprinkled down on them, broken loose around an ugly crack down the middle of the ceiling.

*

TRAVELING THROUGH the shantytowns on the outskirts of Bandary's capital always made Anders tense. Not so much for Peleg, who'd grown up there. But for someone raised in the relative order and opulence of Danevesu, its sights, sounds, and smells assaulted the senses at every turn. It was a filthy, chaotic hellhole—but it was home for seven-eighths of the city's inhabitants, and therefore most of the country.

The structures they passed were regularly blown down by powerful dust storms, only to be hastily rebuilt using whatever spare materials could be scrounged. As a result, most of the buildings lining the streets were newly constructed. But these ramshackle huts merely concealed entrances to the real city below—an underground network of tunnels connecting thousands of habitats and hidey-holes, going down nearly a hundred meters in some places. Few outsiders, including the current regime, had any inkling as to the extent of the subterranean complex beneath their feet.

Anders and Peleg were being led through a winding maze of crumbling pavement and redscale-covered dirt roads in a two-seater rickshaw pulled by a wiry old yishi. The city's main arteries were normally clogged with yishi on foot, but added to that now were fossil fuel–powered transports carrying supplies to Lagar Temu and the homes of government functionaries surrounding the palace. A once-in-a-century dust storm had been forecast to arrive sometime in the next several days.

Lagaredel sat in the lowest part of a long valley that comprised the largest geographic feature left on Bandary, situated between a mountain range to the north and great rocky cliffs overlooking the former capital of Baradel and a vast forest, now buried by the ocean, to the south. The ancient city had straddled the confluence of two great waterways, now dry riverbeds. Once it had been the center of the greatest agricultural region on Our World, producing and exporting grains and a hundred other crops to the far ends of the planet. Now the yishi of Lagaredel subsisted on a combination of jelly mash brought from the port town of Ashedel and what was euphemistically referred to as "seconds," produced by the sewage treatment plants that also provided more or less potable drinking water. Such was the importance of such "recycling" that relieving oneself in anything other than a receptacle connected to the city's plumbing was an offense punishable by death.

As for the once-in-a-century storm, the Lagarenes' ability to forecast weather was something of a local joke. Not that their typical weather was anything to laugh at, but the threat of a once-in-a-century storm was generally understood as the swarm of cyclones that hit about once a year and which, with any luck, brought some much-needed rain. So vigilant but unperturbed yishi lined up to fill jugs with reddish water and collect the seconds that resembled bars of chocolate in all but flavor, odor, and consistency.

Moving as slowly as they were, Anders and Peleg had little to do but watch the yishi of this particular Lagarene slum. Few made eye contact with them, though some who did glared back sullenly, resentful of anyone wealthy enough to afford transportation. A very few showed potbellies of various sizes, evidence of unfettered natural insemination, the kind of thing Anders had never seen in the flesh until being exiled. Children, pregnancy's inevitable by-product, roamed freely, half-naked and sweaty, their feathers mangy and dull. When one little urchin darted into line to join a parent, the next in line raised up a hand to strike him. The parent stepped in and lifted the child out of harm's way, swearing at the irritated yishi and stroking the little one's fluttering wings.

He has a protector, thought Anders. *It's more than I had.* The aloof, officious yishi who had raised young Telesu in the climate-controlled bowels of Danevesu had a habit of taking the side of his persecutors, of whom there were many—until he simply abandoned Telesu prior to the child's equally traumatic adolescence.

News of the closure of Danevesu's harbor had reached Anders and Peleg at Ashedel. Immediately after, their military entourage ditched them as they deployed with the secondary force sent to finish off Danevesu. So Peleg and Anders made their way to the city of Lagaredel and Lagar Temu with Vikram's priceless case in tow.

It was aboard the sub that Peleg realized he had never been in command of anything. He gave the orders to his guards that Telesu told him to. He hadn't approved the sinking of the small civilian submersible, which had no offensive capability. Then the unexpected rendezvous with Bandarian intelligence at the dock in Twenty-six—unexpected to Peleg, at least—had been a humiliating blow. They presented themselves as Bandarian covert operatives, but Peleg was sure they were Hopmoul. It wasn't unprecedented. The terrorist group may have been at war with Bandary, but their common foe—Danevesu—they both recognized as the greater enemy.

Like all Bandarians, Peleg had been raised to expect the Danevesans to one day attack them without warning or provocation. With their love of technology and compulsion for developing more and more sophisticated weapons, it was only a matter of time. As a result, an orientation based on the idea of self-defense had always driven national security priorities. So for Bandary to carry out a sneak attack on Danevesu with a biological weapon like this was more than troubling to Peleg.

Anders was pleased, though. His scheme had been years in the planning, involved numerous actors with often competing agendas, and had played out almost perfectly so far. Berejian had managed his part. The operatives had transported the pathogen to Danevesu's gates and slipped inside the city undetected. They'd created the diversion that allowed two of them to enter the city's ventilation system and release the pathogen inside the canisters while the Danevesans slept. Anders had no doubt the biological agent would be deadly. Berejian had described it to him as a sort of Frankenstein's fungus—a microscopic spore made up of spare parts. It contained genetic material from a stew of Earth organisms—a common species of black mold, a rare Himalayan mushroom, a type of liverwort found only in Antarctica—and redscale. The spore remained dormant while dry or suspended in an inert liquid such as in the canisters. But it behaved more like a virus, multiplying aggressively once it came into contact with a suitably warm and moist organic medium, like the nasal mucous membrane of a sleeping yishi, say. And then it would consume its host, whose immune system was tragically ill-equipped to fend it off.

Really, he couldn't have hoped for better.

As for Peleg, it was hard to tell if he was simply wounded at having his authority usurped, or if he really would have opposed the attack on Danevesu if he could. If that was the case, he certainly wouldn't care for the final stage of Anders's plan. Which was what was occupying his mind at the moment—getting the remaining canisters he'd transferred out of Vikram's case to his Hopmoul contact in Lagaredel. To be safe, Anders would have to keep an eye out for Peleg until he could accomplish a few last errands.

They could see the high dome of Lagar Temu as they turned a corner onto a narrow alley that took them out of the slum. The palace, built more than a thousand years before, rose up from the ground at a gentle slope before turning ever steeper. Its stone walls, pitted and scarred on the outside, were a dozen meters thick at their base, forming a triangle with turret-like rounded corners. It had been a fortress before it was a palace, the seat of a king and his court once, then the legislative chambers of a republic, then the apparatus of a dictator, and now a combination temple and ministry. The warlord who had built it, or rather, had had it built by slaves captured by his armies in battle, had harbored a grandiose vision for what had been at the time a rather modest domain. The building was huge, sprawling over twenty acres, the ultimate expression of what in retrospect was a fairly obvious attempt to overcompensate. Subsequent rulers of Lagaredel would add the great dome and many smaller domes, as well as other refinements and follies over the centuries. As the Bandarian empire grew and the seat of power shifted to Baradel on the southern coast, Lagar Temu fell into disuse. With Baradel gone, the palace endured as it was particularly well-suited to weathering the kinds of destructive dust storms that blew up regularly on Bandary. Also, it made it much easier to separate the elite members of the government, military, and religious orders from the surly, unwashed masses.

Anders and Peleg were deposited by the main corner entrance of Lagar Temu by their elderly driver. They didn't need air-conditioned cloaks here, as the heat in Bandary was a comfortably dry 130 degrees, being further from the equator than Danevesu. But they wore them anyway, as the swirling dust and airborne particles of dead redscale stuck to the skin and infiltrated the feathers if left uncovered. They were admitted into the palace, through three different sets of gates, and finally found the minister Salas awaiting them in what passed for good cheer, having a nosh on his bed.

Peleg presented him the case with a bow, as if he were performing a solemn ritual. Salas eyed Anders curiously.

"Thank you, Dar Peleg," he said with a nod, then turned to Anders. "It must be tempting, Dar Telesu, to hold on to some of these samples, no?" He gave Anders a teasing smile as he took a bite of the special seconds his personal chef prepared for him.

"Not at all," he said truthfully. "I feel no need to hoard Earth organisms."

It was hardly a secret that the regime no longer needed Anders. His expertise, the technology he'd given them, his very heretical presence was only tolerated because of what he'd promised them. And now that he'd delivered it, the question of what to do with him was an open one. But as foreign minister, Salas had more imminent demands on his time. Anders could wait. He wasn't going anywhere.

After they exited the ministry, Anders and Peleg stood together momentarily before parting ways, the silence between them suddenly awkward. "You've done more for your country than you know," said Anders, trying to be polite.

"I, Dar Telesu?" said Peleg. "I did nothing. I just watched it happen." He turned then and walked away.

Anders shook his head and turned in the opposite direction, walking purposefully toward his apartments and laboratory, thinking of all he needed to do in a short time.

16.

THE SPANISH SUN damn near blinded Miles as he dropped out of the wormhole and onto the gravelly path of the Alhambra grounds. He turned around, expecting Anna to fall out any second. But there was no portal. No Anna. He waited. After about thirty seconds that could have been an hour, still no Anna. He looked one way, then the other, then did a complete revolution. She was nowhere to be found. Across the river below him was Granada. He checked over the side of the parapet, just in case. He walked in circles, stupidly searching the same ground over and over again. A vague awareness began to sink in that others were milling around and starting to notice his odd behavior. He didn't care. Thinking about the thing that did matter to him left him wobbly and weak-kneed.

Miles fell on his ass but managed not to flop over completely. He sat and pulled his knees up to his chin. Despair crept up on him as he tried to make sense of what had happened. He had returned to Earth, but Anna had not. Had something terrible happened in transit? Had she convinced them to let her stay and abandoned him? Had he lost his mind and hallucinated the last week of his life? The tourists continued to stare and now it began to bother him. He stood a little too quickly, causing a terrific head rush, but was able to right himself after a minute or so. What if Anna had transported to someplace nearby? He should return to the pension where they'd left their stuff. That was it. If she was in Granada, she would head there.

Miles felt himself float down the hill, his body unused to the weak gravity. The extra oxygen in the air also left him slightly intoxicated. As a result, he had a little trouble finding the pension and walked right by it twice before realizing where he was. He nearly ripped the door off its hinges as he entered.

"Sorry," he said to the door. He approached the front desk and said to the clerk behind the counter, *Hello, how are you?* in flawless Danevesan.

The clerk stared back at him in bewilderment.

My Spanish must be really bad, he thought. "Do you speak English?" he tried.

"Yes, a little," she said.

Miles explained that he and his friend had checked in a few days ago, left their bags, but then had to leave unexpectedly, which was more or less true.

She looked doubtful. "There were backpacks," she said. "But a long time now—wait here, please." She popped her head back and asked him, "How many?" Miles said there were two and described what they looked like, and she disappeared through a doorway. A minute later, she returned with their backpacks and plopped them onto the counter. "These are here more than a month," she said, a little perturbed.

"Right," he said. "What did I say?" He paid for a room for the night, for the night they skipped out on, and a few hundred extra pesetas for storing their bags so long (a miserly tip, but Miles was having trouble remembering what "potatoes" were worth). "If you see my friend," he said to the clerk, "would you let her know I'm here?" He described Anna for her, adding a bit mawkishly, "She's very beautiful."

The clerk listened and nodded slowly, humoring the clearly confused young man before handing him a key.

Miles schlepped their bags upstairs, finding his room after trying the wrong door a couple of times, and threw himself down on a creaky old bed. After a moment, he got back up and stripped off all his grungy clothes, including the red bikini briefs wedged up his butt-crack, which he tossed in a wicker trash basket in the corner. He dug a pair of clean boxer shorts and a T-shirt out of his backpack and put them on. He lay back down and heaved an exaggerated sigh of not quite relief, but resignation.

He lay there in his T-shirt and boxers for a while, just staring at the molding around the dim bulb hanging from the ceiling. He breathed in the fresh air of Earth, tried to appreciate the golden light of the Sun throwing shadows across the walls.

But nothing helped, because he knew Anna wasn't going to show up. And he'd never see her again.

The outline of the bulb blurred as his eyes filled with tears and then spilled quietly down the sides of his face before his chest began to convulse, forcing the sobs to come. He turned on his side and covered his face with a scratchy pillow as he cried for Anna. He cried for Vikram and Danevesu, and he cried for his father. But mostly he cried for himself, unprepared as he was for this life, on this world or any other.

Mercifully, sleep came on suddenly.

With sleep came dreams of the most confused sort, as his mind tried to make sense of the last several days. When he awoke, it was half past midnight and he was starving. A late-night snack of fried potatoes and ham croquettes at a nearby bar turned out to be the most glorious thing Miles had ever tasted and did as much as food could to improve his state of mind. Once sated, he realized he had to return to Barcelona and the Hotel Kashmir. Though he knew that Anna and Vikram would not be there, it seemed necessary that he go back anyway.

It was a kind of circular logic drawing him back to the beginning, a very human impulse.

17.

THE PACKET FLEW out of the Bandarian sub silently but landed in Danevesu with another loud *thump*. Launched several miles offshore from an electromagnetic railgun, it traveled at many times the speed of sound, its impact succeeded shortly after by a sonic boom. The railgun was old-school, of course, in keeping with the ethos of the technophobic Bandarians.

What should have happened next was the same thing that happened the last time Bandary fired a conventional weapon on Danevesu. A large portal should have opened in the path of the incoming ordnance, swallowing the projectile and shitting it out through a second arsehole right back where it had come from, obliterating its sender. It did not merely combine a devastatingly effective defensive and offensive weapon in one, it embodied an infuriatingly smug manner of ironic justice. The first time the Danevesans employed this singularly discouraging defense was also the last time they'd had to.

But that didn't happen this time.

Despite a highly autonomous, artificially intelligent monitoring system in its marine and air defense station, yishi technicians were still an essential part of the process. So, although alarms were blaring and emergency messages being sent to everyone who staffed the station, no one was there to do anything about it until it was too late.

The first packet the Bandarians fired took out the Danevesans' ability to manipulate portals, severely compromising the city's defenses, as well as closing the stationary portal just as Anna was about go through it.

Now several things were going on at once, with a handful of uninfected yishi doing the best they could to perform the necessary jobs of those now confined to sickbeds. They were drastically understaffed, and many had little or no knowledge of what they were doing. Erestu, Dinev, and Shikar were pressed into service by the one remaining member of the marine and air defense station, a yishi named Zino, who had been off-duty and visiting the harbor village the night of the pathogen's release. Although their elegant and devastating defensive weapon had been disabled, they still had conventional laser systems to redirect incoming packets. Given a full squad of experienced technicians, they could have neutralized the Bandarian attack. As it was, they were lucky to thwart half of the packets fired on the city by the two Bandarian ships.

The action Erestu and his crew saw didn't resemble anything Anna would have recognized as combat. Essentially, they sat in a room far from the battle, wearing virtual reality headsets, and guiding specialized remote-control zhinks through the air or underwater to strike at the Bandarian fleet. In some cases, they controlled several at a time—the zhinks moving like a flock of birds or school of fish. When a zhink or group was destroyed, they switched controls to a new zhink, and so on.

Using these defensive zhinks, they were able to disable many of the packets with special lasers that altered their flight paths, crashing many of them into the submerged ruins of Old Danevesu, while Zino worked on figuring out how to restore their ability to create portals for defense.

At the same time, Vikram was working furiously with a young, uninfected bioengineering student. They knew of only about a dozen yishi who had been exposed to the pathogen but not infected. Kalaster was one of them, and Vikram was using him as a lab assistant and a possible source for a neutralizing antibody. Vikram could now study Berejian's pathogen, but he had to hurry if anything useful were to come of it. The more he learned about it, the more discouraged he became, however.

Kerak tended to the sick and wounded. He was the only doctor in the city unaffected by the pathogen. Three physicians who were infected helped minister to the sick for as long as they could. And Anna tended to those suffering the most, trying to at least make them comfortable.

On the morning after the first day of the attack, Danevesu stood in shaky defiance of the Bandarians' steady assault, its once-beautiful gem-like façade scarred and broken, gleaming rows of windows replaced by gaping holes. Despite the damage done and the ugliness it left, most of the city remained intact.

The bombing campaign was more terrifying than anything Anna could have imagined. When they had run out of the portal room shortly after the bombardment began, Anna and Vikram became separated from the others when a hallway collapsed between them. Forced to turn back the way they'd come and past the amphitheater, which, with its central location and large bay windows, served as a convenient bull's-eye for the Bandarian forces, they experienced a bit of the carnage their enemies were inflicting. When a stone and titanium column exploded, Anna fell to the floor clutching her leg as the corridor outside the amphitheater's main entrance filled with billowing dust. A piece of shrapnel was sticking out of her left thigh, the blood showing bright red against the white dust covering everything. Able to stand and walk with some pain, Anna could not see Vikram and wandered into a yishi holding his face in his hands. With blood dripping down one side, into his mouth and covering his neck, she could see that flying debris had taken his right eye and made other new holes on that side of his face.

She didn't know how to help him but tried to hold his elbow and guide him away from the worst of the smoke and debris. To her right, a fire was burning, and two yishi were trying desperately to put out the flames engulfing a third on the floor. They covered him with their cloaks, stamping out the flames as he writhed in pain, too late to save him.

Vikram found Anna and dragged her and the other yishi to safety, further inside the mountain, away from any possible blasts. He and Kerak, who had somehow managed to find his way back to them, carried as many of the injured back as they could. Most of the yishi were also sick and had only gotten out of their beds to move to safety when they were caught in the explosion.

By the next day, Anna was far from the exposed windows of the city, in a hospital ward, but not as a patient. Her leg had been healed quickly by Kerak, who left a barely perceptible half-inch scar where the shrapnel had lodged itself. Anna now helped Kerak tend to the other injured and the far more numerous sick.

The bombing continued, impacts coming without warning. No rumble of guns firing, no whistle of shells in flight preceded them. All at random a low boom would reverberate, rattling their teeth and the floors above and below them, followed by the high-pitched wail and shattering glass a beat later, and then the stone turned to powder floating down around them. The first daylong barrage was intended to smash the ten-inch-thick windows and two-foot-thick walls protecting the city. The packets—no bigger than loaves of bread—sometimes smashed through windows but more often lodged in the thick glass or steel-reinforced stone surrounding it. Immediately after impact they released high-decibel bursts that shattered glass and eardrums in about a ten-meter radius. It didn't matter that Anna was deep inside the mountain, removed from the worst of the blasts. The mayhem kept inching closer. It sounded like the city was being smashed open like a giant piñata, the Bandarians trying methodically to get at the candy inside, which was just sick and dying Danevesans.

The first yishi succumbed to the disease that morning. It was impossible for Anna to know what the usual rituals around death consisted of under the current circumstances, but the body was simply swaddled in a large cloak and fed into a desiccator via conveyor belt before being burned. Later, a slickly edited video of the dead yishi's life was played on every video screen, as though it had been prepared in advance, a kind of multimedia obituary. Anna wondered how many of these they'd see over the next few days, or if anyone would be left to see them.

The pathogen seemed to work its way through the yishi in one of two ways. Some felt the fever come on right away, followed shortly after by body aches, nausea, and incapacitating weakness. But for most the disease began with intermittent coughing fits and shortness of breath, like slowly worsening asthma attacks. These might last half a day before the fever, aches, and weakness set in, finally forcing them into sickbeds while the disease decimated their bodies' defenses.

Kerak had commandeered a little-used warehouse deep in the heart of the mountain for a makeshift hospital. Sick yishi who no longer had homes to retreat to lay on rows upon rows of pallets on the floor. Small zhinks flew back and forth between them, administering pain relief, delivering sustenance, and taking vitals, while Anna walked among them, talking with them and feeding those who couldn't feed themselves. What Erestu had told Miles about the yishi viewing them as near gods turned out to be pretty much true, as Kerak's patients seemed to brighten every time Anna approached. Her improving fluency and ability to converse in Danevesan only added to the reverence she inspired among the invalid yishi. It also helped that she didn't have to wear the gasmask that the uninfected yishi donned at all times. She didn't have to because she'd already been infected.

During the explosion that had caused her injury, either from the infected blood of another yishi or through the air, she'd come into contact with the pathogen. When Kerak tested her, it was in her blood. She hadn't shown any symptoms yet and it was uncertain if she ever would. Vikram, for one, was counting on her not getting sick and analyzed the antibodies in her white blood cells to see if he could develop a vaccine. Anna was counting on it, too.

She found she didn't dwell on it if she kept herself occupied with her charges. If she focused on what she was learning about the yishi, she could think of it as a kind of anthropological fieldwork. Of course, she was observing and interacting with them under duress, their very survival threatened. So she asked her patients to tell them about their lives, and she listened.

One of her favorites was an older yishi named Gedu. He had once taught children drafting and architecture but had left teaching to practice as a structural engineer. He was distressed about the damage the enemy was doing to Danevesu. But he also assured Anna that the city was stronger than it looked.

"It sounds terrible," he said, referring to the intermittent blasts. "But it takes so much to break through each outer layer, and the floors are incredibly strong."

"That's good to know," she said, speaking in Danevesan.

"I worked on the amphitheater, you know," he said.

"It's beautiful," she said, wondering what it looked like now. "When was it built?"

"A long time ago now," he said. "Seventeen, twenty years ago. It replaced the former auditorium, so I suppose it's about time for a new one, anyway." He coughed wetly into the back of his hand and closed his eyes from the exertion. The drugs kept the pain at bay, but it still hurt to move.

"How are you feeling, Gedu?" she asked after the coughing subsided.

"Like I'm dying," he said matter-of-factly.

She was sitting beside him on the floor, studying his eyes while she had a light hold of his hand. "Are you afraid?" she asked.

"At my age, most things frighten me," he said. "Like the way feathers sprout up where I never had feathers before." Anna laughed. "But I'm lucky to have been alive in the first place, and for so long. So I'm grateful. I live in the most beautiful city on Our World at the most momentous time in history."

"You think so?"

"I'm talking with *you*, aren't I?"

Her unwitting role in helping Vikram provide the raw material for Berejian's pathogen was not common knowledge yet, and Anna wasn't going to be the one to tell Gedu.

"Did you know as a child I got to see Araviku's first fluppet?" he said.

"Victor Bass?"

"Yes. Very exciting," he said, his eyes momentarily wide. "Of course, he wasn't in it yet. It just kind of stumbled around like an idiot, but still." He seemed to drift away, whether from the drugs or the memory she couldn't say, then snapped back. "Nothing like meeting an honest-to-Gee human from Earth, though."

"So how old is Araviku?" asked Anna. "If you were a child when he first went to Earth…"

"Older than I, that's all I know," he said. "He never told you?"

Between translating Our World years to Earth years, years spent in other bodies, and whatever Vikram's age was in base-8, Anna realized it would be useless to try for a more specific answer than simply "old." It did make her think about what ever happened to Tor Bass's body, however. *Is it still lying around somewhere?* she wondered. *For that matter, what is Vikram's avatar doing?* "How many fluppets are there?" she asked Gedu.

"Just two that I know of," he said, adding, "they aren't cheap." Which seemed an odd thing to say in a society that didn't use money.

"Did they ever create yishi fluppets?" she said.

Gedu nodded. "Oh, yes, long before the human ones. Of course, they hoped to fool death." Yishi personified death just as humans did, but spoke of *fooling* rather than *cheating* the grim reaper.

"They didn't?" she asked.

"It turns out consciousness dies, just as our bodies do." He managed the barest of movements, which Anna took for a shrug. "When the scientist who'd developed the process for migrating consciousness was dying, he had his own transferred into a healthy young fluppet made from his own DNA. It worked for a while. Then he went mad before slipping into a vegetative state. Other yishi at the end of their natural lives tried to do it and had the same result. After that, no one was allowed to mess around with yishi fluppets. The debate had ended by then, anyway."

"What debate?"

"Between those who believed in pursuing immortality and those who knew that it was unnatural and even unethical for anyone to live forever."

"That sounds like a religious argument," she pointed out.

"Not if you think about it."

Anna had to smile at his pedantic reply. Yishi would have made good, if maddening, professors. "I suppose you can't evolve if you don't reproduce," she conceded. "And if no one ever dies, I guess you'd have to stop reproducing."

"You see? Logic, not faith," he said. "Mortality isn't a flaw in our design, it's a feature. Not that that stopped us."

"Fuck that," said the patient on Anna's other side, Velluk. "I for one want to live forever."

"You see?" said Gedu.

"I wish they had kept some of those old yishi fluppets now," said Velluk.

The regular pattern of noise and shockwaves made by the detonating packets had affected everyone's body clock in an eerily homologous manner, such that, as one, they all looked up when they realized it had been too long since the last explosion.

With their heads cocked, listening, they waited for the bombardment to resume. After a little longer, Anna ventured, "Have they stopped?" No one wanted to tempt fate by answering in the affirmative.

"Nothing's happening," said Velluk.

"Which means something's happening," said Gedu.

Anna rose as she saw Kerak approach. "You noticed it, too?" she asked.

"What? Oh, yes, it's stopped," he said distractedly. "I wanted to show you someone. Can I steal you away from your patients?"

They weren't really her patients. But she appreciated Kerak's new-found civility. She followed him to a partitioned area with infected patients who'd suffered additional injuries during the bombing, beyond which was a much smaller section with casualties who were as yet uninfected. He took her to a jury-rigged section in between with room enough for one patient.

Only a small fraction of the sick were actually inside Kerak's newly created hospital, which was filled to overcrowding. Most could suffer, linger, and die at home in their own bed. The ones on pallets had already had their homes reduced to rubble, which was why they were here.

The few uninfected wounded were quarantined from the sick. For the most part, their injuries required little time to fix. Broken bones, even spinal cord injuries, as Vikram had shown back on Earth, were easy to heal. Internal bleeding, ruptured internal organs, shrapnel stuck in legs—these were likewise duck soup to the doctors in Danevesu. Certain brain injuries posed problems, and losing an eye or a limb still required customized prosthetics and physical therapy that took time. But medicine had advanced to the point in Danevesu that most of these injuries were little more than temporary nuisances. It was the pathogen that stumped them and brought the city to its knees.

"Sanitize first and put on one of these," Kerak told her, grabbing a gasmask from a nearby shelf. "And hurry the fuck up."

So much for his newfound civility.

Curious to know what or whom Kerak wanted to show her, she quickly obliged and entered the special quarantined area he had set up.

"This is Denebasa," he said, introducing Anna. "Denebasa, this is Anna. You've heard of her, I think."

"Call me Deneb," he said, smiling.

From his short stature, budding chest, narrow hips, and high voice, it was obvious he was a child, perhaps approaching adolescence. Kerak told her he'd been infected early the first morning, showing the common symptoms, and had suffered broken vertebrae from falling debris during one of the first railgun attacks. The broken bones were easy to fix, but as with all of the sick, Kerak could do nothing about his life-threatening illness.

"When his painkillers wore off this morning, he informed the zhink nurse his pain was deescalating," said Kerak.

Anna looked at Kerak, unsure what he was saying.

"His fever is down, his coughing has subsided, and he has only a dull headache," said Kerak. "His body seems to be recovering on its own."

"You mean, he's getting better?"

"Isn't that what I said?"

"Sorry, I just—are there any others?"

"None that I know of," he said. "I've been monitoring the patient data coming in from the zhink nurses, but nothing so far. Most of the sick are at home in bed, not here, though. So I don't know if Deneb is unique, or just the first among many who will recover."

"Still, it's encouraging," she said

"I've been trying to reach Vikram, but I think his smartskin is turned off. I was hoping you could find him. When I drew Deneb's blood earlier, it still showed the pathogen, but that wouldn't be unusual if he's still getting well. In any case, Vikram needs to know, to look at him and take samples. He's in the bioengineering lab, blue sector, level fourteen. Could you bring him back here?"

"Of course."

Vikram was drawing blood from his old body—that is, the human fluppet he formerly inhabited, which was now occupied by Tchuvu—when Kalaster led Anna in, now wearing a breathing filter to protect them.

She stopped in her tracks, her mouth open behind her mask. "Vikram?" she asked, staring at Vikram's old body.

"No," he said, "I'm still over here. You remember Tchuvu."

Tchuvu, still getting used to Vikram's old human body (which was in the midst of going through nicotine withdrawal), shook his head and tried to say hello but was having trouble operating his new lips and tongue. "Nhrwvrwhg," he said, more or less.

"Um," she said.

"It's not as easy as it looks, is it?" said Vikram.

Old Vikram looked drunk, and Anna realized she'd never seen him drunk, no matter how much he drank. Tchuvu gave up trying to communicate and just sat there, unable to still a slight Parkinson's-like tremor.

"Kerak needs you," she said to Vikram. "One of our patients may actually be getting better."

Vikram quickly pulled the needle out of Tchuvu's arm, squirting him with blood and eliciting a yelp.

"Sorry," he said, shoving a sponge into the crook of Tchuvu's arm before rising and turning to Anna. "What are we waiting for?"

"Glruhmv?" said Tchuvu, with some difficulty.

"Don't worry," Vikram said, turning back to reassure him. "You'll be fine. Kalaster will see to you."

On the way, Anna filled Vikram in on what little she knew about the patient. Then Vikram started to describe what he'd been working on, which required a little historical background. The mass extinctions on Our World that ended several centuries before, he explained, had not just reduced the biodiversity of large species, but of insects and microorganisms as well. As a result, yishi immune systems had quickly evolved in an environment devoid of the kinds of disease-causing bacteria and viruses that on Earth hopped indiscriminately from man to mosquito, mosquito to rat, rat to monkey, monkey to man, and so on. Since the pathogen's genetic makeup was predominately of Earth origin, it made sense that humans—or at least some of them—might be immune to it. Vikram had tried to isolate what it was in her blood that resisted the disease but had had no luck. Even though the fluppet's blood was not strictly speaking human, it ought to be immune to the pathogen, as the fluppets had been designed to be entirely disease-resistant. Like the flesh puppet as a whole, its blood was an amalgam of both organic material created from the host's DNA and supplemental mechanical parts. Specifically, a mixture of red blood cells, white blood cells (leukocytes), and microscopic machines called nanocytes that functioned like super white blood cells, attacking malignant foreign cells with more precision and reliability than their natural counterparts. The nanocytes couldn't be killed, could learn to differentiate between dangerous and benign foreign bodies they didn't recognize, and could communicate with each another throughout the body.

Of course, Berejian knew well that most Danevesans, as well as wealthy Cardevise and Edrisians, had nanocytes in their blood. They weren't needed to battle bacteria or viruses, but they did successfully fight the one disease that still survived the mass extinctions: cancer. So Berejian would have designed his pathogen to somehow either overcome or simply circumvent the nanocytes.

"So your blood is very interesting to me," said Vikram. "I mean, in trying to figure out a cure."

"I knew what you meant," she said.

"The pathogen found in your blood isn't multiplying," he continued. "And yet, none of the white blood cells attack it, either. It seems harmless, basically inert, but it's attacking yishi systems with or without nanocytes. It settles in the soft tissues of the lungs and disseminates through the bloodstream to the other major systems. So I was curious about the fluppet's reaction to the pathogen. But I'm even more curious to examine your patient and collect some samples."

A packet exploded as he finished his thought, shaking their transport and making its lights flicker. No high-pitched burst followed this time, only a low rumbling like far-off thunder.

"They're attacking again," said Anna, sick to death of it and really starting to hate the Bandarians.

"If the weather holds, we might be in trouble," said Vikram, slightly understating the situation.

By the time they found Kerak, the attack had recommenced in earnest, though the low rumbling sounds of the new packets were almost soothing compared to the earlier bombardment's siren-like shrieks.

Kerak lit up when he saw Vikram and, before giving any kind of greeting, simply dragged him over to the eyepiece of the console he was working at. "Look there," he said. "I took a fresh blood sample. The pathogen is gone. Denebasa is cured."

"What did you do?" asked Vikram, staring into the eyepiece.

"Nothing," he said. "The disease has simply run its course. His body fought it off."

"Any others improving?"

"Not yet."

"None of the other adolescents?"

"That was my first thought," said Kerak, "but no."

"You've done a complete workup?"

"Yeah—blood, feathers, skin, stool—no signs of genetic anomalies. He seems perfectly normal for his age. Except for being cured."

Packets had been going off every couple minutes since they started up again. They all stopped after the last one, however, as the low rumbling noise didn't seem to be abating, but actually getting louder as it worked its way toward them. The closer it got, the clearer it became—not a rumbling but a cascading, metallic cacophony punctuated by small explosions. The latest packets didn't contain high-decibel blasts designed to shatter glass and stone, but millions of insect-sized zhinks working in tandem to skitter and fly their way deeper into the city by any route possible. They had found their way into the ventilation shafts—the same route the pathogen had taken—and were trying to break through the ceiling grates with zhinks programmed to detonate.

Anna, Vikram, Kerak, and Deneb all jumped when the ceiling vent exploded in the large open room beside the quarantine area. The zhinks were too big to fit through the grate, and too small to pack a big enough charge to dislodge it. Helping Deneb out of bed, the four of them entered the sick ward, where the other patients tried feebly to move away from the overhead vent. As the smoke cleared, they could see that some of the little zhinks had attached themselves to the other side of the grate and were cutting through the metal with plasma torches, which from below looked like tiny little welders, throwing off bright violet light and sparks that flew down on the vacated pallets.

Without thinking, Anna went to help the patients she could. Some could manage to stumble away from the vent on their own. Others, like Gedu, were in a drug-induced stupor, wavering in and out of consciousness despite the commotion. Anna found Velluk, who was well enough to help others up, and Kerak led them all through a temporary partition to a dusty, unlit storage area. Behind them they could see the little welders finish cutting through the grate, and hundreds of the tiny zhinks poured out of the opening, crawling over the ceiling of the sick ward or flying down into the space to seek out and attack the slightest movement.

From behind the partition, they all looked up, alerted to the presence of another ceiling grate above them when a swarm of zhinks in the ventilation shaft found it and set to work taking it down.

Soon they found themselves cornered in the storage room by hundreds of the little bastards, as they dropped down from the now mangled ventilation grate. The ones that could only crawl attached themselves to the skin and proceeded to carve incisions into their hosts with the plasma torches until someone pulled them off, which hurt even more. The cuts and burns they caused ranged from intensely irritating to deadly, depending on how many were attached to you. The flying zhinks, however, delivered small electric shocks that, with enough of them latched onto you, were even deadlier.

Anna, Vikram, Kerak, and Deneb tried their best to protect the sickest patients with anything they could find to bat them away as they skittered and flew toward them. Mainly, they swung yishi bedpans, which looked pretty much like bedpans on Earth, except they were able to hover away and empty themselves. The patients who could, likewise armed themselves with whatever was at hand.

After another few minutes, an eternity to the desperate defenders, the zhinks outside breached the partition. Now there were too many zhinks coming at them all at once, from every direction. Anna looked helplessly at Vikram and Kerak, both manic and streaked with blood as they flailed futilely at their relentless little attackers.

When the shock of the current running through her from multiple places at once hit her, Anna's jaw clenched shut, and she could feel her body give way beneath her. Then everything went black.

*

OLIPH SMILED beatifically, his mouth forming a large O, as hormones surged through the pleasure centers of his brain, relief washing over him.

"You see," said Peleg, "I told you the truth would make you free. Doesn't that feel better?"

"Yes. Oh, Gee, *yes*," he said. Peleg had injected him with a psychotropic agent that inhibited the brain's ability to dissemble and rewarded candor. Oliph would've fetched Peleg's seconds or dropped down and fellated him at that moment, so long as he allowed the drug to work its magic.

"He's all yours," Peleg said to Oliph's guards, as he turned and exited the cell deep in the labyrinth of the state's security apparatus under Lagar

Temu. He heard Oliph's head hit the back of his chair as he let out a long, throaty guffaw that completely belied his dire situation.

So Telesu—once again become Anders—had disappeared. With Oliph's help, he had migrated his consciousness back into Bandary's only flesh puppet and entered the portal to travel back to Earth. More disturbing was what Oliph had admitted toward the end of the interrogation, that Telesu had smuggled canisters of the biological agent into Lagaredel, right under Peleg's beak. For what purpose, Oliph had no clue. But Peleg feared the indiscriminate virulence of the pathogen.

Poor Oliph. You almost had to feel sorry for him. He thought that Telesu was going to return from Earth with human DNA and build him his own fluppet. He had really wanted to go to Earth, apparently. Telesu would never come back, though—not on his own accord, at least. Of that Peleg was certain.

Peleg and a crew of Revolutionary Guard agents had ransacked Telesu's lab. The staff were all terrified, of course. Anyone who worked for Telesu was suspect—had been suspect, in fact, since the high-tech lab was formed. The supreme leader and Dar Salas had both sanctioned the project, but no one was enthusiastic about something so antithetical to Bandarian principles. They hated technology. Their ancestors had embraced it, and now Our World was a desert. The Danevesans and others may still worship it, but they at least now knew better.

Their disdain for technology would have been difficult to recognize for Anna or Miles or any human visitor, as much of the technology they did use was a fair bit more advanced than anything on Earth. The Bandarians just refused to use technology that was advanced past a certain point. They were like the Amish, in that way, if viewed by Stone Age time travelers. Technology up to an agreed-upon line was fine, but not beyond it. Any further was evil—a tool of Dan.

So it was an uncomfortable position for the government to create an entire section whose purpose was to develop technology that crossed far over the line that separated good from evil—uncomfortable, but not controversial. Controversy requires dissent, and this was not tolerated in Bandary. Peleg kept this in mind as he stood before Salas and briefed the doughy, lugubrious foreign minister lying in his daybed on what had happened and what he recommended they do.

Peleg was already wary of Salas, who'd masterminded or at least authorized the biological sneak attack on Danevesu. Peleg found it morally indefensible, as he had Telesu's ordering the destruction of an unarmed sub off of Twenty-six and the collaboration with the Hopmoul terrorists, which is what he was certain they were. Hopmoul's enemies included more than just Danevesu. They preached an apocalyptic form of Bahgee, claiming to be soldiers in the battle to cleanse yishikind. To start over, joined only by the righteous in paradise, a new Skygarden accessible only to the faithful, was their ultimate goal. It was crazy, of course, but it had a kind of seductive poetry that appealed to a certain desperate mentality.

If Telesu had worked with Hopmoul to bring down Danevesu, what was their plan for the smuggled canisters? And if Salas had known about the terrorists' involvement in the former, did he know about the latter, whatever it was?

Peleg decided that Salas must not have a death wish—more out of pragmatism than true conviction, as there really wasn't much he could do about it if Salas did. Though his gluttonous appetites and rumored sexual proclivities did suggest a minister having too good a time to wish for it to end. So Peleg told Salas everything he had gotten out of Oliph, and every piece of information they'd gained from tossing the lab and interviewing the scientists who worked there. There was one thing Peleg learned that seemed most pertinent to him now.

"When I spoke with the chief physicist under Telesu," said Peleg, "he said that two handheld devices had been fabricated. These devices permit travel through the spacetime portals—theoretically, travel anywhere—"

"I know what they can do," said Salas, looking impatient and hungry.

"The only one that was in their possession was stolen by Telesu," Peleg added. "The physicist claimed not to know where the other one was kept, or even if it still existed, and I believed him."

Salas nodded, waiting for Peleg to continue.

Peleg looked at Salas steadily, but squirmed inwardly. "I need to know where the other device is," he said.

18.

"EGH, THE BEER'S WARM," said Phil with a grimace, wiping the foam from his upper lip. He was short and stocky, in his early twenties, with dark hair, prominent five o'clock shadow, and eyes magnified behind large-framed spectacles.

"Cheap, though," countered his friend Rob, a tall, well-put-together, dishwater-blond man about the same age.

"Yeah, well, you get what you pay for."

"And you pay for what you can get," said Rob, nodding knowingly.

"I don't even know what the hell that means."

Behind the Hotel Kashmir's bar, Ahmed tried to ignore their conversation by keeping himself busy, actively trying to catch the eye of any of the few regulars in the place while wiping a glass with a moldy washcloth. His eyes came to a stop on Tom, who had fallen asleep on the edge of the bar. Another minute, and he'd fall off, so Ahmed gently nudged him awake. Tom looked around, disoriented, and gave Ahmed a nod. "Cheers," he said and lifted his nearly full mug of beer in *salud*.

Phil and Rob exchanged a nod with Tom and went back to their conversation.

"Did I tell you about my cousin?" said Phil. Rob shook his head. Rob's older brother had married Phil's older sister, so they were legally family. "He's twenty-five, just two years ahead of me, works on Wall Street. Made over half a mil last year."

"Half a million dollars?" said Rob.

Phil nodded.

"Damn....What does he do?"

"He manages a hedge fund," said Phil.

"What's that?"

"It's like a mutual fund, but they make money by shorting stocks."

"I've heard of that," said Rob. "But I have no idea what it means."

"No idea what which means?"

"Shorting stocks."

"It's simple," said Phil, who didn't totally understand it himself. "It's when you sell a stock at a high price and then buy it back at a lower price."

"Oh." His friend sipped his beer and squinted, trying to sort it out. "But…why buy it back? Why not just sell it at a high price and be done with it?"

"Because you don't own it when you sell it," said Phil.

"Then how can you sell it?"

Phil sighed. "You buy it on margin," he said, as if that ought to make it clearer. He was starting to get impatient.

"And this is all legal?"

"Of course, it's legal, dumbshit," said Phil, who regretted bringing it up. "My point is my cousin is raking it in while I'm dicking around Europe with you."

"I thought you wanted a break from business school."

"To be honest, I thought there'd be a lot more pussy."

Rob couldn't complain. He'd hooked up with a girl in Milan and boinked another in Munich. He really wanted to move on to Madrid, as cities starting with the letter *M* seemed to be good luck for him.

"One more year, and I'll have my MBA," said Phil. "But Christ, it's boring. I thought undergrad was bad."

"What'd you major in again?"

"Finance." Phil took another swig of his warm beer. "You know what my cousin majored in? Art fucking history. I mean, can you imagine?"

Rob had graduated from college with a degree in sociology but was planning to go to law school once he retook the LSAT. This excursion was a graduation gift from his parents, and a way to postpone his inevitable move back home. "I don't know," he said. "Maybe art history's a good background for working on Wall Street."

Phil looked at him sidelong. "I can't see how."

Rob shrugged. "Well, anyway, *he'd* probably like it here."

"Yeah, right," he said, downing the rest of his beer. "Jesus, I haven't seen a single girl in here I'd fuck."

Rob looked around, noticing a petite, wispy, dark-haired young woman with glasses drinking with a group in the common room. "What about her?"

Phil appraised her quickly. "I wouldn't fuck her with your dick," he said.

"Just to be clear," said Rob, "I don't want you fucking anyone with my dick."

"We should have gone to Amsterdam," Phil complained. "'The girls in Spain are easy,' you said. 'Why pay for it, if we can get it for free?' Why do you always think Catholic girls are easy?"

"They're pent up."

"*I'm* pent up."

"It's only one bar," said Rob.

"It's the third one tonight," he said, turning to see Tom suddenly standing beside him, an almost full mug of beer in his hand.

Tom had been listening to Phil go on since snapping out of semi-consciousness and hadn't liked what he'd heard. So, without preamble, he dumped his beer in Phil's lap with a satisfied grin. From the look on Phil's face, the beer felt a lot colder now that it was on his privates.

Phil shot up off of his stool and promptly slipped in the pool of beer at his feet. Tom put out a hand reflexively to keep him from falling. Instead of thanking him, however, Phil took an unsteady swing at his chin. Tom turned his head but still caught Phil's bony fist right in his ear.

"Aaugh," Tom moaned. "You hit me in the bleedin' eah." The two stood a little more than arm's length from each other, bodies tensed and fists clenched, and Tom now realized he had no interest in pursuing the fight he'd instigated with this anonymous American. The guy was wearing glasses, to boot.

"If I said s-sorry," Tom slurred, "could we call it even?"

"C'mon," said Rob, getting up. "He's drunk."

"Oh, do you think so?!" said Phil. Then to Tom, "You're paying for these pants, buddy."

"Why would I pay for 'em?" said Tom. "They're soaked with beer."

This just made Phil angrier. "You're gonna pay for the cleaning," he said, trying to make it sound like an ominous threat.

Tom started to laugh. "Are you joking, mate?"

Ahmed, who had seen most of this, interrupted calmly. "Gentlemen," he said, without the irony it deserved, "please, let's not do this here."

Phil, whose sticky, sopping wet crotch would not allow him to just drop this, looked at Ahmed warily. On one hand, Ahmed was of a height with Phil and about thirty pounds lighter. On the other, Phil could see that Ahmed, an Iranian emigré, was clearly Middle Eastern, which, despite his size and manner, automatically made him more menacing and possibly armed or strapped with explosives.

So Phil stood there fuming, incapable of moving, either to slink away or take another swipe at Tom, when an oblivious Miles walked in and called Tom's name with a sense of palpable relief.

Seeing the surprised recognition and an enthusiastic wave, he walked over, barely noticing Phil standing in a sour-smelling puddle. "Tom," he said again, "it's good to see you." He turned to Ahmed and then saw Phil and Rob. "*Hola,*" he said to all with a friendly nod.

"Who's this dickhead?" said Phil.

Miles had had a long day and was still jet-lagged from his journey through the arsehole, so he didn't really know what to make of the unwarranted hostility. "Um," he stammered.

"Look," Tom said to Phil in his calm voice, "I'm sorry I spilled my beer on yeh. But you'd been talking shit all night, and yeh kind of had it coming." He then looked at his empty mug, wiggled it for Ahmed to see, and said, "How 'bout another? I'm empty."

If nothing else, Miles had a better understanding of why this guy was giving off such an antagonistic vibe. It was quaint, in a way—such a minor dustup on such a relatably human scale. Miles found the absurdity of it all almost touching, which showed on his face as a smirk.

"Oh, it's funny, huh?" said Phil, now ready to throw down with the baby-faced Miles, who was standing at the bar between him and Tom.

"No, I—" Miles started, but Phil pushed him out of the way roughly, causing him to stumble backward.

Now Tom was pissed and feeling protective of his friend. As Phil moved toward him, he cocked his left arm to punch him. Unfortunately, Miles decided to intervene just then and caught Tom's clenched fist right in the mouth as he turned to appeal to Tom's pacifist nature.

Miles hit the floor and could taste blood from his upper lip.

"That's it!" Ahmed yelled. "You two out!"

"*Us?*" said Phil. "What about *him?*"

"I worry about him," he said. "You want me to call the police?" And he started toward them, swearing oaths at them in Farsi mixed with Spanish, as the two backed away and made their way out of the bar and down the stairs of the Hotel Kashmir, Phil still sporting a large wet stain radiating out from the fly of his khakis.

Tom bent down to help Miles up, and Miles stood, his head still ringing, his balance a bit off. "Sorry about that," said Tom.

Miles said it was all right and, looking at Tom, could see that, of the two of them, he was the steadier on his feet.

Ahmed returned, saw that Miles was all right, shook his head, and said, "Assholes."

"I know, right?" said Tom.

"And no more starting fights in my bar," he added.

"Cheers."

Miles ran his tongue against the bloody cut in his mouth and wiggled his lower jaw. Ahmed wheeled a bucket with a mop around the back of the bar and put the mop handle in Tom's hand. "Clean," he said and tossed him his damp dishrag. Tom raised an eyebrow but didn't complain as he set to work.

Miles watched Tom mop up the beer and said, "When you're done with that, you wanna get some fresh air?"

*

IT HAD TAKEN Miles a little over a day to reach Barcelona by train, and he got into Sants station around seven in the morning. It was a weekday, but you would've thought the city had been evacuated. Barcelonans were a lot of things—morning people they were not.

Riding in trains, sitting in train stations, walking alone down the Avinguda de Roma, he'd had a lot of time to think. The problems he'd run from when he first came to Spain—the problems of people in general—didn't seem to compare to the problems on Our World. When he ran away from Danevesu, it wasn't of his own will, but he'd welcomed the chance to leave just the same. Passing by the university, Miles felt a pang of nostalgia thinking of the last time he'd been there with Anna and Vikram (which wasn't that long ago). More cars and people began to emerge as he crossed the Plaça de Catalunya and made his way down the Ramblas, still too early in the day for even the most industrious drug dealers and prostitutes. Miles cut over to the Cathedral square, even though it was out of his way, and saw vendors setting up stalls where they sold Christmas tchotchkes. Among the ceramic baby Jesuses, Marys, wise men, and sheep, Miles noticed an odd little guy. Each stall, it seemed, had one version or another of a Catalan peasant in a red cap, pants down, expression tranquil, squatting over a fresh soft-serve swirl of excrement. Miles didn't have any idea what it had to do with Christmas, but he could have said the same for fruitcake, which was equally unappetizing. Perhaps wishing to delay his return to the Hotel Kashmir, he stopped at a stall to buy a small one. This primitive symbol of what—fecundity? organic fertilizer? colon health?—was called a *caganer*, or "shitter," an apt if uninspired name, and reminded Miles of the sign on the door to the head on Erestu's sub.

He wandered the twisting alleys of the Barri Gòtic, examining his little *caganer* and thinking back to what Vikram had said about the Ndzada. Had civilization forgotten something they still knew? He wondered if people were really doomed to do to Earth what the yishi had done to Our World. It took leaving Our World for Miles to see how similar humans and yishi really were.

He tried to see his fellow human beings as Vikram might have. In the six weeks he'd spent traveling around Europe before coming to Spain, Miles had enjoyed people-watching in parks and cafés, on trains. He enjoyed the fact that he couldn't understand the language of the conversations around him. For one thing, he didn't have to hear the stupid things people said. But it also allowed him to pay attention to the gestures and expressions of the people talking, a kind of ballet, with words merely the notes of an improvised musical score. He'd felt closer to people at such a remove than he had among his own family and friends for some time.

Vikram, who had no trouble understanding the various languages humans spoke, had been torn between wanting to help his fellow yishi and remaining on Earth. On a pleasantly cool November day in the Gothic Quarter, it wasn't hard to see why. But was it really preferable to the wondrous Danevesu? True, there were no trees or birds there—except in the menagerie—and outside the city it was hellishly barren and hot. And, he supposed, you could only watch so much porn on so many big-screen TVs before it became monotonous. Maybe Vikram was right to want to stay on Earth. But Miles wished desperately he could get back to Our World.

Miles had walked east of the Plaça Reial and circled back around to a side alley that opened onto the square, where he came upon a cardboard box tipped on its side, partially concealed by a large plastic garbage bin. Inside the box was a cat lying on her side surrounded by a litter of kittens. It was Steve. She was cleaning one of the kittens, who couldn't have been more than a week old, while the others slept or crawled over each other or tried to find one of Steve's nipples for a meal.

Steve looked up and sniffed the air as Miles approached. He reached out a hand and Steve allowed him to scritch her ears and forehead.

"Good kitty," he said.

"*Brrown,*" she said.

A young woman with dark brown hair and wire-rimmed glasses walked up to them with a saucer and small carton of milk. "*Disculpe,*" she said, as Miles stepped aside. She put the saucer down next to Steve and poured some of the milk into it.

She smiled as Steve leaned over to it and lapped it up. The woman was short and thin, wearing ripped and faded jeans with a billowy linen blouse.

"Are you staying at the Kashmir?" Miles asked her, guessing she spoke English.

"Yeah," she said. "You?"

"I was," he said. "I left and came back."

She nodded, and they both watched Steve lick up the remnants of the milk.

"I didn't even realize Steve was pregnant," he said.

"Steve?" she asked.

"The mother," he said.

"You mean 'Stella?'" she said.

"Oh…I guess so."

"Steve is a boy's name," she explained.

"I know," he said. "That's just what they used to call her."

"Didn't they know she was a girl?"

"No, they knew," he said.

"Then why would they call her Steve?" she asked.

"I don't know."

"Well…" she said and bent down to pick up the empty saucer. With a sardonic smile, she turned and shot him a *bye* over her shoulder.

Steve returned to caring for her offspring. It seemed to come naturally to her. Of course, it *did* come naturally to her. Miles couldn't think of anything that came that naturally to him. Not even masturbation, now that he thought of it. The first time he'd accidentally given himself an orgasm, he didn't know what the hell to think. It was late at night, he was alone and scared in his now damp sheets, thinking maybe he'd hurt himself or had contracted a fatal disease.

Steve was clearly a professional at being a cat. Miles knew he would forever be an amateur at being human.

After a quick scan of the hotel's nearly empty common room, Miles hiked up the stairs to Anna's flat. He took out Anna's key and, in the moment before turning it in the lock, imagined finding Anna and Vikram sitting at the kitchen table having coffee and hard rolls—or in Vikram's case, hard candy and a cigarette. But he knew damn well no one would be home.

He unlocked the door and went inside. It looked different than he remembered. The bookcase had been moved. There were new posters on the wall, a different bedspread on Vikram's bed. *What the hell?*

Rapid-fire Spanish flew at him now from the kitchen. He turned to see an angry young woman and man starting to get up from their coffee and cereal at the kitchen table. They weren't Anna and Vikram. They were squatters in Anna's flat. And they were being a little indignant about it, Miles thought. Or, it now occurred to him, they perhaps seemed indignant because they were in fact the new tenants.

"*Lo siento!*" Miles called and quickly backed out the door. The woman and man stood there, staring at each other with shocked expressions. A moment later, Miles opened the door again and threw the man the key. "This is yours," he said with a shrug and closed the door again, for the last time.

Downstairs at the Kashmir's front desk, Miles checked in and got himself some breakfast in the common room before storing his and Anna's stuff in a locker upstairs. When he came back down, the common area was starting to get crowded with backpackers—the new regulars—none of whom Miles knew. *Why did I come back here?* he thought. He found a seat and thought of trying to write his younger sister Sara again. But what would he say? She'd probably like to know he was still alive. So he took out his pen and wrote,

> Dear Sara,
> I am still alive. How are you?
>
> > Love,
> > Miles

He looked at the note with a frown, crumpled it up, and threw it in the trash. He decided to go for a walk and found a nice park bench in the sun to fall asleep on. Later he ate something and walked around some more before returning to the Kashmir.

"Which is when I found you in the bar," said Miles, "right before you punched me in the face."

"How long are you gonna keep bringin' that up?" asked Tom.

Tom and Miles were sitting at an outdoor café near the Cathedral. Tom had offered to buy wine, but Miles declined. "Just a Coke," he said. Tom ordered two Cokes, but when the waiter returned with his small bottle of soda, Tom looked at it like he'd just placed a turd on the table. Miles noticed Tom's hand shaking as he lifted the bottle to his lips.

"So where did you and Anna go?" Tom asked. "Didja ever find Vik?"

"We went to Valencia first, but he wasn't there," said Miles. "He'd left a note for Anna at his apartment, though, and we finally found him in Granada. Then we ended up in Portugal."

"So you've been there the whole time?"

Miles took a gulp of the caffeinated sugar water. "More or less."

As a child of divorce, Miles found it came naturally to omit certain details that he didn't want to share with Tom. Everything starting with his first trip through the wormhole to being deposited on the Alhambra mount was basically implausible. Not that Miles didn't consider telling Tom everything. He didn't think he'd actually believe it, but it might feel good to tell someone the truth.

"So did Vik ever explain how he happened to escape from jail?" Tom asked.

"Not exactly."

Tom raised his eyebrows at that non-answer but didn't press. "And did he ever get his bag back?"

"Yes. Paco...had taken it." Miles suddenly remembered that Paco was dead, that he'd been murdered by Anders, along with Paco's sister and brother-in-law.

"How did he ever find him?"

"Traced him back to where he lived."

"In Portugal?"

"No, Granada."

Tom nodded uncertainly. "Right. But you all moved on to Portugal?"

"Yep."

"But you came back here. And Anna stayed behind with Vik?"

"Yes," said Miles, glad for a question he could answer truthfully.

Tom took a sip of his Coke and scrunched up his face as if the cola were dishwater. "Sorry, mate," he said. "I always liked Anna."

"Me too." Miles looked across the square and up at the dark façade of the cathedral. "Is anybody else still around from before?" he asked.

"Nah, just me," said Tom. "Marie left a few days after you lot. Krissy stayed on for a while, till Tawny returned and they reconciled. They were headed to Greece, I think. The Katyas stuck around for another week or so. Others came and went."

"So what are you still doing here?" Miles asked.

"I teach English at the Escuela de Lengua part-time," he said. "I've also been tutoring Josep at the Kashmir for a few potatoes."

"Josep the manager?"

Tom shrugged. "He's been helping me learn Spanish, as well."

"The wanker?"

"The same," said Tom. "I mean, a fella's gotta eat."

Tom picked up his soda bottle unsteadily, considered taking a drink, then dropped it back down as if it were filled with lead.

"How bad is it?" Miles asked.

"How bad is what?" said Tom.

"Your hand is shaking," he said. "You were falling down drunk when I saw you, and it's barely eight o'clock."

Tom just smiled, a hint of warning in his eyes.

Miles shrugged. He'd known bad drunks in his extended family. Some got violent. Others, like his dad, just got depressed. Tom might have been the worst kind—a happy-go-lucky drunk. The kind people especially liked to be around when he was drinking, a drunk who attracted enablers the way honey did flies. "Sorry," Miles said. "I didn't mean to get too personal."

"No worries," said Tom. "It's fine....I'm gonna stop, you know. I just know mehself too well, you know? I've gotta do it when I'm ready or else....I dunno. I've been here before, so..." Tom caught the waiter's eye and ordered a glass of red wine when he came over. "You want one?" he asked Miles.

"Sure."

So Miles enabled Tom a little longer and let himself enjoy it, even though he knew it was wrong. Tom was good company and seemed to catch his second wind with a few more drinks. Eventually, they wound up back at the Hotel Kashmir bar, where the drinks were cheapest and it was much harder to get lost on your way to bed.

In the common room, Tom introduced Miles to some of the new regulars, including Lisa, the dark-haired Canadian he'd met outside, a couple of Americans from Seattle, a Belgian man in his late twenties, a female college student from France. Inside the bar, it was mostly deserted but for a large blond man chatting up an olive-skinned, raven-haired beauty. The man had his back to him, but Miles would have recognized him anywhere—though he hadn't expected to ever see him again.

It was Anders.

Miles could feel his heart pounding against his ribs as he walked slowly into the bar, keeping an eye on the back of Anders's head and nonchalantly picking up an empty mug on the way. He couldn't believe he was here. Anders, a mass murderer on two planets, come back to the Hotel Kashmir to…what? Chat up young human females? Why would he come back here? Miles realized that, of the two of them, he was the one more unlikely to be here, as Anders had left him and the others on Twenty-six to die.

The girl Anders was talking to got up to go, and Anders turned around to see her walk away when he locked eyes with Miles. Miles was already swinging the thick glass mug at the side of Anders's head. Anders didn't have time to react, and Miles expected the mug to shatter as it connected. Instead, it bounced off with a dull *thumk*, which was not only anticlimactic but made Miles a little queasy. It also just pissed Anders off. So he stood up, grabbed Miles by the neck, and carried him over to the back wall and pinned him to it.

"What is the point of all this technology," he said, gesturing at himself, "if I can't even use it?"

Miles didn't have an answer for that, not that he could answer at the moment.

"I'm not going to kill you," said Anders. "At least not here. But if you damaged any of my happy memories, I will track you down and kill you slowly."

While Miles tried to figure out how he would ever know if he had, he flung his fists about wildly, trying to knock Anders's arm and loosen his grip, to no avail. Finally, he swung his foot upward and connected squarely with what he assumed were the fluppet's testicles. It was a kick that would have made Maradona proud and caused Anders to drop Miles to the floor.

Anders winced slightly and looked at Miles. "Nice one," he said.

Miles launched himself at Anders and managed to stagger him backward a tad before Anders simply threw him off, onto one of the tables. Miles landed on an ashtray and skidded off the table with it into a couple of chairs, crashing to the floor with them. Apparently, nothing broke in a bar fight the way it did in the movies. But that ashtray was going to leave an ugly bruise.

A crowd was starting to gather, but Ahmed had seen enough. He didn't know what was going on—a full moon?—but the Kashmir often went for days without a bar fight, so two in one night was unusual. They certainly weren't paying him enough to break up altercations with people swinging glassware and knocking over furniture, so he brushed past Tom and the other gawkers to use the front desk phone and ring the police.

*

MILES AND ANDERS were hustled into the rear of the Raval police station, handcuffs digging into their wrists shackled behind their backs. In the station, one of the officers patted Anders down and lifted a flat black card from his pocket. It was rigid and metallic, dull on one side, shiny on the other, and the officers passed it around, trying to figure out what it was while Anders looked on unamused.

Miles didn't see officer Amenes, which he was glad of. The officers photographed and fingerprinted them and took their personal effects. Then they were each told their rights in Catalan and Spanish and Miles was given a small pamphlet with his rights printed in English. There would be no translator in until tomorrow, though no one expected the arrestees to be around past morning. One of the officers asked Miles if he needed a doctor, as he was bleeding from a cut on his arm and had scratches and bruises on his face and neck, but Miles said no. Handcuffs removed, Anders and Miles were then each locked into adjacent cells in a small block down a long hallway. The only other prisoner was an older man snoring on his cot in a cage opposite them.

Anders appraised the quarters and took the only seat there was, on the cot, while Miles glared at him.

"So they took your toy, huh?" said Miles.

Anders sort of half rolled his eyes and half laughed.

"Too bad they don't have smartskin in Bandary," said Miles.

"They'll release us in the morning unless the hotel signs a complaint," said Anders. "At which time, I'll have it back."

Miles affected a laugh, but Anders had a good point.

"They're dying in Danevesu," said Miles.

"I know," said Anders, not smiling now. "They'll be dying in Lagaredel too, and in Edrisia and Cardevise."

"Why did you do it?"

"Why did I do it?" he repeated scornfully. "Who the hell are you to question me? What do you know about Danevesu, of yishi, of Our World? I don't owe you any explanations."

"What about Anna? Or Vikram?" said Miles. "Your own father—or mother, parent…whatever."

"Yes, what about them?" said Anders. "I notice you got out. Lucky for you."

Miles wanted to kill him. He looked around for something to throw at him, but the cell was deliberately devoid of potential projectiles. He looked down at his feet. A shoe? It probably wouldn't kill him, though, and his feet got cold at night.

"You look like you did back in the bar," Anders said, as if he were making a casual observation. "Like you want to kill me. Good thing we're separated by these bars. Even without my toy, I'm much stronger than you."

Miles just glared at him some more.

"How did you get off of Twenty-six, anyway? I have to admit I'm curious. I didn't expect to see you back at the Kashmir, or…at all, really."

Miles looked away from Anders and shook his head. "The sub's captain survived and rescued us," he said.

"But we blew up his sub," said Anders. "He couldn't have survived that."

"I don't know what to tell you," said Miles. "I guess you're not as good at murder as you thought."

Anders was trying to figure something out but let it go. "Speaking of murder," he said. "The police here must know about the murders in Granada."

"The murders you committed, you mean."

"I don't think they've solved that case yet," said Anders. "The local cops probably already made the connection between Vikram and Paco. There was a description of the three of you going into the butcher shop, you know. Someone saw you. The police would probably need some help connecting the description there to you here, though…"

Miles lay down on the cot with his back to Anders, defeated. This was a nightmare. *Why did I come back?* he wondered.

"Still, I have to ask myself," Anders continued, standing up and walking over to the barred partition, "do I genuinely want to get involved? I mean, it's really none of my business. On the other hand, *you* are a little inconvenient. Yes, yes...if I'm being honest, I know what I have to—"

Anders stopped talking. *Thank Gee.*

In fact, Anders was not making a sound, as if he had been paralyzed. Miles rolled over to look at him, in spite of himself. Anders *was* paralyzed. He was looking straight at Miles with his eyelids half-closed, his mouth open in mid-sentence, face frozen in that graceless, idiotic expression.

A blue-feathered yishi wearing a familiar military cloak stood behind Anders, pointing a cylindrical device in his direction. Miles recognized him but didn't know his name. Anders tried to move his pupils to the side, but they snapped back. He didn't need to see who it was, though. He knew it was Peleg.

Peleg recognized Miles, too, from the laboratory on Twenty-six. Neither spoke the other's language, but they each knew a little Danevesan.

"Sorry," said Peleg in Danevesan, placing his free hand over his breast. "Sorry."

Miles nodded, noticing the black metallic card strapped to Peleg's wrist. He tried to remember the words in Danevesan. "Go, I...I go," he stammered. Finally, he just pointed to Peleg, put his palm on his own chest, and then said, "I go Danevesu," while pointing up at the sky.

Peleg's eyes widened in surprise. "Yes," he said. He dragged a finger across the screen of his card-sized device and fiddled with it for a few seconds while holding Anders in his paralyzing beam. He swore in Bandarian and tapped the screen angrily a few times before shaking his head and repeating, "Danevesu?"

"Yes," said Miles, a little uncertainly.

A quick tweak of Peleg's fingers on the screen, and a black asterisk stretched open behind Miles. Its center pulled inward at the ragged edges of the portal.

"Danevesu," said Peleg.

Miles looked at Anders and gave him a last nod. "Thank you," he said to Peleg and disappeared into the opening.

*

THE ARRESTING OFFICER, a young man with a baby face and wavy red hair, fiddled with the slim black card, turning it over in his hands. One side was smooth like glass, and the other butter soft in brushed metal. No bigger than a playing card, it had a pleasant weightiness to it. He couldn't stop handling it. It just felt good to touch.

When the young officer had come in that afternoon, the station was hushed and tense. The two drunks he and his partner had arrested the night before had escaped from their cells before they could be released. Their files had also disappeared. It was as if they'd never been there, but for the black card.

This was the third time in a month that this had happened, which probably meant increased oversight, possibly an investigation. There had to be a logical explanation for how these seemingly unrelated escapes occurred.

His partner walked up to their shared desk while he was leaning back in his chair, still playing with the black card.

"What's that?" the other asked.

"Hm?" he said. "Nothing. I don't know. You ready?" He got up and tossed the heavy black card on top of a stack of papers.

"Nice fuck-up this morning, eh?" said the other.

"At least we weren't around when it happened."

"Officer Amenes says it was just a mix-up," said the other. "He thinks they were mistakenly released late last night."

"They must have had the right connections then," he said with an eye roll. "I never even saw Amenes today. Where is he?"

"He left about a half-hour ago," said the other. "He didn't seem too happy."

"Uneasy lies the head that wears the crown."

"Come again?" said the other.

"It's Shakespeare," he said. "Never mind."

A few blocks away, officer Amenes was standing over a rusty steel drum in an empty lot, staring at the Illinois driver's license of Miles Townsend and hoping the fire he'd started in the barrel wouldn't attract much attention. He tossed in the files and Anders Andersen's passport. From Miles's wallet, he took out some paper money, thought about pocketing it, then tossed it in along with Miles's library card and International Youth Hostel Association membership card.

He watched everything burn until he was satisfied it was all ash, then walked away, hoping never to hear the names Vikram Bhat, Miles Townsend, or Anna de Wit again.

19.

MILES FELL ONTO the hard stone of the plateau above Danevesu, right on the already tender ashtray-shaped bruise on his left butt cheek. It hardly registered, however, as Miles's first impression was that he had been dropped into an automatic car wash in the middle of its hot wax cycle.

Fat drops of steaming rain plunked him from every direction, and swirling winds whipped at him in the dark of a scorching night. Short of breath and soaked to the skin by the scalding hot water, Miles tried to gain his bearings. He would not have been able to see anything were it not for the intermittent lightning strikes that enabled him to locate the vestibule he and Anna had exited on their only excursion to the roof of the city. He stumbled toward it, realizing as he approached the entrance that it was completely dark with no one inside to let him in.

Is anyone still here? he wondered. *How long was I gone this time?*

The statue of Arak was illuminated in silhouette by a flash of lightning in the distance. Miles trudged carefully over, feeling his way. As he neared the parapet on the city's edge, he saw smoke rising, dimly lit from below. Beside the thirty-foot Arak, he held onto the rim of the low wall for dear life and looked out on the city's once miraculous façade. It was scarred, blackened, and broken. He could hear nothing over the sounds of thunder, rain, and wind, and the harbor appeared dead, with only a random few lights emanating from windows or openings once covered by glass.

It had probably been foolish to return. And if it was an error, he hoped it would not be a fatal one. But Miles mainly cared that Anna was still alive. Whatever had happened here must have prevented her from following him back to Earth. He was sorry he'd ever left.

He slumped down against the parapet, one hand still gripping the slick, hot stone. The heat was overpowering, making him feel faint and his senses fuzzy. Gradually, the storm lessened in intensity, and a break in the clouds allowed him to see the night sky over the harbor. As the opening passed over him, Skygarden appeared among the stars and illuminated the city and harbor with its diffuse glow.

Looking back over the plateau in the reflected light of Our World's sister planet, Miles could swear the roof was alive, its surface undulating and rippling in waves. As he managed to dry his eyes with his free hand, he was able to focus on the movement around him and recoiled in horror at what he saw. Swarms of miniature black zhinks—resembling millions of cockroaches—were climbing over and circling around each other. They didn't look like the flying zhinks he'd seen in the city. Where these had come from or what purpose they served Miles had no clue.

Unable to look away, he watched them, fascinated. It seemed to him they were fighting among themselves, emitting sparks and puffs of smoke in thousands of tiny clashes. More of them than not lay motionless while the others fought it out on top of them. Rather than dwell on what it signified, Miles looked over the parapet and out over the harbor. He could see small lights on in the harbor town above the docks and decided to make his way down if he could.

The rains began to fall again, and visibility decreased, but the mini-zhinks ignored him even when he accidentally stepped on one. With some difficulty, Miles managed to find the path down to the harbor town. The little harbor village had been hit hard by the attack, as half the buildings were either destroyed or badly damaged. He could see standing water filling some of the houses whose roofs were partially torn off or completely gone, as if the rain had filled them up, though that seemed improbable to Miles. He scrambled down, navigating his way on the switchback and then the stairs carved into the cliff. His skin burned from the rain and his feet slipped, trying to find purchase on the rocky steps. He moved as quickly as he could, as each step in this heat and boiling rain was agony, but fell twice in his haste, scraping and bruising his limbs. Finally, he was down among the buildings of the town. The water stung his eyes and the air burnt his lungs, but Miles at last could make out which building the lights were coming from—a low-slung house, still intact, hugging the rocks that shielded it from the harbor. As he staggered closer, he could hear activity inside. He threw himself against the door and slumped down with a cry. Suddenly, each physically draining aspect of his journey—the heat, gravity, thin air, rain, wind, and grueling trek down—accumulated in him at once. Unable to raise his call for help above a whisper, he passed out with his head resting against the building's front door.

*

WHEN MILES AWOKE, he was relatively dry, though still perspiring. The air felt cool on his skin, and he lay in the softest pile of softness he had ever hoped to experience. He looked around at the yishi looking down at him, and he suddenly remembered where he must be, or at least narrowed it down to the one planet it could be.

The captain from the sub that had returned them to Danevesu from Twenty-six was among them, smiling at him in that by now familiar yishi way.

"I remember you," said Miles. "But I forget your name."

"I am Dave," he said.

Miles just shook his head amiably. "No."

"Excuse me?"

"No, I would have remembered if that were your name."

"Um..." Captain Dave decided to ignore it. "You'll have to forgive my English," he said. "I'm not completely fluent."

Miles closed his eyes in place of a nod. He was still exhausted.

"How did you get here?" asked Dave.

"I walked," said Miles.

Dave shot him a dubious look and laughed. "From Earth?"

"No. I meant from the top of the city."

"Oh. I thought you had transported back to Earth," said Dave. "That was our understanding."

"I did," said Miles. "But I came back."

"How?"

"I had help from a yishi, a Bandarian. I don't know his name."

Dave looked up at his fellow Danevesans in surprise. "That's an unexpected piece of information, I have to say. Was Telesu involved? Did he provide them with the spacetime portal technology?"

"He's in big trouble now."

"Yes. Anyway, you can't imagine how shocked we were to see you."

Captain Dave's English sounded pretty good to Miles. He was starting to feel more awake and began to look around the place, another beautiful interior space, combining intricate decoration and swooping geometric lines with clever utilitarian touches. There were only about five yishi around him, with maybe another five or six scattered around the house as far as he could see. He remembered the desolation he'd seen outside.

"What happened?" he asked.

"The Bandarians attacked us at our weakest," said Dave. "They fired missiles at us from submersibles in the harbor, knocked out our best defensive weapon. It lasted a little over a day. When that big tsunami came in, they had to submerge. Now it looks like they've retreated completely."

"Why?"

"We're not sure."

Miles nodded, not understanding. "Did anyone else survive?" he finally asked.

"That's right," said Dave, suddenly realizing. "You don't know."

*

ANNA'S BODY LAY motionless between Vikram's and Kerak's. They had all gone through a hellish ordeal before being laid to rest on the same pallets where they'd ministered to the sick and dying just a day before.

The miniature enemy zhinks still remained in piles all around them, eerily motionless in the dim light of the makeshift sick ward. Freed from the task of trying to thwart incoming packets after the Bandarian ships submerged, Dinev and Shikar had set to work on dealing with the destructive mini-zhinks in their midst from the relative safety of the command center. They eventually succeeded in hacking into the zhinks' operating system and uploading a virus that overrode their programming and set them against each other instead of on the Danevesans.

Miles knelt down beside Anna and rubbed the back of his fingers along her bare forearm. Despite her cuts and bruises, she looked as beautiful to him as ever.

"Anna," he said, and she opened her eyes, not quite believing whom she was seeing. She sat up awkwardly, the aches and pains evident in her expression, and encircled him in a tight embrace, knocking the wind from him temporarily.

"Miles," she whispered. "I didn't know what had happened to you. I was worried something bad…"

"Me too," managed Miles, "me too."

"Your face," she said, holding him at arms' length to look him over, "what happened?" The blood from his own cuts and scratches had dried a darker red, and the bruises on his neck had turned deep purple.

He shrugged. "Earth," he said, by way of explanation.

She hugged him again, not wanting to let go.

Miles could feel Dinev standing directly behind him, horning in on his moment.

"I thought you'd be glad to see each other," said Dinev, beaming.

Miles resented Dinev for having come between him and Anna, even though a large gap existed between what he knew about it and what he imagined. He knew he had no right to be possessive of Anna, though. She wasn't a lover anymore, just a friend. But it still meant the world to him that he was as important a friend to her as she was to him.

Vikram and Kerak were both stirred from unconsciousness by the familiar voices. They had worked without cease for the past two days, and it was still the middle of the night in Danevesu. On the other side of Miles from Anna, Vikram blinked his eyes open and managed to turn on his side. "Miles?" he said, in uncharacteristic disbelief.

Anna released her grip, and Miles turned to grasp Vikram's four-fingered hand. Vikram pulled Miles down toward him and gave him a yishi-style nuzzle. "I'm so happy you came back to us," he said. "But how?"

Kerak sat up now and looked over at Miles in mild surprise. "How the fuck did you get back here?" he said.

Miles laughed and said, "It's a long story."

"Well, we're up now, ass," he said, "may as well tell it."

*

SO HE RECOUNTED his recent misadventures in Spain for them: arriving alone on the grounds of the Alhambra, his discovery of Anders in the Hotel Kashmir bar, the thrashing he'd received from him, and their subsequent imprisonment. The *deus ex machina* materialization of Miles's mysterious Bandarian benefactor elicited a few raised eyebrows, and the revelation that Tom was now tutoring Josep caused Anna to shake her head and click her tongue. But other than that, Anna and the rest simply nodded along unfazed by most of Miles's tale.

It had been a slightly more dramatic two and a half days in Danevesu, and Miles was anxious to hear the details, including how they managed to survive the onslaught of killer zhinks, trapped in a storage room with nothing but a gaggle of invalids and metal bedpans to protect them. Ironically, it was the invalids who saved Anna, Vikram, and Kerak—and themselves—before Dinev and Shikar's hack ultimately rescued them along with everyone else. According to Vikram, Gedu, in his feeble, drug-addled state, fought like a madman against the zhinks—clumsily, as if in a fog, but drawing strength from some hidden well. He exhorted his fellows—none sicker than he, though some already unconscious. Their numbers, if not their ferocity, sufficed to hold the zhinks off. Numb from the narcotics and natural adrenaline (or its yishi equivalent) coursing through him, Gedu flailed away until he too passed out just as the zhinks began to turn on one another. Miraculously, he survived both his injuries and the illness that had brought him to death's door. Velluk, sadly, wasn't as lucky.

In the end, the contagion, which had spread to virtually the entire resident population of Danevesu, killed about three percent of those infected, about five thousand yishi. The casualties from the bombardment of the city accounted for another two thousand dead. It could have been—was intended to be—much worse, and yet now it was all but over shortly after it had begun. The coordinated attack had failed in its ultimate purpose but left the Danevesans shaken, with thousands of dead to process and a city to rebuild.

They were shaken but also furious. Although part of that fury may have had to do with their hormones. The day after the attack of the zhinks, most Danevesans were still incapacitated by illness, while many were dying of it. Exhausted, Kerak and Vikram could not figure out why Denebasa had fully recovered while no one else had even begun to. Over the course of that morning, however, most Danevesans also received their once-every-twelve-days gift.

"They got a visit from Aunt Flow," said Anna.

"Come again?" said Miles.

"Everyone got their periods."

Why the vast majority of yishi living in the city had simultaneous menstrual cycles was one of those mysteries of yishi biology, but it clearly had something to do with their living in such close proximity to one another over time. That's when everyone who got their period slowly started showing signs of getting better. Kerak was the one who figured out the connection between menstruating and the hormone released in the bloodstream that interfered with the pathogen. (Unlike Vikram, who was well past yishi menopause, Kerak also got his period that morning.) Deneb had had his first period two days earlier, putting the pathogen-fighting hormone in his blood much earlier. He was the only one in the hospital whose menses had begun ahead of everyone else's. Synthesizing the hormone was a simple matter in the lab, and Vikram and Kerak carried out the delivery of the hormone to every infected Danevesan who was either too young or too old to be menstruating, followed by everyone else just in case.

"Is that why I never got sick," said Anna, "because I was having my period?"

"You were infected?" asked Miles.

"I was," she said.

"Your hormones are different," said Kerak. "But there is probably some common characteristic of yishi hormones released during menstruation and follicle-stimulating hormone or luteinizing hormones in humans."

"All right."

"The specific hormone in yishi is only released during menstruation, so we got lucky," said Kerak.

"And Berejian was sloppy," said Vikram. "He didn't take it into account. I'd like to think he goofed on purpose, even if unconsciously. But somehow I doubt it."

"I was carrying the pathogen in my blood," Anna explained to Miles. "But as of yesterday, I tested clean."

"I never should have left," said Miles. "I'm sorry."

"It's not as if you had a choice," said Vikram.

"I know," he said. "But I'm sorry I wanted to leave."

"In my experience," said Vikram, "I've found it's only fair to judge someone by his actions at least as much as by his motives. You came back to Our World the moment it became possible, despite the danger. You don't have to apologize."

"Thanks."

It was still the middle of the night, and everyone was exhausted and in need of sleep. Although they found an empty pallet for Miles, sleep did not come easily for him or the others for some time. When it finally did come, it was a deep, dreamless slumber that lasted well after the artificial lights of the dormitory announced the new day.

When they awoke, they learned why the Bandarians had fled the harbor and not returned.

*

SOME SIXTY-ODD YISHI—the surviving Danevesan councilors and leaders from every guild and group in the city—two humans, and one fluppet crowded into the modest apartment of the translator Geresh. Most had to stand or squeeze onto the scant seating, but, as the amphitheater was now an open-air amphitheater and most of the meeting spaces and prime apartments were damaged or destroyed, Geresh's flat was as good an option as any. Memorial videos played on the screens behind them, a reminder, as if they needed any, of what they'd just survived.

The meeting embodied the yishi need to come together face to face and make collective decisions—it was also broadcast over the network to every Danevesan's smartskin, headset, and monitor. Most of the communications networks had been restored, and news of the outside world was already being shared and discussed. The tsunami that had briefly raised the harbor level past the highest previous tide mark had been caused by a series of underwater earthquakes off the southern coast of

Bandary. Though details were sketchy, one of the quakes had caused a major collapse along the southern coast of the island.

A mountain range stood along the Bandarian coast, holding back the sea from the rest of the island after it had swallowed up Baradel. One of the mountains, perhaps weakened by past centuries of mining, had come down, allowing an enormous tsunami to rise up over the once-towering barrier and inundate the valley. Now Lagaredel was flooded. This all had come on the heels of a severe dust storm that had driven most of the population of the city underground.

The gathered Danevesans were grimly satisfied.

"Maybe there is a Gee," said one sarcastically.

The Bandarian naval fleet at Ashedel had been wiped out by the same tsunami, along with most of the port town. The Bandarian ships that had fled Danevesu harbor were returning to Bandary to rescue whatever comrades they could. Danevesu's own fleet of military subs had been reduced by the Bandarians' surprise attack and subsequent blockade of the harbor that protected the subs firing their packets on the city. But there were still military and civilian subs at sea, as well as the network of Danevesan scientific outposts scattered throughout the islands of the archipelago. This not only gave a recovering Danevesu eyes and ears around Our World, it put them in an advantageous position with regard to the now vulnerable Bandarians.

Danevesan naval subs, however, were never meant to be an offensive military force. They carried no spacetime portal manipulators, no nuclear weapons. No ships did. In fact, the only nuclear weapons still in existence on Our World were stored securely deep in the mountain behind Danevesu. The Danevesans had never intended to use them. On the other hand, a reasonable yishi might ask, if that was so, and no one else had any, why had they kept them?

Vikram's old human form, that is to say, the fluppet now inhabited by Tchuvu, sat in the center of the great room, not saying much, as control over his new body's tongue had yet to progress significantly. So he presided over the argument that was swirling around him in judicial silence. The debate went back and forth, now that Bandary was decimated, over whether to take the opportunity to retaliate for their unprovoked attack, or to leave them to whatever fate nature or Gee intended.

"We have too much to do here," said one, "to recover our health and rebuild our city, to send needed resources in an attack on Bandary. From what we've just learned, it's not even necessary. If the Bandarians survive at all, they'll be so reduced in capacity and resources, they won't be a threat to anyone."

Most of the yishi nodded noncommittally at this.

An older, clearly esteemed yishi, Kovata, stood from his seat near the center of the gathering, and began by addressing the previous speaker. "I sympathize with your notion of focusing on our own recovery. And it's not in our nature to seek vengeance. Like almost all of you, I spent the last three days ill, believing I was going to die, before Kerak synthesized the hormone and saved us." Kerak, Anna was shocked to see, looked embarrassed, shaking his head as if to deny the credit. "But my partner of almost twenty years wasn't so fortunate. He died of the disease before a cure could be found, in one of the temporary hospital wards to which we were evacuated after the bombing began. Before that happened, we got to witness family, friends, and neighbors blown to bits by explosions they had no warning were coming, while they did their best to care for each other through illness inflicted on them by the same enemy. I watched helplessly as the family who lived next door fell to their deaths when the floor collapsed under them. We lived because we happened to be on the other side of the wall. Their child was in his second year of school."

There was silence in the room as Kovata paused to clear his throat. "I have often wondered," he continued, "what it is the Bandarians and the terrorists they sponsor want from us. They blame us for the state of Our World. Maybe they believe things will be better once we're gone. I don't know. And I really don't care what their reasons are. There will never be peace as long as Bandary survives. We may be willing to coexist with a weakened enemy, but they'll never be willing to coexist with us. It just isn't in their nature. They will always be a threat to us. Moreover, if we are to have any hope of peace, I think Bandary must be utterly destroyed."

Almost immediately and at once, many voices rang out in varying shades of agreement and opposition. Further from the center, Geresh translated for Miles what Kovata had said, and Anna hung her head because she realized she agreed with him.

A few actually advocated using the last of their nuclear stockpile on Bandary, more spoke up in favor of doing nothing, while others urged waiting to see what happened. So the choice came down to retaliating or not retaliating—with the idea of putting the decision off until later a compromise option.

Geresh did his best to interpret the goings-on for Miles (less so for Anna, who could understand quite a bit by this point). Miles was shaking his head and asked Geresh, "Can I say something?" Geresh just looked at him, uncomprehending. "To everyone?" he clarified.

Geresh quieted the crowd down and announced that Miles wanted to speak. It would have been impertinent, but the yishi revered Miles to a much greater extent than he deserved.

With all eyes on him, Miles said, "Doesn't anyone see that there's another option?"

The assembled yishi looked at each other after Geresh translated, some curious, others dubious, but all respectful of the Earthling in their midst. They looked at him indulgently, inviting him to elaborate.

"Couldn't we help them instead?" he said.

The yishi were unsure if Geresh had translated correctly. Was Miles actually saying what Geresh thought he was saying?

"Welp dem…bwat?" asked Tchuvu, as translated by Geresh, who showed he at least hadn't lost his sense of humor.

"Save them," explained Miles. "Couldn't we try to save them?"

The silence this produced felt to Miles like a collective and disgusted shake of the head. He wasn't completely wrong, as one of them made clear:

"You want us to help the yishi who killed Kovata's partner, our friends and family?" he began. "Who tried to murder every last one of us in our beds and then sent bombs to cremate our remains? You want to rescue the Bandarians, when we're still half-dead, our beautiful city is in ruins, and, thanks to them, those of us who are still able to get around must be crammed into this windowless little shithole—"

"Hey!" yelled Geresh, before he finished translating. "This is my home."

"Sorry, I…" he trailed off. But others jumped in, talking animatedly, some angry like the previous speaker, a few taking Miles's side, others suddenly unsure what they believed.

"Am I crazy to suggest it?" Miles asked, looking to Anna and Vikram.

Anna shifted uneasily, unconsciously rubbing her thigh where the shrapnel had dug in. "You weren't here, Miles," she said, glancing up to meet his gaze. "You don't know what it was like."

"But, no," answered Vikram, "you're not crazy."

"One of them rescued me," said Miles, "a Bandarian. The one word of his I could understand was 'Sorry.'" Anna looked away, not wanting to say more.

Erestu, who had been monitoring their conversation while listening to the others argue, put in, "You know, I've been thinking, he must have been the one who warned me before our sub was destroyed."

Miles and the others looked at Erestu. "I mean, he did save our lives," he said.

"If we can save yishi lives, I think we have to try," said Kerak.

"Always a physician first," said Dinev, with an inscrutable expression. "I am."

Someone assailed Miles's right to make suggestions or even be present in this forum but was angrily shouted down by others. A few wondered what Cardevise and Edrisia would think of Danevesu if they didn't help Bandary when they were the only ones who could.

It was clear that many were taking Miles's suggestion seriously, which alarmed Tchuvu, who couldn't say much about it in any case. Soon yishi were debating the practicalities of how they could aid Bandary if it was indeed under water, and whether a rescue operation was even possible. The last few vocal supporters of retaliation latched onto the unfeasibility of intervention on behalf of their enemy, pointing out that more Danevesans would die in the attempt.

"There's nothing left to discuss but the when and how," said Gedu finally, standing in a corner with a hand on his neighbor's shoulder for support. "I thought I might be too old for shame, but it turns out I was wrong. Because I am ashamed. Moments ago, like many of you, I was trying to rationalize a nuclear genocide. I had almost convinced myself, too. But our human ambassadors are right." Anna opened her mouth partway and then shut it. "We must try to save Bandary now, not simply because it represents a moral imperative, but because it may be the best and only opportunity we will ever have to end the cycle of hatred between our nations. We have a chance to take the first step in establishing a lasting peace, and it can't be wiping them off the face of Our World, even if we could."

Tchuvu stood up and looked around at the faces surrounding him, larger in Vikram's old body and yet reduced by having lost his own, and now unable to form the words he wanted to. Unexpectedly, his interpreter, Okiva, rose up to speak for him. "Helping the Bandarians is out of the question," he said. "We know what they would do to us if the situation were reversed. In fact, we just lived through what they would do. We don't have to lower ourselves to their level, but neither do we need to waste resources and lives trying to save them from the calamity against which they did nothing to prepare." Tchuvu, standing beside him, nodded solemnly. "They call us devils and blame us for the collapse of Our World's ecosystem, even though all our ancestors played an equal part. They shun our technology. Why should we put it to use for their salvation? We can wait and see what nature has in store for them. We should do nothing."

Some of the assembled nodded and murmured with lukewarm conviction.

"You see?" said Gedu. "Tchuvu doesn't need to think about what he's going to say, it's the same nonsense regardless of the circumstance. Anyone can spout it." There was a good amount of laughter at this. Then Gedu added, "But tell us, Tchuvu, will letting every last Bandarian child die bring back even one of our own?" Tchuvu glared at Gedu for a moment and then sat down dejectedly. Okiva remained standing but seemed to shrink within himself.

"They cling foolishly to their god," Gedu continued, "while we cling foolishly to our technology, the cause of Our World's doom. We each have sound rationales for portraying the other as less than fully yishi. But there is a reason we continue to cling to the technology that at times threatens our very existence. We could use it in a vain attempt to colonize Earth—" Tchuvu looked stricken, unaware that Vikram had already spilled that secret to Anna and Miles "—or we can use the technology we possess to repair Our World, starting with our oldest and most implacable enemy, Bandary."

Between Gedu's words and Miles's preternatural aura, more of the yishi were speaking in support of giving aid to Bandary. It was a hopeful mood among the supporters, and it seemed to be permeating the room.

"I'd prefer we had a consensus," said Elusia slyly, rising up in the middle of the room, "but I think we should first poll everyone here to assess our options. We have three, as I see it. A show of hands—who thinks we should attack Bandary now?"

A few raised their hands, including a dismayed Kovata.

"Who thinks we should do nothing, or at least wait?"

Several more hands shot up.

"And who thinks we should try to help them?"

The vast majority, more than forty yishi, raised their hands. Miles raised his hand belatedly, looking around and shaking his head. "I can't believe it," he said. An air of anticipation mixed with relief filled the room, as excited murmurs grew louder.

Anna had raised her hand, as had Vikram and everyone they knew. Vikram smiled in his crooked old way and turned to Miles. "I think we owe you a debt," he said, holding his gaze on Miles for a few seconds before adding, "I knew I was right to bring you here."

A vote of the entire population of the city was quickly arranged over the network and completed in a matter of minutes, as everyone held their breath.

Elusia nodded after all the results had come in. "The people have spoken," he said. "We come to Bandary's aid. Now we just need to figure out how."

Home

It is fucking great to be alive.

—*Frank Zappa*

20.

"WAIT, DID ANY of this actually happen, or is it all made up?" she asked.

"Well, parts are true," said Miles. "Other parts I embellished. But it's more fun if I tell it as though it all really happened."

"Mmm, okay," she said, playing along. "So Vikram turned out to be a yishi from Danevesu?"

Miles nodded.

"And the yishi are, like, bird-people?"

"They basically look like human females, except for the beaks and feathers," said Miles, who stood leaning against the polished walnut rail of the bar, a student hangout near his campus. "So, you know, humanoid, with avian features and vestigial wings." He was telling Willa, a recent acquaintance, about his travels in Spain and on Our World with the yishi, as he did from time to time, when he liked the person, usually a girl, and knew there was little chance she would take him seriously. He was attracted to Willa, who was a bit of a tomboy with an old-timey-sounding name, and so he was showing off.

Willa knew Miles's thesis had to do with myths and storytelling traditions. He had told her about a custom in the mountains of Kashmir in which storytellers wandered from village to village, telling folktales during the long, cold winter nights. This wasn't a folktale, but it was a cold winter night, so she just went with it.

"They had breasts and womanly hips," he continued, "but they also had something more easily concealed by clothing."

"Vaginas?" she guessed.

"Well, yes," he said, "but since they were all hermaphrodites they also all had penises."

"Of course they did."

"They were very sexually liberated," he added.

"Really. Ever bag one?"

"As a matter of fact…" Miles admitted.

"You sure this wasn't just some cross-dressing dude you picked up?"

"Pretty sure," said Miles, sorry he'd made it sound like a boast. The bartender slid over a gin and tonic, and Miles squeezed a wedge of lime into the glass and stirred the ice with a thin plastic straw. "They were a species free from hatred based on gender, sexuality, or race. So, of course, they had to find other ways to demonize one another."

"Uh-huh," said Willa. "So you think if we didn't have racism or sexism, we'd still have the same problems—oppression, exploitation, war?"

"I'm just telling my story," said Miles.

"Okay."

"There was a war, as it turns out," he said. "Religious and political differences played a role. And resources were scarce, so people acted out of desperation."

"Why were resources scarce?" she asked, puckering her lips after taking a sip of her whiskey sour.

"The climate had changed drastically," said Miles. "The polar ice caps had melted, which had buried the most populated, coastal areas under water, while the remaining land turned to desert. There were natural disasters on a regular basis—earthquakes, tsunamis, dust storms—and the droughts, famines, and mass extinctions that came with them…"

"Sounds bad."

"It was. It was also terribly hot everywhere," he said.

"Sounds nice right about now."

"Trust me, it wasn't," he said, recalling the night he'd landed on the plateau above Danevesu. "Danevesu was probably 160 degrees outside, and that was after dark."

"But it was a dry heat?"

"Not really," he said. Miles began to tell Willa of what life was like on Our World, of traversing wormholes (or arseholes, as the yishi called them), of Vikram and Anna, of Skygarden, of the beauty of Danevesu, of the gene bank and Berejian's betrayal, and of how the Bandarians attacked the city. Willa had nowhere to go, so she indulged Miles, who was a good friend of an old classmate of hers from high school. Miles, for his part, was good at gauging his listener's interest, so he knew when to summarize or simply elide nonessential details. When he got to the part where the Danevesan survivors met in Geresh's flat and agreed to help the Bandarians, he paused, genuinely choked up at the thought. This bemused Willa, who knew as well as Miles that the story was fiction.

A sudden blast of cold air gave them a chill as someone pushed open the door, and Miles held his breath, as he always did, waiting to see who would come in. Drinking in a bar or riding the train, especially, whenever some stranger opened a door, Miles always half-expected Vikram to come walking through and plop down next to him.

But it wasn't Vikram. Vikram was gone, and Tchuvu had his old body. Anna was gone too, still back on Our World, as far as Miles knew.

"So what did they do?" asked Willa, curious now about the fate of Bandary.

"Um…well, Danevesu sent Captain Dave—"

"Captain Dave!" she laughed. "I love his name."

"It was his name," said Miles matter-of-factly. "Anyway, they sent him and Erestu via wormhole to scout out the area where the mountain had caved in on Bandary's southern coast. Apparently, the mountain range had been heavily mined for what we call rare-earth metals."

"What are they?"

"Metals…that are, um, rare on Earth."

"So they don't call 'em that?"

"No, they're pretty common there," he said. "In any case, it wouldn't make sense to call them that on another planet."

"Right."

"Anyway," Miles continued, "the mountain was hollowed out from centuries of extraction, and when the earthquake hit offshore, it collapsed. Then the tsunami came and flooded over the rubble and into the valley. But the main thing they discovered was that the collapsed mountain still stood above sea level. If another tsunami hit, it probably would've flooded the valley again, but we thought we could do something about the situation in Lagaredel before that happened."

The question of how in the world the Danevesans could help Lagaredel—in particular those who had taken shelter from the storm underground and were now trapped by the floodwaters above them—posed a problem.

Assuming they weren't already drowned, breaking through to the subterranean network where the bulk of Lagarenes lived would definitely drown them if the water was not drained first. But there was nowhere for the flood waters to go, as Lagaredel was the lowest point on the large island of Bandary.

Zino had repaired the spacetime portal generator, which had brought both the static portal and their main defensive weapon back online. The senior practical physicist who oversaw the technology had died, but a yishi named Nuin who was widely regarded as the most talented physicist in Danevesu, was at the meeting, still weak from the illness but recovering. He suggested that the portals could be put to further use.

"We've only ever used them for two things," he said. "And yet the practical applications are nearly limitless. We could use them to remove the floodwaters from Lagaredel."

This caused more than a little stir among the yishi assembled. When the spacetime portal technology had first been tested, many of the top Danevesan physicists at the time predicted that it might open a black hole that would swallow Our World, or possibly even the known universe. The reality of travel through the portals still terrified many of them, and having recently learned that Bandary now had a pared-down version of the technology didn't ease their worries.

Nuin continued, "The two ends of the arsehole created by our defensive weapon can be arrayed vertically or horizontally, or any angle in between, up or down, and in much larger dimensions than we've ever used. All we need are precise coordinates." Coordinates weren't a simple matter, however, without the positioning satellites that had gone out of commission and crashed into the sea centuries ago. Someone would have to be onsite to relay the exact positioning.

"What are you saying?" asked one of the engineers present. "Deploy an arsehole in Bandary and bail the water from the city?"

"Create large horizontal arseholes at the lowest points along the flood path," said Nuin, "under the water, probably in the old riverbeds, and position them with the entrances opening up, like drains in a bathtub."

"And have the water drain where?" someone else asked.

"Anywhere over the middle of the ocean ought to do," he said. "Horizontal exits opening downward. Gravity does the rest."

"We've never tried stretching an arsehole under water," said the engineer. "And we don't even know how gravity would behave with the arseholes arrayed that way."

"We could test it here first," said Zino, fired by the idea.

So they did, to less-than-unanimous approval, in Danevesu harbor. And it worked. It was an elegant solution, as everyone had to admit. Beneath the ocean's surface, water flowed into one end of the arsehole on the sea floor and out the other a quarter mile over the harbor, as if falling from an invisible spigot floating in the sky.

"Since helping the Bandarians had been my idea," said Miles, continuing his story, "I volunteered to go to Bandary."

"Of course you did," said Willa, the alcohol from the whiskey depressing her nervous system in a not altogether unpleasant way.

Miles's first impression of Bandary was not of an ancient alien metropolis but of a long, shallow lake set within a flat and nearly featureless desert terrain. The domes of Lagar Temu rose out of the middle of the water, with clusters of two- and three-story buildings peeking above the waterline near the palace and on the outskirts of the flooded city. The water was about seven or eight meters deep over the city center, the old riverbeds going only as deep as another five or six meters beyond that. Debris littered the surface of the newly created lake—debris and the bodies of dead yishi. Gee only knew what was under the surface, but Erestu and Dave had arrived ahead of Miles and the others to dive down into it and find out.

Piloting single-seater amphibious subs, Erestu and Dave had a more difficult task ahead of them than hinted at in Nuin's hypothetical. The water was a thick, silty soup, impenetrable to the naked eye, concealing all manner of floating and stationary building wreckage, the furnishings and personal effects from the destroyed homes of the yishi shantytowns, and anything else not nailed down prior to the flood. They knew where the riverbeds ought to be, but finding an unobstructed trench while dodging and weaving around upended vehicles, free pieces of masonry and construction beams, and the occasional boulder added to the challenge.

Miles and Anna had both gone to help, despite Elusia and Tchuvu pleading with them not to. The truth is they had no business being there, but Miles did feel responsible and couldn't just watch as others wandered into hostile territory on his bright idea. Likewise, Anna wasn't going to shirk her responsibility, even if it hadn't been her idea, or inclination. Once again, their quasi-divine status permitted them to do as they pleased. To Miles's delight, at least, they both had smartskin imprinted on their hands to allow them easy communication with the rest of the group—a pair of cameras and a microphone/speaker tattooed imperceptibly along with them.

In the end, it was lucky they were there, as every Danevesan who came to Lagaredel would be needed and put to use.

Traveling with Anna and Miles were Vikram, Kerak, Geresh, Dinev, Shikar, and about half the Danevesans who had voted to help the Bandarians, including a handful of civil guards fitted out in lightweight body armor. They fanned out around the edges of the floodwaters, helping to spot significant obstacles and communicate with Captains Erestu and Dave, while back in Danevesu Zino and Nuin coordinated the projection of portals at the specific locations given.

Once two suitable trenches were located and portals opened up beneath the surface, the waters covering Bandary began to drain, along with a fair amount of flotsam and jetsam, into the sea just below their north pole. It took most of the day. The more the city was exposed by the retreating floodwaters, the worse it looked. The outer ring of the city, where the shantytowns had stood, was a sea of mud with a jagged crust of obliterated dwellings, punctured here and there by vertical building supports sticking up like giant toothpicks.

While they waited and watched, Miles examined the magnificent, weather-beaten edifice of Lagar Temu palace and marveled at its apparent age and the dozens of variously sized domes that sprouted out of its three sides like mushrooms. He wondered what was going on inside, but could have no inkling of the events that were taking place there while he mucked around the edges of the still submerged slum.

The water level lowered below the rivers' banks, Erestu and Dave drove their amphibious subs out of the sludge and mounted higher ground. The entire force gathered and quickly formed into several small groups. With an armored civil guard walking ahead of each, they spread out to search the wreckage. The Danevesans, though none had ever been here before, knew of the underground dwellings the poor of Bandary had carved out below the city in the centuries following the cataclysm and loss of their old capital in the south. So they began to look for hatches, anything that looked like it could be an entrance to the underground. After only a short while, however, confronted by the grim reality facing them, their mission suddenly struck them all as utterly hopeless. To start with, any opening to the city below would undoubtedly be buried under mud and debris. And, even if they found one, they had to hope that the waters hadn't infiltrated the makeshift underground hatchways and drowned the Bandarians in the rooms where they had sheltered from the storm.

This wasn't helped at all when the group led by Erestu uncovered the first underground entrance. He, Geresh, and Anna pulled aside the wall of the shack that had partially covered it and cleared away the mud gumming up the edges of the hatch. Erestu signaled to the nearby group led by Captain Dave, which included Miles and Vikram, who looked over hopefully.

Lifting the corroded metal door on its creaky hinges, they discovered a chamber filled to the brim with murky water. Aiming powerful flashlights into it revealed bodies inside, dead for half a day or more. They dared not disturb anything below, as they could only hope that the underground room either didn't connect to others, or that the tunnels between were sealed watertight.

With the sun nearing the horizon in the east, everyone returned to the search in silence. No one needed to speak the thought they all shared, that this looked like a rescue mission without the possibility of saving anyone. Miles, Vikram, and Dave passed by one of the bloated bodies that hours ago had floated on the surface of the floodwater and made a mental note of its location. Earlier they had discussed the need to properly dispose of the bodies once they'd brought up the survivors. The conclusion that burning corpses would likely be the only part of the plan that they would accomplish was becoming harder and harder to ignore.

Two things then happened simultaneously to inject both hope and fear into the Danevesan rescue party.

A message dinged through on everyone's smartskin. Written in the customary universal Script, Miles could easily interpret the words. "Survivors!" Vikram exclaimed, in case he couldn't. "Dinev says they're over there." Vikram pointed to Dinev's group frantically pulling away wreckage from the ground a few hundred meters to the east of their position.

Then, "Lagar Temu, look." It was Anna replying to all over the smartskin's voice transmitter. "The southwest entrance. Yishi are coming out. Military, from the looks of them. They look armed."

They were, and slightly outnumbered the Danevesans as well, of whom only the civil guards were equipped with anything like weapons or armor. The Bandarians were headed in their direction.

Miles's and Anna's groups came together, joined by the nearest group to them, while the team next to Dinev's helped them pull damp but relatively unscathed survivors up from a door in the floor of a collapsed home. The most forward group started to double back toward Miles, Anna, and the others gathered in a loose bunch.

Erestu signaled to the Bandarians, holding up his hands with palms outward, in the universally understood gesture for "I'm unarmed" (or at least not hostile). The main group of Bandarians headed toward them, weapons drawn, while a small detachment walked toward the Danevesans hauling up shaken but grateful Bandarians, of whom five or six were now aboveground. They were staring at their rescuers in mild disbelief, unaware of the series of events that made this a truly improbable occurrence.

Erestu and Geresh stood in front of the others, awaiting the primary force of Revolutionary Guards. As they came closer, slowly as they navigated the piles of wreckage, one of their number burst ahead of his comrades and stood about ten meters away, staring at Miles in stunned surprise. He removed his helmet and dropped it to the ground in front of him. Miles recognized him at once as the Bandarian who had freed him from jail. Peleg turned and motioned for his fellows to lower their weapons, then turned back to Miles and the others before stumbling over his helmet and falling face first in the mud as Miles rushed to meet him.

Miles helped him up, and after wiping the mud from his eyes, Peleg gave him a nuzzle, the affectionate greeting common to both Danevesans and Bandarians.

"I'm Miles," he said, as Geresh came up behind him to translate.

"Mai-oolz," said Peleg, nodding. "My name is Peleg. Did you do this?" he asked, meaning the startling absence of water everywhere.

The other Bandarians behind Peleg still eyed this group warily. With two aliens in their midst, Danevesans were in their city, with what purpose they honestly couldn't fathom. For their part, the Danevesans behind Miles were mostly just as, if not more, suspicious of the armed Revolutionary Guards in their bulky body armor, staring at them darkly from behind tinted glass visors.

Erestu and Geresh both recognized something off about the force that had come out to meet them. They were in loose formation, not a tight, two-row deployment, for one. For another, there was no doctor-priest among them, usually distinctive in brightly colored cloak. And the lack of discipline that would allow one of their group to run ahead of the others and embrace a potential threat was unheard of. What did it mean? Under the unusual circumstances, perhaps nothing. But it raised some questions that needed to be asked.

"Where is your faith representative?" asked Erestu, who spoke fluent Bandarian.

Peleg nodded toward Erestu politely. "There have been some changes at Lagar Temu," he said. "The One and his ministers have been deposed. The attacks on Danevesu were orchestrated by them in coordination with the Hopmoul. Though, in truth, I don't believe they ever understood Hopmoul's ultimate goal. They could only see and revel in your destruction. Do I take it from your presence here that the attacks failed?"

Erestu shrugged in acknowledgment of the fact.

"My friends don't believe you would come to our aid," said Peleg. "Not after what our government did. I'm hoping that they're wrong, and that I can tell them you've come to help us. Did you somehow manage to drain all the water away?"

"Yes," said Erestu. "Was it you who warned me of the destruction of my sub off of Twenty-six?"

Peleg smiled. "That was you?"

Erestu described for Peleg and his siblings-in-arms how Danevesu had decided, after surviving the attacks on the city, to send a rescue delegation to Bandary in hopes of finding and helping the survivors of the flood.

"It was your idea," said Peleg, looking back at Miles.

"It was a group decision," Miles pointed out. "The entire city voted." Erestu explained how they drained the water away and then tried to find survivors. "We'd been looking for a while before we came across them," he said, indicating the yishi being brought up as they spoke.

"We can help you," said Peleg, who turned to his comrade, who seemed to be the one nominally in charge, and spoke a few words in his ear. The squad leader turned away to talk into his headset while the two groups regarded one another awkwardly.

"Peleg," said Vikram suddenly, pulling him aside and speaking Peleg's native tongue, "do you know whatever happened to the case Telesu took from me?"

Peleg recognized Vikram from their one encounter in Berejian's lab. "We brought it to the minister Salas," he said, "who kept it safe." Vikram nodded in relief. "But...after we executed him, I had the case and its contents incinerated."

"Oh," said Vikram. "Well...that's just as well, I suppose."

Erestu, who had overheard, looked agitated, as if he were holding something in. "You executed the minister?" he said finally. Peleg nodded. "And the One?" Another nod in the affirmative. "Who else?"

"There were many traitors," said Peleg unapologetically. "The penalty for such acts is clear. We've imprisoned others who aided them. What would you have us do with these mass murderers?"

"It's not that," Vikram cut in. "It's just we don't put a yishi to death for any crime in Danevesu."

"Perhaps if you had when Telesu betrayed you," said Peleg, "the attacks would not have happened."

Vikram nodded ruefully at Peleg. "You may be right," he said. "Was he executed as well?"

Peleg shook his head. "We're still questioning him," he said. "He's under guard in the palace," he added, motioning over his shoulder to Lagar Temu. As he said it, another group of Bandarian soldiers emerged from the palace, carrying what turned out to be a small pump and a coiled length of five-inch-diameter hose. "I know these tunnels and underground dwellings," Peleg said, returning to the task at hand. "If we can pump the water out of some of the entry rooms, we should be able to find survivors in the rooms beyond."

Erestu nodded, and they started to formulate a plan of action between their forces. Small mixed groups fanned out to find entry points. When they found survivors, they would pull them up and, if able, put them to work aiding in the search. If they came upon a flooded room, they would use a pump to empty it of water and search for hatches to rooms or tunnels beyond.

The first time they started up one of the pumps, it sent up clouds of white smoke, and the acrid-sweet stench of petroleum permeated the air. Miles and Anna couldn't help but notice the Danevesans react with visibly more horror at that than they had at the news of the executions.

Peleg led a group of searchers with Vikram, Miles, and another Bandarian soldier, and he found the entrance to a tightly sealed hatch he knew well. If they had survived, members of his family and others would be huddled in the rooms below.

The Bandarian soldier was the first down into the hole. Muddy water was up to his knees, but no one was in the first room. He heard knocking on the hatch at one end of the room and helped pull it open, revealing two dozen or more frightened survivors standing behind it. To Peleg's relief, the soldier called up to share the good news, that they could begin to help them up.

Miles started to climb down into the hole, but Peleg put a hand out and gently barred him from entering. He said something, almost apologetically, which Vikram translated: "He's worried you might freak them out," he said.

"Oh," said Miles.

Bandarians had of course heard of Earth and the human beings who populated the planet, though many put no more stock in their existence than grown humans did in the Easter Bunny.

So Vikram went down instead, while Miles waited at the entrance to the hole. And to every Bandarian Vikram helped out, he said, "By the way, there's a real human from Earth waiting at the entrance to give you a hand up. Don't be afraid, he's harmless."

Soon there were hundreds of yishi survivors aboveground. The more who emerged, the more who were able to help search, the more who knew their way around the underground networks. But it was getting dark, making the work more difficult. As the electricity had been knocked out everywhere, they carried flashlights and lit fires near entry points. Kerak administered to those who were injured, as most of the Bandarian doctor-priests in Lagar Temu had been imprisoned or executed, and in any case their anachronistic medical practices made them about as useful as medieval barbers. Food and drinking water were scarce and had to be rationed, so many were thirsty and hungry. The plants that purified liquid and solid waste had been rendered inoperable by the flood. Supply ships from Danevesu were on their way but would not arrive for at least another day.

They all worked through the night, pulling up survivors as well as the dead. When there were more than enough yishi to search for and uncover entry points to the underground city, some were assigned the morbid task of dealing with the corpses. More fires were lit, large blazes far from the holes, as there was no more practical thing to do with the dead Bandarians. In the heat and mud, they were already beginning to rot.

Anna, bringing up survivors with a search party near Miles, found the Bandarians' reaction to her presence a stark contrast to the Danevesans' reverence. The Bandarians reacted with barely concealed terror and disbelief when encountering her, a human, no less so than with Miles, despite her rough resemblance to the yishi. Most of them, upon seeing her, would stroke their beaks and touch a forefinger to their foreheads two or three times in an apparent ritual of warding off evil. Unable to speak their language, the best Anna could do was to make exaggerated gestures conveying passivity and amity. After her time in Danevesu, seeing the variation in their physical appearance was startling, as was their natural deference and timidity. Their dress wasn't colorful or fashionable, merely functional—well-worn verging on ragged. The children were both more numerous than in Danevesu and more integrated within households, as they tended to stay with their parents, who raised them.

Anna realized then that she had barely dipped a toe into the ocean that was yishi civilization as a whole, reduced though it was. She observed the Bandarian survivors interact with each other and the Revolutionary Guards, listened to the sing-song babble of their native tongue, a more musical language lacking the clicks and guttural consonants characteristic of Danevesan. They grew accustomed to Anna the longer the night wore on, the more they saw her rescuing their neighbors, bringing water to the thirsty, and helping those with injuries.

It was nearly daybreak when Peleg insisted that their group take a rest. They'd been at it relentlessly for most of the extended Tonshuan night and believed they'd discovered every entry point there was to find in their sector. Peleg sat down with Vikram and Miles along the foundation of a crumbled stone wall, the remains of one of the few solidly constructed buildings outside of the city center. He surveyed the scene in front of him, thousands of his countrymen, now refugees in their own city, looking dazed and anxious and surprised to be alive. Dark clouds flowed eastward overhead, blocking out the light of a setting Skygarden.

"We have a great deal of rebuilding ahead of us," said Peleg.

"As do we," said Vikram.

Peleg nodded wearily. "I wish we were in a position to offer you the help you've given us."

Vikram translated for Miles, who appreciated it, used as he was to not comprehending most of what he heard. "You said yesterday that your leaders have been deposed," said Vikram. "What happened?"

"When I interrogated Telesu, we learned of the minister Salas's involvement with the Hopmoul," said Peleg. "We learned how the One had approved it all, of the other ministers' collaboration. Once we verified what Telesu had told us, we had no choice but to act."

"The Revolutionary Guard?" said Vikram.

"Most of the generals were ignorant of the conspiracy," said Peleg. "They would not have gone along with it had they known."

"Even though the conspiracy's goal was to destroy Danevesu?"

Peleg considered the rather pointed question. "We tolerated the Hopmoul, and others, because we shared the same enemy. Some in the Revolutionary Guard believed in the destruction of Danevesu by any means, but most rejected any kind of unprovoked offensive. But using a genetically designed pathogen as a weapon violates every tenet of our faith. And the Hopmoul wouldn't have stopped at the destruction of Danevesu."

"Wouldn't have?" asked Vikram. "Does that mean you know where the spare canisters are?"

Peleg nodded, surprised by how much Vikram knew. "Before the flood, no one could leave the city because of the dust storm. Telesu told us where his Hopmoul contact was hiding. We retrieved every canister, all of the pathogen."

"You didn't incinerate them?" said Vikram.

"There was some disagreement, as you might imagine," said Peleg. "Ultimately, they decided to hold on to them in restricted storage deep inside the palace. Much like Danevesu did with its nuclear weapons."

Vikram shook his head and smiled wryly. "We found a cure, you know," he said.

Peleg raised an eyebrow. "Good to know."

Across two lots of debris and sludge, Miles could see Anna by the light of one of the fires, standing next to Kerak, who was busy administering to an injured survivor. As Anna's eyes met Miles's, her expression seemed to capture all that was both grim and hopeful in the situation. She acknowledged Miles and Vikram with a slight smile, and Vikram gave a quick wave.

"What will you do when we get back to Danevesu?" Miles asked him.

"Like Peleg said," replied Vikram, "rebuild. What about you?"

"Go back home," he said.

"What if this is your home?" said Vikram.

"Our World?"

"Not necessarily," he said. "Not any one place, per se. I mean, maybe you're a nomad like me. You might not like going back to being stuck in the same familiar place."

Miles considered that. "I miss home," he said, realizing as he said it that it was true.

"Going back won't change that," said Vikram.

"Look, it's almost dawn," said Peleg, pointing to the horizon.

A faint magenta glow began to lighten the western sky, announcing the sun's imminent appearance. It looked to be a dramatic sunrise, with hints of color reflected in the clouds moving overhead, and Miles waited for the first rays of the sun to peak over the edge of the world.

As Our World and its sun prepared a vibrant show for the devastated city, and the survivors and rescue workers continued to clear away the wreckage and think about how they could start to restore a modicum of order, the universe took the opportunity to remind everyone that chaos was its true nature.

Just to the west of Lagaredel was a slight rise, a low continental ridge extending hundreds of miles along the larger of the two old riverbeds.

"What's that?" asked Miles, doubting his eyes as usual.

Four distant figures crested the ridge, like the Four Horsemen—if they'd had horses, that is, or there were such a thing as the Four Horsemen of the Post-Apocalypse. The Danevesans and Bandarians had already faced pestilence, war, and death, and were close to meeting famine when the first of the Hopmoul death squads descended on them with the rising sun at their backs.

Peleg stood, thinking perhaps his comrades from Ashedel had managed to make the trek to Lagaredel overnight. But when the first explosion hit about a quarter mile away from them, Peleg leapt toward the smoking crater before the flying debris had even settled. The Hopmoul launched small but powerful explosives from low-slung Cardevisi EM cannons and aimed for the most populated areas—anywhere survivors and rescuers were gathered in sufficient numbers to inflict mass casualties.

Miles and Vikram stood and watched in shock as Peleg ran toward what was soon a perimeter of fire set by their attackers on the far side. Vikram yelled into his smartskin as he and Miles ran toward Anna and Kerak, surrounded by a crowd of rescued Bandarians. Vikram was alerting the Danevesans about what was happening, but they already knew, and he and Miles saw Erestu fly past them to help Peleg fight the Hopmoul.

"We've got to get them back!" yelled Vikram. The group surrounding Anna and Kerak weren't moving. They seemed to be transfixed by the sudden mayhem and noise.

An explosion near where they'd just been sitting with Peleg flung them forward, causing Vikram to stumble. Miles extended a hand, and Vikram stood with a laugh.

"And to think," he said with a crooked smile, "you were sorry you'd missed this."

The group they were moving toward had begun to scatter and retreat, and they were looking to see if they could find Anna or Kerak when the next grenade exploded about twenty meters to their right. This one knocked them both to the ground. Miles was spun around and landed on his chest, knocking the wind out of him. As he struggled to regain his breath, he could hear the violent clash of Peleg, Erestu, and the other armed Bandarian and Danevesan guards as they fought with the nearest death squad.

A layer of hot ash had coated one side of Miles's face, but his heavy cool cloak had offered some protection from both the blast and his landing. Miles could see Vikram lying on his back a few feet away, and he crawled over to him on his belly. Vikram's eyes were half open, and he was bleeding from an ugly gash on the side of his temple.

"Vikram!" Miles shouted. He shouted his name again, shook his shoulder, but got no response. "Kerak!" he yelled toward the crowd of yishi running away or taking cover, but there was no way Kerak could have heard Miles, even if he were near.

Miles's hands shook as he activated his smartskin. All he knew how to do was communicate with the others, so he shouted into his hand for help, hoping Kerak or Dinev or Anna, or someone might hear him. He stared at his glowing blue hand and remembered how Vikram had fused Tom's fractured spine his first night in Barcelona. He was sure he could save Vikram if he just knew how to use the miracle tool tattooed on his hand, but he had no idea.

Vikram continued to lose blood, and his chest began to rise and fall in steadily diminishing breaths, as his eyelids fluttered, only the orange of his eyes showing. Miles covered Vikram's head wound with his right hand, in an attempt to stanch the flow of blood, but it was no use. The wound was too deep and too wide. All Miles could do was hold Vikram's head in his hands and plead with him not to die as his life slipped away.

"Wait," said Willa, setting down her whiskey sour. "You mean Vikram dies?" She seemed annoyed. "How could he die?"

"Unceremoniously," said Miles.

Willa frowned. "Well, that's too bad," she said. "I liked him."

"Me too."

"Though I suppose he has to die in the end," she said, rubbing the side of a finger across her chin. "It's that whole Joseph Campbell thing, isn't it?"

"If that helps." Miles continued with his story.

By the time Anna and Kerak found Miles, Vikram had stopped bleeding. His chest had ceased to move. Miles looked up at them, his sooty face streaked with tears, his hands covered in blood, and said, "I couldn't help him." Kerak gently moved Miles out of the way and knelt down next to Vikram. He did all of the things a physician from Danevesu knew how to do, but Vikram was beyond help. Anna knelt down beside Kerak and wept, while Miles tried to console her and Kerak beat his own head in his anger and his grief.

The Hopmoul attack was soon after put down.

A traitor inside Lagar Temu had alerted the Hopmoul to the arrest of Telesu and the subsequent coup. They came for the canisters of pathogen, to finish the job they'd started. But they didn't know about the Danevesan rescuers and couldn't guess that so many survivors would be out of their holes milling around the ruins of Lagaredel. The survivors, as much as the Bandarian and Danevesan military, thwarted the death squads. All the Hopmoul accomplished in the end was to add to the piles of dead and to the number of fires burning around the city.

After the Danevesan subs arrived at the ruined port of Ashedel and supplied the survivors of that city and Lagaredel with food and water, the first Danevesan expeditionary force went back home. Kerak, Erestu, Anna, and Miles accompanied Vikram's body on the long return trip via submarine. The choice not to burn his corpse in Bandary was a purely sentimental one. It wasn't as if they were going to bury him in Danevesu. In fact, if anything, the method of disposal there was arguably more ignoble than burning his body with a bunch of others atop the rubble of Bandary. Vikram was fed into a conveyor for desiccation, after which his dried carcass was ground into a mulch that could be used in a number of ways that usually weren't discussed in polite company.

Upon returning to Danevesu's harbor, the first thing everyone noticed after the sorry state of their city was the area around the exhaust vents on the upper story on the outer edge of the plateau. The redscale had disappeared in halos that radiated outward from the vent openings. It hadn't taken much for the biologists in Danevesu to figure out that the airborne pathogen had killed the redscale. A little investigation showed that the pathogen devouring the redscale plague was a mutated form of the original disease-causing organism.

At first, in dealing with the dead after the outbreak of the pathogen, they burned the desiccated bodies to prevent the spread of the infection. Now that a cure was in hand and a possible use for the biological agent loomed, they decided to sprinkle the dried, ground-up bodies of its victims on a far-off section of plateau. As hoped, the pathogen killed the redscale in the section and began to spread. Like the samples from around the exhaust vents, the organism mutated after contact with the redscale (from which the frankenspore contained genetic material) and continued to reproduce as long as it had redscale to consume, but died out once its food source disappeared. Berejian couldn't have devised a more effective eradicator of redscale if he'd set out to do so.

"Vikram would have appreciated the irony," said Kerak.

This was a big fucking deal, as Kerak would probably also say. They still did not know, however, if they were simply replacing one plague with another—or if they could rehabilitate and reclaim soil long ago lost to the redscale for agricultural purposes. It also brought up the thorny question about what dangers the mutant pathogen might pose to the yishi, or any other living thing. Still, there was at least a basis for guarded optimism.

Miles had the opportunity this time to make his good-byes properly. To Erestu, Kerak, Geresh, Captain Dave, Shikar, and even Dinev. Miles had many more well-wishers and admirers besides, whom he knew only from sight or not at all.

Anna, as he knew she would, decided to stay.

Once again, Miles stood in the room with the portal to anywhere. Once again, standing beside Anna. Only this time, he knew she wasn't coming with him.

They'd said a lot to each other over the previous few days without saying much really. Anna gave him a motherly kiss and squeeze and held him at arms' length to look at him.

"I'm sorry," she said.

"Me too," he said. And then he entered the arsehole and returned to the Hotel Kashmir, where he hoped to find his stuff still in the locker where he left it, with his passport and traveler's cheques. Where he hoped the Mossos d'Esquadra had by now forgotten all about him.

Miles downed the half-melted ice rattling around the bottom of his gin and tonic. "What were we apologizing to each other for?" he said. "I have no idea."

"So was Anna a real person?" said Willa.

"Still is, as far as I know."

"You didn't keep in touch with her?"

Miles shook his head.

"It's hard, I know," she said. "What about Vikram? Was he real?"

"Yeah, he was real."

"And Anders?"

"Him too."

"What really happened to him?"

"I don't know what became of Anders," he said. "But I heard what happened to Telesu."

"All right," she said, humoring him.

"Telesu was set free by the Hopmoul sympathizer inside Lagar Temu," said Miles, "the same one who informed the death squads about the loss of the canisters. There was still a functioning portal in the palace, a static console."

"So he escaped Lagar Temu?"

"He did," said Miles. "But with no handheld device, it was a one-way trip."

Telesu planned to travel to Cardevise, where he had contacts, or once had. He couldn't return to Earth or his human form, but he could at least avoid execution. The arsehole stretched open in front of him, but some inner voice warned him not to enter. He shook it off and plunged ahead. There could be no worse place for him than Lagaredel right now. The only thing to do was to go.

Where he ended up was almost completely dark, the only light coming from the stars and a half-lit Skygarden obscured by clouds. It was unbelievably cold—not just for Our World. It was cold for Scandinavia. This wasn't Cardevise. Telesu looked around in dread and soon realized he was struggling to breathe. He was hyperventilating just to get a fraction of the oxygen he needed into his lungs. He couldn't say he'd never been warned. Araviku knew it could happen under even the best of circumstances. The effort to breathe was exhausting him, making him sleepy, and the cold was making him shake uncontrollably as he fell to his knees on the frozen ground. Now he could see the dead sister planet more clearly. It wasn't Skygarden, it was Our World—his world—staring down at him from the heavens. He wished he found it beautiful then, but it still looked hateful to him, and he spat his last ragged breath at the yishi who called it home.

"Hold on," said Willa. "How could you know all that?"

"Hm?" said Miles. "Well…I'm allowed a little artistic license, aren't I?"

"So what's the moral?" she asked. "What are we supposed to take away from your story?"

"That's what I've been trying to figure out," he said.

Just then, a beautiful tune came on the jukebox, one of those sappy mid-seventies soft-rock songs about growing up or lost love or both that no one ever openly admits to liking. Time seemed to stand still for a moment while the music filled them with longing and melancholy and the desire to love everyone and everything. Then the lights came up, and the bartender started hustling out the suddenly self-conscious patrons.

"You can't go home again," said the bartender and American lit major to a few confused stares, "and you also can't stay here."

*

ANNA SHIVERED as the El train passed overhead. She wasn't prepared for the cold or the noise of Chicago in February. She could see her breath. She couldn't remember being able to see her breath since her undergraduate days in Groningen. So she practiced making little puffy clouds around her head to pass the time.

She recognized Miles immediately as he made his way down the steps of the station's exit. He was a block away, but he looked older, like he'd grown into his height, the baby fat giving way to a little more muscle. Two days' stubble shadowed his formerly boyish face, and his once unkempt hair was cropped short. The sapling that should have snapped in a strong wind looked thicker with a few more growth rings. But he still looked like Miles.

She thought of calling out to him before he started walking, but fell in behind him instead, observing him in his natural habitat. Stalking him, really, if she were being honest.

He turned down a side street, where it was quieter away from the train line and bustling six-way intersection. It was past two in the morning, and a thin veneer of ice seemed to cover everything, including the bare branches of trees and street signs. No moon or stars shone in the night sky, which was lightened by a thick blanket of gray winter haze. He came to a three-story graystone and took the stairs two at a time to the raised front door, his keys already in his hand.

Miles was in the vestibule, about to unlock the inner door, when he was startled by a *knock-knock* on the glass of the door behind him. He turned and stopped upon seeing Anna outside, her teeth chattering in the cold. He opened the door and said, "Anna?" She was wearing a black leather jacket with a thick pink scarf wrapped around her chin. Her dreads were longer, but otherwise she looked the same. Beautiful.

"Can I come in?" she said, visibly shivering.

Miles shook his head by way of apology and opened the door wide for her to enter. Once inside the relative warmth of the entry, he gave her a quick hug and opened the inner door. "Come on," he said.

She followed him up the stairs to his apartment on the second floor. The one-bedroom flat was at the rear of the hundred-year-old building, vintage for Chicago, but not in a good way. Anna stood inside the front door as Miles turned on the lights. She could see pretty much the whole place from there—the main living area with a TV and a brown garbage-picked sofa, a small tacked-on kitchen from the 1960s to her left, a tiny bedroom through a door to her right, a closed door that presumably concealed an even tinier bathroom beyond it. The wood floors were warped, the finish long since worn away, the original plaster molding around the high ceilings was crumbling, and the glass of the windows overlooking the alley was wavy like the melted sugar panes of a gingerbread house.

"This is a real dump," she said matter-of-factly.

"Well, it's home," he said, just as a breeze blew up outside and rattled the windows in their frames.

"I like it." She walked over to the couch and plopped down on it.

He moved over to where she was sitting and stood a few feet away. "Make yourself comfortable."

"You look good," she said.

"So do you," he said, feeling his face flush.

"It's been a while, hasn't it?"

"Yeah, five years." He nodded, then remembered something. "I almost forgot," he said and started toward his bedroom, where he disappeared for several seconds, making noises like he was digging in his closet. He came back out with her old backpack. "This is yours," he said and placed it on the couch next to her.

She examined it as if it were an artifact from a past life. "You kept my pack this whole time."

"It was with my stuff back at the Kashmir," he said. "I think it still has your passport in it, though I'm not sure you need that anymore. I didn't know if I'd ever see you again, but I doubted you'd be going back to your old apartment."

"No."

"I got out of Spain as fast as I could. Took a train across the border into France and then on to Italy."

"Rome?"

"Yeah," he said. "The ruins were…different than I expected."

"Yeah."

"Then I flew home."

Miles hadn't been prepared for how miserable he'd be when he first came home. He'd made it back just before Christmas, which was a good time of year to come home. He was happy to see his sister Sara and some of his old friends, and even his mother who, for all her faults, loved him. He got together with high school friends who'd gone off to college and were back for the break. There were some colorful stories he could share, more he couldn't. Then things returned to normal. Where four months had gone by for everyone else, a lifetime had passed for him. Conversations drifted to the weather, what was happening at school, what TV shows they liked, how the football team was doing, and Miles feigned interest. Soon his friends headed back to their universities downstate or across country, and all he felt was relief.

It had taken more than a year to settle into a tolerable routine. He managed to acquire new friends at new schools. An associate's degree from the local community college, a bachelor's from the University of Illinois at Chicago, and an assistantship to attend grad school at the same.

"You're studying anthropology?" Anna asked with a surprised smile.

"Don't laugh," he said. He liked his studies, which perhaps shouldn't have been surprising, as it was a kind of connection to Anna and Vikram.

"It's been hard not being able to tell anyone about Our World," he said. Anna nodded. "I mean, I do tell people about it on occasion"—she raised an eyebrow, and Miles felt a twinge of guilt for having lied to Willa—"but I pretend it's just a story I made up. Sometimes I embellish the truth to make it a better story."

"We're still the only two people who've ever seen it," said Anna, turning to her purpose. "You know, I spent the last year and a half traveling around Our World. It's been amazing....They live on all these separate islands and still speak with reverence about their old underwater cities. You can see how some of them cling to the past while others—particularly the young—just want to move on. I've been to islands in Cardevise and Edrisia and to tiny islets that are all that's left of other once-important nations. They're all so different—different languages and customs, different ways of adapting.

"Part of me thinks that I should only be observing them, but I'm afraid I'm not an ideal observer. You can see it in their eyes when they first encounter me. My presence—my existence—changes something basic about the way they understand things. They're never the same afterward. I'm going around Our World planting seeds, not knowing what will sprout up."

Miles nodded. "It's not exactly what Vikram intended, but..."

"No," she agreed. "Nor Tchuvu. His support sort of vanished after Lagaredel. There's no more talk of colonizing Ecuador, or sending new fluppets to Earth. But the redscale is disappearing everywhere. They've already begun sowing fields again in Danevesu and Bandary. That *is* what Vikram intended. And other things are changing—they seem to change quickly there."

ALEX LUBERTOZZI

Miles smiled, glad to see Anna happy. He stood there, feeling nervous around her again. He thought about how easy they'd been with each other once, and about how brief a time that was.

"Did you know," she said, looking up at him, "that there's a statue of you in Lagaredel?"

Miles laughed. "Really?"

"Yeah. I mean, it looks nothing like you, but it's right outside the palace."

"Wow," he said, taking a seat on the couch next to her backpack. "I'd like to see that."

"You could—we could," she said, turning to face him better.

He looked at her hazily. "Just drop everything and go?"

"Sure. Why not?" she said.

He looked hesitant.

"Do you have a girlfriend?" she asked.

"I did."

"So that's a no."

"What about school?" he said.

"It's not going anywhere," she said offhandedly. "Besides, I could write three dissertations from what I've learned about cultural patterns and linguistics over there."

"Yeah, but they'd lock you up in a nuthouse if you did."

"True." She looked at him closely. "It's not just about being selfish, you know. It's not simply an academic field trip. Someday, when the yishi are in a less desperate position, they'll want to make contact on a larger scale than inviting two nobodies for a visit. We could be a lot of help then."

Miles nodded.

"Yishi might not be perfect," she said. "They still exploit one another, they still hate. But the ones who use others and try to divide them are at a disadvantage. They don't have any inborn differences to separate them, so the divisions can't take root as easily. There's a lot we can learn from them. And a lot we have to teach them." *As a cautionary tale*, she could have added but didn't. "Honestly, I thought you'd be itching to go back by now."

"It's not that," he said. He'd fantasized about it for years. About Our World, about Anna. "It's just I'm not sure what you want from me now."

"I thought we could at least be friends," she said.

"I was in love with you, you know," he said.

"I know," she said. "You told me so, remember?"

"Yeah. It's just…you kind of broke my heart back then."

"How old were you at the time?"

"Eighteen."

"And what are you now? Twenty-two?"

"Twenty-three," he corrected, "and a half. What's your point?"

"You've had time to grow up."

He wondered if that was true. "What about Dinev?"

"What about him?"

"You're not still…together?" Saying it out loud and seeing her eyebrows go up in genuine surprise made him realize how much he may have incorrectly assumed. But now he'd gone and said it out loud.

"We were never 'together,'" she said. "I haven't even seen him in half a year. To be honest, I never really thought about him romantically, or any yishi, for that matter. I mean, they're wonderful. And they do have all the equipment. But they're aliens, aren't they?"

"Of course," he said, shaking his head.

"Speaking of," she said, "Erestu asked me to say hello."

Miles sort of froze. "You…know about that?" he said.

"I do now."

Miles may have been older, but Anna was still smarter. He looked down at the floor. "That was a weird time."

"I bet." She looked at his older, suddenly redder face, and smiled. She was enjoying this a little. "It's okay. We'd been broken up for, what, six hours?"

He knew she was teasing him, but he still felt repentant. "When we were first together," he said, "I felt like maybe I was becoming the person I wanted to be, someone I might actually admire. More confident, maybe, less wrapped up in my own bullshit. At first I thought it might be Spain, then I was sure it was you. But, from the moment we arrived on Our World, I was afraid of losing you, and I stopped being the guy I wanted to be."

"I admired you then," she said. "I admired you when you convinced us to help the Bandarians when all I wanted to do was forget them, let them…die. I think your memory of the way things were back then might be skewed. I wanted to stay, and I knew you wanted to go back. Plus, you were still very young, and our age difference—"

"Our difference in age hasn't changed," he said.

"Well…actually, it's only been three years for me," she said.

He looked surprised, then remembered the disconnect in timeframes when he'd returned from Our World. "How does that work, then?"

Anna shrugged. "I don't know."

"You don't know?"

"Do you know how your TV works?" she asked.

He looked at the TV sitting on the foot locker in front of them. "Not as such," he admitted. "I wish I did. This one's kaput."

She looked at the boxy Japanese television set with its bulbous little nineteen-inch screen and shook her head. "You were still running away from something then," she said. "You and Vikram had that in common. Until he returned home."

"Look what happened to him."

"But he had to do it," she said. "Just like you had to. Even though it was hard."

Miles thought of the small service they'd held for Vikram back in Danevesu before sending his body along the conveyor belt to be desiccated and then ground up. Someone had edited together a movie of his life—mostly video clips and still pictures from when he was young, from after he returned from Earth the first time, and before he left again. Odd music played over it, and it ended with a slow-motion close-up of Araviku's face recorded in the amphitheater after he'd come back to Danevesu with Anna and Miles. It was fascinating to see the young Araviku, before they knew him. But there was nothing from his time as Tor Bass or Vikram, his human forms. So the images Anna and Miles held in their heads of Vikram from his days with them on Earth belonged to them alone.

Miles thought of the snapshot he'd taken of Anna on the Alhambra mount in Granada, how he'd kept it in his mind and held it close for the past five years.

"I'll go with you," he said.

Anna knew he was making a leap of faith. But it was okay. She knew what she was doing. She'd found her Skygarden in Our World. Sure, the planet could barely sustain life. Catastrophic climatic and geological events happened almost every day. Yishi represented practically the last vertebrate species left on land or in the sea—and they had just been trying to wipe each other out. But, unlike here on Earth, things were looking up. She saw a glimmer of hope for Our World.

About the Author

ALEX LUBERTOZZI has been a writer and editor since the Clinton administration. He has coauthored two works of nonfiction—*The Complete War of the Worlds* (2001) and *World War II on the Air* (2003)—written for numerous books and magazines, and had his short fiction published in *The Arcanist*. He has been composing fiction for most of his life (if you count lying), but this is his first novel. He lives in the Chicago area with his wife and son.

Photograph by Nick Lubertozzi